Miranda
Sherry

Bone
Meal
for
Roses

HEAD
of ZEUS

PART ONE
MOUSE-BABY AND
THE METAL-HAIRED MAN

CHAPTER ONE

ACCORDING TO WHAT she's gathered from watching television, Poppy is a person. She's got two arms, two legs and the right number of things on her face, all arranged correctly. But Poppy's not convinced. Nothing on this side of the TV screen is as it should be. For one thing, the curtains are all shredded from sun damage and hang down in front of the grubby apartment windows like brownish seaweed. Television windows sparkle and have things like slatted blinds on them, or wafting drapes that filter the light. And then there's the carpet. On this side of the TV screen the carpet is filthy, and there are piles and piles of things crowding the edges of it. Jason keeps picking things up and bringing them home, saying *I'm definitely going to need that one day* but he never does, and there's a perpetual congregation of *stuff* creeping in to block the path that Poppy has carved between the TV, the kitchen and the bathroom.

The seaweed has been hanging in the windows since they moved in. Poppy can't remember what the windows were like in the place they stayed before, or the place before that, but she knows that they were no closer to the ones in television homes than this one is.

Outside the front door there's a bleak hallway with other doors on it leading to other flats which aren't up to much.

Some of the people living behind the doors are nice to Poppy, and a few give her things to eat when she asks. Other doors she dashes past as fast as she can. Down the main stairs is the street, which isn't very convincing either. It just seems to have more long dirty buildings with more corridors and more doors in them, or small scruffy houses falling to bits. Nothing is as it should be, on this side of the screen.

Poppy watches the television from right up close. That way, she can look into the real world with its bright colours and neatly arranged furniture and not have to think about the dirt, or Jason smoking and looking at magazines while sitting on the stained toilet with the bathroom door open, or her mother sprawled out on the couch. Her mother, Yolande, hasn't woken up yet today. She smells of cigarette smoke and sweat and something sharp and chemical. Poppy doesn't need to turn around to know that her mother's mouth is slack, and her bad teeth are showing between her chapped lips with the sores on the corners. Television mothers have white straight teeth with no brown bits and nobody flinches at the smell of their breath. Nothing on this side of the screen is as it should be.

Poppy doesn't know how long she and her mother have been living in the seaweed-curtain place, but it feels like a long time. Maybe that's because at the place they stayed before, there was a yard outside that Poppy could go to when Yolande wasn't waking up, or *was* awake, but shouting. The yard had old bits of car in it, and a stained mattress leaning up against the concrete wall, and the ground was always covered in lines of ants that would bite the tender skin at the top of her legs if she sat down on it too long, but there were places to hide. Sometimes Poppy would pretend that she was a giant walking through a city like she saw on TV one time, and all the bits of junk lying around were buildings with

4

tiny people in them, screaming their heads off when they saw her coming.

The day after Poppy gets her first wobbly tooth, she goes out into the corridor because her mother and Jason are talking too loudly as they wave their brown bottles of beer around, and she knows that that means there will soon be fighting. The corridor is the best she can do in the absence of a yard, even though it smells of garbage and wee and other people's cooking. At the food smell, Poppy's stomach gives a growl so loud that she's not surprised when one of the doors opens. It's the door with a '7' on it. Jason's has a '9'. Poppy knows numbers because she watches the TV show with puppets that teach you things.

'Oh, hello there,' the number-7-woman says when she pokes her head out of the door. Her hair is grey and tied up on top of her head in a knot.

'Hello.' Poppy sees that the number-7-woman is carrying a plastic bag also tied at the top with a knot. 'Were you going to take that to the bins?'

Sometimes, Poppy goes to where the dustbins are outside on the pavement and waits to see if anyone throws anything interesting-looking away.

'Good guess. You're a sharp one, aren't you?'

'I can take it for you, if you want.' Poppy eyes the packet. Could there be something to eat in there? The knot doesn't look too tight.

'Oh that's very sweet of you.' The number-7-woman smiles and her cheeks wrinkle up and almost cover her eyes, which are brown. 'What a dear. Give me a moment, I think I've got just the thing to say thank you.' The number-7-woman disappears back behind her door, taking the top-knot packet with her. After a few moments, she's back.

'See this little fellow?' The number-7-woman waves a small stuffed dog in Poppy's direction. 'It came free with a promotional pack of loo paper. I was keeping it for my youngest grandchild, Suzy, but I think it's getting lonely from having to wait too long.'

The stuffed dog is tiny and clean and is the colour of oats. It has a little red scarf sewn on around its neck. Poppy can barely breathe because it's so beautiful.

'Come on, dear, take it if you want it. Consider it payment for taking out my rubbish.' The number-7-woman holds out her other hand with the top-knot bag in it.

'Thank you.' Poppy rushes forward to grab the dog and the bag and then dashes down the corridor towards the steps and the street before the woman can change her mind.

Poppy calls the dog Wombo. She hides him under her T-shirt when she goes back to the apartment later that evening. Then, she changes into her other pair of shorts. They were once pink. They're now a sort of brown, but they have big pockets, which means that she can have Wombo with her all the time.

Two weeks later, Poppy hears loud crying and shouting outside the seaweed-curtain apartment. When she peeks out and sees that it's the number-7-woman weeping, her stomach goes fluttery. The number-7-woman's top knot is coming all unravelled and strings of grey hair hang in her face and catch in her mouth as she cries. There's a man with her who keeps saying, 'Come, Ma, come in. Stop now, Ma.' And eventually he manages to get her back behind the number 7 door.

Poppy never gets to find out if the number-7-woman is OK, or why she was crying so much, because three days after that, Yolande makes them move out of the seaweed-curtain place. She and Jason shouted at one another all night and when

Yolande shuffles into the kitchen in the morning, her eyes have a flat look. Poppy knows it well.

'Put that down, Poppy. We're leaving.'

Poppy gives the cereal bowl another swill under the tap before climbing down from the chair that she's been standing on to reach the sink. She rummages for a cleanish plastic supermarket bag in the cupboard and then moves through the apartment, selecting the few things she thinks of as hers. She takes her one pair of tackies, even though they're too small and squash her toes, her socks and T-shirts and jeans that haven't been washed in weeks. She takes the bowl she's just rinsed, and checks three times to make sure that Wombo is in her pocket.

When she goes back to the bedroom, Yolande is standing in the centre of it with an armful of clothes and a hopeless look on her face. 'Ma?' Poppy whispers. 'Here's a packet to put your stuff in.'

'Stop nagging at me, for Christ's sake.'

'You said we were going.'

'Listen to you. Anyone would think we had a nice hotel or something waiting for us or some such shit. You do know we've got nowhere else to go, right?'

'You always find someplace.' *Maybe the next one will have an outside yard.*

'That's true.' Poppy's mother jerks to life again. 'I do. Don't I?' She gives Poppy a jagged grin, and jams Jason's favourite sweater into a suitcase along with her motley collection of things. Poppy's pretty sure the suitcase is Jason's as well. They'd better move fast or there's going to be trouble.

When they're ready to leave, the afternoon sun is burning through the seaweed curtains, and the ghost shapes of the original pattern suddenly reveal themselves in the sharp light.

After months of thinking that the fabric was just dirty, Poppy can make out what looks like bunches of roses. Or she thinks she can. In some spots, the floral motifs morph into grimacing clown faces.

'Move it, Poppy.' Yolande shifts the suitcase from one hand to the other. 'Or do you want me to leave you here?'

Poppy spins around, but her mother is wearing an almost-smile. She was teasing, not serious. Relief jellies Poppy's knees.

'No, Ma. I'm coming with you.'

'Well, come then.'

Poppy walks over to the television and switches it off. The real world gives a flicker and then goes dark.

The next place they stay in is not as full of stuff as the one with Jason was, but it doesn't even have curtains on the windows, seaweedy or otherwise. Instead, there are long decaying paper-like strips all joined together at the tops and bottoms with bathplug chain. Office blinds, Karel calls them. He swells with pride each time he says it, as if having such items in his apartment automatically gives him the air of someone rising through the corporate ranks. Poppy doubts Karel's ever worked in an office. The television people who work in offices walk fast through corridors in shiny shoes and do important-looking things on gleaming laptops. Karel wears sandals made out of bits of old tyre, and whenever he's in possession of a laptop he sells it almost at once.

He steals computers, along with cameras and cell phones and expensive sunglasses, so that he and Yolande can sell them and buy their medicine. After a successful trip to the chemist, they sit in the lounge with the office blinds closed and smoke their medicine through the broken necks of glass

8

Coke bottles. Poppy sits even closer to the TV when they're doing this. The smell on her empty stomach makes her nauseous. The yard she was so glad about when they moved in is useless. There's a dog out there with a big fat head and a booming bark. Poppy doesn't know whose it is. It seems to own the whole street. No one called it off when it jumped on her and knocked her down the first time and last time she went outside alone.

One evening, Karel sells the TV. He and Yolande already owe too much to the Nigerians for their medicine and they're itching. *Itching* is what Yolande screams at Karel after stomping across their shared mattress on the floor and kicking him in the ribs to wake him up.

'I know you've had the last bit without me, you asshole.'

'What d'you want me to do?' He is bleary, blinking, rubbing his kicked ribs. 'We've got nothing, and nothing to sell.'

'Make a bloody plan!' Yolande hisses. Her breath is so rank that Poppy can smell it from all the way across the room.

Karel marches to the TV, yanks the cord from the socket, and heaves the dead black rectangle up in his arms. When he carries it away, Poppy cries for the first time since she can remember. She stops when Yolande smacks her in the mouth, but then the sobs start all over again when her mother's stony expression crumbles.

'Sorry,' Yolande whispers, and pulls Poppy in to a hard, uncomfortable hug. Poppy doesn't know whether it will be one of the OK-hugs, or a scary one, so she stands, frozen, her upper lip wet with snot.

'It'll be OK, Poppy,' Yolande says. 'Once Ma gets her medicine everything will be fine.'

But Poppy knows that it won't.

*

'I know who'll lend us some bucks,' Yolande says two days later when the TV money is all smoked up.

'Let me guess, you're going to get a loan from the bank?' Karel's laugh sounds like something between a bark and a retch. Poppy, sitting in the far corner holding Wombo, is careful not to look up. When Karel's in a laughing mood he keeps looking for 'funny' things. Lately, this seems to involve Poppy in some way. He likes to make her dance, sing, or act out scenes from TV commercials, like some ridiculous marionette. When he makes her do 'bits' on command, Poppy wishes that the walls would melt and the floor catch fire, and the whole place blow apart like the explosions she's seen on television. It never happens though. Nothing on this side of the screen is as it should be.

'Not the bank, you fool. I know some guys.'

'What guys?'

'Money-lender guys.'

'Well why didn't you say anything earlier?'

''Cause I already owe them a lot from before.'

'Like how much?'

Yolande shrugs. Her shoulders look like shards of broken glass covered in grey skin.

'So I'll meet with them, then. You can wait around the corner or something. They don't need to know you're in the picture.'

'They'll know. Money-lender guys know everything.'

'Think they won't lend us anything then?'

'They might, but they'll make us piss blood to pay for it, you can bet on that.'

'So what? Aren't you itching?'

'I'm itching.' Yolande glances at Poppy, which she hardly ever does, and Poppy shrinks from the changing weather that flickers inside her mother's eyes. First sorry then angry then sorry again, and finally settling on hard and made of glass. 'I'm itching bad.'

Karel stands up. As always, there's too much leg sticking out of the bottom of his shorts, skinny and white and covered with little frizzes of black hair. Poppy wishes he would wear longer shorts. Trousers would be even better.

'Come, bitch,' he says to Yolande, and Poppy feels cool relief when her mother's gaze moves off her and back on to Karel. 'Let's go make a deal.'

Poppy is alone in the locked apartment for a very long time after that. With no real world to plug in to, she reluctantly picks up the stolen Nintendo Game Boy that Karel gave her a few days ago to stop her *goddam whining about her goddam tooth*. Poppy's sure she's never whined, unless the word means something that she doesn't understand. She hardly ever talks at all about anything, tooth included, but Karel seems to go off about her *whining* every time he sees her mouth. *Ag, leave the kid alone,* Yolande sometimes says, but never loud enough to make it stick. The tooth got chipped when Poppy slipped scrambling to pull her pants up when Karel barged into the bathroom while she was on the loo. It's the third time he's done that in the last few weeks. There used to be a key for the bathroom, but Karel lost it.

Poppy presses a few buttons on the game, but without new batteries, the device gives a sad little moan and blinks into blackness. She shakes it a few times, holding it up to her ear to listen for life, and then, thinking she's broken it, with panic whirling in the pit of her empty belly, she hides it under the decrepit sofa, pushing it as far as she can reach into the embrace of the dust bunnies. Hopefully, if he doesn't see it, Karel will forget about it, and won't find out that she killed it.

For a while, she walks up and down the length of the window, brushing the 'office blinds' with one hand so that they all sway in unison, like a chorus of dancers on a bright stage. Poppy's stomach hurts. She goes to the kitchen and eats the sweet-salty red goo out of a small sachet of tomato sauce that once came with a takeaway meal that she finds in the cupboard. There's a little plastic envelope of vinegar, too, but she reels back when she bites it open, eyes burning from the acid fumes. She pushes a chair up to the sink and pours the contents down the plughole, watching the trail the clear liquid leaves in the scum at the bottom of the sink. She turns on the tap and drinks and drinks, trying to fill up her insides, but it just makes her feel strange and sloshy when she climbs down from the chair.

When it gets dark, Poppy carries a few cushions to the cupboard, makes a nest in the bottom, curls up on them, and sleeps until it is light. When she wakes, she lies on her side for hours, finding faces in the knotholes in the pine cupboard walls.

Much later, Poppy is sitting in the empty bathtub playing with Wombo when she finally hears the front door open. She freezes, her fingers tight on the dog's greying plush body. Yolande's laugh stabs through the quiet, followed by the sound of falling, more laughing, Karel's voice. Poppy doesn't know whether to get out of the bath or not. Its solid walls make her feel safe, like she's in a little box. But then, people are buried in boxes, and Poppy can't shake the image of lumps of earth raining down on her from someone's shovel above, just like she saw happen on the TV one time.

Poppy scrambles out of the bath, pockets Wombo, and creeps out to see if, by any chance, Yolande and Karel have brought some food home with them. When Yolande, who is slumped down into the corner of the sofa with a dull look on her face, sees Poppy, she opens her mouth very wide, stretching her lips back over her gums like a baboon from a nature documentary. Yolande holds the expression far too long for it to be a yawn, and no sound comes out so she's not planning on saying anything. The menace in the gesture is riveting. Poppy stares at the raw red hole, unable to move or look away.

At last, Yolande closes her mouth. She pulls a bent cigarette out of the pocket of her jeans and places it between her lips.

'You wouldn't mind being sold, now, would you?' Yolande asks. The lighter in her hand hisses up its flame, and she leans forward to suck her cigarette to life before looking back at Poppy. 'You must be dying to get away from me, hey? Just think. Maybe end up in the lap of luxury.' Poppy is silent. She covers the lump in her pocket that is Wombo with one hand and gives him a squeeze. 'More likely, you'd end up in the lap of some sick old fucker, though, wouldn't you? Because life is just like that for ugly little girls with snot on their faces.' Yolande pulls hard on her cigarette and Poppy can see her eye-weather changing from black frost to something wet and dripping and filled with sadness. It only lasts a moment before the wind blows the hardness back in. Ice chips and stone.

'Just remember, even if you do manage to get rid of me, Poppy, I'll always find you. You can bet on that.' Yolande gives a strange, thin smile, eyes squinting against a wreath of smoke. 'Hey, then I could sell you again. Twice the profit.' Poppy squeezes Wombo so tightly that her fingers are shaking. 'Although second time around I'd have to lower the cost for damaged goods.' A cough-laugh, and at last, her mother looks away, releasing Poppy from her terrible trance. 'Stop staring at me, for God's sake. I don't know why you always have to fucking stare like that. Go out and play. Go on. Out.'

CHAPTER TWO

THE METAL-HAIRED MAN arrives in Pretoria one windy Tuesday afternoon in late September. He climbs over a small heap of discarded rubbish and unopened junk mail to get to the front door of Karel's shabby cottage. His knock sends the dust motes whirling and makes Poppy look up from the game she's invented: using old matchboxes to build a little town on the floor in the corner of the room. The knock comes again. Yolande, awake and itchy, shuffles over to the front door and pulls it open. There's a wide silence and then a sudden clatter of sound as she steps backwards into a pile of old CDs, sending them scattering across the floor.

'Dad?' Yolande tries to slam the door, but her reflexes are slow. It bounces against the worn farmer's boot the man has placed in the gap and swings back open to reveal an upright figure in clean, car-rumpled clothes. His sun-wrinkled features are topped with a thatch of hair so uniformly grey it appears metallic in the fading afternoon light.

The metal-haired man's face pales when he sees the state of his once beautiful daughter. Her hair hangs in greasy strings around a thin, greenish face. There are mauve blotches around her nose and on the sides of her mouth. Some of her teeth are missing.

'Yolande?'

'What do you want?' she snarls. Her breath smells like stale smoke and rotting meat. The metal-haired man tries not to flinch.

'The child. My granddaughter, where is she?' He's speaking in English. Poppy knows English from all her television watching, but she's unused to hearing it spoken by people on this side of the screen and is slow to catch all his words.

'Who told you there was a child?' Yolande's laugh is shrill and cracked like the caw of a crow. 'Someone's been telling you fibs, Dad.'

'One of your loan sharks found us, Yolande. They were looking for the money you owe them.' Two days have passed since that phone call, but the metal-haired man can remember the exact sound of the stranger's voice on the other end of the line. It had been hard-edged and threatening, trying to scare an old man into paying off his daughter's debts. But then there had been a pause and then the voice had gone high and soft and filled with horror: *There's a little girl. She offered to sell the kid to us. What kind of sick filth does that?* It was the first the metal-haired man had heard of his daughter in seven years. It was the first time he discovered he had a granddaughter.

Now, he looks down at the toes of his boots and balls his hands into fists, clenching tight. 'Thanks to those low-lifes you've gotten yourself mixed up with, your mother and I managed to find out you were living here in Pretoria. We hired a private detective—'

'How the hell did you two get it together to do that?' Yolande lets out a screech of laughter. 'Finally decided to come in from the garden?' She crosses her arms, which are marked with scratches and little scars that look like they could be cigarette burns. 'I notice you guys never bothered to get a detective to find me before.'

'For God's sake, Yolande. We tried. All the times we tried to get you to go to rehab. We've been wondering and hoping for years, and now, here…' The unfinished sentence hovers, fading at the edges. The metal-haired man softens his tone: 'Your mother isn't well. She was diagnosed with rheumatoid arthritis soon after you left.'

Yolande wipes her nose with the back of one wire-thin wrist.

'She's in a wheelchair quite a lot of the time now, but some days are fine. Some days you'd hardly know she was sick at all.'

'Did you tell them?' Yolande bites the corner of her scabbed lip.

'What?'

'The money-lender guys.' Her eyes dart over his shoulder.

'I was talking about your mother, she—'

'Did you tell them what the PI told you… where I live?' The metal-haired man is quiet. His large hands, sun-freckled and used-looking, clutch into fists and release. Clutch and release. Poppy can't take her eyes off them.

'Hey!' Karel shuffles in from the bathroom. He scratches the pale patch of emaciated belly that shows between his boxers and his decaying T-shirt and scowls at the metal-haired man. 'Who're you?'

Silence. Clutch and release.

'Who's this, *bokkie*?'

'This is my dad, Karel.'

For some reason, Karel finds this information hilarious. He doubles over and wheezes with laughter. Tears pool amongst the sparse lashes along the fuchsia-coloured rims of his eyes.

'You're both high,' the metal-haired man says.

He's aching for air and is about to step backwards towards the exhaust-fume and uncollected-rubbish smell of the street, when he sees the child. She seems to materialise into being against the jumbled contents at the back of the room. For a moment, the metal-haired man isn't sure if he's looking at a human. She could be a creature from another world. She has large, terrified eyes, mouse-grey hair matted with dirt, and cheekbones that stick out too far.

'Hey, little one?' he whispers, taking a step further inside. 'I'm your grandpa.' He speaks in Afrikaans this time, but Poppy stays frozen still. Only her eyes move, flicking from her mother to the tall, metal-haired man in the doorway. He's the cleanest, calmest-looking person she's ever seen on this side of the television screen.

'Go into the bathroom and lock yourself in, Poppy.' Yolande has forgotten that Karel lost the bathroom door key weeks ago. 'Go on.' Poppy doesn't move.

'Her name's Poppy?' says the metal-haired man.

And then he starts to cry. The first unexpected sob ripples through the stale air and ricochets off the grubby walls. When it reaches Poppy at the back of the room, it releases her, as if from some kind of spell. She takes a step, and then another. The oversized pink sandals she's wearing make sucking sounds as she crosses the sticky linoleum and edges past the hysterical Karel and her frozen mother. She walks right up to the metal-haired man and places her small, filthy hand in his.

The man looks to his daughter. For a moment, he sees fight flame inside her bloodshot eyes, but then, as if milk has been spilled somewhere behind them, it flickers out. Yolande gives an almost imperceptible nod and then drops her gaze.

'You can come too,' the man whispers to Yolande, but she turns and walks towards the bathroom. Her back is hunched beneath her T-shirt, making Poppy think of a cockroach shell. 'Yolande?'

'Fuck off out of here before I change my mind, Dad.'

No one says another word, but Karel's wheezy, retching laugh follows the metal-haired man and the little girl as they walk out of the flat and down the stairs and away.

The metal-haired man drives Poppy out of Pretoria in a well-used old bakkie with springy seats that send her shooting into the air every time they hit a bump in the road. Each time she flies up, the seatbelt cuts into her collarbone, but it also means that she can catch a glimpse of the pale grey stripe that unwinds like a ribbon ahead of them, ending in a grey fuzz of blocks on the horizon.

'That's Johannesburg.' The metal-haired man has stopped crying, but his face looks burnt out and hollow. 'But we're not stopping there. We're going all the way to the Cape. Have you heard of the Cape?'

Poppy says nothing.

The metal-haired man's large brown fingers tighten over the steering wheel. Poppy thinks he might be about to cry again, but instead he says: 'My name's Jeremy. Your ouma calls me Jem, but you can call me Grandpa, if you like.'

Silence swims back into the hot cabin. Beneath the grinding noise of the bakkie's engine, Poppy's sure she can hear the echo of Karel's laughter. She cranes her neck to make sure that he's not hiding in the back somewhere, but she's too short to see around the seat.

'We've got a long journey ahead of us, I'm afraid, but we're stopping at the next garage for some food. How about a burger? That sound good?'

Poppy looks at her grandpa with wide eyes. Burgers are what television people eat.

Jem phones his wife from a payphone while he's waiting for Poppy to use the bathroom at the rest stop south of Johannesburg. The roadside air smells of diesel and dried grass, and his fingers slip on the buttons. The phone rings and rings. He can imagine Anneke making her slow way over to answer it in their small, bright home. He can almost hear the soft thud of her walker on the wooden floorboards.

'Hello?' Her voice comes through clear and strong.

'I've got the girl, dear heart, I'm bringing her with me.' His wife, Anneke, sucks in air as if she's been holding her breath ever since he kissed her goodbye two days ago.

'What's her name?'

'Poppy.'

'Poppy,' Anneke repeats. 'But Yolande always hated plants and flowers.' A granddaughter. 'How old is she? Is she all right? What's she like, Jem?'

'She's a tiny little thing. Needs some feeding up.' It's a pathetic skirting-around of the facts but Anneke will see for herself soon enough. 'It's a good thing we found her when we did.'

There's a pointed silence where Anneke doesn't ask about Yolande, and in the uncomfortable space between her breaths, Jem can hear the loan shark's voice: *Sell the kid. Sell the kid.*

His heart suddenly skips and then thunders. The little girl is all alone inside the echoing tiled expanse of the female bathroom where he can't enter. What if someone's taken her? What was he thinking, letting her go in there alone? He's about to drop the receiver and rush off to check when the tiny, grimy rodent-like creature emerges from the bathroom and takes a cautious step towards him. His insides liquefy with relief.

'Jesus.'

'Jem?'

'It's all right. It's going to be all right, my love. Your grand-daughter will be with you tomorrow afternoon. I'm driving through the night.'

'Be careful.'

'Always.'

Clutching her Styrofoam container of leftover burger, Poppy sleeps with her cheek pressed up against the seatbelt for most of the long journey from Johannesburg through the dry flat vastness that lies between the cities of the north and the mountains and valleys of the fruit-producing farmlands in the south. Dawn comes as they cross the last of the Karoo, and when the sky begins to lighten, Jem searches for signs of himself or his wife in the girl's mouse-tiny, slumbering fea-tures, but beneath the dirt and the smeared hamburger sauce, and with those hollow eye sockets and angular cheeks, it's hard to tell. She looks nothing like Yolande did when she was little, with her chubby rounded limbs and curly brown hair. Poppy's hair is grey, which puzzles Jem until a sudden shaft of morning sunlight reveals that it isn't at all. Beneath the accu-mulated dirt, Poppy's hair is a creamy, lemon-pith blonde.

Anneke's hair was the exact same colour when they first met. The forty years that have passed since then have aged her blonde to an unearthly white, so that now his wife looks as if she's wearing a silky veil made of dandelion seeds. Jem's throat tightens. He didn't want to come on this trip without her, but the pain has been bad this month, and the bumpy roads and poor suspension of the old vehicle would've been torture for her. He calculates the hours that have to pass before he sees her again, and presses a little harder on the gas.

Once the rusty sand of the flat Karoo is behind them, the road twists and bends its way first between low brown hills, and then larger greener ones until, finally, they're in the mountains. By the time they reach the winding road that leads towards town, Poppy still hasn't said a word.

'Town' is little more than a wide dusty main street with a shop that sells a small bit of everything, a liquor store, a church and a post office. A few side streets with quaint old houses sprawl out on either side, just waiting for the tourism board to notice their charm and put the town on the map like its bigger, prettier neighbours. Jem drives through the town and out again in minutes. A short while later, they crest the last rise before the valley dips towards the dirt track that will take them home.

'We used to own a lot of this land, you know, Poppy.' Jem's voice is scratchy from lack of use, but after the hours of silence, it still seems too loud. 'It was all part of your ouma's parents' farm. We inherited our half from them long before we had your mom. I became a farmer! Fancy that? An English city boy like me. It was falling in love with your *plaas-meisie* ouma that did it. A real farm girl, I would've become a dung beetle herder or a rocket scientist if that's what it would've taken to spend my life with her.'

Poppy's finger makes a squeaking sound as she collects the last remnants of sauce in the now empty takeaway container.

'Luckily, with her help, it so happened that I wasn't too bad at the whole farming thing. We grew plums and olives and walnuts, just to begin with.' He glances across at Poppy. She is still not looking at him, but something about the tilt of her head tells him she's listening. 'And d'you want to know something? Each time I dug into the soil, something burrowed deeper into me, some kind of love. You see, Poppy, you have to love a piece of earth in order to make it grow something for you. I fell in love with your ouma, and with the ground she walked on.' He's said this to Anneke so often over the years, and still, she indulges him with a burst of laughter every time. Poppy, however, remains expressionless.

'But your ouma isn't well, I'm afraid, Poppy. She's got something called rheumatoid arthritis, which is a sickness that makes her sore and tired a lot, and means that a lot of the time, now, she has to be in a wheelchair.' Poppy sits motionless. Jem keeps on talking.

'Seven years ago, when we found out that she was sick, we sold off most of the farm, and kept just a little piece of it for ourselves. But don't you worry, there's more than enough space on our corner of the valley for a lovely little Poppy.'

Jem counts off each familiar clump of trees, each cairn of apricot-skinned rock that marks the track back to Anneke.

'I can tell you're wondering why we sold the farm.' In truth, Jem has no idea if Poppy even understands what he's saying. *Does she speak English or Afrikaans?* Yolande grew up speaking both, but the person who was once his daughter is now a gaping chasm in his understanding of the world. His mind slips over the thought of her, threatening to skid into darkness until he brings it back to the hot, silent cabin.

'We sold it because we didn't know how much time we'd have left together, you see.' Jem's hands are sweating on the steering wheel as the sun burns in through the windshield. 'We didn't see the point of slaving away to keep it all going. All those hours and hours. Farming is hard, you know, Poppy, not just the planting and growing and harvesting but dealing with the buyers and the farmhands and money and paperwork. Why would we want to spend our last years together, not-together, I ask you?'

The little portion of land that they chose to keep was the source of an age-old dispute between Jem and Anneke and their neighbour, Tertius le Roux, because it contained a natural spring. This made the ground swampy, not much good for crops, but le Roux wanted to reroute the water flow to irrigate his vast vineyards. 'Waste of bloody resources,' he'd bellowed at Jem when he'd refused, once again, to sell. How could he sell? The land, which sported nothing but a cluster of worn-down farm buildings arranged in a large U, long unused and falling to ruin, was special to Anneke. Despite le Roux's efforts to rally the community to support him in his battle to take ownership of the spring, Jem and Anneke spent two years converting the stables into a long L-shaped house that showed only a blank, solid wall to anyone approaching from the road, but which opened all along its hidden length on to the sun-filled courtyard on the far side. Flanked by a raw, rocky hill and an old barn set at right angles to the stable, the courtyard was utterly private.

There they hollowed out a pond and created drainage rills to manage the swampiness from the underground spring, piled on layers and layers of well-rotted manure and compost, planted a lemon tree, an olive and two kinds of plum. At one end, they planted flowering quince, to grow into a hedge along the bottom of the hill that divided their land from the le Roux's. They created a small grove of silver birches which flourished in the sheltered space, protected from the unforgiving African sun and the buffeting wind. They built a set of raised beds for vegetables in one corner, and filled in the rest of the space with a multitude of seeds that, over the years, have grown into a lush wonderland of flowers, fruit and herbs.

It is the fragrance of this garden that seeps into the bakkie when, at long last, Jem and Poppy's journey comes to an end. They're parked inside a large, wooden barn with shafts of sunlight slanting through the gaps and knotholes of the slatted walls. In amongst the bars of light lurk mechanical shapes of various vehicles wearing blankets of dust. Poppy can make out another, older bakkie, something that looks like a tractor in pieces, and two motorbikes, one splattered with mud, and the other blotched with rust. Jem opens the driver's door, letting in a rush of cool, scented air.

'We're home.' Jem walks around the van, unbuckles Poppy's seatbelt, and lifts her out. The smell is fuller and sweeter than anything she's ever encountered. She can't even dare to imagine where it's coming from. As Jem carries her through the vast barn to the wooden door in the back, the impossible fragrance causes two tear tracks of clean pink to snake through the grime on Poppy's cheeks. The smell grows stronger, and when Jem opens the door, it fills her completely.

The garden.

At first, it's just an onslaught of green, but as Jem carries her further in, Poppy sees fuzzy-bodied bees buzzing between long pale green stalks topped with purple flowers. When she looks up, there are tiny green birds with white rings around their eyes bouncing and peeping high in the limbs of a tree studded with bright lemons. As Jem's ankle brushes past one of the shrubs beside the path, a delicate cloud of butterflies rises up and then settles back down again, as if someone has lifted an invisible net with silk bows tied all over it.

In the heart of the garden, in a clover-covered clearing surrounded by yellow, white, red and pink roses, sits a wheelchair, and in it, a soft, cream-skinned creature with wispy white hair who must be made from rose petals herself.

'Poppy, it's time to meet your ouma.'

CHAPTER THREE

IT TAKES THREE consecutive bathtubs of warm, soapy water to eliminate Poppy's carapace of accumulated dirt. The first lot of water is dark grey-brown in minutes, and Anneke picks up the child from the scummy puddle, wraps her in a towel, and holds her close while Jem drains the tub, cleans the grime off it, and runs a fresh one. The second time around, Anneke kneels on the bathmat, despite her aching knees, and gently, so very gently, soaps Poppy's skin. Patches of what she thought were dirt turn out to be welts and bruises, and as Anneke scoops water over tiny sharp-boned shoulders and knobs of spine, a whipping storm of rage hurtles through her, battering her insides until her soothing mutterings and croons of comfort are unable to make their way out past the thick paste of bile lodged in her throat.

The third bath takes place in grim silence. Jem crouches down to help comb conditioner through the child's matted hair, starting at the very ends and carefully working upwards. Now that it's clean, the similarity between Poppy's hair and the way Anneke's used to be is startling. It is as if sopping strands from the past are slipping between his fingers.

When the child begins to shiver, Jem and Anneke exchange a wordless look and begin the final rinse, despite the fact that half her head is still a knotted mess. Poppy watches them both with huge, light-coloured eyes that flick from Jem to Anneke and back again. She hasn't made a sound the entire time, but responds to whispered instructions like *Close your eyes now, Poppy, we're going to rinse*, acquiescent as a doll as she's finally lifted from the water and dried with a clean towel.

By the time the ordeal is over, and Poppy is dressed in one of Anneke's vests and a cardigan that they have to wind around her twice like swaddling and tie closed with a ribbon from Anneke's sewing box, Anneke and Jem are as pale-faced and silent as the girl. Jem bundles her in a blanket and sits at the kitchen table with Poppy on his lap, wrapped up like a pupae, while Anneke prepares something to eat.

Night presses in against the kitchen window, dense with the solid buzzing song of the frogs around the pond. Inside the room, now warm with the scent of scrambled eggs and buttered toast, the contrasting wordlessness almost becomes a tune in itself, a silent harmony in the symphony of the clicks and screeches and calls of the garden and the wild hills beyond.

Later, in bed, with the girl asleep between them, Jem and Anneke reach out to touch one another's hands in the darkness. Both of them are weeping.

Poppy wears one of Anneke's old floral blouses gathered at the waist with another sewing-box ribbon. The clothes she arrived in are clean and dry, no longer soaking in a tin bucket and sending tendrils of brown-grey filth into the water, but neither Poppy nor Anneke has touched them since they were taken from the line. Even Wombo, washed and pegged up by his tiny tail, has been ignored.

Poppy stands in the garden and waits for Jem to return from his shopping trip into town. He's been dispatched to buy small T-shirts, underpants, shorts and sandals in a suitable size. It would've been easier to have the girl with him, but when he tried to take her out of the garden and through the gate to the bakkie, she'd gone stiff with horror. Jem had looked into those wide, mortified eyes and had set her down, back in the cool green, heading out to do his shopping alone.

Now Poppy stands as still as she can and closes her eyes. She can hear secateurs going snip pause, snip pause as Anneke deadheads the first of the season's roses. She listens to the soft plish-splash of the fountain in the herb garden. Somewhere close by, a bird calls in liquid notes. Somewhere far, another answers. She tries to breathe away her gathering fear: *this will end.* Any moment now, her mother will arrive and caw her name in a gust of reeking breath and wrench her out of this sanctuary and back into hell. Claws of panic scrabble inside Poppy's throat until, finally, they escape in a shattering scream. The bird goes silent. The secateurs stop snipping.

'Poppy?' Anneke makes her slow way round the flower-studded bank of greenery to where the child stands, trembling, beneath the wild olive tree. Her tiny legs stick out from the billow of pale fabric like a pair of tweezers. 'It's all right, it's all right.' Anneke draws the girl into her arms. 'We won't let anyone take you, Poppy. This is your home now.'

When Jem returns with a shopping bag of new clothes for Poppy, he finds them both lying on the grass, the little girl in a tight ball, and his wife curled around her, her frail body forming a protective cowl across the child's back.

That evening, Anneke and Jem sit at the kitchen table while the cried-out child sleeps on the sofa. All that can be seen of her is a tuft of white-blonde hair sticking out from under a quilt that Anneke sewed last winter out of scraps cut from Jem's old shirts.

'She must be terrified that Yolande will come for her.' Anneke turns her mug, making circles in a patch of spilt coffee on the worn old oak.

Since her first glimpse of Poppy's emaciated, bruised little body, Anneke has been battling to contain her increasing fury. The monster responsible seems to have no connection to the daughter she raised and lost and grieved for. There's a new hard dark piece inside Anneke where the Yolande-sadness used to be.

'Could that happen, do you think, Jem?'

'Yolande won't. Unless…' There's always an 'unless' with Yolande.

'My sister will probably try and get hold of her, you know how Sussie is. And even if she doesn't, Yolande could change her mind at any time, Jem. You know how she…' Jem watches the way that Anneke grips her mug, even though it clearly hurts her swollen thumb.

'Annie, when we walked out of that hell-hole, Yolande let us go. She caught my eye and the hazy look vanished from her face for an unguarded moment. I saw relief, I saw acquiescence.'

'You're sure?'

'Yolande knew what was happening. She let it happen. I know this sounds crazy, considering all the neglect and abuse, but I think she was doing it for Poppy. I think she *knew* that she was ruining her child's life. By letting her go she was… was being kind.'

'But,' Anneke's voice breaks, and she fights for breath, 'Yolande was never one for *staying* kind. She'd always forget her promises, remember?' For long minutes, they sit in clock-ticking silence.

Jem remembers Yolande as a baby, chubby-cheeked and curly-lashed, yelling her lovely little head off when she couldn't get her way. From day one, she'd been unsatisfied with her lot as the only daughter of a pair of aging farmers. *Planting compost worms. You're obsessed with dirt*, Yolande declared in disgust. Nothing was ever how she wanted it to be. The farm was too quiet, the village was too small, the local primary school was too boring, the school she boarded at later was too strict. Jem thinks back to an early morning one spring when Yolande was about nine or ten. He'd glanced out of the kitchen window to see her racing around the yard. The cool air was thick with pollen and birdsong, and he'd imagined it drawing back from her furious little fists. *Why does nothing ever happen?* she'd screamed, throwing her body into ever more frantic spins as if trying to create her own tornado.

Yolande craved discord, but harmony clung to Anneke and Jem and wouldn't be budged no matter how many tantrums she threw. She'd left home as soon as she'd turned sixteen and, despite all their efforts, they'd not heard from her again.

Until two weeks ago.

Now each of them hope that she'll stay away for good.

Jem knows that this is not the first time he's wished Yolande gone, and a familiar stab of guilt twists his guts. *Did we do this to her? Did we make Yolande like this?*

Yolande seemed to have come into the world self-serving, needy, desperate to escape her life and who she was, but that isn't fair, and Jem knows it. Something *made* Yolande hate herself so. Her frustration with her parents' contentedness was the result of something deeper, wasn't it? It wasn't really about worms and soil. He glances across at his wife, with that dreamy distant expression she so often wears as if she is somewhere else entirely, somewhere where you'll never be.

He's spent most of his life trying to get in there with her, into that private secret space, and little Yolande must've tried too. Jem shifts in his chair, the guilt is now a taste in his mouth, something that the sugar in his coffee cannot sweeten.

'We can't do to Poppy what we did to Yolande,' he says in a soft voice. 'We can't leave her out.'

Anneke touches his work-rough hand. 'Don't start that guilt stuff again, Jem. Don't. We need to be here for *this* child, right now.' They both look over to the wisp of blonde hair sticking up over the quilt. 'We loved Yolande, we gave her everything we could. We didn't leave her out, Jem.'

'But we did.' Jem knows *he* did. He knows he resented the intrusion of the difficult demanding child on his Anneke-devotion. And although he could never say it, he knows that Anneke in her gentleness, in her quiet dreaminess, without ever meaning to, leaves *everybody* out.

In a little over two weeks, the purple stripes caused by the bakkie's seatbelt digging into Poppy's collarbone and fleshless thighs start to fade, and when they do, they take her other old bruises along with them, leaving her clean-skinned and new. One warm afternoon, Anneke holds out Poppy's old clothes and motions to the kitchen dustbin.

'Shall we chuck them?' Poppy nods. She still hasn't said a word. 'You want to do it, my love?' Another nod.

Poppy takes the tatty rags from Anneke and hurls them into the bin, looking up at her grandmother for reassurance that she's done the right thing. At Anneke's smile, Poppy dashes off into the house and returns with the pink sandals. With a nervous look over her shoulder, and just the very beginnings of a grin, she sends the shoes into the bin as well. Wombo stays, but Poppy hides him away in a drawer, unsure of his place in this new bright world of warm wooden floorboards, patchwork scatter cushions, and green green green.

After three full weeks, one doctor's visit, and worried conversations held in hushed tones as the girl sleeps, Poppy finally breaks her silence.

Anneke is stirring their breakfast in a pot on the stove while Poppy sits, quiet and motionless, on a pile of cushions that Jem attached to one of the kitchen chairs with a length of old pantyhose so that she can reach the table. The shaft of morning sunlight that slices across the room is so bright on the girl's pale hair that her whole small self seems to blur and glow.

'While we wait for your oatmeal to cook, would you like to see the flowers you're named after?' Anneke asks. She knows not to wait for an answer. She turns down the heat on the stove and holds out her hand. The girl slides off her chair and follows her grandmother outside onto the path where a row of Iceland poppies flaunt their end-of-season flowers in a showy display of tissue-paper petals. Tangerine, lemon and hot pink.

'These are poppies. Your namesakes. Aren't they lovely?' Poppy's soles are growing chilled on the flagstones. She rubs one bare foot against the warm top of the other.

Beneath the blowsy blooms, the hairy poppy stalks remind Poppy of Karel's legs. All those dark strands poking outwards. She can still see his calves, pale and skinny, protruding from the horrible grey shorts he always wore.

'See, that's a bud, just waiting to become a flower.' Anneke points to the swollen hairy oval hanging from the end of one stalk. At the sight of it, Poppy gasps, dashes off along the curving path and disappears into the depths of the garden. Anneke, who is having a good day, follows slowly behind.

She finds the child standing at the edge of the pond, staring across at the little wooden grave marker in the furthest corner of the garden, beneath the old oak tree. The wood of the marker has rotted away and been replaced many times since it was first dug into the soil, and each time, the carving of one word has been done anew.

'That?' The girl points towards the grave marker and speaks in hesitant English. 'What's it say on there?' *She's speaking!*

'It says "Sam".' Anneke keeps her voice level, careful not to scare that little voice away again by making a fuss of the fact that Poppy's silence has finally been breached. 'It's to mark a grave.'

'Someone dead?'

'Some*thing*. Yes.'

Over the years the large mound of soil has sunk and dissolved into the carpet of periwinkles, clivias and arum lilies that grow wild in the shade of the oak tree. The flame-coloured clivias are no longer in bloom, but the arum lilies are crisp and white against the dark green, like freshly ironed linen napkins that have been folded into flutes for an elegant dinner party.

'Who was Sam?'

'He was my horse,' Anneke answers. 'My very best friend. He was buried there when I was fifteen.'

'Horse.'

'Do you know what a horse is?'

'Yes.' Poppy makes a little motion with her hands as if holding a set of reins, jogging them up and down in a mimed trot. Clearly another lesson learned from the TV. 'What colour?' she asks, picking her way through the reeds to edge around the pond towards the far corner.

'Brown. With a white bit on his nose.' Anneke remembers exactly how it felt to kiss that white bit: the tender, velvety skin on the flare of Sam's nostrils, and the scent of chewed grass and dust and horse sweat in her own.

'Did you love him, the horse?'

'I did.'

The child walks around the wooden marker three times, as if performing a ritual. Each time, her toes catch on the periwinkle stems that snake between the lily plants, the dark leaves and blue flowers twitch. She runs her fingers over the letters in the rough wood and then turns to look at Anneke.

'Ouma?' The word is halting and new in her mouth. 'Can I be called Sam?'

'What, instead of Poppy?'

'Yes.'

'Short for Samantha?'

'No, just Sam. Only Sam.'

'Are you sure? It's more of a boy's name.'

'I won't be Poppy any more.' Her mouth twists. 'I can't be. Any more.' One heavy rain storm, the girl imagines, and those fluttering petals will end up bruised and broken in bits on the ground.

'It's a big decision, changing your name.'

And then there are those hairy bits. That horrible oval bud. 'Please?'

Anneke leans hard on her walker and gives the child a long look.

'You really don't like Poppy?'

'I hate it.'

'Well that's no good, is it?' Anneke says. 'Sam it is then.'

'Will you tell Grandpa also?'

'Absolutely.'

'Sam Sam Sam,' the girl whispers, circling the wooden marker again.

'Come along, Sam, it's time to go in and have some breakfast.'

PART TWO
THE HORSE-GARDEN

CHAPTER FOUR

WHEN SHE WAS still Poppy, Sam subsisted almost entirely on stolen sweets and scraps. Sometimes, when Yolande forgot about food for too long to bear, she'd go scrounging through whichever neighbourhood they were living in at the time, knocking on doors and asking for biscuits. On bad days, she'd hunt through the litter for crisp packets so that she could lick the broken, salty remnants out of the seams. Now, after three months of home-made peach jam and farm butter on freshly baked bread, mutton stews, butternut sprinkled with cinnamon, thick vegetable soups and oatmeal served with grated apple and honey, Sam has transformed. Her shins are no longer blades, her cheeks have filled out and she's shot up almost two centimetres according to the markings on the doorframe of Anneke's sewing room that has now become her bedroom. Even her hair has grown and thickened. She wears it in two puffy braids that reach to her shoulder blades.

This afternoon, Anneke is in the kitchen rubbing crushed cardamom and orange rind under the skin of a big, bald bird in preparation for tomorrow's special feast. Sam is outside in the rose garden, and every now and then she catches a whiff of citrus and spice wafting out from the open doorway. Tomorrow is Christmas. It used to be just a TV word, but the mysterious event is happening for real this time. Sam helped

Jem string Anneke's collection of old trinkets over the potted cypress in the lounge that serves as a Christmas tree, and they've been having dark, fruity mince pies with their afternoon coffee for the past week. Sam is in love with mince pies. She wonders if it's too soon after breakfast to ask for another.

Out amongst the roses, with the heavy summer heat cloaking her back and shoulders, the clover is cool and yielding beneath Sam's bare feet. She stops at each rose bush, checking for acid-green aphids on the tender sprouting tips. When she finds them, she squishes their fat, sap-filled bodies between fingers already stained a brownish green, just like Jem showed her.

Suddenly the quiet is interrupted by a loud cry:

'Koewee!'

Sam freezes, baffled by the shrill sound she's never heard before. Is it a bird of some kind?

'Anneke!' Not a bird. Sam's body goes limp with fear, and she sinks down on to her haunches, oblivious to the scrape of rose thorns on her knees. 'Anneke!' A stranger's voice strains through the wooden barn gate. The latch rattles, as if someone is trying to open it from the other side. 'I know about the girl,' the voice says in Afrikaans. 'I know you've been dodging my calls. Come on, you have to let me in!'

Who is here? Sam quakes. *I know about the girl*, the voice had shouted. Yolande has sent someone to fetch her back.

'Ouma? Grandpa?' Sam whispers. 'There's someone... someone at the gate—'

'Hold your horses, Sus.' Anneke emerges from the house. Her face is white. She wipes her trembling hands on her apron and makes her slow way down the path. 'Promise you won't make a fuss, Sussie?' she calls through the wood.

'Oh, good heavens, Anneke, I'm not going to thump you or anything like when we were kids. I just want to know what's going on. You can't drop off the radar like this and expect me not to come barging round.'

'No, you're right there.' Anneke pulls back the latch and a cloud of alien perfume overwhelms the green smell of the garden.

Sam peers through the rose stems to see a bigger, smoother, more carefully put together version of her grandmother muscling her way in through the barn gate.

'A grandchild, Annie? Seriously, you thought you'd keep that from me?'

'I was going to tell you, but it's been... I... we had to give her a chance to settle in.'

'What's going on, for goodness sake?' Sussie glares into her sister's pale face. 'Why on earth do you look so frightened?' Anneke clutches the corners of her apron, and Sussie lowers her voice. 'You're scared she'll come looking for her, is that it?' Sussie lets the question dissipate, unanswered, into the hot, thin air before resuming her rant.

'Did you think I'd let Christmas pass without demanding to know why you just vanished off the face of the planet for the past three months?' She peers around at the leafy garden. Sam squeezes her eyes shut to keep herself hidden.

'And then I heard about the girl. Where is she? Yolande's child?' Sussie asks. Sam holds her breath. *Yolande's child.* It's been months since she's heard the name out loud, and hearing it now, spoken as if Sam is *HER* possession, brings the memory of the feel of Yolande's nail-bitten fingers encircling her wrist, stretching the skin till it burnt. Sam can feel the wrench inside her shoulder joint as her mother pulled her along the pavement, and the way her feet skidded in their oversized sandals, sending her toppling down. Blood on her chin and a dirty brown-pink blob of discarded chewing gum on the ground, like some kind of hideous creature that had crawled out from a crack in the pavement, waiting to jerk back to life and suck her down.

Sussie's voice brings Sam back to the garden: 'I can't believe you've been hiding your granddaughter from me for three whole months!'

A light breeze stirs the leaves of the olive tree, showing their secret silvery undersides. Sudden colour flows back into Anneke's cheeks.

'Ag, come inside, have some coffee and calm down to a mild panic, would you?' She jostles her sister's arm to uproot her from her spot in the gateway. 'It's true, we do have a new little family member here, but it's complicated, Sus. There are reasons for my silence.' Sussie allows Anneke to propel her towards the house. 'You'll understand when I explain.'

'Why didn't you ask for my help?' Sussie's voice has softened. She puts a protective arm around Anneke's shoulder to take her weight as they walk up the path.

'The girl has been adjusting to a new environment. The last thing she's needed is you swooping in here and bossing everyone around.'

'Me? Bossing everyone?' Sussie says, and both the women burst out laughing as they disappear into the house.

Sam lies down in the clover and tries to remember how to breathe.

Sussie brews the coffee while Anneke unpacks a plastic tub of home-baked *vorm koekies* from the depths of Sussie's voluminous handbag. Sussie always bring something sweet. *Vorm koekies*, with their jammy, coconut centres, are Anneke's favourite.

'So you brought her back here, and just like that, she's yours?'

'Well, we hope so. Jeremy said that Yolande was in no state to look after herself, let alone a child.'

'I heard from Sanet van der Westhuisen that you and Jem brought a little girl in to see Dr Cilliers in Robertson. She said she was as skinny as a spider leg and covered in sores.'

'That Sanet must be in seventh heaven working as a doctor's receptionist. She always was a gossip, and now someone can't even have a corn on their toe without her releasing a bulletin to the whole of the Western Cape.'

'Well if it wasn't for Sanet's great big mouth, I'd still be in the dark about the child. I can't believe I had to get the news through a gossip, Annie!'

'Enough with the guilt. I haven't been able to talk to anyone about her yet, Sus.' Anneke takes the offered coffee mug. 'We just want her to be safe here first, that's all. Didn't want anyone… Yolande…'

'You're scared she'll come back and take the child?' Sussie asks again.

'We are,' Anneke admits. Outside, unseen in the shrubbery, Sam listens in, her whole body quivering.

'From what Sanet said about the state of the child, it doesn't seem like Yolande would care enough to bother.'

'Yes, but with Yolande you never know.' Anneke takes a sip too soon. She breathes out to cool her scalded lips. 'You never know what idea she'll get into her head.' Just outside the doorway, a gasp of breath, too soft for the women to hear.

'Jem said Yolande and her current man were living like feral animals in a forgotten cage. Nothing clean, no food, scratching around in filth to find something to get high on.'

'Ag, that's terrible.'

'Little Sam was just a scrap when he found her. You wouldn't believe how much she's grown since.'

'Sam? Same as your old horse?' Sussie asks with a raised eyebrow.

'She chose it.'

'Ja, but really?' Anneke shrugs, and Sussie changes direction. 'Any idea of her age?'

'We think about five going on six. The doctor said that undernourishment may have stunted her growth, which is why she seemed so much younger when Jem found her.'

'You *think*?'

'Well who are we going to ask, Sussie? Guessing is all we've got to go on.'

'You could… Yolande might—'

'No,' Anneke snaps. The kitchen is very quiet in the wake of the word's violence.

Sussie looks around the room, looking for a change of subject to fill the humming-fridge silence. She frowns at the sight of the half-seasoned goose on the kitchen counter. 'I'm guessing you two bringing Sam to the main house tomorrow for a decent family Christmas is out of the question?'

'It's too soon for her, Sussie. She's only just becoming herself.'

'Is she, you know, all OK?' Sussie bites into a cookie and apricot jam squelches out and sticks to the corner of her lip. 'Don't give me that look, Anneke, it's a perfectly fair question to ask, given the circumstances she was raised in.'

'If you're trying to find out whether she's retarded or anything, she's not. She was undernourished, frightened and dirty. She had bruises on her skin and, I've no doubt, bruises on her soul, but she's clever and loving and she's ours now, so everything's going to be fine—'

42

'Don't cry, Annie. I didn't mean to make you cry.'

'It's just...' Anneke rubs wet cheeks. Her fingers smell like rosemary and orange rind. 'I'm just so glad we found her, that's all.'

Slowly, throughout that first long, hot summer, Sam softens, like a lump of hard wax held in the palm of a warm hand. Her English vocabulary grows, helped along by Jem, who reads to her every night before bed, sitting with her on his knee in his favourite easy chair in the lounge and letting her turn the pages. She seldom smiles, but sometimes Jem can coax a light flutter of a giggle out of her, and the sound of it is so wonderful that he finds himself playing the clown more and more of the time.

Every morning, Anneke brushes Sam's hair, taking her time to tease out the night's knots and smoothing the cream-coloured strands until they shine. Sam sits with her eyes fixed on Anneke's in the mirror during the brushing, her features relaxed and unguarded, and her small shoulders releasing some of their perpetual rigidity. Once Sam's hair is brushed and braided into two pale ropes, Anneke sits in the chair and passes the hairbrush to Sam. An hour can easily pass at the dressing table in Anneke's bedroom.

'Groom, groom, groom. You two are like a pair of monkeys,' Jem likes to tease. 'Some days I'm scared to come in here in case you both grab me and wrestle me to the ground and start picking nits out of my hair.' Sam smiles, and Jem tugs at the grey woolly hair on his forearm and asks her: 'How many braids could you give this, do you think?' He is rewarded by a burst of breathy, delightful laughter. He catches Anneke's eye in the mirror, and then sits on the edge of the bed to watch

Sam weave her grandmother's hair into a wonky, lopsided braid. At his back, the curtains move in the breeze, ushering in the scent of the roses.

Sam is at her most relaxed, however, when she's in the garden with a job to do. Jem and Anneke soon learn to give her little tasks, because as soon as she gets going, Sam seems to transform. She scurries around busily if the job requires it, or sits at her duties with a look of quiet intensity on her face, humming to herself. With a vital place in the running of things, Sam seems to grow more solid, to fill out around the edges, as if she's suddenly realised that she has value. She is not afraid of working hour after hour on the dullest of tasks, like carefully extricating the roots of items to be transplanted from their clinging soil, and isn't the least squeamish about picking fat, white cutworms out of the turned compost and putting them into a bucket of suds.

'Couldn't be less like Yolande,' Anneke whispers to Jem, and he nods and thinks that *they* are the ones who are really different. No more shutting out. No more just the two of them. Not like the old days when Yolande was young.

Winter brings a dusting of white to the distant mountain tops, a chill wind that sneaks in beneath the door and around the edges of the window frames, and even more rain spiders than usual. There's one near the kitchen ceiling, right now, high up above Anneke's head. *It knows*, Sam thinks, and stares out of the window, trying to see through the icy rain to the place where she once put the spider-jar.

It knows what I did.

When she first arrived at the farm, Sam had been terrified of the large spiders, with their long, curved legs and motionless watchfulness. One afternoon, she managed to catch one which had been haunting her bedroom, using an old jam jar. She closed the lid tight and carried the jar outside, where she left it, with the spider still inside, pushed beneath the shrubbery at the far end of the garden. Every day, she would go and check on the spider. Every day, she found the spider feeling along the smooth curve of the glass with its delicate feet, looking for an exit. She wanted to release him, she meant to, but each time she went to check on the jar, she couldn't do it. And then one day it was too late and the spider stopped moving and she felt even worse. It took weeks for the creature to die, and Sam ached each time she thought about how she never set it free. When Jem finally discovered the jar with the dry, spider husk in it, he took Sam onto his knee and gave her a hug and explained that rain spiders were the good guys.

'They don't bite people,' he'd said, 'they just like sitting near the ceiling and chomping on mosquitoes all night long so that you can sleep in peace without getting itchy bites.'

Why didn't I just let it go?

Anneke, trying to warm her aching fingers around a mug of hot soup, watches as the girl's shoulders tighten, and her face seems to pale and shrink in on itself.

'What are you thinking about, Sam?'

'I just wish I could go into the garden.' She needs to go to the spider-jar place, crouch down, and whisper sorry. Again.

'You'll be able to, soon. Just wait and see what Grandpa's bringing home from town. That's him arriving now. Can you hear the bakkie?' Sam nods, her gaze fixed on the rain.

'I got the catalogue,' Jem announces when he walks in, treading puddles of brown water onto the kitchen floor. 'Take a look at this lot.' He hands Anneke the thin booklet, and she spreads it open, on the tabletop.

'Come, Sam, come and choose your gumboots.'

Sam approaches the table with slow steps, and sucks in her cheeks as Jem lifts her up onto her cushion-tied-with-pantyhose chair. She blinks at the bright printed colours. She knows something is expected of her, but she isn't sure what.

'You can pick any ones you want. Aren't we lucky that the local store doesn't sell such small sizes, hey? Because look at all your options in here.' Anneke taps a picture of a pair of gumboots in sky blue with a pattern of sunny yellow polka dots. 'What about these?'

Sam stays silent.

'If we get you some gumboots, lovey, we can bundle you up to go outside, even if it's raining,' Jem says.

Sam stares at the catalogue, glancing up at Jem and then back again, touching the flimsy paper, running her hand over the rainbow of options.

'Do I get just the picture or the real thing?' she asks, and Jem and Anneke exchange a look.

'The real thing, Sam. They'll be your very own special gumboots for gardening in the rain.'

'These.' Sam points to a pair at the bottom of the page. They are a sober olive, just like Jem's.

'Are you sure? Not the pink ones, or these juicy-looking red ones?'

'These,' she insists.

'Good choice, dear heart,' Anneke says, and gives the girl a squeeze. 'Very good choice.'

Spring. Beneath a new blue sky, the espaliered rows of fruit trees burst into clouds of blossom, covering the valley with a chequerboard of fluttering pink and white. In amongst the fynbos, dense patches of wild vygie flowers blaze luminous pink against the brown. From the sheltered, secluded garden, however, it's impossible to see any of this.

'You're missing out, Sam,' Anneke encourages when Jem suggests a short drive, but Sam has not stepped foot out of the boundaries of the garden since their trip to see Dr Cilliers in the week after she was rescued, almost a full year ago.

'Come for a drive, lovey, just a short little one. We'll be back here before you know it.'

'I'm coming too,' Anneke coaxes, already waiting by the gate. 'Look, even with my sore hips, I'm dying to see the fairy kingdom.'

'I don't... want.'

'The orchards are beautiful, row after row of blossoms. Don't you want to see?'

Sam bites her lip. Jem takes her hand, and Anneke the other one, and together they walk through the gate and into the barn where the bakkie is parked. Sam's fingers tighten around her grandparents' and her breath comes in sharp little snorts.

'No,' she gasps, coming to a stop.

'We'll just drive up the road, look out over the orchards, and come back again, dear heart.'

Sam starts to tremble and her face goes chalk white, and Jem thinks it is as if she has become embedded in the garden, like a plant with filigree roots that will be broken and damaged if someone tries to move it. He is tempted to give up and take her back in, but he knows that if the girl continues to stay inside, her fear of leaving the place will only grow, and her sanctuary will one day become her prison. Steeling himself against her heart-wrenching expression and the tears that now gallop down her cheeks, Jem picks Sam up and carries her to the car, fighting tears of his own as he buckles her limp body on the front seat beside him. He helps Anneke into the vehicle beside the girl, and walks around to the driver's side.

'We're all coming back here, I promise,' he whispers as he starts the engine. 'The three of us, together. You'll see.'

Jem and Anneke weren't exaggerating the magnificence of the flowering fynbos, or fruit trees in blossom, but it's only when Sam spots a horse and a rider moving between the white-petalled limbs of an orchard that she comes to life. She sits up and cranes to see better, unbuckling her seatbelt to clamber over Jem's lap and poke her head out of the driver's window.

'There!' She points at the chestnut horse, tears drying on her cheeks. 'Sam.'

'Not Sam,' whispers Anneke, 'he was more chocolate-coloured than that.' Sam gazes at the rider, a teenage girl with a long, dark ponytail, guiding her horse between the rows.

'That's the le Roux girl, isn't it?' Anneke asks Jem. 'She's all grown up. Must be about sixteen or so by now.'

'A laroo-girl?' Sam breathes, enchanted, eyes glued to the horse and human who move, as one, amongst whirling con-fetti-white petals. 'Can I be a laroo-girl?'

'No, le Roux's her surname, dear heart, that's our neigh-bour's daughter, Liezette.'

'Oh. The bad people,' Sam scowls, 'on the other side of the hill?'

'What have you been telling her, Jem?'

'I once mentioned that le Roux didn't want us to make our garden home where we did, that he wanted our water for his big fancy farm.' Jem glances at his wife. 'What? It's the truth. I didn't realise that it would make such an impression.'

'*She* can't be bad, though,' Sam points at the dark-haired girl, now moving out of view, 'or the horse wouldn't let her ride him.' She wiggles backwards off Jem's lap and tucks herself in close to Anneke. 'Tell me the story again, Ouma, the one about how you first got Sam?'

'You sure you want to hear that old thing again?' Anneke smiles, delighted that Sam's terror of the outside world seems to have abated a little. 'All right, I'll tell it while Grandpa drives us home.'

CHAPTER FIVE

SAM'S SECOND EVER Christmas goose has been reduced to a container of congealing scraps in the fridge, and the last days of the old year hang motionless over the valley, pressing down on the baking soil with heavy fists. When Sussie's 'koewee!' sound comes, Sam is sitting on a rock at the cool edge of the pond with her feet in the water. She glances across to Jem, who is turning the compost heap in the shade beside the shed. He gives her a reassuring smile, and she knows he's reminding her not to run off and hide like she usually does when Sussie comes round. Sam has been assured over and over that Sussie, who is her grandmother's younger sister, is a good person, just a bit bossy. Nothing to be afraid of. Sam needs to be brave, just like she was the first few times when going for a drive in the bakkie. Sam has made a promise not to hide, but her resolve is faltering as the 'koewee!' rings through the garden. She can feel Jem watching her, and can hear Anneke, in a wheelchair today, as she rumbles over the flagstones to open the gate. The drawing of the latch. The smell of store-bought perfume. Sam doesn't move.

'There now, Sussie. I got here eventually.'

'Good grief, Annie, why you insist on trekking out to let me in each time, I just don't know. Would it kill you to leave this gate unbolted? What on earth do you have to lock yourselves up for?'

'To stop busybodies like you barging in whenever they want.' Anneke kisses her sister hello, and then both women turn towards the pond. Sussie takes in the child with her thin limbs and pale blonde hair, tousled where bits of it have escaped their plaits. She opens her arms as if expecting the girl to run into them. Sam, who can see this out of the corner of her eye, digs her fingers into the squelchy mud at the edge of the pond.

'She won't. Not yet.' Anneke reaches for her sister's hand. 'Come inside and have some coffee.'

'In this heat?' Sussie tries not to look put out. She's used to being greeted by children, especially related ones.

'Iced, of course.'

'Ah, Anneke's famous ice-coffee.' Sussie turns back for one more glance at Sam, and then pushes Anneke's wheelchair towards the house.

'You're going to have to meet your great-aunty properly sometime.' Jem grins at his scowling granddaughter. Sam picks up a clod of mud and lobs it in his direction. It splats into the still green water of the pond and Jeremy laughs.

After a bit, Sam laughs too.

SUSSIE WEARS HER hair short and immaculately styled in an upswept halo, but in the time between exiting her air-conditioned car and entering the blessed cool of Anneke's kitchen, the carefully arranged wisps at the back of her neck are already sweat-glued to her skin.

'Sit down, Sussie,' Anneke orders, and rolls her wheelchair over to the freezer.

'Let me help—'

'Stop fussing. I do this a hundred times a day, you know.' Anneke waves an ice tray at her sister in a menacing fashion until she sinks down into a chair. Anneke gets out two tall glasses and pours cooling coffee over the ice cubes that she made earlier using condensed milk.

Sussie stares out at the garden. The heat has leeched the greenery of its colour, and the borders blur between the plants, the pond water, and the white-haired, skinny-limbed child.

'Sam's grown a lot, hasn't she?' Sussie takes the proffered glass. The iced milk cubes are already sending creamy tendrils snaking through the dark coffee. 'She has hair just like you did when we were girls.'

'I know.'

'She must be six now, hey? Or seven?' She sips the bitter warmth. As the ice melts, each progressive sip will be colder, creamier and sweeter.

'We think so.'

'She'll be needing to go to school then, won't she?' The town is too tiny to warrant having a school of its own. All the local kids are bussed to and from a bigger town in the area each day.

'I don't want to send her to the primary in Robertson. She refuses to speak Afrikaans.' Sussie raises an eyebrow. Anneke plunges on: 'I think it reminds her of her old life or something. Understandably, she wants to forget the whole thing, poor child.'

'Well there's always boarding school, if it needs to be English.'

'Nope.'

'Come on, Annie, it's been almost a year and a half and you haven't heard a peep from Yolande. Don't you think it's time you and Jem relax the guard a bit?'

'It's not that. Or not *just* that. I can't possibly send the little thing off to board. After what she's been through, not a chance.'

'So take her to mad Mrs McGovern in town. She teaches the English curriculum from her house to her own sons and those fancy-schmancy Ndlovu kids whose folks don't want their precious brown babies shipped off to a big bad boarding school either.'

Anneke remembers her own petrifying first day of grade one. There were vast cold rooms with windows too high to see out of, bristling with screeching, elbowing girls. Compared to her parents' warm, ramshackle farmhouse, it had felt like she'd arrived at the other end of the earth. Three decades later, she'd deposited a singularly unterrified Yolande into those same dark, socks-and-floor-polish-smelling corridors.

'You've heard of Mrs McGovern?' Sussie continues. 'She's the wife of that big-shot engineer whose working on the dam project in—'

'I know who she is, Suss, I'm in a wheelchair, not an isolation tank.'

'Could've fooled me, the way you and Jem carry on.' Sussie spears a spoon into her glass and the melting cubes skitter. 'She's a bit of an odd bird, but then again, she's English.' Sussie's shrug manages to convey the ludicrousness of all English speakers, Jem (and now Sam) included. 'Look, Sam's around the same age as the youngest McGovern kid, so I'm sure she'd be accommodated. I could make a call.'

'You'd love that, wouldn't you, Sus? Taking charge.'

'I'm just saying, she needs to become socialised, integrated into the community. She can't just bugger about in the garden all day like you and Jem do, never going out, never seeing family.'

'And here comes the obligatory lecture.'

'Look, Annie, having your own kooky ideas about things is fine when you're a little girl who wants to talk to invisible creatures in the fruit orchard rather than play with real humans... But it makes no sense now. Not in your condition, with Jem not getting any younger. The two of you all alone out here without any help, and now with a child to look after—'

'Good grief, you make us sound like a pair of decrepit old fools.'

'Someone has to be practical, is all I'm saying.' Beyond the window, in the green garden, Jem is crouched on the grass beside Sam, their heads bent over something small and wriggly in his soil-covered hand. 'Learning how to faff around with worms is one thing. But that girl is going to have to go to school.'

Mrs McGovern's home school is to regular school as a cupcake with icing primroses covered in sprinkles is to a stale bran muffin. Despite this, and regardless of the fact that each flagstone leading up to the front door of her house has been painted a different cheery colour by each of the four pupils in Mrs McGovern's care, Sam can hardly breathe as Jem lifts her down from the bakkie.

'See, what's this planted here?' Jem tries to distract her. Sam bends down briefly to finger the tiny leaves and woody stalks of the plants growing between the coloured flagstones, but doesn't loosen her clutch on Jem's hand.

'Don't know.'

'Course you do. Give it a whiff.'

'Lemon thyme.' She curls her scented fingertips into a fist.

'Good girl. See, it can't be so scary here if there's lemon thyme, now can it? Mrs McGovern probably planted it on the path so that each morning you'll be enveloped in a cloud of refreshing scent on the way to school.' Sam's scowl deepens.

'Why can't I just stay home with you and Ouma?'

'We've talked about this, darling, and I hate to admit it, but your ouma's busybody sister is right for a change. You don't want to just sit and deadhead daisies with old folks all day for the rest of your life.'

'Yes I do,' she sniffs. 'I really do. Sussie doesn't even know *anything*.'

'I'll be right here waiting when it's time to come home, and then you can help in the garden for the rest of the afternoon.'

'But what if *she*... somehow finds...'

'Yolande's a hundred miles away. Remember that long drive we took to get here from Pretoria?'

'Yes.'

'Well she's all the way on the other side of that. And she hasn't got a bakkie like mine to drive here, now does she?'

'She doesn't have a car at all.'

'Exactly.'

'Or a motorbike,' adds Sam, thinking of the two old machines parked in the shed back home. She feels a little better.

Jem pulls her gently up the steps to the stoop. As they approach the open front door, a small boy darts out of it. He's clutching a painted paper plate with two cut-out eye holes over his face. The ragged fringe of orange wool around the plate hints that it's supposed to be a lion. The boy roars with gusto and Sam just about levitates into Jem's arms.

'Gosh, Keegan, that's quite a welcome for our new friend. Perhaps it's time to put the lion mask away and let Sam see how friendly you really are, hey?'

Mrs McGovern looks exactly like the sort of person who would encourage children to paint flagstones with their fingers, and then give them herbal tea with honey and oatmeal cookies afterwards. Unlike the other women in the area who favour practical jeans and men's shirts, saving their coloured slacks and chiffon blouses for Sunday church services, Mrs McGovern is wearing a long flowing outfit that seems to be sewn together out of different bits of old saris and cushion covers. Her feet are bare. There's a silver ring on one of her toes. She smiles at Sam, and despite herself, the girl doesn't scowl back.

'She'll be very well looked after here, Jem. You don't have to worry about a thing,' Mrs McGovern says as Jeremy hugs Sam close to his soil-smelling shirtfront.

'Remember,' Jem says, working to keep his voice steady, 'she goes home with nobody but me.'

'You have my word. Come on, Sam, say goodbye to your grandpa and let's go in and show you around.' Mrs McGovern takes her by the hand, and Keegan rushes up, lion mask abandoned in the flower bed, to grab the other. Between them both, Sam is almost carried into the house.

CHAPTER SIX

BY THE TIME December returns, bringing hot winds and flying beetles with domed coppery shells that munch on the rose leaves at dusk, the terror of Sam's first day at school has been reduced to a shifting, shadowed memory. Over the eleven months that have passed, she's relaxed into the company of her classmates, Zama and Thuli, can tolerate ten-year-old Nathan's teasing, and is devoted to earning Mrs McGovern's smiles of approval. Early on, Keegan's chatter wore away Sam's brittle shyness, and now the two of them, laughing, race down the main street.

'Last day, last day!' Keegan shouts into the midday heat. 'No more school for a whole month.' And then, when the Super Saver comes into view: 'I'm going to buy... like ten Fizzers!'

'I'm also getting some. Green ones.' Coins rattle in the pockets of Sam's shorts, and puffs of silky dust billow up around her bare feet.

Suddenly, Keegan skids to a halt.

'Hey!' Sam yelps, just managing to stop from slamming into the back of him. 'Why are you stopping?'

'*They're* back.' The dread in Keegan's voice jellies her muscles and freezes the marrow inside her bones. Her breath is gone. The world tilts to one side. *Yolande and Karel are here.* Her mother has finally come to take her. Sam feels as if her insides are filled up with ice-cold porridge, sludging in her veins, slowing her heart. She ducks behind Keegan and stares at the Super Saver, now only half a block away. At any moment, Yolande and Karel are going to step through the doors and out into the street.

They will turn their heads and they will see me. Sam remembers the wiry strength in Karel's skinny arms, and the way Yolande could run when she needed to, chewing up distance in greedy, gulping seconds. Blotches of white-hot panic cloud the edges of her vision.

'Who's "they"?' she whispers through dry lips.

'Boarders.' Keegan's voice is faint with horror. 'I just saw two of them go into the Super Saver. I thought they'd only come tomorrow.'

Relief nearly drops Sam where she stands. She sways, light-headed, almost laughing. *Not Yolande.*

'What are boarders?'

'Some of the other kids that live on the farms and stuff around here get sent away to boarding school, but now they're back for the holidays.'

'Is that bad?'

'Yes, that's bad. They're Afrikaans.'

'*I'm* Afrikaans.'

'Only half. And you're not… you don't… They once tried to—' He breaks off, gulps air, and tries again: 'They like picking on me and Nate.' Keegan places the arch of his foot over a small sharp stone and pushes down. Sam can see him wince. 'Let's get out of here.'

'But the Fizzers—'

'Come ON!' Keegan tugs Sam's T-shirt to spin her round, but in his clumsy desperation, he knocks her over. Gravel stings the palms of her hands.

'Hey, that's no way to treat your girlfriend!' someone shouts in Afrikaans. Sam looks up from her shredded palms, and through hot tears, sees two big boys with khaki shorts and bony hard feet striding towards them. One of the boys has hair on his legs, but it's not wiry like Karel's was, it's mielie-silk yellow against the brown.

'Is your English willy so small you have to show your little girl who's boss by hitting her around, hey, salt-dick?'

Sam hasn't heard anyone swear in Afrikaans since her Poppy days. The harsh cadence of it sends her spinning back into the past. She can feel the pressure of Yolande's hand on her shoulder, and her nostrils fill with the vomity cigarette smell of her mother's claw-fingers.

'Get up, get up!' Keegan wrenches Sam upright and the two of them belt back up the road towards the schoolhouse, feet pounding on the dirt.

The boarders must have better things to do on their first day of summer freedom, because a breathless Sam and Keegan make it back to the safety of the lemon-thyme pavers without any further incident.

'Oh no, you're bleeding,' Keegan whispers when he sees the state of her hands. 'I'm so sorry. Come.' He drags Sam past the schoolroom and into the never-seen-before depths of the McGoverns' home, taking her to a bathroom that smells of something lemony with an undertone of peed-on bathmat. Sam notices a small plastic ship on the edge of the bath as Keegan leads her to the basin.

'Here. You need to rinse.' He guides her hands under the running tap, and she sucks in her breath. Flaps of translucent skin lift and move in the cold water. There are bits of grit embedded beneath.

'Ow, it looks really sore, Sam.'

'It's not that bad.' Sam moves her hands to try and wash the grit out. For a moment, the two of them are engrossed in watching the thin trails of blood snake down the plughole.

'Do the boarders come every year, Keegan?'

'Ja.'

'And are they always so…'

'Ja.'

'Hey, what's going on?' Nathan appears in the doorway, scowling. 'Why's *she* in here. You know my rules about school people on home turf.'

'It's holidays, she can come in if she wants,' Keegan retorts, and then lowers his voice. 'They're here already, Nate.'

'Seriously?' Keegan nods. Nathan picks at a scab on his elbow. 'Crap.'

'Two of them were coming out of the Super Saver and that's why Sam fell and hurt her hands.'

'Which two?'

'Driekus and Morné.'

'Oh God.' Nathan's face loses some of its colour. 'OK then,' he says, nodding his head towards Sam, 'I guess she can game with us if she wants.'

Sam dries her hands on a wad of crumpled loo paper and follows Keegan into the lounge. She stops short when she sees the black blank face of the McGoverns' television against one wall. It's the first one she's seen since she stopped being Poppy. Her mouth goes dry. Her legs feel funny.

'You're going to have to wait your turn, Sam.' Nathan is holding a plastic device with buttons on it that reminds Sam of the long-ago Game Boy that Karel once gave her. 'You can play with Keegan after this but I'm going first.' Sam runs her tongue over the new, perfect tooth with slightly frilly edges that grew in when the chipped one fell out. Her ears are making a whooshing sound.

'Have you played PlayStation before? It's awesome.' Keegan's face is flushed and eager. 'I'll show you all my games. If it wasn't for this thing, Nate and I wouldn't survive the summer holidays.'

'Are you...' Sam's mouth is having trouble shaping itself around words. She can taste road dust. 'Are you going to switch the TV on to play?'

'Well, duh. Obviously,' Nathan says and points the remote. The screen bursts into light and colour and Sam reels backwards. 'Welcome to the summer sanctuary,' Nathan grins, pressing various buttons on the gaming console. 'Make yourself comfy. Those bloody boarders can't touch us in here.'

All of a sudden, Sam is on the ground staring upwards. The McGoverns' lounge carpet has softened her second fall of the day. Her eyes swivel sideways. There are little fuzzy dust balls under the couch.

'What the heck!'

'Sam, why are you on the floor? Did you faint?'

'Hey, is she crying?'

Sam rolls over and crawls towards the door, desperate to get away from the blue flicker and the onslaught of sound.

'Come back, Sam, you can't go out there, those boarders will get you.' She's barely breathing. She scrabbles for the doorknob, and then, at last, she's out in the yellow-layered brightness of real daylight. She crawls down the steps till there is grass beneath her body. Living, prickling grass. She drops her face into it and gasps sharp, green-smelling lungfuls of air.

'Sam?' Keegan's voice is a whimper from the front steps. She looks up into his wide, shocked eyes. 'What *was* that?'

'I don't like television.' Each word is wrapped in a sheath of ice.

'What? Are you nuts or something?'

'Or games or consoles or anything… like that.' Sam sits up and checks the palms of her injured hands. Her breathing is calming down now, and she can no longer feel her heart thump.

'But it's the best, you haven't even tried—'

'Go back inside.' Sam gets to her feet. She's a little wobbly, but her gaze is steady, cold. Keegan takes a small step backwards. 'I'm going to wait out front for Grandpa. He'll be here soon to take me home.' The word 'home' brings the scent of lemon blossom and compost. Roses, pond mud, coffee and condensed milk.

'Your grandpa won't be here for a while. Remember, we were going to play because it's the last day—'

'I'll see you next year when school starts, Keegan,' Sam says, and then she runs.

Keegan wants to call out that he'll play outside with her, wherever she wants, even if the boarders come, but she's already disappeared around the corner of the house. His hands feel numb. His mouth tastes strange.

'Sam?' he calls, but it's only a whisper. He realises, with a dropping heart, that he's not going to follow her. It's not just the boarders he's afraid of, or the uncomfortable memory of his friend crawling, sobbing, to the door, it's the way her too-pale eyes changed so fast. From water to ice.

On Christmas Day, Sam sits wedged into the front seat of the bakkie between her grandparents. They're going to a Christmas lunch with the extended family at Sussie's house.

'Do we have to?' Since the last day of school and the awful PlayStation incident at Keegan's house, Sam hasn't left the sanctuary of the garden. During the long hot afternoons, while Jem and Anneke have napped beneath an old whirring fan in their curtained bedroom, she's been playing alone in the cool corner by the pond. Nourished by the long-dead body of Sam-the-horse, the oak tree is a sprawling wonder of knotted branches and dense foliage, and in the relief of its shade, wearing a bridle made from plaited wool that she scavenged from Anneke's knitting basket and a pair of torn pantyhose tucked in the waistband of her shorts as a tail, Sam has spent her summer pretending to be a horse.

But there's no tail and bridle in evidence today. Sam has been buttoned into an unfamiliar dress, and Anneke has brushed out her braids so that her hair falls, hot and heavy, down her back.

'It's unavoidable, my love.' Anneke pats Sam's leg as the bakkie lurches over the humps and bumps of the dirt road leading into town. 'You know what a fuss Sussie made the last two years when we opted out. Your gramps and I are in enough trouble as it is, living out here on our own as we do.'

'Yup, we don't want to start World War Three.'

The backs of Sam's bare legs are glued to the baking seat after only a few minutes.

'Do they have a TV?' Anneke and Jem share a glance.

'They won't put it on today. It's Christmas lunch.'

'Do you promise?'

'We'll make sure.'

Sussie and her husband François live with their youngest, unmarried son, Gerrie, in what once was Anneke's parents' old home. Their elder son, Franz, his wife, and their two boys live in the adjacent plot, but they're here today. Everyone in the world is here today, it seems to Sam. She clings to Anneke's arm as they approach the house. Under Sussie's command, the front lawn is snooker-table-smooth. Inside, the floorboards gleam, and the scatter cushions on the sofa look like they've been arranged using a spirit level and measuring tape. The large Christmas tree has wire arms covered in green plastic needles, and sports a perfect arrangement of baubles and lights. There are no bare spots, unlike the decorated mini-cypress at home.

Sussie, dressed in lime green slacks with a floral chiffon blouse to match, swoops at Sam, kissing her hello on the lips as she does with everyone. Sussie's under no illusions that Sam enjoys this, but she's making no more allowances. Enough time has passed for Sam to stop being offish and mopey and to join the loving ranks of the family. Sussie embraces Sam for a little too long, trying to squeeze some affection into the strange girl. She knows it's in there somewhere, because the child clings to Jem like a limpet. In Sussie's fragrant grip, Sam is on fire inside with the urge to squirm.

'See? We came.' Anneke smiles at her sister. 'Now you can stop losing your mind about "not having the whole family together".'

'Sussie's a true collector,' François agrees. 'She gets ants in her pants if she doesn't have a full set.'

'We *still* don't,' Sussie mutters, leading them through into the lounge. 'There's someone missing, in case you hadn't noticed.'

'Don't, Sus.' Anneke flashes her sister a dark look. 'You're not to mention her. You promised.' The dense silence is filled, edge-to-edge, with Yolande's unspoken name. Sam is sure she can smell cigarettes. She pushes herself as hard against Jem's ironed shirtfront as she can.

'Come on now, it's time to get festive.' François banishes the hush. 'There's a present for you, *meisiekind*,' he says to Sam, pointing her towards a pile of brightly wrapped boxes beneath the tree.

The sight of the shiny parcels reminds Sam of the very first birthday she celebrated with Anneke and Jem, four months ago. Last year, Sam hadn't known about birthdays, but after singing songs and watching her classmates blow out candles at Mrs McGovern's, she realised that she needed one too. Because her real birth date was unknown, Sam chose her own, picking the twenty-third of September, the day that Jem rescued her from Pretoria. Anneke had made a delicate vanilla cake sandwiched together with rose-petal-flavoured cream and topped with eight candles, even though they couldn't be absolutely sure that this was the right amount. When Sam saw it, she'd burst into tears.

'Ag, my love, it's all right,' Anneke had whispered as she held her close. 'You'll find that sometimes even sweet things taste better with a little salt.'

After the cake, Sam had unwrapped a pale turquoise jersey which Anneke must've knitted in the dead of night because Sam hadn't seen even a scrap of turquoise wool around the house, and a book called *The BFG* which Jeremy reads to her before bed every night. They've almost finished it for the second time.

None of these presents look like books, but Sam pretends to be pleased when she unwraps a plastic-faced baby doll wearing knitted booties and a pink, floral dress.

'Thank you, Auntie Sussie and Uncle François,' she says, and braces herself for another round of kissing.

More family members arrive.

Crackers, fairy lights, carols blaring out from a sound

system somewhere, lots of talk in Afrikaans about Jesus. Sam's head swims.

Sussie's grandsons are loud and large. Sam is startled to recognise the younger one, Morné, as the boarder with the mielie-silk leg hair who terrorised her and Keegan in Main Street the other day, but he seems oblivious of the fact that their paths have crossed. He barely looks at Sam, focusing only on eating as many of the wrapped chocolates from a bowl on the coffee table as he can.

Soon, the room is full to bursting with big people with shiny faces. Sam dodges their uncertain attempts to get her to engage, and clamps herself onto Jem's side because Anneke, surrounded by her sister and her family, seems oddly unavailable all of a sudden.

At last, Sam manages to slip away. Compared to the bright colour of the festive front rooms, the rest of the house is cool and dark, and she's able to breathe better. In the corridor leading to the bedrooms, she comes across a wall of framed family photographs, and challenges herself to find all the ones featuring Anneke. It's easy. No one else has their shared white-blonde hair. Even in the black and white pictures, it glows like a silver halo around her grandmother's head.

In one photograph, Anneke is holding a little baby girl with brown curls. Sam's stomach lurches when she realises that she's looking at her own mother. She reels back and then moves along the display, preferring the pictures from a time when Yolande wasn't even thought of. She stops. Hanging low, just at her eye level, is a black and white photograph of a young Anneke with a horse. Sam lifts the picture from its hook and carries it to the light of the window to study it better. Her grandmother looks about fourteen. She sits astride the animal with her head resting on the elegant curve of its muscular neck and her smile lighting up the world. It's Sam-the-horse. It has to be. He is just as she imagined.

'Your ouma loved that horse.' Sam jumps, startled to find that Sussie has been watching her from the doorway. 'And the horse loved her right back.' Sussie steps closer. Sam's fingers tighten on the frame. 'The two of them together... it was a special thing, I tell you.'

'I'm sorry I took the picture down. I just wanted to see it better.'

'I've an idea,' Sussie says. 'Why don't you take that home with you? That way you can look at it whenever you want.'

'Really?'

'Sure.'

'To keep?'

'Why not? Christmas is all about giving, after all.'

'Thank you, Aunt Sussie.'

It's only later, as she clutches the framed photograph to her chest on the drive home, that Sam feels uneasy. She's pretty sure that no gift comes from Sussie without hidden costs attached.

That night, Sam-the-girl dreams of Sam-the-horse. He comes to her in a blur of wind and whipping leaves so that she's not sure where his mane and tail end and the rest of the world begins. He is huge, a monolith of smooth brown warmth rising upwards. He lowers his massive head and she touches the swirl of hair between his liquid eyes.

Sam wakes up at that moment. She lies still, with the orange gold of early morning glowing through her bedroom curtains, and tries to will the dream to return, but it is gone.

CHAPTER SEVEN

SAM WAKES TOO early on the morning of her first day back at school. She touches the framed photo of the girl-ouma and her horse which now lives on her bedside table, and then kneels up on her bed to open the curtains. She blinks, rubs her eyes, blinks again. There are a thousand white butterflies streaming across the pale sky like petals blown from a smashed up bridal bouquet. Sam watches, breathless, until the last fluttering insect has flown out of sight.

After they're gone, she tiptoes through the house and lets herself out of the kitchen door. There's a dead butterfly lying in the centre of the path. Sam picks it up as carefully as she can. Its tissue-thin white wings are veined with a tracery of brown. She looks up into the quiet sky. There's nothing but blue.

Later, in class, when Mrs McGovern tasks her and Keegan with drawing something from nature, Sam places the dead butterfly on her desk and copies the pattern of its wings into her workbook with soft, reverent strokes of her pencil. Just remembering the mass of fluttering creatures makes her whole body feel charged.

'That's beautiful, Sam.' Mrs McGovern places a large, important-looking book beside the girl's work and taps the page. 'Here's some more about butterflies, if you're interested.'

Keegan scowls at Sam from behind his own drawing. He's done Superman battling a Ninja Turtle. Turtles are from nature, aren't they? Sam catches his eye and glances away, fast. Last year's PlayStation incident has discoloured the air between them, and neither one is sure what to do about it.

At lunch break, Sam is slow to leave her desk. In the past, she and Keegan would've dashed off to play something involving superheroes (Keegan has always been the ideas-man behind their games) but now she's not sure if this is still on the cards, or even if she wants it to be. Keegan, hovering in the doorway, has just built up the courage to ask her to come outside with him, when Zama strides up to Sam's desk.

'Hey, that's a really good drawing.' She adjusts her glasses and takes a closer look at Sam's pencil butterfly.

At thirteen, Zama is the eldest pupil in Mrs McGovern's care, and she wears her seniority, along with her flower print skirts and coloured T-shirts, with an air of quiet entitlement. Sam has been enchanted by Zama since she first saw her, but it's the older girl's sturdy-framed spectacles that she covets most. If Sam also had to wear glasses they would help hide her eyes. Sam's eyes, she's realised, are too light and strange-looking to be fully acceptable. *Pools of reflective water hiding goodness knows what in their depths* – Mrs McGovern once described them, but Sam doesn't want water-eyes. She wants brown serious eyes with fringes of curly black lashes like Thuli and Zama.

'I didn't know you liked art,' Zama says, and in the face of her up-close, spectacle-wearing awesomeness, Sam can only manage a nod.

'I've been doing extra drawing lessons. Do you want to see my portfolio?' Zama spots Keegan waiting in the doorway. 'Unless you want to go...'

'No.' Sam can't look at her old friend. Her face has gone boiling hot. 'No, it's fine. I'd like to. See.'

Only after Keegan has turned away does Sam look up to watch him leave.

For the next two days, Sam spends her break times with Zama, looking through her portfolio and watching over her shoulder as she turns the pages of the fat art book filled with glossy coloured prints that Mrs McGovern keeps on the shelf. Zama's unexpected attention makes Sam feel all puffed-up and special, but she wishes they could be special outside, rather. She tries not to fidget, but she aches to be in the wind and the sun with her shoes off and her feet in the grass.

On the third day, as Sam is poring over a picture of a painting that seems to be nothing but blurry strips of colour, Zama reaches into her bag and pulls out a dark plastic oblong. It beeps. It has a screen that lights up, and buttons. Batteries. Buttons. Bile. Sam freezes. She tries not to look at the cell phone. She forces her attention back to the book. The colours on the page blur, and her eyes are drawn to the menacing device with its rows of neat buttons sitting on the desk between them. In an instant, she's back in Karel's filthy lounge. She feels the horrible slick warmth of his fingers touching hers as he handed her the Game Boy. All the time and distance between that moment and this seem to melt into nothing.

'Why do you have that?' The apricot jam sandwich that she had for lunch is trying to crawl back up her throat.

'My cell? It's so I can SMS my mom to tell her when to fetch me from all my extra classes and stuff. Thuli's getting one for her birthday this year, but you're not allowed to tell.'

Sam has to concentrate really hard not to drop the heavy art book as she places it on the desk. She rises to her feet. 'I'm going to go outside now.'

The bright outside pulls in tight around her, slamming into her senses and banishing the sick feeling in her gut and the taste of metal on her tongue. Above her, the sky is a clean, perfect arch of blue. She throws her head back and searches for the flicker of a white butterfly wing, but there's only the pale grey shape of a very high-up aeroplane heading towards the mountains, the sound of its passage lost in distance.

Sam spots Keegan across the mowed green square of lawn. He's stomping with miserable resignation around in the flower bed amongst the cool strappy leaves of the agapanthus. Keegan's face lights up when he sees her approach, but he quickly checks his grin. The look he gives her instead is cautious, questioning.

'Let's play,' is all she says, and then they do.

The PlayStation incident and the recent days of silent strangeness are never mentioned, but the old ease between them is now clouded, as if strung across by a myriad of spider-web-like strands, invisible until a sudden breeze blows and they float up and catch the light.

The two new computers are the ugliest things Sam has ever seen. They sit on the desk by the classroom door like dark entities from another dimension, sucking power with their black cables and blank, dead screens. On the floor, wired up to the monitors, are two humming black cases, 'towers' Keegan calls them in a know-it-all voice. Mrs McGovern starts explaining how computer science is now going to be included in their studies.

'I'm no expert myself, but I've found a wonderful online tutorial that you can use to teach yourselves basic HTML, and my husband has organised for one of his interns at work to come in two hours a week and work with whoever is interested. Yes, Keegan, I know that's you, no need to jump around so, darling.'

'Will we have the internet?'

'Yes, Nate, but we can't get broadband out here, and there's going to be strict rules about using it. I'm going to explain those to everyone after break.'

'We have a computer at home, and I already know how to use Word,' Zama says. 'Can I bring my files here on a flash drive to copy over?'

'Of course. Perhaps you can teach the others how to use the program.'

'I already know how.'

'No, you don't, Thuli, you just know how to play solitaire,' Zama shoots back at her little sister, who scowls.

'Do we have to?' Sam's voice is high and panicked. She clenches her hands into fists to stop them from shaking.

'It's important for you to give it a try, Sam. I'm afraid you'll be doing yourself a huge disservice if you don't get to grips with the digital age.'

'It's the future of EVERYTHING!' Keegan is still bouncing up and down with excitement.

'Yeah, this *is* 2006, you know.' Nathan has never forgiven Sam for her PlayStation meltdown. 'Not the last century where people rode donkeys and minced about in bloomers.'

'That's enough, Nate.' Mrs McGovern places a hand on her son's head. 'Now, everyone get back to your desks and carry on with your assignments. We'll all have a computer and internet introduction session after lunch.'

72

During break, Sam leaves Keegan on the jungle gym pretending to be Spiderman and heads back to the classroom. She feels as if an invisible line of fishing gut is pulling her inside, towards those new computers with their smug, rectangular faces.

She pauses on the threshold of the room. The invisible line tugs. From their corner, the machines radiate an air of menace that seems to pulse out in waves, washing over Sam and making her stomach all nauseous and swishy. She takes a step towards the computers, and then another, and before she really has time to process it, she is standing right in front of them, breathing in their terrible electrical exhalations, ears throbbing from the sickening sound of their mechanical beating hearts. Sam's own heart is thundering in her chest as she reaches out to pull the wire from the back of one of the screens in an attempt to make the noise stop. Her hand bumps the mouse and the screen blazes to life. Sam gasps, staring, transfixed, into the dead blue oblong eye of the monitor she's awoken. Her nose is inexplicably filled with the garbage and smoking tik smell of her Poppy days. She can taste hunger and cigarette smoke. Her breath comes in quick little rasps. Sam remembers the television people with their blurred static edges and too-bright colours. She remembers them right up close to her nose, while her mother lay slack and drugged on the floor behind her back. Goosebumps leap out all over her skin.

It only takes a moment for Sam to clamber up to the special shelf where Mrs McGovern keeps the big fat art book, grasp it in her slick fingers, and approach the computer once more. The smell of vomit and beer and dust is thick in her nostrils now. Yolande's voice seems to whisper from every corner of the classroom.

No!

The book leaves her hands and flies into the monitor. Sam

watches it happen as if from a great distance, sees the spine open and the pages flap like the wings of a dying bird, sees the crack shatter outwards from the point where the heavy cover slams into the screen and splits the blue light like a terrible smile.

'No!' Keegan cries out from the doorway behind her, his shocked voice only raising the volume of her mother's spectral voice. Sam puts her hands over her ears. The humming hasn't stopped. The voices are still there.

'Sam, how could you? What have you done?' Keegan rushes to the monitor and touches the cracked plastic as if ministering to an injured animal. Blue light haloes around his finger and static crackles.

'Stay back, it's going to get you,' Sam implores, grabbing onto Keegan's arm and pulling to try and get him away from the danger.

When Keegan turns to look at her, the confusion and despair on his face jolt her from the past and back into the sunny room. She can hear Mrs McGovern's footsteps, and Thuli's singing outside the window. She lurches backwards, gasping for breath.

'I'm sorry. I didn't mean—' but Keegan's back is towards her again, he grabs the mouse and starts clicking urgently, checking if there's damage that goes deeper than the crack in the screen.

Sam watches the little squares open and close on the blue screen in response to the movement of Keegan's fingers. Blood rushes from her face, and she sways on her feet.

'You're going to be in big trouble for this, you know that, Sam.'

Sam sinks down to her knees, tears pouring down her cheeks. Big trouble.

They're going to send me back.

The afternoon light drapes the garden in golden bands, and where it catches a rose, the bloom seems to glow as if each petal is alight. Sam stares at the brand new yellow one that just unfurled its petals this morning before she went to school and saw the computers. Before she ruined everything. Her whole body feels as if it is filled with dark, claggy mud. She can barely move her legs to take a step. Her hand, when she reaches out to touch the new petals, which look like they've been carved out of butter, is almost too heavy to manoeuvre. *You're going to be in big trouble for this, you know that, Sam.*

Sam's hand drops to her side, leaving the flower untouched. She's so absorbed in her misery that she doesn't hear the noise Jem makes as he pushes Anneke's wheelchair through the clover towards her, nor his careful footsteps as he walks away.

'Mrs McGovern phoned, Sam.' Anneke's voice is gentle. 'She's very worried about you.'

'Worried?' Sam is not expecting this.

'She said you weren't yourself.' Sam can smell the flowery-powder smell of Anneke's skin lotion. She closes her eyes for a moment to block out everything else but that. 'She said that the Sam she knows would never vandalise a piece of classroom equipment. She said it was as if you went into some kind of panic at the sight of those computer-things. What happened, my love?'

'Are you going to send me back?' Just whispering the words makes Sam's legs go weak.

'What? No! Of course not. I'm just trying to understand.'

'The computer screen – *all* electronic screen things… they…' Sam stares so hard at the yellow rose that it seems to unfold further in front of her, ready to swallow her into its golden centre. 'They remind me.'

'I see.' A warm wind picks up and gives the branches a gentle shake.

'And it's like I'm there again.'

'Well then.' Anneke nods to the roses. 'Which one are you going to choose?'

'For what?'

'To remember that you're not back there, that you're not Poppy any more.'

'A rose can help me do that?'

'Pick it very carefully, concentrating hard all the while on the fact this is a *special rose*. You then put it in water, and watch as it fades, and each petal that browns and falls represents a little more of the old Poppy-life falling away. When it is done, and the rose is all gone, you will know that you can face the computers and the cell phones with nothing to fear.'

'But I still won't *like* them.'

'That's fine, you don't have to like them, as long as you don't try to destroy them. Or allow them to destroy you.'

As Sam stares at the roses, her breath comes more easily and her hands stop trembling. The white ones look clean like just-washed linen, and there's a big orange one that's going pink at the edges, like a sunset, but it's the newly opened yellow rose that calls to her. She points it out to Anneke, who nods, indicating the pair of secateurs lying in her lap.

'And then tomorrow morning, before school, I want you to come out here and pick another bunch of roses. A big bunch.'

'Why?' Sam pauses, secateurs at the ready.

'To give to Mrs McGovern, along with the apology letter you're going to write tonight after supper.'

'OK,' Sam says. One corner of the sky is turning indigo. She turns back to the butter yellow rose, takes a deep breath, and makes the cut.

CHAPTER EIGHT

BY THE TIME Sam's next 'made-up' birthday comes around, the lemon tree blooms with such exuberance that there are more pale stars than green leaves on the thorn-spiked branches, and the centre of the garden vibrates with a permanent halo of bees. Every corner of the evening garden is perfumed by the lemon blossom, and beneath the tree, the scent is so powerful that Sam can feel it at the back of her throat. Even inside, from her spot on the bedroom floor, her head swims with the sweetness of it, and she has to pause mid-drawing because the brown pencil crayon almost slides from her fingers.

Sam is drawing another horse. Her bedroom walls are already rustling with tacked-up pieces of paper featuring her artwork. There are horses with peculiar perspective problems, different length legs, necks that are too short, and others far too long, and manes and tails with such volume as are never seen in nature. Stuck to the wall beside her bed is her prize work so far: a painstaking copy in pencil of the photograph Sussie gave her last Christmas. She never managed to get Anneke's face quite right, and now her ouma's skin looks grey from all the rubbing out, but Sam feels she can forgive herself for that because her rendering of Sam-the-horse is almost perfect.

Today, she is drawing a dark-haired girl on a chestnut

horse riding through a white-blossomed orchard. That one sighting of the 'laroo-girl' has stayed with Sam ever since her first, raw spring in the valley, and even now, years later, she's determined to try and capture something of that moment. She has no idea if the laroo-girl from the far side of the hill still rides her horse, but Sam still aches to *be* her: half human, half animal, an otherworldly thing of strength and speed.

It's her birthday tomorrow. Sam knows that she won't get a horse. She knows that it's impossible. Ouma is so sore these days, and Grandpa so bowed under the weight of her pain, that Sam didn't even think to mention that she wished for one. If, by some miracle off-chance, a horse were to turn up, where would they keep it? They're living in the stables already.

Perhaps Sussie and Oom François could keep a horse at the main farm, but how would she get there to visit it? Sam is secretly glad that Anneke has been too delicate for that bakkie ride lately. At Sussie's there are always too many questions about school and pointed comments about church, and worried looks at Ouma and hugs and kisses and more kisses till she wants to scream.

It's been two months since her ouma last went out in the bakkie, and the memory of that trip is a sore place in Sam's world, like a scab that won't heal because she keeps picking at it. Jem, Sam and Anneke had been on their way back from the big hospital in Paarl, and the bakkie cabin had felt like a small core of warmth in the middle of the empty Karoo road. Although it had been too dark to see the granite mountains rearing up on either side, Sam could feel their presence beyond the windows: cold and distant. Observing. At each bump and curve in the road, her ouma had sucked in a soft hiss of pain-breath.

'What did the doctor say, Ouma?' she'd asked.

'Ag, my child, don't you worry yourself about it.'

'Are you going to get better?'

'The problem with my sickness is there is no cure, my love. My silly old immune system is attacking itself. It has decided that I'm an intruder in my own body.'

'But you said maybe they could do an operation, or something?'

'They did, but they don't recommend it any more. The surgery might be too much for my system to take.'

'It could make you worse?'

'It could.'

'Oh, Ouma.' Sam had found Anneke's hand in the dark and covered it lightly with her own, feeling the swollen balls of Anneke's knuckles like the humped backs of tok-tok beetles beneath her palm. She'd imagined the beetles eating away at the stuff inside Anneke's joints with their serrated mandibles. Relentless.

'But they gave me different pills. Stronger ones. I'm sure it will be better.'

'I'm sure,' Sam echoed.

'It will,' Jem had added in a too-loud voice.

There in the confiding dark, the words that Sam had been afraid of speaking for so long suddenly leaped up the back of her throat, and out:

'If something happens to Ouma, if there's only Grandpa to look after me, will *she* come back?'

Her grandparents had exchanged a look. An invisible twine of tension seemed to twist and wind its way between them, tightening everyone's throats.

They're scared too! Sam had thought. *They're scared Yolande will come back.*

But then Jem had said: 'We honestly don't know where

79

Yolande is or what she's doing now. We feel bad about it, Sam, but ever since you came to live with us, we haven't tried to contact her again.'

'We used to try and get her to get help for her drug problem, we tried to get her to go to a special hospital to help her get clean, but she never wanted to, and then she made sure we couldn't get in touch with her so she wouldn't have to listen.' Anneke's voice had been soft, and Sam had to strain to catch her words over the engine. 'When we saw what she had done to you, we stopped trying.' There'd been a silence filled with engine noise and wind and then: 'She is no longer my daughter, Sam, only you are.'

'She was *Poppy's* mother. Maybe,' Sam replied. 'But not Sam's. Only *you* are.'

Beneath the wheels of the old bakkie, the road suddenly turned from tar to earth, and Jem had slowed down to try and minimise the jolting.

I don't want Yolande ever to see me again. I want her to think that I'm dead. Sam realised that she'd been holding Anneke's hand too tightly, and quickly lessened her grip.

'Promise me I can stay with you, Grandpa.'

There had been a pause and then: 'We promise, Sam.'

The rest of the drive had been spent in silence.

Now, on her bedroom floor, Sam breathes in the lemon-blossom scent and colours in a section of flank, and then pauses to listen to the noises coming from the kitchen. She's not allowed in there this evening because Jem is making her a surprise for tomorrow. Sam knows it's a chocolate birthday cake because she saw Ouma writing down the ingredients and instructions in a slow, careful hand and handing it over to Jem when she thought Sam wasn't looking.

*

Jem has never baked a cake before. His entire front is covered with flour, and there are sticky strings of raw egg on the floor between the table and the dustbin. He wants to ask Anneke if he's supposed to sieve the cocoa powder, but when he cranes his head to look into the lounge, her eyes are closed. He decides to sieve it anyway, because the brown stuff comes out of the tin in stuck-together clumps. All the while as he works, there's a small fluttering deep in his belly, as if an insect with sharp wing-cases and clawing legs is trying to burrow its way up through his intestines towards his throat. Jem takes another sip of coffee from his sticky, floured mug to try and quell the feeling, but it soon comes back. It always does. Jem knows that it's here to stay.

'Koewee!' Rattle, rattle goes the garden gate. When Jem pulls back the latch, Sussie marches in and gives him a big hug. Her youngest son, Gerrie, makes his way through the gate behind her.

'Hello, Oom!' Hug, kiss, pat hand on Jem's back goes Gerrie. Sam watches from her spot by the herb fountain, bracing herself for her turn. 'The chair's in the back of the bakkie. Shall I bring it in?'

'After coffee, my boy, after coffee. Come on in.' Jem has always had a soft spot for Gerrie. He is careless and jocular and full of undirected, enthusiastic ambition, all of the things that Jem wasn't when he was that age. When Jem fell in love with Anneke, he had only one goal: to be worthy of her. That meant that he had to be worthy of her land too, and of the rows and rows of fragrant fruit trees that flourished on it. Having grown up in Cape Town in a small city home, he felt he needed to make himself bigger to fit the vastness of the valley. Big enough to take on the massive task of running the farm with her. Now, he has just one small corner of it to look after, but the pressure on his shoulders is larger than ever. Her last years, in this garden, must be beautiful ones.

'Jeez, would you look at this place!' Gerrie's eyes go huge when he takes in the full glory of the summer garden. 'It's like a frigging fairy kingdom in here.'

'And there's the fairy herself,' Sussie says as she spies Sam lurking in the lavender by the fountain. Despite looking the part with her pale-morning-sky eyes and cascade of creamy hair, Sussie notes that the fairy in question is scowling like a troll.

'No, seriously, look at this place,' Gerrie breathes in wonder as he walks along the slate paths between the exuberant flower beds. 'And look at the old stables!' He stops dead and stares at the undulating old plaster of the walls, now painted a soft dove grey, interspersed with large wooden-framed glass doors that all lead out into the courtyard. 'You did this, Oom? It's better than one of those fancy-pantsy B&Bs in Albertville and such. You could charge a small fortune for city folks to come out here and stay for holidays. And weddings!' His voice gets higher and higher as each new thought occurs to him. 'People would be killing themselves to have their wedding in this garden. *Killing* themselves, I tell you.'

Well they can't. We live here. Sam, having been duly hugged and kissed, has retreated to Jem's side. The unspoken words strain against the inside of her, biting on the bones of her skull to get out.

'Glad you like the garden, Gerrie, but that's not going to happen any time soon.' Jem's smile is tighter now. He folds his arms across his chest.

'I know, I know, but, Oom…' Gerrie grips Jem's shoulders

and grins into his face, 'Sussie says you're going to have to move the three of you guys in with her because Aunt Annie is not doing so well, and I say the sooner the better. What you have here, my friend, is a goldmine.'

'We're not going anywhere.' Jem breaks away from his nephew's fevered clutches and rounds on Sussie. 'What have you been saying, Sussie? If Anneke so much as heard a whisper of this, she'd clip you around the ear. Arthritis or no arthritis.'

Sam's whole body throbs. She always liked her uncle Gerrie until now. Her fresh hatred for Aunt Sussie is a raging red fireball lodged in her throat. Sussie's always pushing and prodding, like a frenzied, voracious bird poking its long sharp beak into the ground to pull defenceless earthworms from their soil world. Snap gulp, and down her merciless gullet they go. *How dare she try and make us leave here? Why does she always want to ruin everything?* Sam glares at her great-aunt as hard as she can, sending imaginary poisoned darts shooting out of her eyeballs.

'Perhaps I need to spell this out to you, Sussie, because it seems that you've got some kind of busybody mental block when it comes to your sister, but the three of us are not budging, not to your house, or to anyone else's.' Jem's voice is low, almost a growl. 'This is our home, full-bloody-stop.'

At his words, Sam's pounding heart lifts and soars above the fruit trees. Sussie huffs out a breath and heads inside to see her sister. Jem looks at Gerrie, who stares at the play of sunlight over the leafy garden with an enchanted expression on his face.

'I'm just saying, this place would work like a bomb for a guest house, Oom. If you ever want to sell it, which I can see that you don't,' Gerrie adds hurriedly. 'Give me a call.'

*

That night, Sam dreams of the brown horse again. This time, it is standing on top of the hill behind the garden, a sharp cut-out against a green-grey sky. When she looks again, the horse *is* the hill. The russet boulders and fynbos scrub have become assimilated into the creature's vast body, somehow. Its eyes are as big and deep as pools fed by a mountain spring, and its nostrils two moss-covered caves.

Sam runs towards the horse-hill, dying to touch it, to climb up on its vast, majestic back so that she can look down from up there and see the other side, see the whole valley and the world beyond. Her dream-feet pound and her muscles strain, but each stream of hot, grassy breath that rushes down from the nostril-caves blows her back to where she started. Again and again.

The horse-hill is always beyond her reach.

CHAPTER NINE

IN EARLY FEBRUARY, on an evening when the blistering afternoon heat shows no sign of relinquishing any of its fury, Anneke refuses to get up from her afternoon nap. The ceiling fan stirs the bright, hurtful light of late summer slanting in through the window into a burning wedge that echoes exactly how Anneke feels beneath her skin. It's been a bad week in a bad month. Yesterday evening, she'd only heaved herself off the mattress and into her waiting wheelchair when Sam had put the spaghetti in the pot to boil for dinner, but now, as dinner time approaches once more, she's asked to be served in her bed.

She lies propped up against hot, heaped pillows and bites her lip as Jem hovers at her side, trying to encourage her to rise.

'You need to keep moving, dear heart, the doctor said, remember? The stiffness can get worse if you don't.'

Stiffness? What a ludicrous word for what Anneke's feeling. *Stiff* is how her legs used to feel the morning after a long outride, *stiff* is aching shoulders after an hour hunched over a weed-ridden vegetable patch. This is the slow turn of spiked steel screws in each joint. This is her hips, her ankles, her elbows, all screaming. This is hell.

'I'm sorry, my love,' Anneke turns her head so as not to see the tears in her husband's eyes, 'I can't tonight. I just need a little more rest.'

'It's OK, Ouma.' Sam, who's been watching the exchange from the doorway, jumps into action. 'We can *all* eat in here.' She goes over to the dressing table and starts to clear away the little bottles of lotion, pills, tissues and random assortment of life-junk that has collected on the surface. 'I'll bring in two kitchen chairs. Grandpa and I will sit here so we can all eat together. It will be fun. Like a picnic.'

Jem doesn't move from his position at Anneke's side, but his gaze follows his little granddaughter as she trots back and forth between the dressing table and the already heaped top of the chest of drawers where she's relocating the clutter. Sam's quick movements feel alien in the stillness of the room. Such comfort to be taken in the busyness of someone else getting on with things. He'd never realised it until now.

'How long has it been, Annie? Tell me, how long since you got out of bed?' Sussie's eyes shoot green fury across the padded quilt that covers Anneke's legs. At any moment, the down stuffing could smoulder and catch fire.

'Just this morning, when Jem helped me up to go to the loo.'

'Don't be clever, Anneke, you know what I mean.'

'Well don't speak to me like I'm an imbecile.'

'So then you don't act like one!' It could be an argument right out of their childhood, whipped through the intervening decades and transplanted here in this small bedroom where the winter sun leaks through the window and fades the patchwork squares that Anneke once stitched together in the days before her fingers ached.

'What do you want from me, Sus? To leap up and start waltzing around the room?'

'Of course not.' Sussie's hands clench into fists. 'It's just – you never told me you weren't getting up any more—'

'Because I knew you'd act like this—'

'And they say that once you're bedridden, you never... I want you to let me look after you until you're better.'

'No.' It's a small word, spoken softly. 'There won't be any *better*, Sus.' Sussie's face crumples and her legs sag. She sits on the edge of the bed beside the slender mound that her sister's legs make beneath the bedding. 'Jem and I have known this was coming from the moment I got my first diagnosis. You already know that it's not just my joints that are affected, it's my heart, my arteries, my kidneys. My body is eating itself.'

'Ag, don't say that, Annie.'

'It's true. Even if there was something they could really do for me at this point, or better drugs to dull it all, I've no wish to claw myself along through the days like some half chewed up thing.'

Sussie shakes her head, unable to speak. She leaves the room with its sad little bottles of pills and flowery smell laced with something bitter, like the rind of a grapefruit, and follows Jem as he walks her back out to the barn where her car is parked. Through stinging eyes, she sees that the garden has been pruned and cut back, brown stalks waiting for new life. Sussie stops. The heels of her shoes sink into the wet earth.

'I don't know what your problem is, Jem, why the two of you have given up, but *I'm* not going to.' Her voice is fierce. Sam can hear it from all the way over by the pond where she's carving the letters 'SAM' into a new chunk of wood that will soon serve as a replacement grave marker for the horse's burial mound. The old one has rotted and splintered, and the carved-out letters are almost invisible. Jem will dig it out and replace it with this new one as soon as she is finished. This is the first time since her horse died when she was fifteen that Anneke is unable to do the carving on the replacement 'Sam' marker herself. She'd cried about it earlier, when she'd thought Sam wasn't looking.

Sam pauses at the sound of Sussie's voice, her chisel placed inside the etched outline of the 'A' that Jem made earlier using a bench knife, listening.

'I pray for Anneke every day, and I'll continue to do so,' Sussie says, and Sam seethes at the implied reproach in her voice. *As if she's better than us because she prays. As if we don't deserve Ouma.* The wind sweeps a chunk of hair into Sam's mouth. It tastes sour from the lemon juice that Anneke makes her squeeze into the last rinse water every time she washes it to keep the blonde from going yellow.

'That's good, Sussie,' Jem says. 'Prayers certainly won't hurt.' Jem's tone reminds Sam of the many times he's soothed her own terrors. This casts Sussie in an unexpected role. Sam frowns. For a moment, a small gap appears in the rigid hatred she nurtures for her interfering great-aunt.

'But you need to know that we're not giving up,' Jem continues in the same, calm voice. 'We're letting her life play out as she's lived, with grace. With quietness.'

'But this is ridiculous. She needs proper care.'

'She's got it.'

'She needs her family.'

'What do you think Sam and I are, then?'

'She needs—'

'She *wants* peace.'

'You and Annie… you're both fools, Jeremy Harding,' Sussie declares. Sam's hatred gap closes up again and stitches tight.

'That's what you've always said.' Jem sounds weary, now. Sam can hear the squeak of metal on metal as he works the gate bolt open. 'Nothing new there.'

'Shall I come round tomorrow?' Sussie's voice has changed again. The frightened child is back.

'Give it a week, Sus,' Jem replies, and the rest of his sentence is swallowed up by the barn as the gate closes behind them. Sam lets the tools drop to the ground at her feet, and tucks her chilled hands into the warmth of her armpits. The wind gusts again, and Sam's sure that she can make out the faint whinny of a horse on the air. She stands dead still and stares hard at the periwinkle-blanket over the burial mound, straining her ears for more, but there's nothing but rustling leaves and the high, raspy peep of a Cape sugarbird.

Sam-the-horse, it's clear, only rises up in her dreams.

CHAPTER TEN

WINTER RAIN DRIPS from the eaves outside the Super Saver, and Sam and Keegan, although already wet from their walk to Main Street, dart between the drops and under the awning.

'Hello, Mr Vosloo,' Sam says to the spherical figure of the shop owner, who is leaning up against the outside wall, staring at the wet.

'Hello, my girly. How's your ouma doing, then?' Sam shrugs her answer, and Mr Vosloo nods, then looks back out at the rain. 'I'm having my break now, so Betty will help you guys. Don't think that because she doesn't talk she doesn't have eyes like a hawk, hey? No snitching.'

'We would never, Mr Vosloo,' Sam says as she pulls Keegan inside. The Super Saver is gloomy compared to the brightness outside, and they stand in the doorway, rainwater squelching from their shoes, as their eyes adjust.

'Let's not,' Keegan says for at least the tenth time since Sam pulled him by the hand and dragged him from the McGoverns' to Main Street. 'They could be anywhere.' It's true. Mid-year break is even more perilous than December because there are no festive celebrations and beach holidays to thin out the herd of boarders that have migrated back to town.

Sam squares her shoulders and marches deeper into the store.

'Come *on.*'

'They could come in any minute.' Keegan is pale. Why has his friend suddenly gotten it into her head to go to Main Street on a day when she knows the boarders are lurking?

Sam has been strange all day. If Keegan is honest with himself, she's *always* strange, but today it seems to burn right through her skin, like a fever. Her cheeks are pink, and her hair, ever unruly, has worked even more of itself out of her braids than usual. The stray wisps stand up around her head like antennae.

'I'm getting a Bar One.' Sam knows this is Keegan's favourite. She holds up the black and red wrapped chocolate like a trophy and waves it in his direction. 'Want one too?'

'I guess.' Keegan takes a step further into the store. He nods to silent Betty, waiting behind the till, and scurries to Sam's side in the sweetie aisle. 'Just hurry up.' He selects a chocolate bar, and then shoots a glance over his shoulder towards the door. He freezes. His stomach drops. There, silhouetted in the Super Saver doorway against the grey-blue daylight, are three shapes. Big ones, but not big enough to be adults. Boarders.

There are two boys and a girl, all older. He recognises them straight away. They are wearing big farm boots and jeans and their faces are clouded in shadow despite the buzzing neon overhead. Keegan makes a little mew of despair deep in his throat, and Sam spins round to see the three approach. They are wet from the rain, and the girl, who is wide-shouldered and athletic-looking, has a slick of brown fringe glued to her forehead.

'Look who it is!' the girl says in English.

'It's the little *soutpiel* who's always hiding from us.'

'Haven't seen you in ages, *soutpiel*.'

'Ja, we thought you'd died or something.'

'Of fright!'

'Hey, where's your big, brave brother, *soutpiel*?'

'Why do you ask, Chantal?' The smaller boy gives the brown-fringe girl a shove. 'I didn't know you had a crush on Nathan.'

'Shut up, Dewalt.' She shoves back. 'Don't be a dick.'

'You're all dicks,' Sam says. She's speaking in Afrikaans. They all look at her in astonishment, Keegan included. Sam turns her attention back to the chocolates. Her voice is matter-of-fact, as if she's talking about the weather: 'Even you, big girl. Maybe that's why you're wearing those boy's jeans. To hide it so no one will know.'

There's a long silence while everyone digests this. Sam picks up a chocolate bar. Puts it down. Selects another. Keegan is dry-mouthed and staring. He's not sure he caught everything that his friend just said in her rapid Afrikaans, but for her to say anything at all to a bunch of strangers is astounding in itself.

'*What?* What did you say?' The brown-fringe-girl's face has gone violet. Her companions are pinking around the ears, their mouths hanging open.

Sam turns to face the boarders. She seldom speaks Afrikaans because doing so reminds her too much of being Poppy, but the few, short sentences she's just uttered have opened up a sluice somewhere inside her. Sam's past hurtles through it in a deluge that seems to fill her whole body with brackish water and when she next opens her mouth, it's as if she's channelling Yolande, the scabbed users she hung out with, the bull-necked drug dealers that used to drop by, and all of her loser boyfriends at once.

A volley of filth spews from Sam's mouth, splashing over the horrified boarders, filling the Super Saver aisles, and trickling out to mingle with the winter mud on Main Street. She's not even sure what she's saying any more. The vile words, of which she has no idea of the English equivalents, pour out of her from a hidden vault that taps directly into the years before she came to live with Anneke and Jem. What emerges is stinking and putrid. The boarders turn tail and run as if they've had scorching acid flung in their faces.

Sam stops. Now that the words are out of her, she feels emptier. Lighter. She turns to Keegan, who hasn't blinked since she began her rant, and smiles.

'Maybe they'll leave us alone next time,' she says, speaking English once more. She takes her Bar One to the till, and Keegan grabs a chocolate bar and trots obediently behind. He has no idea what she said to the boarders, but the guttural sounds seem to have left a residue of something behind in his friend. He watches in admiration as she pays Betty for her sweets. Sam is taller. Stronger. He's sure of it.

In her dreaming, Sam looks up into the cooling twilight and sees that Sam-the-horse is on the hill. At first, he's a cut-out with twitching ears, small and distant against the indigo sky, and then, quite suddenly, *she* is the horse. She has high-stepping long limbs and twitching skin where the flies try to land. She is the one watching over the garden below with her large brown eyes, and sniffing the air for danger. Sam stamps a hoof in a frustrated panic, sending up curls of dust. She can sense creeping, stalking figures out beyond the valley, trying to find a way in, but no matter how hard she stares, all she can see is grass.

October heat prickles the back of Sam's neck and sends trickles of sweat sliding down her chest, along her arms, and pooling into the fingertips of her gardening gloves. Her fingers ache from squeezing the cutters. Often, she has to use both hands together to get the blades through the woody stems. She's working in the patch of garden at the base of the hill which has gotten overgrown, limbs snaking into vines and thickening, locking into place. The quince hedge is taking over a lavender bush, and is casting too much shade on the tomatoes. Sam makes each cut with ferocious determination, bracing her shoulders and clenching her jaw.

Now that she is a big girl (she's stopped wondering what her real age might be; she *feels* ten, and that's enough) and Anneke is no longer able to do any of the tasks she once carried out in the garden, Sam has taken it upon herself to fill her role. There seems to be a never-ending list of things for her to do when not at school: prune this, cut back that, dig in compost here, pull up old plants there, pick these, tie those back. This overgrown bed has been taunting her lack of discipline and effort. She works till her shoulders burn.

'Come, Sam.' Jem walks up and gives the pile of ravaged branches at her feet a long look. 'It's time to take a break.'

'I just want to finish this first.'

'No, my love. Give it a rest.' Jem's quiet words send Sam's frantic energy spinning free and away, and when it does, she finally feels the ache in her hands, and the sting of salt and sun in her eyes. She pulls off her sticky gloves to find raw burnt-looking patches on her fingers where the blisters are starting. Sam goes over to the tap and winces as the cold water sparks the pain to life. When she's drunk deeply and washed the sweat from her face, Jem is still waiting. He holds out a tube of sun block, and as Sam reapplies it to her arms and face, she notices he's carrying a small, faded khaki backpack.

'What—'

'Tuck the bottom of your jeans into your socks in case of snakes,' Jem instructs, and then: 'Come.' He puts the sun block back into the backpack and starts heading for the hill that rises up behind them.

'Where are we going?' Sam scampers behind him.

'Up there.' They've never gone up the hill before. *Too many snakes*, Jem's always said, but Sam knows that it's really because of the le Rouxs on the other side. What would happen if they encountered Jem's old enemy? Would there be a fight? She can't picture her grandfather's large, strong hands being used for anything but gentleness.

'But Ouma?' Sam says. They never go anywhere if they can help it these days. What if Ouma needs them for something? What if something happens while they're gone?

'Remember to make a noise with your feet.' Jem keeps moving. 'We want the snakes to hear us coming and get out of the way. Nothing more dangerous than a surprised snake.'

Sam swallows her questions and follows Jem as he steadily climbs, stepping between the tufts of fynbos that cover the hill. No snakes so far, just khaki-coloured crickets, black-bottomed beetles and dusty lizards.

The climb gets steeper. After a while, all Sam can focus on are the soles of Jem's boots pushing ahead, balancing over stones and kicking up sand. She's exhausted now, and starving. It's lunchtime, isn't it?

Finally, they reach the top. Jem sinks down and rests his back against the cool slant of a red rock and pats the stone beside him. When Sam sits, he pulls a bottle of water and a sandwich out of the backpack and hands them across. She tucks into both. The cheese and tomato sandwich tastes like heaven. She can smell the fishy tomato-tinned-pilchard goo oozing out of Jem's.

The sky is enormous from up here, with a depth of blue that seems to tug her breath right out of her, leaving her giddy.

'I used to come up here all the time, once.' Jem breaks the companionable silence once his pilchard sandwich is finished. 'I'd forgotten what it's like. So wide open.'

'It's great,' Sam says, but now she's dying to scamper beyond the rock and look down the hill on the other side. *What's it like?* she wants to know. She's never seen the le Roux farm. *Can you tell that the people who live there are nasty?* Jem told her that they're not allowed on the property since the dispute over the spring, when Anneke and he moved to the stables. No le Rouxs on this side, and no Hardings on that side, those are the rules.

'Go on,' Jem says, responding to Sam's unasked question. He jerks his thumb behind him, towards the le Roux side of the hill. 'Take a look if you want.'

'But won't they see me?'

'Not from down there. But keep low. Who knows what that old lunatic would do if he thought we were trespassing.'

Sam tries not to look too eager as she gets to her feet and walks towards the other side. When the land starts to slope, she drops to her haunches and stares down at another whole world. There are tractors and machinery, a stable, a large barn with a corrugated iron roof, and a sprawling white, gabled house in the distance that looks like all sorts of new bits have been added onto it over the years. There's a pad-dock with horses in it (*laroo-girl laroo-girl!*) and beyond the house, stretching into the distance, rows and rows of pale green grapevines.

'Which cultivars?' she asks, sounding so much like a local now that Jem grins.

'Cinsaut, I think. And palomino.'

'They live so close to us.'

'I know. Down in our little spot, you'd never think we had neighbours, hey?'

'No.'

'You're never to go over there, Sam, do you hear me?' Sam turns back to see that Jem is watching her, squinting against the sunlight. Her grandfather's mouth is a small, hard line. 'That le Roux is an angry, vindictive old bugger. It wouldn't be safe.'

'I won't.'

'Promise me.'

'I promise, Grandpa.'

As Sam stands and walks back, wiping her buttery hands on the pockets of her jeans, she feels the intensity of Jem's look soften. Together, they gaze down at their own side. Home. The garden is a dense patch of green nestling at the bottom of the brown, bristly slope, embraced within the ragged-roofed arms of the U-shaped buildings. Sam watches, mesmerised, as the wind shifts the leaves on the top of her familiar old oak tree. It's another creature entirely when seen from up here.

'It's all so small,' she says at last.

'I know.' Jem closes his eyes and leans his head back against the rock. 'It's good to sometimes remember that, Sam.'

But as Sam stares down at the curving slate paths twisting between the green, and the bright spots which must be the roses, she knows that it doesn't matter how big the world that sprawls on either side is, all that matters is this perfect piece. The place where she is safe.

CHAPTER ELEVEN

ON NEW YEAR'S Eve, Sam decides to sleep outside in the garden. The midsummer air is no cooler out here, but the movement of the wind creates the illusion of it. Earlier, she laid out her bedding on an old camping mattress in the middle of the clover patch, and now she lies with a ring of rose bushes framing the black sky above.

Without the barrier of walls and windows, the garden sounds press up close. To one side, there's the house, with the soft ticking of metal as the roof cools and the electric whirr of the fan in Anneke and Jem's bedroom, and on the other, the pond with its watery splashing and serenading frogs. The chittering of bats and the zinging of crickets are punctuated by the eerie screech of big-eyed ground birds calling to one another through the darkness.

Every so often, Sam switches on her torch and shines it onto Anneke's old watch. The watch was her recent Christmas present. The metal on the back of it is dull from decades on her grandmother's wrist, and the strap feels warm, as if it carries something of the essence of Anneke's skin even now, clutched in Sam's fist, out in the night.

She is waiting for the moment when the old year will be over and the new will begin. Will she be able to tell? Will the sky change, the winds shift, the sounds alter slightly?

It's close now. Her hours of patient wakefulness are almost up. She glances at the watch face, then switches the torch off and counts the last three minutes under her breath.

There. It's happened. It's 2008.

Nothing is different.

Sam's body fills up with something she can't define: a restlessness and a squeeze of doubt stirred in with a new ache beneath the skin of her chest.

When she finally falls asleep, the rose beetles zub down and investigate her hair. A moth flutters past her face, its wings vibrating with her breath. A small, brown scorpion marches across the sheet that covers her still limbs and scuttles off into the darkness on the other side.

As Sam sleeps, she dreams that she wakes. In dream-time, the night wind that brushes her face has become breath. She can smell ground-up grass, and when she looks upwards, it's into the wide nostrils and the long muzzle of Sam-the-horse. In the dark she can make out little more than the patch of white, and somewhere higher up, the gleam of his huge eyes, but she can feel his vivid, shocking presence all around her. She gets up from beneath her twisted sheets to stand before him, and reaches out a hand to touch the velvet of his nose. When she makes contact, a shock, like electricity, jolts up her arm and through her body and she is flung backwards. She flies through the rosebushes and continues on, falling fast back and down and down through the space where the ground should be but isn't. Her stomach swoops and clenches until she jerks to real wakefulness with a gasp. With her cheek pressed against the cool, soft clover beside her pillow, Sam waits for her heart to slow back down.

*

'We're not sure what we're going to do without the two of you,' Mrs McGovern says to Zama and Thuli once they've all finished singing the 'jolly good fellow' song. The 'best of luck' banner that Sam made with coloured felt-tip pen letters on pieces of paper Sellotaped together and strung up across the blackboard has buckled under its own weight, and now seems to be wishing the sisters 'best ofuck'. Keegan nudges Sam to point this out with a grin, but she struggles to smile back. Since she heard the news that Zama and Thuli's father has been relocated to Botswana, and the sisters are leaving the area, she's had an itchy uncomfortable feeling. She wants things to stop changing. She wants to find her ouma pottering in the garden when she gets home from school like she used to, instead of inside that close little bedroom. She wants Zama and Thuli to be here every day with their wide, perfect smiles and their dark brown eyes. But no matter how itchy she feels, nothing is staying the same.

At the beginning of the school year, Sam was startled to discover a new member of the school group in the form of a tiny, six-year-old boy with auburn hair called Dale, the child of an English-speaking family, new to the valley. Even now, months later, his small autumn-toned presence in their midst feels like an intrusion. Dale's arrival has also nudged Sam and Keegan out from their positions as *youngest in the class*, and Sam can't help feeling that Mrs McGovern now expects more of her, somehow. She had to watch from the other side of the room as Mrs McGovern helped Dale to blow up the balloons for today's party. She's sure that *her* balloons were fuller and rounder and less inclined to deflate.

At the front of the room, Zama and Thuli are now cutting the cake. Zama turned sixteen three weeks ago. She no longer wears floral skirts and coloured T-shirts. Now, she's in black jeans that are so tight they look like pantyhose, and a white

T-shirt with a skull on it. The skull comes dangerously close to the icing as she leans over the farewell cake to cut a slice.

When her family moves out to the middle-of-nowhere in Botswana, Zama's going to finish her schooling via correspondence like a grown-up. Mrs McGovern thinks it's best to continue working with her this way as she's so close to writing her matric finals, and starting a whole new school in a whole new country would be too much of an upheaval before the exams. Thuli will be enrolled in a boarding school to finish her education, and, after existing on a diet of 'jolly hockey sticks' type books over the past few months, has been talking non-stop about all the things she's going to get up to with her new friends living in a dorm. It sounds awful to Sam. Just imagining being shut up in a place where she can't leave to go home in the afternoons brings the dirty walls and sallow corridors of her Poppy days sliding in to the edges of her vision.

'Here's some cake for you.' Sam is brought back to the sunny schoolroom when Nathan hands her a plate. He's been different lately too. No more teasing Sam about her technophobia, no more ignoring her as if she's one of his little brother's toys that he couldn't be bothered to play with.

Sam doesn't know that Keegan recently told his elder brother about her tirade of Afrikaans at the Super Saver a year ago, the one that sent the boarders scattering like startled pigeons. She's no idea that the two boys scoured the internet for meanings to some of the words that Keegan could remember from her torrent of curses. It wasn't easy finding translations for them, but what they did unearth left them wide-eyed and stunned. In their minds, Sam transformed from a familiar girl with a long white braid into a mysterious being with almost supernatural powers and sinister depths.

*

This winter, there's snow on the tops of the highest mountains that ring the valley, and Sam can taste its white-cold breath in each of her own. The garden is a wet, icy quagmire filled with blackened stalks and silence. Sam is forced to remain indoors more than usual, and finds herself exploring deeper into the archives of Jem's old book collection. One Sunday morning, she finds an aged paperback with a worn beige cover with the picture of a compass on it: *Survival. A guide.* The spine is soft and creased, and who knows how long it's been lurking beneath that pile of detective novels with moisture-wrinkled edges.

Sam turns the yellow, musty-smelling pages with their dense, small type, and starts to read. She rests her spine against the bookshelf and learns about the various ways in which you can collect water from overnight condensation if you're stuck in the desert. She discovers how the patterning of moss on the trunks of trees can tell you where north is if you're lost in a forest.

I could survive on my own, she thinks. *If I had to.* This new knowledge is intoxicating. If she had to escape from Yolande again, she could run, and survive. If she found herself without Jem or Anneke to come home to, she could live wild on the hills around here, safe on her own, where no one could touch her. Sam draws her knees up beneath her jersey and reads about how best to skin a deer carcass. The mug of tea goes cold on the floor beside her.

By the time Sam is about to turn eleven that September, she's read the survival book from cover to cover, and reread parts of it more than twice. As soon as the weather warms, she uses the book's illustrated diagrams to experiment with building different kinds of campfires, and tries some of the suggested water-collection techniques, checking her buried Tupperware traps in the mornings before school and drinking each small, earth-flavoured yield.

She is keen to try her hand at shelter-building, and starts planning how she'll make one on one of the flatter spots on the lower hem of the hill. She chooses a location that's just high up enough to allow her to see out beyond the U-shaped buildings and towards the road. From up there, hidden behind its camouflaged walls, she'll be able to see if anyone suspicious approaches their home. Anyone too-thin with ratty brown hair and wrecked teeth and stone-filled eyes. As Anneke grows weaker and quieter, Sam starts to think of her planned shelter as 'the lookout'. No longer an experiment, but a necessity.

'You need a proper knife for that,' Jem says when he finds her trying to strip the green bark from a selection of fruit tree canes that were recently pruned from the plum tree. Jem is startled to realise how much Sam has grown over the long, cold winter without him having noticed. It is as if the ice in the air has simultaneously shrunk his wife, now such a deflated little shape beneath her bedcovers, and nourished the girl into the beginnings of growing up. Sam's white-blonde hair is so long now that she has to wind her braid back on itself in a loop to stop it from getting in her way when she works in the garden. As she battles with the bark on the fruit tree canes, Jem watches the rope-like bundle at the back of her head let loose new escapee wisps each time it swings.

Sam's eleventh birthday is dwarfed by Anneke's worst flare-up episode of rheumatoid arthritis yet, and the day is a blur of pain management and fright. Late that night, while Anneke finally sleeps a doped-up sleep, Sam and Jem eat an improvised dinner at her bedside. Crackers spread with peanut butter and home-made plum jam for Sam, and the obligatory pilchards for Jem. There, at Anneke's bedside, a pale-faced Jem finally hands his granddaughter her birthday gift. It's Anneke's father's old hunting knife. It has a bone handle and a time-hardened leather sheath that fastens closed to ensure that you can wear it in a belt without any accidental stabbings. It even comes with a hard grey oblong of well-used whetstone. Sam gazes at the knife for long moments, and when she looks up to thank her grandfather, her eyes are full of wonder.

As September ripens into October and the garden breathes again, Sam starts work proper on her lookout shelter. The knife is strange in her hands at first, big and quick and dangerous, but she soon masters the slice and the sweep of it. Her wooden building material is finally twig-free and smooth, and a pile of green bark strips lie softening in water, ready to be used to tie the construction together.

Every evening, Sam sits at Anneke's bedside and tells her how progress is going on the shelter. Neither one of them pretends that Anneke will ever see it, but Anneke is as invested in its construction as Sam is, keen to discuss the details and make suggestions. *Does Ouma also think that I need to watch out for Yolande? Does she also think we'll need a place to hide?*

'And for the roof?' Anneke asks. Her face seems pale, tiny and childlike within its cloud of white pillows and even whiter hair.

'Well, I don't want it to be too hot in there, so I'm going to grow one, Ouma, for insulation.'

'Grow one?'

'Using the grasses and some smaller fynbossies from the hill.' Sam moves closer to Anneke to show her the picture in the survival book about creating a living roof using a water-proof barrier and a grid of wooden battens to hold the soil from slipping.

'It looks heavy.'

'Ja, I'm going to have to do a lot of reinforcing.'

'You'll have to water it.' Anneke smiles at the image of her granddaughter teetering on a ladder with a watering can.

'Especially at first, to get it established, but then because it's indigenous, it should be OK. I'm worried that one big storm will wash it all away, though.' Sam closes the book and rubs her hands. They ache from lashing poles together. Her fingernails are rimmed with a faint green colour from the strips of bark she's been using. 'Or the wind could just blow it all off. It's probably not going to work.'

'Then you can try again.' Anneke shuts her eyes. The lids look as if they've been replaced with crumpled lilac silk. 'A living roof. How magical. It would be like sitting inside the earth. If I had known it was even possible I would've done it to this place.'

The scent of lemon blossom enters through the open window and washes over them both. There are fewer flowers on the tree this year, and the garden is slow to come to life. While the winter was particularly harsh, Sam knows the real reason: it's because her ouma is no longer able to walk through it. The plants feel her absence like a vital nutrient is missing from the soil around their roots.

Without Zama and Thuli, the schoolroom feels huge and quiet. After break, Mrs McGovern sometimes reads out emails that she's received from Zama in Botswana. Very hot, seems to be the prevailing theme. Zama appears to be studying for next year's upcoming final exams from inside a spit-warm swimming pool, with her notes and books spread out on the baking ground beside it. Sam's imaginings of middle-of-nowhere Botswana did not include such things as swimming pools, and she has to reconfigure her mental image to fit one in.

The new boy, Dale, has finally stopped crying every morning when his mother drops him off, and has taken to following Keegan around like a small, russet-headed duckling. Keegan doesn't mind. Sam is no longer particularly keen on playing superhero games at lunchtime, and Dale makes a willing sidekick, and is much easier to boss around.

Sam usually spends her lunchtime reading out on the lawn by the agapanthus plants, shifting into the patch of shade and out again to warm up in the October sun. *Like a cat*, thinks Nathan, who has been watching her through the window of the classroom instead of looking at the computer screen. *Only cats don't have such strange pale eyes.*

He leaves the computer and wanders outside. There's a robin on the grass, right by Sam's foot. Her stillness has made the little creature brave. *Either that, or stupid*, Nathan thinks, imagining her as a cat again.

'What's that you're always reading?' Nathan's voice startles both the girl and the bird, and one of them takes flight with a shudder of wing-flaps. Sam looks up at Nathan, but with the sun at his back, she can't make out his expression. She can smell him, though. It seems that along with the sudden height and the hardening of Nathan's limbs, turning fourteen has switched on something inside him that leaks out in the heat of the sun. An oniony, mannish smell, reminiscent of the farm labourers that Sam greets whenever she passes them in Main Street. Reminiscent, too, of the shadowy man-shapes from her Poppy-days. It makes her think of the frizz of Karel's leg hair and the lump of Jason's Adam's apple beneath his scrubby stubble.

'It's an old book of my grandpa's,' Sam answers at last, when it becomes clear that Nathan won't leave until she does.

'It must be riveting.'

Sam shrugs. As if protecting a secret, she covers the book with both hands.

'Clearly more interesting than my little brother, hey?' Nathan's grin goes unseen as Sam turns then to watch Keegan and Dale on the jungle gym. 'But it's a normal thing that you guys are no longer so close, you know. Girls develop faster than boys.'

Something about the way he says 'develop' makes Sam's stomach lurch. She stands and moves past him towards the classroom.

'Time to go in now,' she says.

CHAPTER TWELVE

AS THE HEAT of summer continues to build, Jem and Sam carry Anneke out into the garden every evening and place her, as gently as they can, onto an old garden lounger puffed with pillows that has now found a permanent place in the centre of the clover between the roses. Each time they make the journey out into the fragrant air, and then back into the house again later, Jem can tell that his wife is just that little bit lighter in his arms than she was the last time. It is only Anneke's silver hair, which Sam combs and braids into a long rope just like she does with her own, that seems to be unaffected by the illness that is eating at her. Whenever he can, Jem holds this braid in his garden-rough hand, clutching it as if it is a lifeline that can tow him back in time to when his wife was solid and worried about her weight, and laughed loudly, and banged about in the kitchen when baking rusks.

One warm evening in late November, Anneke sits up from her garden pillows with a startled grunt.

'Sam?' she says, staring beyond the yellow rose bush.

'I'm right here, Ouma.'

'No, my sweetheart,' Anneke turns to smile at her granddaughter, 'not you.' A soft breeze lifts the hair at Sam's temples. She feels a sudden chill rising up through the earth and the clover and into her bare feet, into her bones.

'What is it, love?' Jem's fingers tighten around his wife's springy braid as if letting it go would send her drifting off and up, like a fairground balloon from a sleepy child's fingers.

'Nothing really. I just… I thought…' Anneke gives a little laugh and places her misshapen hand onto her husband's knee.

Sam looks up at the sky. It's still too early for stars. The sky is still pale blue with a pinking edge to the west. A wisp of unseasonal cloud hangs high and quiet above their heads.

'Who were you talking to, Ouma?'

Anneke lifts her hand as if to touch something in the air before her.

'Glowing white, like the arum lilies,' she says, still smiling.

'Oh God.' Jem drops the hair rope and rubs his hands over her face. 'I gave you more this morning, because the pain was so bad in the night. The doctor said I could increase the dose. But this…'

Sam's feet feel numb on the cooling clover. Her mouth is dry, and she can't seem to swallow. She knows her grandfather is talking about the brown glass bottle with the black lid and the pharmacy prescription label that reads 'morphine' that sits on Anneke's bedside table.

'Oh God,' he says again. There are puddles of shimmering wetness in the lower rims of his eyes.

'Grandpa.' Sam reaches across Anneke to touch his hand. In her survival book, there's a section all about soldiers and survival in the fields of war. She knows that they carry little vials of morphine to administer to the injured, the dying.

Sam's whole body gives a shudder and her throat aches, but then, quite suddenly, the urge to weep is transformed into something else. Something new. Sam feels totally clear and empty inside, as if a flash storm has rushed through her and washed everything out. She blinks at the yellow rose-bush. She's sure, for a fleeting moment, that she can detect the edge of something moving in the deepening dark beyond it. She hears the faint, raspberry blowing noise of a horse huffing out a breath. She leans her head against her grand-mother's side and closes her eyes.

In the hushed charcoal-coloured hours of early morning, Jem starts awake. There's the shrill peep of a cricket coming from the space beneath the chest of drawers, and he can hear the whump-whump whirr of the fan. He pushes himself up onto his elbows and blinks into the gloom. What woke him?

'Je…' It's a croak, inhuman-sounding.

Anneke.

He fumbles for the switch on his bedside lamp, and with the sudden yellow burning his sleep-sore eyes, turns to where his wife lies beside him in the bed. Anneke's eyes are wide, and she moves her mouth as if trying to talk, but all that comes out is a slurred rasp of breath.

'Love? What is it?' Jem takes her hand, and her thundering pulse beats beneath his fingertips. Her gaze swivel towards his for a moment, and then away.

'No.' He stumbles from the bed. 'Wait. Not now. Not yet.' Jem knows, as he races out of the room, slipping on the rug and just catching himself on his way to the telephone in the kitchen, that he's breaking their agreement. He knows that he is doing exactly what he promised he wouldn't. But now, in the middle of the night, with the shadows pressing in against the windows and the floorboards hard beneath his bare feet, he also knows just what a fool he was to think he could do otherwise. To think he could let her go without a fight.

The receiver is slick and solid in his trembling hand. He promised *no hospitals, no ambulances*. He dials, shuts his eyes, leans against the wall, and sucks a frantic breath through the tight band that has pulled in around his throat. As the phone rings on the other end, he indulges in a brief fantasy of his wife, alive, furious, sitting up in a hospital bed and admonishing him for not being strong enough, for breaking their agreement. Every particle of his being urges the universe forward to that longed-for moment.

It must happen.

Anneke.

Sam stands on the cracked, baking tar of the hospital parking lot. The blue has bled from the sky, leaving a bleached, agonising whiteness that burns. When she closes her eyes, dizziness engulfs her and she has to sit down heavily to stop from falling.

'Sam!'

Her nostrils fill with alien parking lot smells: hot rubber, grease and petrol. Someone close by starts a car with a roar, and she breathes in the stench of its exhaust fumes. Her stomach twists and lurches. If she'd had a chance to eat anything today, it would be pouring out of her in a hot snake of sick and splashing down her T-shirt.

'Sam!' The clomp of feet running towards her is followed by hands in her armpits, pulling her upright. It's her uncle Gerrie. She can tell without opening her eyes. He always wears so much deodorant, it smells like he baths in it.

'You could get run over out here. What are you doing?' Gerrie lifts her up in his arms as if she is seven rather than eleven, and carries her back to the safety of the hospital lobby.

The sure movements of his muscular frame are comforting. She rests her head on his shoulder, eyes still closed.

'*Yissis*, I'm so, so sorry about your ouma, *kind*,' he croons once they're inside, swaying with her in his arms. 'Such a terrible thing. And so sudden, even after her being sick so long, hey?' Sam breathes in. She can now detect a salty layer of sweat beneath the overpowering deodorant. She's glad of the onslaught of smells. It's something to focus on. 'And I'm sorry about how I made you worried because I wanted your grandpa's land for a guest house, that one time.' His voice is thick with tears. 'I never meant to make you think you'd lose your home. Especially after all the *kak* you've been through, *kind*.' It seems the drama of the morning has opened a sluice gate of sorry inside Uncle Gerrie. He keeps on talking, calling her '*kind*' every so often, but Sam stops listening. It's too much to manage: both breathing and listening. Not now. Not today.

'Right, then,' Sussie says as she steps out onto the stoop. She and Gerrie have stripped the bed, bundled the bedding into the wash, and carried the mattress outside to dry in the sun.

Ouma peed herself, Sam thinks. *Dying must be really scary.*

'You won't be able to use the mattress for a day or two, Jem.' Sussie's voice is brisk and businesslike, but the rest of her seems to have dissolved. She stumbles a few steps before sinking down into one of the cane chairs. She stares in front of her, hardly blinking.

It's taken Sam all day to figure out why her great-aunt looks so strange, but now she gets it: Sussie is not wearing any make-up. Sussie always wears make-up.

'But in any case, I think you two should definitely come back with me tonight,' Sussie says.

Sam turns away and glares at the garden. The green swims and shimmers.

'We need to talk about the funeral, Jeremy.' As soon as she utters the word 'funeral', Sussie starts crying again. Sam digs her fingernails into the palms of her hands to stop herself from starting up again too. She glances at her grandfather. He is sitting dead still with his back straight. His brown hands, loose and lost-looking, rest in his lap.

'She wanted to be buried here.' Jem knows that he's already broken one promise so easily. He tries to fight away the image of his wife in the ambulance earlier. Again, he sees the tube shoved between her teeth and fed down her delicate white-skinned throat, watches needles puncturing her flesh, medics handling her precious body with cursory professionalism.

'There's the family graveyard at the farm. Every member of our family has been buried there since my grandfather's father. You *know* that's where she'll be buried.' From the way that Sussie's jaw juts out, Sam can tell she's clenching her teeth.

'But…' Jem's voice comes out soft. Weak. 'She wanted—'

'You can't put her in the bloody garden, Jeremy.' Sussie turns on him, tear-streaked and vicious. 'This is the real world, man. For one precious moment, will you stop being such a damn dreamer?'

'Anneke—'

'She was my *sister*. She wasn't just your wife. She was…' Sussie gasps for breath between heaving sobs, 'ours too.'

'Ma?' Gerrie steps out onto the stoop. 'Come now. It's OK.' He puts a hand on her shuddering shoulder and darts an apologetic look over the top of her head towards Jeremy.

'Before you. She was ours,' Sussie whispers, hands over her face. Sam digs her nails into her hands even harder. She will not cry. Not now. She bites her bottom lip.

'I think we need to head back to the farm and give these guys some space. Come, Ma.' Gerrie helps Sussie stand. 'We will discuss the funeral plans and that tomorrow. I think that's best.' He looks at Sam and tries to smile, fighting his mouth which keeps pulling down into a sob, and then turns to Jeremy. 'I am so sorry for your loss, Oom.'

When the wooden gate rattles shut behind Sussie and Gerrie, the whole garden seems very still and quiet. Sam holds her breath along with it. Her head thumps with blood in time with her heart. She stares out over the garden to the dark patch in the far corner beneath the oak tree where Sam-the-horse rests.

'She should be buried here, Grandpa.'

'I know.' If he hadn't called the ambulance, if he'd behaved like she'd asked him to, she would've died here. Her body would still be his to protect.

'But that's not going to happen.'

'No.'

And then at last, looking out of the garden that they planted together, with the sunlight touching the tops of the bright leaves of the lemon tree, Jem begins to weep.

CHAPTER THIRTEEN

YOLANDE LICKS THE scab at the corner of her lip and tastes metal. Some thin type of stuff, without shine. Tin. She tastes like tin. The thought makes her smile, and the crusted blood tugs at her skin when she does so, pulling her out of shape. Yes, tin is malleable and dentable, but endlessly recyclable.

Yolande is recyclable. She's eco-friendly. Greener than green. She's filling no landfill, not yet. She's gotten herself a whole new life once more. Like a used tin can, she's melted herself down again and again, forming up into the same shape each time. A vessel to pour chemicals into. A can of worms.

But there's a blank space inside it where an aching memory used to sit. Yolande can sometimes feel the jagged edges of the forgotten thing, raw and sharp. Whenever she senses it, her persistent need for oblivion sprouts vicious teeth that rip at her until she smokes something to push them under again.

Yolande is wearing clothes that have been worn and faded to the colour of leaking rubbish bins and dark corners, perfect for blending in with the city night. Yolande dislikes the term 'cat burglar' to describe her craft because cats are sneaky little buggers and too clever by half, always sucking up to people and purring to get what they want. Yolande's days of sucking up and purring have been used up and wrung out. Only the blind-drunkest of men, or the dead-eyed-empty ones, fall prey to whatever wiles she can thrust at them. She's got far too few teeth for one thing (although to some, that *can* be a selling point), and has found that robbery is more lucrative than getting some guy to be interested enough in her scrawny beef to let her freeload off him and his stash like she used to in the old days.

No. Yolande thinks of herself as a 'rat burglar'. Twitchy, quick and skinny enough to squeeze through places people never think to lock. She's been operating her own little thievery concern for over a year now, and she's thriving. She's living 'hand to mouth', or more accurately 'needle to vein', so she doesn't need much. She scuttles from city to town to another city to another town before she can get too complacent and get nabbed. She's always one step ahead on her scaly little paws. Ducking out of sight just in front of the sleek clever cats and the big, stinky dogs that like to run in packs, robbing with brute force and working for syndicates. Yolande tried that for a bit, but she's not a team player. She had to leave Durban in a hurry to prevent things from getting ugly. Uglier.

For now, she's the rat-bitch, tin-can queen of Port Elizabeth. Small towns can make things tricky if you're not careful, but it's always easier to get to grips with the local scene. It didn't take Yolande long to sniff out the right types to score from, the right types to sell to, and some nice dark little corners where she can take her medicine in peace.

Yolande slips around the edge of the beachfront parking lot. Salt-rimed sand crunches beneath her flip-flops and jumps over their rims and in between her toes. She doesn't notice. Her attention is elsewhere. This is a good place for lucky-dipping and sneaky-snitching. At this time of year, the beach is packed, and holidaymakers often leave their phones and wallets in their cars so they can flop about on the sand and run into the sea unencumbered. Sure, they hide their precious goodies, but Yolande can spot the telltale bulge of something slipped under the floor mat on the passenger side, or a too-carefully placed cardigan hiding a handbag or an iPad. She's getting better and better at jimmying the locks, and makes her way over to the spot where she hides the wire she keeps handy for the job.

'Hey, skinny.' Yolande just about jumps out of her skin when Sabelo calls out to her, but she scowls instead, plays it cool. She saunters over to where he stands in the shade of a scrubby tree.

'Fuck do you want?' she asks when she's close enough to smell the sick-herb stench of the permanent weed-cloud that surrounds him. Sabelo's eyes are salmon-pink-stoned in the deep brown of his face. A puff might lessen the mad sun heat, but Yolande needs to be sharp for her lucky dipping. She's rushing nicely anyway, no need for a downer. She waves the offered joint away and asks again: 'What makes you think you can order me over like some kind of waitress, hey?'

'You came, didn't you?'

'Ag, bugger off, Belo, I don't have time for this now.'

'No wait,' he drawls as Yolande turns away. 'I've got a message for you.'

'A message?'

'From someone through someone who called someone else. Reg passed it on. Think it's from your Pretoria days. Some money-lender guys, maybe.'

'What the hell are you rambling on about?' A hot scratch of worry rises up the back of Yolande's neck. Who's she pissed off now? Which someone from what past wants to tell her something? For the first time today, Yolande can smell salty ocean, and the sweet-sour of dropped ice cream cones on hot tar. She waits, but Sabelo just raises the joint to his lips again, moving in slow motion, his lids lowered against the smoke. 'Ag, you're just baked, Belo.' Yolande starts walking away. 'I'm not hanging around for this shit.'

'Nuhuh. You're going to want to hear this one, Ratty. It's about family.'

'Ha, well that's where you're wrong.' Yolande barks out a laugh. 'I haven't got any.'

Sabelo leans back against his tree trunk and raises one of his patchy eyebrows. Yolande's forced cackle splutters and dies. She shifts from foot to foot. She can feel the sand now, grinding between her sweating toes.

'OK then, tell me, if you've got something to tell me,' she relents. Sabelo smiles.

'According to my sources, you've got an aunty trying to get hold of you.'

'A what?'

'An aunty, man. You know, some nice old tannie from back at the farm or whatever. Determined old *gogo*. She's been try-ing to get a message to her lost little niece out there in the big bad world.'

Yolande's head spins. The skin suddenly feels too tightly stretched across her jaw.

'What, Sabelo?' All pretence of cool has gone from Yol-ande's voice. She steps closer. 'What's the message?'

Sabelo pinches out the last, gritty end of his joint and looks at Yolande with his pink, down-turned eyes. He shakes his head, then scratches a scab on his arm.

'It's your mama,' he says at last, and Yolande's mind scram-bles for purchase on the word. She sees a flash of silver hair, a pair of muddy gardening gloves lying on a wooden table.

An alien ache begins to claw at the space behind her eyes. 'They say she's dead. There's going to be a funeral.'

For a moment, the ache becomes blindness, and Yolande has to reach out and grip the front of Sabelo's stained T-shirt to steady herself.

'Shit,' he says. 'Sorry, man.'

Yolande is very still, and then suddenly she steps back and straightens her spine.

'Well don't be.' Yolande wipes her hands on the seat of her jeans. 'She was a bitch.'

'Right.' Sabelo resumes his lean against the tree and crosses his arms over his sunken chest. 'So. Would the bitch have left you anything, then? Money? Inheritance?'

Yolande looks out over the parking lot towards the beach and the blue stripe of sea beyond. She's remembering the rings on her mother's fingers: a wedding band and a pretty diamond on a strand of white-gold. They never suited the woman's too-rough, garden-mud fingers.

'Dunno,' she says. Something about Yolande's too-wide, brown-toothed grin slices through Sabelo's weed-induced fog and turns his belly to ice. 'Maybe I'll have to just go and see.'

CHAPTER FOURTEEN

THERE ARE TWO, ragged-barked gum trees standing in the graveyard, but their dappled shade is no match for the blazing heat. Dry grass crunches beneath the new shoes that Sussie bought for Sam to wear to the funeral service. They're hard and shiny black, and look to Sam like two lost beetles poking out from beneath her new dress. The beetles seem to have no idea which way to go to escape either the boiling glare, or the suffocating blanket of sadness that cloaks the valley.

Sam holds Jem's hand very tight. In contrast to her trembling, he is motionless and solid, a rooted tree. The black beetles shift closer to his shade. Sam finally lifts her gaze from her shoes and squints at the gathered crowd. *A big turnout*, Gerrie had said before the service, and Sam thinks that everyone who lives in town, and on all the outlying farms, must be here. She spots Mrs McGovern with Keegan and Nathan accompanied by the seldom-seen Mr McGovern in a dark suit. Keegan sees her looking, lifts a hand to wave, and then thinks better of it, blushing an awkward pink.

Sam looks back down at the beetles, and then up again.

There's the Vosloos and dour Betty from the Super Saver. There are a large group of farm workers, neat in their Sunday best, with gleaming combed hair and sweating faces. Sam even spots the boarder girl she shouted at that one time, with her brown fringe and her shoulders too wide for her navy blue dress, standing with her family. Everyone is blinking their eyes against the burning light.

'Le Roux.' Sam's not sure if Jem has spoken the word, or merely exhaled, but the syllables somehow coalesce in the still air, making Sam turn her head to follow his gaze. There, at the back of the gathering, stands a large, bearded man beside a soft-faced wife. Beside them, *it must be, it has to be*, is the laroo-girl. The laroo-girl is a woman now, tall and elegant in black strappy sandals and knee-length skirt, but Sam recognises the dark silk swish of her ponytail, remembering the way it had blown out in the wind on that day in the orchard, just like the horse's tail. Two whipping, brown flags in a rain of white petals. The memory brings with it a rush of Anneke's flowers-and-lanolin scent. Sam can almost feel the pressure of her grandmother's arm against hers, just as it was on that day long ago in the front seat of the bakkie.

To avoid the ache that builds behind Sam's eyes each time she thinks of her ouma, she concentrates hard on staring at the all-grown-up laroo-girl. Instead of the reins of a horse, the laroo-girl is now holding the hand of a young man with tousled hair who looks like he doesn't quite fit into his suit.

'Ah, the much talked-about fiancé,' Sam hears someone whisper in Afrikaans. 'I hear he's an Englishman, from Cape Town.'

'Old le Roux can't like that much. How's some city-boy going to look after his precious grapes?'

'That's what everyone said when Jeremy Harding married Anneke, and look how that turned out. He grew the best nectarines in the whole Western Cape.'

'Ja, but Jem is different. His love for Annie was... something else.'

'I know, and now… so sad, hey?'

'Ja.'

So sad.

The syllables shuffle and rustle like dry leaves, and Sam closes her eyes, leaning against her grandfather to keep herself upright. *So sad so sad.* The words are too small to describe the horror of the quiet bedroom back home, with the quilt that Anneke once stitched now so flat on the bed without her beneath it.

On long-ago early mornings, Sam used to crawl in beneath that quilt beside her ouma. To the background soundtrack of the running-tap-and-clanking noises of Jem making coffee in the kitchen, Anneke would take Sam on imaginary journeys through the landscape created by the different fabric squares. Walking their fingers across the quilt, they would explore perfect planted rows of grapevines in a striped patch, and then the complex grid of a city played out in plaid. They would take their finger-people (Sam's small and grubby, and Anneke's sun-spotted and swollen-knuckled) wandering across lawns and seas and through sandy deserts. Sam's favourite squares were the rare 'forest ones', which Anneke had snipped from a treasured piece of Liberty print that she'd once gotten as a gift. The fabric was deep green with repeating, complex swirls, and Sam had imagined tiny forest creatures watching them from between the stylised fronds.

So sad.

Sam clutches Jem's hand and feels a tiny part of herself, deep inside, curl up and crawl away to where she knows she will never be able to find it again.

After the earth has been replaced over the coffin that Sussie insisted on, despite Jem's suggestions of a cremation, after the ham sandwiches and milk tartlets that Sussie served for the funeral tea have all been eaten, and after Sam and Jem have climbed into the bakkie to head back to their too-silent house, a figure emerges from behind a clump of bushes on the rise leading up to the family graveyard.

It's a woman, but barely. Living has worn her thin. Even her hair is emaciated, its colour leached out to a dusty, hessian grey. The woman is dried out and ashen like the shed skin of a snake, but one that walks about wearing men's dark glasses, skinny faded jeans, and a T-shirt with a stain on the front of it.

Yolande trudges up to the grave and stops. She touches the freshly turned earth with the toe of one scuffed trainer. Her foot sinks a little into the soft soil. She pushes harder, grinding her sole over the place where she imagines that her mother lies. With her father, evidently, still alive, there will be nothing for her here. Not yet. She's going to have to wait some more. Yolande flicks the butt of her cigarette into the divot her foot has made, turns and walks away, back down the hill to wherever it is that she came from.

Nobody sees her but the waving blue gums and the sky.

CHAPTER FIFTEEN

AFTER THE SOLITARY, silent weeks that followed the funeral, the first days back at school are dreamlike and strange for Sam. For a while, everyone treats her as if she's made of fragile blown glass, liable to shatter at any moment, but by the end of February, the classroom regains its rhythm and there are moments when Sam almost forgets that her life is no longer what it used to be.

Today, the wind is on edge, buffeting the eaves, shaking the plants and scouring sand across the classroom window panes. By the time classes are over, it has died down, but the fine Karoo silt that's been blowing in all morning, travelling up the mountains and over the vineyards and fruit trees, seems to have coated everything in a peach-coloured powder. Sam can feel it clinging to her sweat-sticky limbs as she climbs on to Keegan's bicycle for her turn to freewheel down the hill, and when she pushes off, she can taste its bitter grittiness in her mouth. The rushing air whips Sam's hair back from her boiling neck, and she gives a high laugh as the bicycle swoops down the wide, empty street.

'Nice one,' Keegan calls out after she brakes and swerves at the bottom of the hill and starts pedalling back towards where he waits for his turn at the top. 'Told you you'd like it.'

'I never said I wouldn't.' She's out of breath when she

brings the bicycle to a stop beside him. 'I just wasn't sure I felt like it in this heat.' Keegan's hand is clammy with sweat as he takes the handlebars from her. 'I'm surprised that *you* do, to be honest, Keegan. I thought you stayed inside playing computer games in the afternoons these days.'

'No need. With the boarders back in their barracks,' he grins, 'the town is ours again.'

He gives a whoop as he barrels down the hill, and his slender shape seems to dissolve into the heat haze that hangs over the road. Now that she's no longer moving, Sam can feel the hot thick blanket of summer pushing down on her once more. She wipes the sweat on her forehead with the back of her wrist, but then has to lift the corner of her T-shirt to wipe away the resulting smear of pale orange mud.

'If you're planning on stripping down…' Sam turns to see Nathan sauntering up to her with his hands in the pockets of his shorts. A sheen of moisture glistens over the faint new fuzz on his top lip. 'Don't let me stop you.'

'What are you on about?'

'Lifting your top up like that. Could be taken the wrong way, you know.'

'Oh, shut up.'

Nathan's cheeks redden, and Sam turns away before he can say anything else. She watches Keegan cycle up the hill, elbows out and knees pumping. There's an urgency to his movements that wasn't there earlier when it was just the two of them. He skids to a stop and scowls at his elder brother.

'What are you doing here?'

'Just chatting.'

'Here, Sam, it's your go.' Keegan thrusts the bike at her.

'Maybe she's had enough of playing around with your baby toys, Keegan.'

'What do *you* know?' Keegan hurls back. Sam stares at them both for a moment, and then launches off back down the hill on the bike, biting the wind and relishing the stomach-swoop as her speed builds towards the bottom of the dip.

When she turns the bike around, she sees that Keegan and Nathan are still arguing. She can't hear what they are saying from here, but the two little figures at the top of the rise are gesticulating furiously. She wheels the bicycle into the grass beside the road and sits down in the shade of the old karee tree. She leans her back against its rough bark and closes her eyes, but the heat still pricks and pulls at her, itching her skin.

Eventually, Keegan wanders down the slope, kicking up dust with his trainers and muttering curses. Every so often, he turns back to make sure that Nathan is no longer watching him. The road is empty, except for a small, dome-shelled tortoise that is making its way across the orange sand.

'Hey,' he says when he gets close enough to Sam, who is still sitting, eyes closed, against the tree. Her eyes fly open. As always, Keegan is taken aback by their impossible pale watery blue. He jams his hands into his pockets. He pokes at a tuft of dry grass with his toe. 'Too tired to cycle up the hill again?'

Sam shakes her head and closes her eyes again. 'Too tired to get in the middle of your and Nathan's sibling *stuff*.'

'Right.' Keegan sits down beside her with a huff of breath. 'My brother's being a dork.'

Sam says nothing. A breeze moves the long tapered leaves on the branches overhead, and the dappled spots of shade dance across Sam's cheeks and closed eyelids.

'He thinks you're too grown up to be playing with me but that's not true because we're the same age.' Keegan steals a look at the long white braid draped over Sam's shoulder. It reminds him of the twisted-looking horn of a unicorn in one of the picture books he used to love when he was little. Would the braid be warm to the touch? Springy or soft? His heart is hammering beneath his sweaty T-shirt. 'Don't you think, Sam?'

'Of course. Nathan doesn't know what he's talking about half the time.' She blinks her eyes open again, but doesn't look at him. She is gazing up the road. 'Is that a tortoise?'

Keegan doesn't hear the question over the sudden swish and thump of the blood rushing through his ears. He's going to do it. He has to. He knows that it's too soon, *far* too soon, but if he doesn't, he gets the feeling that Nathan just might, and that cannot happen. It just cannot.

'Sam.' His voice comes out in a strange croak, and she turns to him then, her pale eyes on his, unreadable. With a funny little gasp and a jerk, he moves forward and kisses her, quickly, on her slightly open mouth.

Sam pulls back. 'What are you...'

Keegan holds his breath. Everything is very still, even the breeze has stopped. Sam frowns.

'Why did you do that?'

Keegan blinks at her. *Surely it's obvious?* But Sam's frown deepens. She seems genuinely baffled.

'I don't... know,' he lies. He tries to smile. Sam turns to look up the road again, wiping her mouth with the back of her hand. Wiping away his kiss. Keegan's chest crunches in.

'Look, it *is* a tortoise!' She jumps up and trots towards the dark little creature that's trundling through the dust. 'Let's help him off the road in case a car comes.'

Keegan's eyes fill with sudden tears and the red road and the girl and the tortoise all blur into a shimmering hot mess. He touches his mouth with the back of his hand as if to hold the taste of her on his lips: fresh and strange and almost sweet, like water.

The bakkie's headlights snake along the bottom of the dark bowl of the pre-dawn valley. It overpowers the moonlight that Sam knows is bright tonight. She knows it is because they've timed this carefully. They'll need a full moon.

She forces her sleep-gritty eyes to stay open by staring at the stripes of light from the headlights illuminating the road ahead. Jem is silent in the driver's seat beside her, and in the back of the bakkie, tucked up against each other and rattling around under the stars, are the plants.

Months ago, Jem showed Sam how to take cuttings from each of Anneke's rose bushes. He showed her where to snip with sterilised secateurs, how to remove the buds and leaves and moisten the end of each cutting in her mouth before inserting it into a raw potato. *It's important to make the hole in the potato first so that you don't damage the end of the cutting*, he'd said, handing her a screwdriver whose shaft was about the same diameter as the rose stems. She'd slotted a licked stalk snugly into each potato before Jem showed her how to bury them in good loose soil, tamp them down hard, and make a little greenhouse with a plastic bottle over the top for each of them. Now, three months later, they have a new little rose plant for each of the bushes that Anneke nurtured and watered and whispered to for so many years. The stalks have hardened off well and the roots have grown, feeding first on the starchy tuber and gaining strength before venturing out into the soil. All through late summer, autumn and early winter, the new bushes grew, sending out small leaves and a few cautious buds, until last week, when they were pruned back along with their parents in preparation for spring.

Yesterday evening, Jem and Sam dug up the baby rose stalks and wrapped each little clod of dirt and roots into careful bundles of sacking before tying them with string. Now the new plants, little more than thorn-covered twigs, bounce against each other in the bakkie basin along with piles of compost and a tub of bone meal, two spades, a trowel, and a sack of brown bulbs, collected from the garden and rustling their oniony skins against each other in the darkness.

Jem parks the bakkie as close as he can to the little family graveyard beneath the blue gum trees in the dip behind a low hill. Without saying a word, Sam climbs out of the cabin and goes to the back to help him unload. With the headlights switched off, their eyes begin to adjust to the blue moonlight, and Sam is astonished at how much she can see: the snail-trail-silver road winding down the hill behind them, the dark trees against the darker sky with the mountains rearing up in the distance. She can easily make out the little granite headstone that marks her grandmother's grave.

For the past few nights, in the lighted warmth of the kitchen, she and Jem cradled their mugs of coffee and planned where they would plant each rosebush and bulb, how they would dig into the poor orange earth of the graveyard and backfill the holes with good compost. The weather has been on their side. A light rain fell all day, leaving the cold soil wet and friable. Their spades scrape and stab into the tomato-coloured mud. It's hard work. The night air is chilling the sweat as soon as it appears and Sam's hands are starting to ache but she pushes on until at last the ground is ready.

As the eastern sky turns from navy to deep blue, she and Jem unwrap the little hessian bundles and plant the baby rosebushes into their fresh burrows of bone meal and compost. Then they push bulbs into the turned earth between them. Some will flower next winter when the roses are bare, some in spring, and others will bloom in summer, their strident faces poking up between the rose buds.

Jem stretches out his back and surveys their handiwork. There's not much to see, just a bunch of sticks poking out of disturbed soil. He's sure nobody will notice before the sap rises and the leaves burst out.

'Now all we need is some more rain for their first watering.'

'That shouldn't be a problem.' Sam points west to where the sky is being swallowed up by a dark shadowy shape blowing in over the mountains.

'Perfect timing, hey?' Jem looks to where the scudding clouds are just starting to fold over their helpful moon. 'Clearly your ouma put in a good word for us.'

'She sure did.'

Jem pulls the girl into a hug, and Sam breathes in his familiar smell of soil and sap and green things waiting to grow.

'It's going to be beautiful come spring,' she whispers into the scratchy wool of his jersey. The tears are hot and then icy on her cheeks, but she lets them fall.

PART THREE
THE COPPER-FEATHERED EAGLE

CHAPTER SIXTEEN

SAM RIDES JEM'S old motorbike into Main Street. When the tar was first laid a few years before, it had been raw and gleaming, turning the town into the equivalent of a khaki-clad farmer wearing a shiny leather belt, but since then, the constant coatings of Karoo dust have made it barely discernible from the surrounding farm roads.

Sam brings the bike to a stop outside the Super Saver. The heat of the road rises up and simmers between the skin of her calves and the cracked leather of Anneke's old horse-riding boots. Sam's been wearing the boots, along with a motley assortment of Anneke's old clothes, ever since she's been big enough to fit into them. The boots are her favourite. Without their hard soles, she'd never be able to kick-start the arthritic old Yamaha to life.

She climbs off the bike to wrestle the bent kickstand into doing her bidding. It hasn't been the same since she lost control of the bike on a patch of loose sand last month and skidded into a boulder. She curses herself, again, for having been so thoughtless.

'When's your grandpa going to fix that old thing?' Mr Vosloo asks when she walks into the store. After the glare of the street, the shop is gloomy, even with the buzzing blue light coming from the fluorescent tubes above the aisles. Sam blinks, spots Mr Vosloo restocking the hanging rack with packets of batteries, and remembers to smile.

'It's not like that old *Engelsman* to let something go unmended, is it?' he says.

'I haven't told him yet, Mr Vosloo. Don't want a lecture.' Sam adds just the right amount of conspiratorial tone into her answer. Mr Vosloo grins.

'You kids. Dewalt's just the same. Wants to be a big man and go playing with the grown-up's toys, but is too *poep*-scared to take the fall when something goes wrong. Isn't that right, Betty?'

Betty, dark and wordless at her post behind the till, gives what is most likely a nod.

'Hi, Betty.' Sam picks up a basket and heads to the aisles. She hears another customer enter the store behind her, and freezes when she hears Mr Vosloo's obsequious greeting:

'Good day, Mr le Roux!' She glances sideways to see Mr Vosloo almost bowing to the great grape-grower. Tertius le Roux. Jem's sworn enemy seems to have grown taller since Sam last saw him almost six years ago at Anneke's funeral, and his farmer's moustache is even bristlier. She ducks down behind a shelf, pretending to read the ingredients on a packet of biscuits that she has no intention of buying.

'I hear your lovely daughter has returned to the bosom of her family,' Mr Vosloo says, and Sam scowls. Who the hell says 'bosom of the family'? Does the shopkeeper think le Roux will spend more in his store if he talks like an idiot from the eighteen hundreds?

'She has.' Le Roux's answer is brisk, but polite. 'With her husband, Charlie, and my little granddaughter.'

'Ag, that's lovely, hey? Must be nice to have all the family together.'

'Ag, ja, it's good to have Liezette home.' The warmth in le Roux's voice doesn't sit neatly with Sam's mental picture of him. This is the man who thought Anneke's garden wasn't worthy of the water which he had no rights to. She resists the urge to peer around the shelf to check if his fingers are crossed behind his back.

'And her daughter, little Delia, is a treasure,' le Roux adds.

The laroo-girl is a mother? Sam can't imagine her as anything other than an otherworldly creature galloping through a blossoming orchard.

'I heard you bought Liezette a new horse, to celebrate her homecoming,' Mr Vosloo says, and for a moment Sam smiles to think of the laroo-girl riding out again, half human, half horse.

'What a lucky girl, hey?'

'Yes.' Le Roux must have had enough of discussing his daughter with sweaty old Mr Vosloo, because he is suddenly back to business: 'Just the newspaper today, please, Betty.' Le Roux pays Betty, says polite goodbyes, and then leaves. Sam exhales. If he'd noticed her, would he know who she was? Probably. Her Anneke-hair is always a dead giveaway.

She returns the biscuits to their shelf and gives a little jump when she realises that Mr Vosloo is now staring at her, folded arms resting on the bulge of his prodigious gut.

'You and my Dewalt are about the same age, aren't you?' Mr Vosloo's chatty mood has obviously not been satisfied by le Roux's brief visit. Sam remembers Dewalt Vosloo. He was one of the boarder boys she and Keegan used to run from each time the school holidays came around.

'Yup. Seventeen next week.' Sam selects a packet of green Sunlight soap bars, a box of Five Roses tea.

'I heard that your arty-farty teacher said that you're not going to classes at her house any more.'

'That's right.' Sam picks up a bag of oats.

'You've got to be careful. Can't do much in life without a matric, you know, girly.'

'I'm still going to do matric next year. I just decided correspondence would be better.'

Bottle of orange juice. Small block of white cheddar. Sam adds it up in her head as best she can to make sure that she's got enough cash to cover it.

'Isn't studying by correspondence just making things more difficult for yourself?' Mr Vosloo shakes his head and his jowls quiver. 'Not to mention all you're missing out on by not hanging out with kids your age. My Dewalt just wants to party non-bloody-stop!'

'Yes, well, you know.' Sam gives a vague sort of shrug and shoves her basket onto the counter by the till. 'Ring me up, please, Betty.'

Betty punches the price of each item into the ancient cash register in silence. Mr Vosloo eyes her like a hawk. He always has, even though she's been working in his store for ten years and in all that time, has neither made a mistake nor said a single word.

'Aren't you forgetting something?' Mr Vosloo gives Sam an exaggerated wink.

'I'm not sure what you—'

'The pilchards! Your grandpa's pilchards. I know that old *souty* can't go a day without a stinky pilchard sandwich.'

'Of course.' Sam's face blazes hot. She almost trips in her haste to reach the tinned food aisle. 'Thanks for reminding me, Mr Vosloo.'

Her fingers tremble as she hands the tin of pilchards to

Betty. 'Add that on, please.' Betty looks at Sam with wet, black eyes before returning her attention to the till.

'Good girly. Your grandpa will thank me, hey? Don't forget to tell the old man I say hi and that he needs to pull himself towards himself and get better soon.'

'Will do. Thanks.'

Sam leaves the Super Saver as fast as she dares.

When the familiar roar of Sam's motorbike splits the drowsy hush of Main Street, Keegan is hunched at his computer, annihilating alien civilisations with clicks of his mouse. From his bedroom, the sound of the engine is faint, but he's kept his earphones off to ensure he won't miss it. He pauses the game and is out of the house, on his bicycle and out of the gate in moments.

Keegan pedals hard, jolting over scrubby lawns and hurtling around corners. Sam's forays in town have become progressively fewer and briefer over the past few weeks. Even with all his planning, he might miss the chance to talk to her today.

Relief shivers through him when he arrives outside the Super Saver to see Sam's mud-spattered old Yamaha leaning on its wonky kickstand. He just manages to slow his breathing down and wipe the sweat from his face with the sleeve of his T-shirt when she comes out of the store. Wisps of Sam's lemon-pith hair are sticking up all over the place from where she took off her motorbike helmet earlier, turning her head into a dandelion that glows as she steps into the sunlit street.

Her face, however, is tired and tight-looking. Keegan imagines the thick braid sucking the strength out of her to make itself more magnificent.

'Hey,' he calls, and then again louder, because his voice came out all croaky. 'Hey, Sam.'

'Keegan.' His name in her mouth is bone-marrow-melting. He grins and trots over.

'It's weird at school without you,' he says. *Nice way not to sound needy, Keegan*, he thinks. *Way to go.*

Sam glances back to where Mr Vosloo lurks in the gloom of the shop. She fidgets with the straps of her backpack.

'You'll adjust, I'm sure,' she says, and smiles to see that the lock of brown hair on Keegan's crown is standing up, just as it always has. 'Speaking of adjusting, have you recovered from the shock of me asking to borrow your old laptop?'

'Not really.' Keegan had been speechless last month when Sam had handed him a newly purchased 3G dongle and asked him to set it up so she could use the internet at home. 'I never thought I'd see the day.'

'Your mother insisted. She said she couldn't let me do the rest of my schooling via correspondence without it.'

'You must really have been dying to get away from me then, hey? To let evil technology into your house?' Keegan says, trying to pretend for both of them that her leaving doesn't hurt.

'That's not why I did it, man.' Sam gives him a playful push on his shoulder. 'I needed to be home more, that's all.'

'Is your grandpa doing OK? He's been sick for ages.' Sam bends down and wipes at the dust on the scuffed toe of her boot. 'Is he getting any better? Is that why you dropped out of school? To look after him? There are people that can do that, Sam, you don't have to like… stop your life or anything.'

'I didn't *drop out* and I'm not stopping my life.' She hefts the backpack on to her back. 'Don't be so melodramatic.'

'I know your grandparents went all weird and reclusive when your ouma got sick all those years ago, but it doesn't mean you have to do the same thing now.'

'Honestly, Keegan, when have I been anything *but* weird in your opinion?'

'Well, either way, it's strange without you there, like I was saying.'

Keegan follows Sam back to her bike, and watches as she pulls the straps out from inside her helmet before sliding it on. It's an old-style one without a visor, so she has to wear sunglasses to stop things flying into her eyes. Keegan wonders how many bugs she's swallowed since she started riding the bike into town, instead of sitting beside Jem in the bakkie like she used to.

'Think you'll change your mind and come back?' In the ensuing silence, Keegan sees his own reflection in the dark lenses of Sam's sunglasses. Skinny and stupid. He looks away, suddenly shy.

'I guess I'll see you round here, then,' he mutters.

'Of course.' The refrigerated orange juice bottle in Sam's backpack is a patch of cold against her spine.

'Email me next time you're coming in to town.'

'I'll try and remember.' She fights the kickstand up again, and straddles the bike.

'If you owned a cell phone like a regular human, you could SMS or WhatsApp me when you get here, and we could meet up.'

'Bye, Keegan,' Sam says, and kicks the motorbike into life.

Keegan stands in the centre of the wide street and breathes in the dust cloud that Sam leaves in her wake. It tastes dry and bitter, like the Karoo itself.

CHAPTER SEVENTEEN

ON THE RARE, clear days when he's working on a piece that's going to turn out just right, Charlie Rowan ceases to exist. His breath becomes the hot-sugar smell of maple on the lathe, and his heartbeat the jump of the saw in his hands. On days like this, the timber seems to know what he wants it to be, bending and shaping itself into the back of a chair, or the base of a side table, without him having much to do with it at all.

But on all the other days, wood is war.

It bites and hisses beneath his useless fingers, lashes out and trips him, splits and splinters and draws blood where it can.

As soon as he opens the workshop door and the morning sunlight falls past him and on to the battered bench and the worn woodworking tools that he inherited from his late teacher, with their scuffed handles, brass fixings, and coal-coloured points, he can feel it. What was merely a pile of logs and planks the evening before has transformed into something needy and sentient overnight: a moody lover. Sometimes it's all blissful curving openness that greets him, and the waiting wood is smooth-limbed and spice-scented. Those are the days when Charlie becomes every knot, grain and notch of it. But on the wilful days, the workshop smells musty when he pulls open the doors, and a claggy grime of dust and resin seems to cling to every surface. At once, his body is heavy with doubt and all he can hear is the mechanical grinding of the 'fear-of-fucking-up' gears turning behind his temples.

Charlie doesn't want to associate this feeling with Liezette, but each time he feels that weight and that pressure, it's *her* voice he hears in his head.

When he first met Liezette, his woodworking concern was little more than a few commissioned pieces for friends and a few items sold at local market stalls on Sundays. Despite the fact that he was sleeping on an old mattress in the draughty built-in veranda of his dad's little house in Plumstead, the 'kind-wood' days far outweighed the bad. At night, he would drop onto his sleeping bag beside his dad's muddy-pawed mutt called Elmo and sleep like the dead, wood shavings still curled between the hairs on his forearms.

And then an exclusive store in trendy De Waterkant began hounding him for pieces. In amongst the brushed steel and glass items that adorned the immaculate shop floor, his creations stood out like vital, growing things, seeming to burst from the polished floorboards in an effort to reach the light. It was here, in amongst the wildly priced goods (his own included, he was wide-eyed to note), that he met Liezette.

Liezette had huge green eyes made even larger by carefully applied black eyeliner, dark hair and long, white limbs with freckles that looked like sprinkles of cinnamon. She'd run her slim fingers over the solid chunk of burnished wood that Charlie had worked into a lamp base with an intensity that had left him breathless. He didn't know it then, but despite her thrift store outfits and cultivated urban arty-girl look, Liezette was a creature moulded from wine and money. She shared a shabby flat with a friend in Gardens, but a steady stream of support from her daddy flowed down from a vineyard north-east and into her charity-shop-bought pockets. Privilege seemed to coat Liezette like the bloom on a ripe grape, and every time Charlie touched her, he imagined a little bit of it rubbing off on him. As soon as they moved in together, the demand for his work went into overdrive. Hand-crafted artisan furniture had suddenly become *the* 'must have' item.

Soon Charlie was working such long hours that the calluses he'd cultivated over years of carpentry wore right back into blisters, raw patches that Liezette would soak in bowls of warm water and cider vinegar before kissing them gently and bandaging up his hands before bed. In their wedding photographs, you can see the pink shiny bits of sore skin on the edges of his fingers.

Back then, there were still more kind-wood days than bad ones, but Charlie was starting to find it harder to feel his way through each piece. He felt shaved down too thin and lifting at the edges, like a poorly worked veneer. Some days, he just lay on the floor of his workshop in amongst the sawdust and tools, and slept.

And then Delia arrived.

Charlie had not been in any way ready to have a child. He'd been furious with Liezette when he discovered she's gotten pregnant on purpose despite his well-aired views on the subject, and then hated himself for resenting her obvious, glowing joy. Every millimetre of girth that grew around her midriff added a fresh layer of pressure, each one like a coating of varnish, thickening and hardening over the grain of him until there was nothing to see but rigid dark.

Of course, his heart had just melted when he first held the tiny, black-haired little bundle that was his newborn daughter. He'd gazed down at her squidged up features and impossible eyelashes and felt the same sense of oneness that he did on a kind-wood day.

But the wood didn't feel that way.

In the years after Delia's birth, it became more and more recalcitrant. It rebuffed his advances like a jealous lover, spitting and furious, refusing to be shaped. His hands bled and his eyes stung and the flow of finished pieces slowed in direct proportion to the orders that poured in.

'I'm losing it, babe,' he'd said to Liezette as she lay beside him in the dark, her musky-grape scent already infusing the new Egyptian cotton sheets she'd purchased that morning.

'Oh Charlie, you're being daft.' She'd brushed his hair back from his furrowed forehead and laughed off his doubts. She seemed to believe that continually telling him how talented he was would bind the cracks that he was battling to keep in check. But each word of praise was a wedge being hammered in, splitting him apart.

And then, he noticed that Liezette had started dawdling in the infant section of Woolworths whenever they were out shopping together, holding the tiny flannel suits to her face and breathing in as if she could somehow inhale a new baby into being.

'It's not going to fucking happen, Liezette,' he'd snapped one terrible winter afternoon. The lashing rain had trapped the three of them indoors for the entire day, and Delia's ear-splitting three-year-old shrieks seemed set to shatter his skull bones.

Once her shock had subsided, Liezette's tone had become soothing and honeyed: 'We'll get away from all this, Charlie. You need somewhere where you can work properly. My parents have been begging for us to move out to the farm with them. There's a barn that they no longer use. It would make the most perfect workshop for you. It's huge. You're always saying that you don't have enough space in your dad's old garage.' Liezette was really the one who'd complained about this. She was often on at him about getting more professional premises. 'The business will thrive in all that space. *You'll* thrive. Not to mention what all that clean air will do for Delia.'

And yes, in that tiny apartment with the endless flotsam of plastic toys forming a candy-pink crust over every surface and his little daughter leaping from the back of the sofa and yelping like a basket of poodles, he'd been too ragged to think of an objection.

But now, each morning after coffee and rusks in the farmhouse kitchen served by Liezette's silent, smiling mother, Antoinette, Charlie approaches the workshop that Liezette's parents have set up for him in one of their old barns with an escalating sense of dread. Despite the fresh air rushing down from the mountains, the rows of vine stalks in the late winter sun, and the space so wide beneath the sky that even Delia cannot fill it, Charlie knows that he has lost his way with wood.

It no longer wants him. Simple as that.

Charlie stands in the barn and clenches his fists. On the floor at his feet lies the chunk of tambotie that he ordered last week. He stares at the rich, two-toned, chocolate-coloured grain, but just cannot fathom how on earth it could possibly become part of the chair that he's been asked to make. The design is simple, he's made many like it over the years, perfecting each joint and curve, but right now, the concept of turning *this* into *that* seems ludicrous. Laughable. He's astonished to see strange, dark spots suddenly appearing on the surface of the wood, and it's only when he looks up and feels the wetness on his cheeks that he realises he's been gazing at his own tears. He steps back, rubs his hands over his face and then walks out of the barn, closing the large doors and bolting them behind him.

Right outside the back of the barn there's a patch of dirt, and then the land slopes up and soars into a large raw hill that marks one edge of the farm boundary. Unlike the startling green of the lucerne fields, the groomed fruit trees, the rows of immaculate vines, the grand whitewashed homestead and surrounding cluster of well-kept utility buildings, this little piece of land has a refreshing wildness to it. The fynbos fights with the weeds at the foot of the hill, and then gathers confidence, marching up its slopes towards the sky. There's something of a relief in the chaotic scrubby mass of it, interspersed with long, beige grass and bleached rocks. Charlie would like to sit in the sun and gaze up at the hill for a while, but the empty hum of the workshop at his back won't let him.

He strides around the barn, away from the hill, and makes his way to where his van is parked beside a small orchard of plum trees. The farm is so huge that the best way to get from the house to the barn and back again is to drive there. Charlie doubts that he'll ever get used to it.

As Charlie nears the van, he sees Liezette walking towards him, squinting into the sunlight. She's wearing riding boots and dusty jodhpurs, and an old tracksuit top that looks like it belongs to her father.

'Hey, I was just coming to see how you were doing.' The Liezette that lived in Cape Town with him wore silky printed tops with skinny jeans and ballet pumps and always looked immaculate. This version could do with a hair wash.

'Hey, Liez.' He leans in to give her a kiss, but she turns her head and he bumps into her jaw instead. She smells ripe, but no longer of grapes. She smells of horse. The first thing that Liezette's father did when they moved here last month was reward his beloved daughter for returning to the fold by buying her one. Turns out, Liezette is horse mad. He'd had no idea before. From what he's gathered, the first time she ever climbed down off one of the things was to go to university in Cape Town.

Since the massive, nut-brown animal made its appearance at the farm, Liezette has spent hours grooming it and cleaning its tack and walking beside it and riding it, fast and wild, along the farm roads and between the rows of trellised grapevines. Even Delia has been sidelined, somewhat, although his daughter is only too delighted with her new occupation: bossing her devoted grandmother around.

'Where the hell are you going? I thought you'd be working, Charlie,' Liezette scowls. 'There are three orders that need to go out, quick-quick.'

'I know that. Jesus, Liezette, can't a person take a break?' He moves past her towards the van.

'So, where are you going now?'

'Into town.'

'Why?'

'To buy something from the shops, if that's OK with you.' He climbs into the driver's seat and slams the door. He rolls down the window when she raps on the glass.

'What's your problem, Charlie?'

'Ag, forget it.'

'No I won't "forget it". You're being a total prick.'

'Thank you for the update.'

'And anyway, what could you possibly want to buy? There's nothing in town.'

'They've got a liquor store, don't they?' he yells over the roar of the engine as he turns the ignition.

'Of course. But—'

'Well then, I'm going to get some beer. There's only so much bloody wine a person can drink, you know.'

There's been so little reason for Charlie to drive anywhere since they moved here, that as soon as he turns out of the farm gates, he's not sure which way to go. The vehicle vibrates, pent-up and eager to run. He takes in the scattered blue mountains and the miles and miles of stunted-looking, leafless, winter vineyards. The whole landscape looks as if it's been neatened by a giant with an enormous comb.

Which way?

He notes the same ragged hill that he can see from the barn in the rear-view mirror. Surely that means he needs to go left? The tyres spin in the dirt as he urges the van onwards. It doesn't really matter where he's going, as long as it's away.

Twenty minutes, and a couple of double-backs and wrong turns later, he sees the tiny town approaching on the horizon. As the van jolts over the bump where the tarred road begins, a small, dirty motorbike zooms towards him in a cloud of dust.

'Hey, slow down, moron!' Charlie yells. He's not going to be driven into the ditch by an asshole on a shitty old bike. Not today. As the motorbike nears, he sees that the rider is small and light. *Just a kid.* The roads out here are full of kids on motorbikes. They use them to get around the farms and stuff because it's too damn far to walk anywhere.

The motorbike passes. *Was that a braid snaking out from under the helmet?* He looks in his rear-view mirror to be sure. Yup, there's a thick rope of blonde hair streaming out behind the rider.

It's a girl, all right.

There's no way in hell he's going to allow Delia to ride around like that when she's that age. *If we're still living here then.* His guts lurch. He flattens his foot on the accelerator, trying to outrun the spectre of the empty workshop. He's surprised to note, however, that its screams at his retreating back have lessened, softened by the new memory of that flying braid, pale, like a piece of turned ash glowing in the sun.

CHAPTER EIGHTEEN

SAM DOESN'T HEAD straight home. Instead, she rides to the little graveyard that huddles in the hollow behind Sussie's farm. When she switches off the bike engine, the silence swims in like a caress, heavy with the scent of flowering bulbs. It's now almost impossible to see Anneke's grave through the thick-stemmed tangle of exuberant bushes that surround it. It's still too early for roses, but spring daffodils and freesias bob their bright faces in amongst the green. Sam moves between the plants, checking the tiny new rose leaves for signs of aphids, and remembering that night long ago when she and Jem first drove down here in the dark with a bakkie-load of twigs.

Over the years, they've had to replace some of the plants that didn't take, and heap mulch on the ground between the ones that did to help keep the soil cool around the roots. Water has always been a problem in midsummer, especially when the plants were first struggling to establish themselves. Jem and Sam have spent many night hours over the years ferrying buckets of water from the old collection tank on the hill.

This early in the season, though, the ground is still spongy from the winter rains, perfect for pulling out the numerous sprouting weeds. Sam crouches down amongst the bushes to do so, using the old hunting knife that Jem once gave her, and which she now always wears on her belt when she comes to town, to lever the deep ones out. She is so absorbed with weeding that she doesn't hear the car. It's only when the sound of a heavy door slams the silence in half that she realises she's no longer alone. Sam freezes with her hands pressed against the moist earth, heart thumping, poised as if about to start a race. Only there's nowhere to run.

Damn it.

'Sam?' *Well, at least she didn't say 'koewee'.*

Sam doesn't move. A rose leaf tickles the back of her neck.

Desecration, Sussie had spat at Jem when she first realised what they'd done to the graveyard. *My family's remains, our heritage, lying undisturbed for centuries and then you come along and you just have to have your bloody way. Nothing is sacred to you, is it? Nothing anybody else cares about matters nearly as much as you getting to stamp your precious mark all over everything.* Jem had been shocked at the accusation. Stupefied. He'd been shaking. Sam can still remember it. His big, worn hands, trembling against the worn green of his muddy trousers. *How are roses and dahlias and freesias a desecration? They are part of who Anneke was, Sussie. I planted them to honour her.* Jem had started shouting too. Sam remembers that, because it's one of the few times she'd ever heard him do so. *Unforgivable*, Sussie had said, weeping with fury. And that had been that. No more Sussie in their garden, no more Sussie in her big car bringing *vorm koekies* for tea on the stoop, no more Sussie in their lives at all.

But she's here now. Sam dares a peek. *And she's not going away.* She can see Sussie's sensible sandals and sky blue trousers through the leaves.

When she realises that she has to move, to do *something*, Sam stands, wiping her dirty knife on her jeans and tucking it back in its sheath. Although she's spotted Sussie from a distance over the past five years, it's the first time they've been face to face since 'the desecration'. How fitting that Sussie should accost her here, in the midst of the crime scene. *Did she follow me here? Has she been waiting for me?* Sam's breath squeezes in her throat. She knows she's being paranoid, but paranoia has become necessary.

'My God,' Sussie breathes, 'you look just like her.'

Sam is not expecting this. She is ready to carry on Jem's fight, but Sussie looks limp and wide-eyed, staring at Sam as if she's seen a ghost. Sam notes that some of Sussie's immaculate gloss has worn away. There's a slight stoop in her shoulders and her hair has thinned so that, with the bright sky behind it, Sam can make out the vulnerable shape of her great-aunt's skull beneath the carefully styled helmet.

Sussie covers her mouth with a trembling hand. Tears collect in the creases of her face before dripping down to join the pattern on the fabric of her blouse. Sam doesn't move. The air is still and dense with hush. Sussie drops her hand, opens her mouth to speak. Nothing.

At last, she turns and makes her way back to her SUV. The engine starts up with a diesel roar, and the vehicle reverses and then drives off. The mud is drying on Sam's fingers, tightening her skin and pulling them into stiff claws. She waits, motionless, amongst the rose bushes until the dust cloud has moved along the farm road, over the rise, and away.

Sam parks the motorbike in the barn beside her grandfather's old bakkie, and unlocks the padlock on the door separating the barn from the courtyard beyond. The padlock is a recent addition, one of her 'extra precautions'. Sam locks it behind her with a click. The wind that blew up while she was riding back from town has ushered in a leaden sky. It presses low over the garden with a belly full of waiting rain. A sudden gust whips the lavender stalks back and forth and curls around her back, chilling the sweaty patch caused by the backpack.

A distant crunch of thunder churns around the valley and an answering whisper seems to rise up from the shadows beneath the greenery. Sam glances back to the barn door with its gleaming padlock, unable to shake the feeling that she has locked herself on the wrong side of it.

Don't be an idiot. There's a chunk of softening cheese in her backpack that needs to be put in the fridge. *Come, on, get a move on.* Sam marches into the gloom. Her boots sink into the wet ground and the leaves that brush her jeans release a herby-bitter smell. She glances across to the darkening pool of shadow beneath the oak tree with its proud new coat of bright leaves. Sam-the-horse's grave marker could do with replacing again. A fat raindrop splats down, followed by another.

Sam holds her breath as she passes the rose garden. Unlike the ones planted in full sun around Anneke's grave, these in the cooler valley are only just showing signs of coming back to life. The pruned stalks poke out of the mulch like clawed hands, and new maroon-coloured nodules that promise spring leaves are popping up all over them, like little blood-filled sacks.

Sam runs. She crashes into the kitchen and shuts the door behind her.

'I'm home!' she calls out to banish the silence.

The rain has left the sky clean and pale, and from her seat on an old cane chair in the lookout shelter, Sam can see where the lowering sun tinges the edges of it with stripes of lemon. With Jem's help, she's rebuilt the structure twice since Anneke's death, and it now sits squat and solid on the hem of the hill, blending in to the surroundings thanks to her much-discussed sod roof with its indigenous plantings.

'Why do we need a lookout?' Jem had asked as they had worked together to nail the thick plastic over the split-pole ribs of the roof to create a waterproof layer beneath the soon-to-be-laid earth. 'Expecting an army to invade?'

'I just like to see the road,' Sam had replied, pointing out to where the track wound into their valley. 'In case some-one's coming. It's impossible to see anything from down in the garden.'

'That was the whole idea when we built the place,' Jem had said with a grin. 'Nice and private.'

'I like that,' she'd agreed, pulling the plastic taut and hammering in a panel pin. 'I don't want people to see me, but I want to see *them*.' She'd folded the plastic over and hammered in another pin to ensure that the nail holes wouldn't result in leaks. 'First, at least.'

Now Sam leans forward in her chair and rests her elbows on the wooden rim of the window opening. She closes her eyes as the clean breeze blows across her face, carrying the faint herbs-and-honey smell of wet fynbos. There's a deeper layer of scent in the wind, something new. Her eyes open with a start and she sucks in her breath. She leans out of the window and stares into the murk of the evening garden. It's impossible to make out the wooden grave marker through the oak leaves. She can smell it, though. The unmistakable, gamey scent of horse.

When the valley is dipped in black and the garden beyond the kitchen window pulses with the song of frogs and the whirs and clicks of nocturnal insects, Sam heads back down towards the house. Her stomach growls. She's planning on making macaroni with cheddar grated from the block she bought earlier, and although she tries hard to concentrate on how it will taste, she can't ignore the whispers.

The garden is full of them.

Sam can hear the hiss of voices beneath the splash of the fountain in the herb bed, and the rustle and rattle of branches in the wind. She stops for a moment, heart beating fast, and looks back the way she's come. There's no moon tonight, and she can see the dark shape of the oak, the hump of the hill, and the pale points of stars reflected on the still surface of the pond. *Macaroni. Cheese.* She swallows, and forces herself to keep moving. As Sam gets closer to the pruned roses, her ears begin to hum and her heart gives a strange gallop in her chest, and before she can stop herself, she begins to run.

CHAPTER NINETEEN

AT THE LE ROUX dinner table that evening, Charlie Rowan drinks his fourth newly purchased beer straight from the bottle. He gets a bitter little stab of satisfaction each time he raises it to his lips, somehow vindicated by the disapproving look on his wife's face. Feeling righteous about drinking beer at his wine-growing father-in-law's table is pathetic and he knows it, but Charlie is too panicked by yet another day having passed without him completing a stitch of work to care. Tonight, he's letting the downy brown haze of the alcohol do the thinking for him.

He thunks the bottle down on the white tablecloth, then tries, and fails, to suppress a beer burp.

'*Sis*, Daddy.' Delia frowns at her father across the table. 'Say pardon me.' Sitting in her highchair, his daughter has the air of a diminutive princess issuing commands.

'Haven't you had enough, Charlie?' Liezette is sitting up very straight, just like Delia. *A pair of princesses. Any moment they're going to order my head to be cut off.* Something about the grandeur of the dining room with its heavy furniture and properly set table makes Charlie restless, not to mention the fact that their dinner is brought to them by a servant, for Christ's sake. Who does that any more? Charlie tries to give the guy a sympathetic 'you-and-me-are-on-the-same-side' look, but the man refuses to catch his eye. Charlie moves his gaze up to the wooden ceiling beams that have been treated to look like aged oak from the 1800s. The whole place is doing its best to pose as an old Cape Dutch manor. *What a pile of crap.*

'Wasn't this house built in the eighties or something?' Charlie spears a sweet potato with his fork. *Too sweet*, he thinks. *What is it with these people? Why must every damn vegetable be coated in sugar?*

'What are you on about now, Charlie?' Liezette's expression is willing him to shut up.

'Nineteen seventy-three,' Old le Roux answers. With his neatly trimmed moustache, Liezette's father looks like he's just stepped out of 1973 himself. *I bet he misses the old days*, Charlie thinks, glancing at the coloured chap who stands by the door and waits to clear their plates for them. *If the old fool has even realised that the apartheid era is over.*

'A good vintage, was it?' Charlie struggles a little with the word 'vintage'. *How many beers is this now?* It was only when they moved here a month ago that he learned that the old man doesn't even *make* any wine, he just sends off his grapes to the cooperatives to be crushed and added to their communal fermenting vats.

'Delia, why don't you tell Daddy what you found today?' Liezette steers the conversation into the three-year-old zone. *Smart move.* Delia, once prompted, can talk about herself for minutes on end without taking a breath. Something about the atmosphere at tonight's dinner table has rendered his daughter silent, however. She looks at her mother with wide, worried eyes.

'We found an old photo album, didn't we?' Liezette's mother prompts. Her voice is so soft, and her comments so rare, that everyone leans forward in their seats a little. Delia looks from her mother to her grandmother, her fingers gripping the plastic handles of her child-size cutlery. Her small face begins to pink, starting with the rims of her ears.

'Looks like your plan to change the subject has backfired, Liez,' Charlie mutters to Liezette. He can feel the sneer curling his mouth, but is unable, somehow, to stop it. Delia's own lip begins to tremble in response. 'Look what you've done to the poor kid.'

'It's OK, my baby.' Liezette rises from her chair and goes around the table to pick up their daughter. She holds the little girl against her chest and Charlie feels a cold spot opening inside his. He stares at the tender hollows in the back of his daughter's knees and fights down the sudden urge to weep.

'It's all right, Delia,' he says, pushing his own chair back and standing up too quickly. His head spins. 'Naughty Daddy is going to go to his bed without any supper.'

'Good.' Liezette's eyes glitter at him over her daughter's dark pigtails. Charlie swipes at the table to grab his beer and clips the edge of le Roux's wine glass as he does so. It wobbles, but the old man manages to steady it in time. He doesn't look at Charlie.

'Perhaps you should get a move on before you cause any more damage,' Liezette hisses, and Charlie stumbles from the dining room with her voice fizzing in his ears.

Charlie sleeps on his back with his arms flung above his head and his knuckles grazing the walnut headboard. His snores fill the bedroom with the yeasty stench of breathed-out beer. Liezette would normally wake him and make him turn over, but she's sleeping in Delia's room tonight, so there's nothing to shake Charlie from the clutches of his dreams.

In his dreaming, Charlie finds himself sitting beside his

mother at the little craft table that she'd set up for him when he was six. The craft table had been painted yellow, and on it, Charlie's mom used to arrange little tubs of things for him to create with. There was a tub of old buttons, one of pebbles, and numerous others filled with bits of things that they'd collected together. There were delicious-looking packages of Fimo clay for sculpting, a tin can full of coloured pencils, and heaps of paper, cardboard and glue. Every afternoon when he'd come home from school, his mother would sit with him at his craft table, helping him build castles and superhero badges, pencil holders, bows and arrows, and dinosaurs. She taught him simple origami, and sometimes let him use a sharp awl to punch patterns into her leather belts. She always wore them, even after he'd messed up.

After his mother died from leukaemia when Charlie was twelve, he'd abandoned his craft table, unable even to look at it without feeling as if he was drowning. It was only when he started high school a year later and was introduced to compulsory woodwork as a subject that he felt he might be able to breathe again.

Now, in the dreamtime, his mom looks just as she did in the years before she was diagnosed. Her face is tanned and her hair is brown and the harmonic of her shampoo makes it smell sweet and slightly fruity, like jelly babies. She's wearing it plaited up into a single, long braid that pours down over her shoulder.

Wait.

His mother never wore a braid.

The braid is from somewhere else. For a moment, his dream scene slips from the room and skids out onto the dusty road he drove earlier today, where a girl rides a motorbike with silvery hair streaming out behind her.

'Charlie?' his mother says, and he's back at the yellow craft table. Dream-Charlie is too big for the thing, and his adult legs cramp as he tries to squeeze them under.

'What are we making today, Charlie-chops?' his mom says, picking up a chunk of green Fimo. 'Dinosaurs? Dragons? Daisies?' She grins and nudges him with her elbow. Real. Alive.

'Mom, I can't make anything any more.'

'What are you talking about, darling? Look at all this stuff. We've got the whole afternoon.'

'No, I... you don't understand. I can't.'

Charlie's dream-mom turns to him, her face full of encouragement. He notices that the lump of lime-coloured clay she's holding has become patchy with dark mould. Something like watery tar drips out of it and through her fingers and splats down onto the yellow tabletop. 'Why not, Charlie-chops?' The dripping from the clay is getting worse, with more and more thin fluid sloshing out of it. Charlie suddenly realises that the more it drips, the less of his mother is left. She's dissolving into the lump, all of her self being swallowed up and dripping down until there's nothing but a slick puddle of dark slime.

Charlie jerks awakes when his fists slam into the headboard above his head. He is drenched in sweat and panting for breath. He stares into the pitch-dark bedroom, waiting for his heartbeat to slow. When, at last, it does, he gets up and puts on the clothes that he left lying on the floor before he collapsed into bed earlier. He follows the trail of discarded items and puts each one on as if trying to rewind back to a time when he hadn't had that dream. No, before that, before dinner. He winces at the memory of it. He is fully dressed when he reaches the bedroom door. He opens it slowly, then creeps through the silent house and out into the night.

It's drizzling outside. The cold spray on his face clears his head a little. He tiptoes over the gravel drive towards his van, gets in, turns on the headlights and lets down the handbrake, rolling the vehicle down the hill and away from the house so that he won't wake anyone when he starts up the engine.

He sits in the cabin staring at the track that diverges up ahead. One path points towards the gate and the road beyond, and the other winds deeper into the farm, leading to the workshop. After five long, humming minutes, that's the route he takes, navigating through the mud towards the looming shape of the black hill against the dark purple sky, and the barn with its double doors and corrugated iron roof.

The lights flicker and then blaze on when he presses the switch, and everything is just as he left it: the chunk of tambotie on the floor, the rows of tools that have been extensions of his hands for so long, and the workbench with its waiting holes and little wooden dogs poking up into the stillness. Perhaps dense, dark tambotie was the wrong choice. He needs to work in something pale and silvery. *Curly maple?* He blinks away the image of a streaming blonde braid and takes a breath. *Ash.* Carefully, as if approaching a half-tame animal that might turn and snap at him at any moment, Charlie Rowan walks towards the wood.

CHAPTER TWENTY

EVER SINCE HE saw the white-braided girl on the motorcycle, and then dreamt about his mother and the yellow craft table, Charlie has barely left the workshop. He is up and dressed and driving to work before the spring sun has had a chance to soften the mountain air. It tastes clean, each breath filling his lungs with a freshness that finds its way into his work. Charlie, it can be said, is on a roll. The finished pieces that now stand at the far end of the barn have a life to them that seems to go beyond the warm tones of the finely sanded, painstakingly polished wood. As the sunlight strengthens into midday, and bands of gold slide through the open double doors and pool around Charlie as he works, the completed pieces in the shadows seem to glow in response, as if they're still nourishing themselves on his fervent energy.

As he closes up the barn each night, he touches each item as he passes, his brief caress somehow refining the curves even further.

He missed dinner last night, only coming in long after everyone else had finished. Liezette had watched from the kitchen doorway as he'd stood at the counter and shovelled down the plate of dried-out lamb stew and creamed spinach without even noticing she was there.

Liezette wakes early. The curtains on the bedroom window

are the same ones she had as a child, and in those first, fuzzy moments between sleeping and waking, the familiar pink glow of the day shining through them whisks her back into the past. It's only after a minute that she remembers that she's no longer a girl, and that there's supposed to be a husband in the bed beside her.

When she sees that Charlie's already up and gone, a little nagging feeling twists at the bottom of her belly, and despite spending the morning busy answering emails, collating orders and trying to stop Delia from destroying her grandfather's study, by lunchtime the worry has wrapped itself tight around her insides.

And so, armed with a bag of sandwiches which she asked Angie the maid to make, Liezette drives down to the barn, her now-seldom-used city car bouncing over the rutted dirt road. On either side of her, the grafted vines shake their velvety new white-green leaves at the empty sky.

She cuts the engine and glances in the rear-view mirror to check her make-up. The twist around her guts has transformed itself into a nervous flutter. She pauses for a moment before striding towards the barn.

'Charlie?' she calls. 'I brought you lunch.' Liezette walks into the resin-scented hush feeling as if she's entering a church in the middle of a service. The light streams through the open double doors at the far end of the workshop, and she has to blink to see Charlie there in the middle of it, his head and back haloed by a swarm of slowly descending fragments of wood dust.

'Hey, babe?' she says, and when he turns, the expression on his face is one of such intensity that Liezette realises what an intrusion her visit must be. She wishes she hadn't come. 'Sandwich?' The wobble in her voice makes the word come out as a threat rather than an offering.

'Oh yeah, hi.' He wipes his forearm across his face. 'Thanks, Liez.' There are shavings of sawdust stuck all over his sweating skin, making him fuzzy around the edges, as if she's unable to see him in anything but soft focus. Liezette approaches with the sandwiches held out in front of her: *like one of the bloody three wise men in a Nativity play*, she thinks, feeling like an idiot.

'Put them down anywhere. Just in the middle of something.' Charlie turns back to the workbench. Liezette places the packed lunch down, and watches him in silence for five long minutes before realising that this is it. This is all she's going to get.

Liezette is very aware that when she exits the barn, Charlie doesn't even register her leaving.

Liezette's new horse is called Rolo, and while she wasn't the one who named him, she's in full agreement with whoever did. He's exactly the colour of milk chocolate, and his large eyes are warm toffee brown. Rolo's nature is just as sweet as the treat he's named for, and when she walks towards the paddock with tears drying on her cheeks, he trots over and whiffles his soft nose all over her face in welcome.

Together, they head towards the stable so that she can put on her boots and saddle him up. She walks with a hand pressed against the warm velvet of his neck, feeling the huge muscles moving beneath his skin, and every now and then he gives her a little nudge with his shoulder, as if they're both in on a private joke.

When she rides Rolo between the grapevines, with the mountains curving around the bowl of the valley and the sky open above their heads, Liezette doesn't think of Charlie.

She doesn't think of how both strange and comforting it is to be living with her folks again, she doesn't even think of Delia, who has occupied her every moment since she emerged, yelling, into the world three years ago. Riding Rolo is all about sensation. The curve of his ribs between her boots, the movement of his shoulder blades beneath her hands, the tickle on her fingers from that humorous little tuft of mane that bounces as he moves, and the sound of his breath and her own. Each hoof fall vibrates through the earth and up through his strong legs and into her spine, melding land, horse and human together into one, joyous, thought-free thing.

'Mama!' Delia's sharp yell spears through the still evening air, and Liezette gallops back towards the paddock with her heart in her throat. 'Hello, Mama.' Her daughter is grinning. The yell was merely outrage that Liezette's attention was elsewhere. Delia rides her grandmother's hip with an air of entitlement. Liezette has the momentary impression that all that's missing is a bit and a set of reins clutched in her daughter's pudgy fist.

'Ma, did you carry her like this all the way from the house?'

'Ag, it's no trouble.' Antoinette le Roux gives Delia a kiss on the cheek and squints up to look at Liezette. 'She was asking for you.'

'We were just stretching our legs.'

'You've been riding for *ever*.' Delia scowls. 'Come inside now.'

'I will. In a minute. I have to brush him down first.'

'Ooh, can I brush too?'

Rolo gives a snort as if he's objecting to the idea. Liezette is equally reluctant to relinquish the quiet of the stable for Delia's high-octane mix of babble and squealing. The realisation brings a stab of guilt.

'Of course you can, my love. Come. You can help Mama brush Rolo down.' Liezette dismounts. Her legs feel light and anchorless without the dense, vital body of the horse between them. She lifts her arms over the fence to take her daughter.

'Thanks, Ma,' Liezette says to Antoinette. Her mother looks small without her granddaughter on her hip. 'For everything. You know.'

'Shush, it's just lovely to have you all here.' Liezette knows that Antoinette has been waiting for her to return to the farm from the moment she left to go to university years ago. Liezette always resisted, and now here she is. She's not sure if it's a victory or a failure.

'Where's Daddy?' Delia asks her as they walk hand in hand back towards the stables.

'Daddy's working.' Rolo gives another well-timed snort. Liezette can't help smiling.

'He's *always* working,' Delia whines.

'Now that's not true,' Liezette says, thinking of the past months of infuriating inactivity. 'It's just he's got a lot of catching up to do.'

'*Always*,' Delia insists. 'Can I brush Rolo now?'

'Soon.'

CHAPTER TWENTY-ONE

'IT'S SAM'S BIRTHDAY today, you know.' Keegan interrupts his mother in the middle of her explanation of a geometry theorem. Mrs McGovern smooths her hand over the textbook page with its network of intersecting lines, and glances at her son.

'I know that, love.'

'We always used to have cake for her birthday. Vanilla was her favourite.' From across the classroom, the scratch of Dale's pencil stops.

'I can't stand vanilla,' Dale says. 'What a waste of a cake. ALL cakes should be chocolate, don't you think?'

'How's that cross-section diagram coming along, Dale?' Mrs McGovern says with a pointed nod at his many rubbings out.

'It's coming,' he mutters, and bends his head back over his work. With only two students left, Mrs McGovern's concern can no longer really be called a school. The classroom has a brittle empty feel about it. She's thinking of bringing in some couches or something, just to make it feel less cavernous.

'Remember how last year she only wanted yellow balloons?' Keegan says. Last year, they'd both turned sixteen. *Sweet sixteen and never been kissed*, Keegan thinks, and reddens at the memory of his clumsy attempt to kiss Sam years ago at the bottom of the bicycle-riding hill. In the years since then, his courage seems to have shrunk in direct proportion to her growing. He's never summoned up the nerve to try again. And now she's gone.

'I remember.' Mrs McGovern places a hand on Keegan's, and then removes it again before he can get all cross and accuse her of embarrassing him.

'Think she'll come back, Ma?' He sounds so young when he says this that Mrs McGovern's heart clenches inside her chest.

'I don't know, Kee.'

'She should. You should tell her to.'

'She's a very independent young lady. You know that.'

'I know. But aren't you worried that she's not studying and stuff?'

'A little, but I'm checking up on her, don't you worry about that. She has to come in to write her cycle tests next week, remember? I'll soon know if there's something amiss.'

'But it's not really fair that she has to stay home to look after her grandpa because he's sick, is it? It's like something out of the Victorian ages or whatever.'

'Look, I'm not going to pretend that I think this is ideal, and I told Sam that when she spoke to me about studying from home, but she's over sixteen, and she has the legal right to make this choice. We have to respect that, OK?'

'Unless she fails her cycle tests.'

'Exactly.' Mrs McGovern smiles. 'Now no more dodging this geometry theorem, Keegan. Come, we're going to nail this bugger down.'

The lemon tree blooms, filling the garden with memories of Anneke. Each perfumed inhale hurts. One moment, it is her ouma's hand on Sam's cheek, and the next, the click-tick of knitting needles, or the sound of condensed-milk ice cubes clinking the side of a coffee-filled glass. Sam ties her hair up extra tight in the mornings, so that the sight of the silvery strands, caught out of the corner of her eye, will not make her heart squeeze in. There are too many memories out here in the garden, and, without Jem's usual pottering around and whistling, and making toast for his pilchards every few hours, there's too much silence inside the house. So Sam, glad of the warming weather and clearer skies, has set up her studying spot in the lookout shelter a little way up the hill. Each morning, after oatmeal and coffee, Sam takes her books and notes and hikes out beyond the boundaries of the garden and up into the wild. She's become a diligent student since dropping out of Mrs McGovern's class. She has to be, with so much to prove.

'I'm just going to study at the lookout, Grandpa,' she says, her voice too loud in the morning hush.

Today, the smell of sprouting green and white, waxy lemon blossom is undercut with something meatier, something almost animal. Sam clutches her books to her chest and dashes past the rose bed and through the lavender, under the lemon tree, around the pond, and out beyond the deep shade of the greening oak. Her heart hammers as if she's being chased.

But then Sam sees something that stops her dead. She gasps for breath, and the books tumble out of her arms onto the ground. There, on the hill, silhouetted against the morning sky, just as he has stood so often in her dreams, is Sam-the-horse.

She blinks. He's still there. She steps over her fallen school work and walks a few steps closer. The horse is still there. *He's real.*

You're never to go over there, Sam, do you hear me? Jem's voice is loud and clear inside her head, as if he made her promise this yesterday, rather than all those years ago when they'd once climbed the hill together.

That le Roux is an angry, vindictive old bugger. It wouldn't be safe. Sam looks back towards the house, but lush garden growth blocks it from sight. She turns back to the horse. *Still there!*

Promise me.

The animal turns its head. Sam swallows. Her mouth is dry and tastes of the grassy dust from the breeze blowing down from the hill. *It's looking at me. It wants me to come closer.*

Before she realises that she's made the decision to do so, Sam begins to run.

She scrambles up over the rocky face of the rise, brushing through bushes and jumping over clumps of grass. She forgets to stamp and sing to scare away the snakes as Jem always taught her to do. Up and up and closer and closer. The horse is brown. She can see that now. Is that a scrap of white on its nose? Just as she's getting close enough to tell, the horse turns and trots away.

No, wait!

She speeds up, panting, scratching her calves on thorny scrub and slipping on stones. *Wait.*

But Sam-the-horse is moving faster, high-stepping over the rocky ground as he heads around the hill to the far side. Sam sees his tail swish as he saunters out of view. She follows.

The horse from her dreams is real. Breathing. Alive.

What other choice does she have?

Liezette bears down on the stable hand with a purple face.

'What do you mean, he just *went*?'

'Like I said, missus, he was out at the end of the paddock

and then he wasn't.' The stable hand is holding the handle of the stiff broom he uses to sweep the stable floor, clutching the wood and twisting it between his dark hands. 'He a good jumper that one, missus. He must've just felt like going out.'

'But where? Good grief. What does my father pay you for?'

'To clean and care for the horses, missus.'

'Oh, for Christ's sake.' Liezette knows she's being unreasonable. She knows that this young man with his frightened brown eyes and twisting hands cannot be held responsible for a horse that decides to bolt, but the idea that Rolo might be gone for good makes her want to double up in pain. She marches out of the stable and into the fresh air of the paddock. Her father's four other horses are eating grass at the far end with an air of studied innocence. What do they know about it? Did they gang up on the new guy? Do something to drive him off?

She shields her eyes from the sun and scans the pinstriped vineyards, revolving slowly on the spot and searching for his brown bulk amongst the rows.

'Rolo! Come here, boy!' Her voice cracks, and Liezette is horrified to realise that she wants to open her mouth and bawl, just like Delia does when something she wants is taken away from her. She's seconds away from stamping her foot. Coming back home seems to be reversing things, turning her into a spoilt little girl again. *And now Rolo's gone.*

Liezette storms across the paddock and grips the rough wood of the split-pole fence so that splintery bits jam into her skin. From here she can just make out the hump of Charlie's barn and the brown hill rising up behind it. She spots some sort of movement at the bottom of the hill. She strains to see better. The shape disappears behind a clump of trees. She holds her breath, waiting. There! The shape is now on the farm road and moving fast.

'Rolo!' she calls, and the shape speeds up, resolving itself into the unmistakable figure of a horse. Coming towards her, racing back to be with her. She scrambles over the fence poles to get to him.

Sam stops running when the absurdity of her fevered horse-chase finally crashes through her hope.

She's all the way on the le Roux side of the hill and the animal, which she now realises cannot possibly be Sam-the-horse, is out of sight, no doubt trotting back to wherever it is he belongs. She fights for breath, coated in sweat that stings in the new scratches on her legs, and so dizzy that she has to sink to the ground to stop from falling. She lies on her back at the foot of the hill. The empty blue sky spins above her. Her legs are shaking. *Everything* is shaking.

I really thought it was Sam.

She fights to suck in air, then curls up on her side and sobs.

It is here, wedged in behind a boulder on the le Roux side of the hill, surrounded by scrub and with a clump of grass pushing into her spine, that the truth finally catches up with Sam. It opens its inescapable jaws and swallows her down into its hollow throat.

I am alone.

There is no dream horse on the hill, no ouma in the lemon-blossom breeze, and no grandpa, with a backpack of sand-wiches and sun block, who can stand at her side.

After a long while, Sam sits up. She rests her aching forehead against the warm bulk of the boulder, and when she raises her gaze, she's shocked to realise that she's been right up close to one of the le Roux farm buildings this whole time. A few metres down the slope is an old barn with peeling plaster walls and a tin roof and wide open doors.

Someone could've seen me!

She peers over the boulder and blinks to clear her salt-raw eyes. In the barn doorway, lit by the mango-coloured light of the late afternoon sun, Sam sees some sort of sculpture carved out of glowing wood.

No, it's not a sculpture. She ducks back behind the rock, heart racing. *It's a person. Has he been there the whole time?*

Sam knows that she should creep away before the glowing-wood-man looks up and sees her. The best thing to do would be to wriggle backwards to that thicker clump of bushes that she passed earlier and sneak out of view. But for some reason, she doesn't. Instead, she holds her breath and peeps out again.

The man is wearing jeans, but no shirt, and the sweat on his bare arms catches the light in such a way that it looks as if his flesh is morphing into the gleaming piece of timber in his hands. The man is not motionless as Sam first thought, he's polishing the piece of shaped and sanded wood with a rag, using tiny movements to work it carefully into the curves. Every so often, he dips the corner of the cloth into a can of what Sam figures must be some kind of oil, bending low over his work so that his brown hair flops down and she cannot see his face.

As Sam watches the man's muscles slide beneath his skin, a strange hot swish of blood rushes beneath her own. Down from her head to her soles and all the way up again, pooling with a warm liquid feeling somewhere in her centre.

A line of industrious ants begin marching their way over her calf, but she's unaware of the tickling of their tiny legs. Then, suddenly, the man stands up and turns and goes back inside, too quickly for Sam to see anything but the wings of his shoulder blades and the hollow of his spine bisecting his broad back. Sam waits, biting her lip, but the glowing-wood-man doesn't return.

She waits some more. Nothing.

Get moving, Sam. You need to get back and now's your chance.

Sam inches backwards from the boulder and then dashes to the next clump of cover. Slowly at first, then speeding up as she gets further and further from the le Roux side of the hill, Sam heads back home.

That night, Sam dreams she hears the repeating screech-cry of a martial eagle echoing through the house, high-pitched and urgent. She follows the sound, walking through into the dream-kitchen. The room is empty, but the sunlight streaming through the kitchen window is butter-yellow. She holds her hand up to the light and it's so dense that her fingers look as if they're coated with it. She could place them in her mouth and suck the sunlight off them as if it was pancake batter. She touches her finger to her lip and a low throb pulses out from the tip and down her throat, dropping into her belly and then further. She squirms, gasps. Almost wakes.

But the dream is not done yet.

There, in the middle of the kitchen table, is a small wooden carving of a horse. Sam picks it up. It is warm against her palm. The wood grain swirls across the miniature creature's flanks. Its eyes are mere notches gouged out with a carving tool, but the moment Sam looks into them, she can feel herself falling.

She wakes before she hits the floor.

CHAPTER TWENTY-TWO

YOLANDE THE RAT-BURGLAR has worked her way along the coast, picking what she could and selling it on and smoking it up or spiking it in, and now here she is in the mother city. *The mother lode.* Cape Town is rich with ignorant foreign tourists and big spenders and rat-pickings, but it's dangerous too. Lots of cats out here, and packs of rangy dogs with gold in their teeth and hard eyes.

Yolande returned to Port Elizabeth after making sure that her mother was dead and in the ground for good, but ever since then, she's felt something tugging her westwards, inching her back in the direction of the valley. She feels the pull, despite the fact that her father, with his too-straight back and silver hair, was clearly still alive. Just thinking about him makes Yolande feel itchy and uncomfortable, with a hollow hurt in the middle that she's in no mood to investigate. Even from here in the city, with the ocean in the wind and the shelter of the massive flat mountain at her back, Yolande can sometimes catch it on the air: Karoo dust and fruit sap spiralling down from the farmlands that lie to the northeast. The smell sings of childhood frustration, of straining at too-tight leashes, but there's something else in it now, a yearning. Yolande is plagued by an image in her chemical-sickened dreams of a pair of brilliant gold rings, one of them alive with sparkling stones, on a mud-spattered, swollen-knuckled hand.

I want what's mine. What's owed to me.

But the old man with his disappointed sneer is not going to let her get near them. Nope, Yolande's going to have to wait, but that's OK, she's got other plans brewing, rich, juicy plans, and she's not going to let a stinking breeze stop her from making Cape Town her bitch.

For the past few nights Yolande has been scoping out a place right on the side of the 'oh-so-special' Table Mountain. The neighbourhood is not her usual hunting ground. It's far too fancy. Yolande has learned that it's easier to take from those who have so little that they're not equipped to guard it too fiercely. A phone here, an old wallet there, that special something someone working double shifts has saved up for months to buy. Even if there's only one paltry item worth taking in a break-in, Yolande nabs it and then sells it, and then buys her medicine: something brown and sticky to spike, or something white and crystaline to smoke. She's going to be able to stock up good after tonight. Get a room for a few days. Suck up the goodness and float away.

Yes, tonight she's ready for something bigger. She's been planning this, hiking through the City Bowl and up into Higgovale each night for almost a week. It's a posh suburb filled with angular modern houses hugging the mountain-side like sparkling gift boxes propped up on stilts, all nicely wrapped in their electric fences and alarms and armed response signs, brimming with iPads and Xboxes and lovely little shiny things in drawers by bedsides. Yolande knows that the wrappings tend to tear with time, and after a while nobody realises that there's a hole at the bottom of a fence, or a broken branch resting on a wall post, or a sensor that's lost its war against the raging Cape winds and has become disconnected.

And now, she's found her mark. She crouches down in a scrub-filled hollow on the other side of the road where the ground drops down. Mountains, she's discovered, even the ones featured on postcards, are full of hidey hollows for rats. It's cold with the wind whistling down the rocky flanks, and her dirt-coloured balaclava is doing double duty tonight. She digs into the pocket of her jeans and pulls out a baggie containing three crushed up Thinz tablets. Compared to all the substances she's snorted and smoked and sunk into, these are not going to do much, but they'll keep her alert and thinking. Extra ratty. Rat tabs. She smiles again and her scab pulls and she snorts up a quick fingernail of gritty powder before sucking the remains from her finger. The bitter chemical taste pulses at the back of her throat as she folds up the baggie and slides it back into her pocket. The car, one of those big poser 4 x 4 things that rich assholes like to drive these days so that they can sit up high and look down on the regular people, moves off. Yolande watches the cherry-red glow of its tail lights moving off down the road and around a bend. She's been waiting for this. She flexes her rat-fingers and darts across the street.

CHAPTER TWENTY-THREE

SAM FEELS THE familiarity of Mrs McGovern's classroom wrap itself around her like a comfortable old sweater that she'd forgotten she owned. She's back here to write her first test, and even after weeks away, everything is as it always has been: the caramel colour of the pine desk beneath her papers and the way that particular patch of sky looks through the window. The smell is familiar too: a chemical sweetness of Xylene whiteboard markers mixed in with the lemongrass essential oil that Mrs McGovern believes helps to keep the mind alert, and beneath that, the particular foot and armpit aroma of *boy*.

The boys responsible for this are fidgety in Sam's presence. They've got tests to write too, but neither of them is going to do very well. Dale is to her right, his elbows spread wide on his desk, rumpling his papers. He stares at Sam without pretending not to, until Mrs McGovern taps his desk and gives him a stern look. Keegan, to her left as always, darts little glances as if taking surreptitious sips of something cool and delicious.

Sam is too nervous about the tests to notice. The stakes, she believes, are high. She bends over her papers with an intensity that makes her even more watchable. Her study regime was going just fine until she betrayed her grandpa and followed that horse to the other side of the hill. She's been trying extra hard, but yesterday, she couldn't stop herself from going back there and spying on the wood-man again. He was inside the workshop, so she'd had to creep out from behind her boulder and stalk closer to watch him. The memory of it makes her shift on her chair and she momentarily struggles for breath. She grips her pen tighter. *Concentrate*.

'Well, Sam, you certainly haven't been skimping on your studies.' Mrs McGovern smiles at Sam over the top of the completed test paper. 'I'm going to mark this properly tonight, but it looks good at first glance.' She slides it onto the pile. 'How are you feeling about tomorrow's algebra and biology?'

'OK, I guess.' Sam shakes out her right hand which has gone stiff from all the writing. 'I want to ask you something about this one thing in algebra, though.'

Keegan waits while Mrs McGovern helps Sam with her equation, and is still lingering close when Sam starts packing her things back into her backpack for the ride home.

'You're going already?' Keegan tries to sound casual.

'I need to get back—'

'To be with your grandpa. Of course.' The word 'grandpa' seems to hang in the air and vibrate. Sam can almost see it. Mottled red and charcoal grey. She battles with her bag, which keeps snagging on one corner of the file she's trying to jam into it.

'Yes.' She can suddenly smell roses. There are no rose bushes in Mrs McGovern's garden. Her mouth goes dry. 'And to study for tomorrow.'

'How's my old computer treating you?' Keegan tries again.

'Fine.'

'If it ever gives you crap, just let me know and I'll come and take a look at it for you.'

'Oh, Keegan, Keegan, Keegan.' They both turn, startled, to see Nathan slouching into the classroom. He was already tall before he left to go to university in Cape Town at the beginning of the year, but now he seems to almost brush the ceiling with his carefully asymmetrical haircut. 'Don't you know the way into a woman's pants is not through her keyboard?'

'Oh thrills, the so-called deflowerer of first years is gracing us with his presence,' Keegan says, although his ears have turned almost luminous pink. 'When does varsity half term end, again?'

'Don't worry, little brother, I'll be out of your nerdy way by the weekend.' Nathan seems to sway on his thin legs in their skinny jeans, bending towards Sam like a stalk in the wind. 'Hi, Sam, how's it going?'

'She's fine.'

'I think she can speak for herself, there, kiddo.'

'I'm fine,' she echoes, turning back to the business of getting her file into her bag.

'You look… fine.' Nathan's grin looks like a slice of some wet and slightly rotten fruit peeking through the stubble of what he's clearly hoping is going to end up being a trendy beard. Sam shrugs as if to slide the laden word from her shoulders. 'I hear you've gone all lone wolf now, hey? What's the deal with you studying from home? You'd better watch out being stuck away like that, or you're going to turn out even more socially inept than my dear brother here.'

Sam raises her eyes at last. Her expression is flat and cool. 'So great to know you're looking out for me.'

Nathan refuses to be ruffled. He rubs his long fingers through the sparse hairs on his chin.

'Do you have a Facebook profile?'

'Christ, Nathan, Facebook? Have you actually *met* Sam?' Keegan can see that Sam is edging her way to the door.

'You should get one. It's a great way to stay in touch. Oh, and it's excellent for spying on people.' At the word 'spying', Sam suddenly sees herself as she was yesterday afternoon, crouched down on the le Roux side of the hill. She remembers how the wood-man had looked bent over his workbench, so intent on his measuring of something that he'd no idea she'd crept right up to the side of the barn to see him better.

Spying on people.

She blushes and turns away, but not fast enough. Nathan catches her eye and raises an eyebrow at the flustered expression on her face. For once, he keeps his mouth shut, but she can just about *smell* him wondering: *what's up with you?*

Later that evening, despite promising herself and Jem (but only silently, inside her head) that she wouldn't, Sam crouches down behind the boulder to watch the wood-man work.

He is planing a selection of planks that have been set up across two trestles on the patch of dirt outside the barn. The power tool whirs and buzzes in his hands, and each time it touches the wood, it whines into a scream, echoing something winding up inside her. Sam feels as if an unseen hand is pouring some kind of molten metal between her legs, letting it run into her in a steady stream. She can feel it filling her up with heavy heat till her whole body aches. When she shifts a little to try and find some relief, pins and needles rocket up her released leg, and she has to clutch at the cooling rock to stop herself from falling over. She's been here, on her haunches, for far too long.

I should go. Now, while he's busy and the noise from that thing can give me some cover.

But she doesn't. She watches.

By the time the man goes back inside, and Sam finally scrambles up the hill, darkness is seeping into the valley and filling the fynbos with shadow.

Snakes. They must be everywhere. What were you thinking, Sam? Jem's voice scolds inside her head.

Nothing. She wasn't thinking at all.

CHAPTER TWENTY-FOUR

'THESE ARE BEAUTIFUL, Charlie. I can see why you've been in here every hour God sent. The workmanship is...' Liezette runs her fingers over the immaculate joins in one of the occasional chairs that she's helping Charlie wrap for transport.

'Are you going to help bubble wrap, or are you going to just stand there and stroke the thing?' Charlie grins. He's holding out the scissors, waiting for her to snap out of her reverie and take them.

'Seems a pity to cover up this loveliness.' Liezette uses the scissors to slice through a piece of plastic, and the large sheet comes away from the roll and flaps around her like a futuristic cloak.

'Are you talking about yourself or the chair?' Charlie's laughing now, and Liezette joins in, aware all the while that she can't remember the last time she heard him do so. 'I'm happy to take you to Cape Town with me in the cabin, Liez, you don't have to bubble wrap yourself up to go in cargo.'

They work in silence for a while, side by side beneath the hard fluorescent lights of the barn. Even with the white glare and the dead blue shadows everywhere, Liezette can tell that the pieces they're packaging are sensual and extraordinary, and she feels vindicated about insisting they move out here to the farm. The orders are only going to increase once they've delivered this lot to De Waterkant tomorrow. She's married to an artisan rock-star.

She's been feeling giddy and girlish at the thought of the upcoming trip. It will just be a day in a car driving to Cape Town and back, nothing to get excited about, but the idea of just the two of them together has a sheen about it, like something treasured that she thought was lost, poking unexpectedly out of a pile of junk.

But when she glances across at her husband, whose skin looks greenish in the awful light, Liezette can see that the joking and laughter just lie like a thin, trembling skin over the new, roiling deep that has opened up in Charlie. From the look in his eyes she knows that he's already moving off somewhere she cannot follow. *Christ, can't you give the tortured-artist thing a rest for a minute?*

'Are you sure you're OK with me coming?' As soon as the words are out of her mouth, Charlie's lips tighten.

'God, Liez, I've already said it's fine. What do you want, an embossed invitation with gold frigging edges?'

'No, it's just…'

'Why are you making such a big deal about this?'

'I'm not, you just seem…'

'What?' He rounds on her, roll of packing tape in one hand like a shield. 'What have I done wrong *now*?'

'You have to admit that you've been bloody distant, Charlie,' she snaps back. 'I barely feel like I'm married at all any more.'

'Look, do you want me to work, or do you want me to bound around your ankles like a needy puppy? A month ago you would've given anything to have me chained up in here, slaving away like a demon, and now that it's flowing in to me, now that I've got it back…' Charlie breaks off. He can't talk about what

183

has happened to him since his dream about his mother and the yellow craft table. Words might shatter the spell.

Since driving to town to buy beer that one time, Charlie has been focused on only the work, whereas before he couldn't even see it through the tight, knotted mesh of responsibility that has been steadily obscuring his process for years. He feels as if he's returned to something he once had as a child, something precious that he was entrusted with before his mother passed away. It feels as if he's fought a long, aching and bloody battle to reclaim it, and that his tenuous grasp could slip at any moment.

He turns his back on Liezette and winds packing tape around a wrapped pedestal. He's pulling too hard, rucking up the bubble wrap, using far too much tape and making a big plasticky mess. *This is going to be a nightmare to get into on the other side.*

'Babe, calm down.' Liezette's touch on his arm makes him jump as if burnt.

'Jeez, you startled me.'

'Sorry, I was just...' The fright evident in her large eyes makes Charlie hate himself just that bit more.

'No, it's OK. Ignore me, I'm just tired, Liez.'

'I didn't mean to—'

'Forget it.' It takes all his effort for Charlie to pull Liezette into a brief, hard hug. Even though he knows it's crazy, he can't help thinking, *She did it. She took it away from me.*

When Sam creeps round the last bend on the hill and sees that the barn doors are shut and the yard is silent, a strange hollowness yawns beneath her ribs. She crouches behind her boulder and waits. The morning is giving way to noon, and the sun burns down on her scalp. Sweat seeps out all over her skin, and dust and bits of dried vegetation stick to it and make her itch. Her nose is running. The surface of the rock sears the palm of her hands.

No one throws open the barn doors.

A sunbird flits past, so fast that she barely has time to register the frantic beating of its iridescent green-black wings before it is gone again.

Long minutes tick away, and the hollow feeling inside her grows until Sam is nothing but thin, hot skin surrounding emptiness. She imagines herself with a puncture somewhere, slowly leaking stale air, finally folding up on herself and drying away to nothing under the baking sun.

She begins the hike back home.

'The wheels on the bus go round and round, all day long!' Charlie sings, with Delia joining in from her kiddie seat in the back of le Roux's double-cab. They've borrowed it from Liezette's father for the trip as it's far roomier than Charlie's old beat-up one, and the bubble-wrapped pieces were bulkier than he thought. Because this van has a back seat, Charlie suggested they bring Delia along.

'I've been neglecting the poor little moppet,' he'd said to Liezette when she reminded him how trying their daughter could be on long car journeys. 'I really need to spend some quality time with my kid.'

And now it's late, they're almost back at the farm again, and the day that Liezette was so looking forward to has passed in a churn of engine noise, Charlie's off-key singing and Delia's bright chatter from the back seat. Liezette hastily tamps down the thought that she might be jealous of her own little girl, and chooses instead to fume about Charlie's rudeness at the store earlier.

Just as she suspected, the pieces were received in Cape Town with wide-eyed looks of wonder and little 'oohs' of delight, but Charlie had been offish, refusing to talk about his work or his process when asked, and then running off to play catch with a shrieking Delia inside the store. She and the other 'grown-ups' had stood around making polite conversation and pretending not to flinch each time the pair careered close to one of the expensive hand-blown glass vases or glazed ceramic pots. After a day swinging between irritation, loneliness, and rigid embarrassment, Liezette has a vicious purple headache pounding behind her left eye.

'Daddy, are you going to stop working so much now that you've taken your things to Cape Town?' Delia asks through a mouthful of gummy bears once the 'bus' song has reached its merciful conclusion.

'No, my angel. I'm afraid there's still lots and lots to do.'

'But why?' Her little face crumples, and Charlie's heart responds in kind when he catches sight of her expression in the rear-view mirror.

'Ag, I'm sorry, my moppet. I know it doesn't seem fair. I've missed you too. I have an idea: why don't I take over bedtime story duty from now on, hey?'

'Ooh, yes yes, the one about Kipper, read that one first.'

'That OK, hon?' Charlie finally addresses his wife.

'You're never in by bedtime story time.' She stares straight ahead, face set.

'I can change that. I can always pop out again to the workshop for a bit afterwards, if I need to.' Charlie glances at Delia in the mirror again. 'Can't I, Delly?'

'Yes!'

'Liez? You don't mind me hijacking story time for a bit?'

'Sure,' Liezette says with a shrug. Her headache blooms out behind her eye, trying to push out tears. She clenches her hands into fists against her thighs.

'You don't think I'm going to manage it, do you?'

'I never said that.'

'You'll see, I'll be there like clockwork. Every single—'

'Ja, right, I get it.' She cuts him off. 'Clockwork, story time. Whatever.'

'Are you a clock, Daddy?' Delia seems to find the idea hilarious for some mysterious, gummy-bear-addled reason.

'You tell me, Delly. Do I look like one?'

'No.' Giggles.

'You mean I don't have numbers all over my face and big pointy arrows sticking out of my nose?'

'No.' Shrieks of laughter from the back seat.

'Are you sure?'

'Yes!' Delia can barely breathe now. *The child's going to wet herself in a minute.* With each delighted yelp, Liezette's headache sends out tongues of dark flame to lick at her temples.

'Because if I have—'

'Enough.' Liezette's command slices through Charlie's words and kills the laughter. A shocked silence fills the candy-scented cabin. In the back seat, Delia's eyes go very round.

'What the hell, Liezette?' Charlie finally mutters. 'What's up with you?'

'Nothing.' Her eyes never leave the darkening road ahead. 'It's just… enough.'

After a day away from the workshop, Charlie is cautious when he returns to it the following morning, but after five minutes, it's as if he was never gone. Relief softens his muscles and makes his movements fluid, perfect for the new work he's starting on. Against one wall of the barn wait chunks of trunk with knotholes and roots, twisted branches, and misshapen boles of bulging timber. Rather than sketching out the designs first and then measuring and cutting and working the wood to fit the plans, he's been collecting this selection of offcuts and oddities, and finally feels brave enough to use them. He is going to allow each one to tell him what it wants to become.

Hours pass. He feels none of them. He is nothing but the singing surfaces and hollows beneath his hands. At last, Charlie raises his head to look outside. Beyond the doors, the day is brightly coloured, as if someone has just finished painting it. The long grass moves in languid strokes and each leaf on the bushes growing up the hill seems sharply outlined. But then he freezes. He's staring straight into another set of eyes. The strange eyes are wide open and a very pale blue, and as soon as their owner realises they've been seen, they vanish behind a boulder. Charlie blinks at the solid, red rock. *Did I just imagine that?*

Charlie steps outside, and a cool breeze slides over his sweaty skin like a caress.

'Hello?' he says in a cautious voice, feeling daft.

Nothing. The hill is decidedly lacking in blue eyes. Just as he's about to turn and go back inside, the wind snatches a strand of blonde hair from behind the boulder and waves it aloft like a strange, pale flag. *There's someone there, all right.*

'Hey!' His sudden shout, which comes out louder than he intended, startles the intruder from their hiding spot. Charlie watches in astonishment as a slender person with a long blonde rope of hair dashes out from behind the boulder and up the hill, slipping and scrabbling in her haste to make her escape. 'Stop, please!' Charlie cries out, but while he can hear her panting, frantic breath over the sound of the loose sand and stones that she's sending skittering down the slope behind her, she gives no indication that she's heard him.

He watches the creature, who is wearing an odd combination of an old floral blouse, men's shorts that are far too big for her and hiking boots, vanish behind a clump of vegetation and then reappear again, further up the hill.

'What are you doing here? Where are you going?'

But his call goes unanswered. The strange girl keeps on running. In moments, she is out of sight, and there's nothing for Charlie to see but a big brown hill rearing up against the sky.

CHAPTER TWENTY-FIVE

FOR THREE WHOLE days, Sam stays away from the wood-man and the barn on the far side of the hill. Each morning, she wakes exhausted, enmeshed in sheets that are twisted and damp from the exertions of her dreams. She sits at the kitchen table with one of Jem's old le Carré novels and drinks black coffee and eats oatmeal with cinnamon and sugar but no milk. Dairy has been a luxury ever since she's had to bring it back on the motorbike in the sun, and it doesn't keep long enough to make the effort worthwhile. She's gotten used to being without it.

See, I told you, it's better black. Jem's voice inside her head makes Sam think of how she betrayed him every time she climbed that hill. Her oatmeal becomes a solid lump in her mouth.

And now you've been seen, Sam. Now you're in trouble.

When she's finally managed to force her breakfast down, Sam goes straight into the corner of the lounge where she's set up her laptop on Anneke's old writing desk, plugs in the 3G dongle, and checks to see if she has any new email assignments from Mrs McGovern. This is where she stays, researching and writing a paper on the Treaty of Versailles and the causes of the Second World War. She crunches through the dusty old facts like dry autumn leaves, enjoying the relief they bring from the pulsing heat that has taken up permanent residence inside her mutinous body.

When the effort to resist is too much, Sam reaches for an old tin box that has lived on the top of the desk since she can remember, and pulls it towards her. The stamped metal surface, a raised pattern of flowers and leaves that have tarnished black in the grooves, is cool beneath her fingertips. She opens the lid and takes out the bundle of letters that lie within. They're love letters, all addressed to Anneke, all written by Jem in the months before they married, when he was wrapping up his life in Cape Town in order to come and be with her. A letter a day. Sam has read each one over and over in secret during the years since Anneke's death, and now she knows her favourites by the feel of their creases and the velvet of the much-touched, yellowing paper.

My dearest-heart, she reads. Jem's handwriting is a mixture of jagged slashes and long swoops. *The moon is a thin little slice over the city tonight, like a cut-out piece of cloud, barely visible. Does it look the same to you?*

Further down the page: *It comforts me to think of you in your parents' kitchen, laughing over roast chicken with pumpkin and peas drenched in that gravy which your mother makes and you love to pour on everything...*

And then, at the bottom, Jem signs-off, as he does all his letters: *Love me.*

Sam looks up from the paper in her hands. The silent shadows of late afternoon slide across her shoulders. She folds the letter with care and places it back in the box before selecting another.

I think of your skin, creamy, with a bit of pink, like the inside of a red apple that's just been sliced, and I want to taste its sweetness.

I long to run my tongue up the inside of your wrist, to your elbow, up to your armpit where the sweetness becomes salt, and the scent of you makes my head spin.

Sam's breath quickens. The wood-man on the far side of the hill has skin that makes her think of buttered toast. She closes her eyes, opens them, and reads on:

I will be there next Friday, if the car decides to behave itself this time around. Even if it doesn't and, again, I end up in the sun on the side of the road with a wrench, cursing at all the forces of the world which are suddenly in cahoots to keep us apart, I will force the mechanical monster into action. I cannot live another week without breathing you in again, my dear heart.

Love me

Love me love me love me, letter after letter. Each one ending the same way.

Sam's fingers tremble as she folds the paper back along its creases. Her breath sticks in her throat. She can feel her heart thumping, beating out through her skin and reverberating throughout the silent house.

Sam wakes with the taste of butter in her mouth. It is there when she goes into Jem's room to open his curtains, and all through breakfast, and its creaminess lingers below the mint of her toothpaste even as she brushes her teeth. When she sits down at the laptop, the taste turns into a strange tingling feeling that starts in her mouth and is soon spreading out everywhere, down her throat and into her fingers, and all the way down into her feet, making her limbs so restless that she cannot stay still.

She gets up from the desk, walks through to the kitchen, and puts on her hiking boots. There are burrs in the laces, and bits of broken grass all over the toes. She walks outside. The butter taste gets stronger. Saltier.

'I'm just going—' Her voice breaks, she swallows and tries again: 'Into the garden.'

The scent of lemon blossom is taking centre stage now that the roses are gone. The smell seems to linger on her tongue alongside the butter, and Sam feels so filled up with sweet and salt that she's unable to think. She can only move. One step and another and another and soon she is past the oak tree and climbing the hill, past the lookout shelter and up into the land of wild scrub and skittering scorpions.

A tiny brown mole snake flicks its muscular body across her path, and for a moment, as she catches her breath, Sam almost turns back.

But she doesn't.

As soon as she climbs high enough to see the other side of the hill with its immaculate rows of vines and its well-irrigated fields, the butter taste gets even more overwhelming, as if the warmth of her mouth is melting it to coat everything inside her in slippery gold.

Sam slows down and drops to the ground when she comes in sight of the barn. She creeps forward, taking her time. The barn doors are open, and she can hear the sound of sawing coming from inside. She makes it to the boulder in a final burst of speed, with her heart hammering and the buzz building to a frenzy inside her ears.

That is when she sees the note.

This is no paltry message scribbled on a piece of paper.

This is a work of time and care, meant to be read from a distance, like 'help' scrawled in the sand of a deserted island beach in the hope that a plane flying past will see. Someone has taken a rake to the flat bit of dirt between the barn and the hill, and then, on the smoothed earth, has laid out different pieces of wood to spell the letters:

IT IS OK.

WATCH IF YOU WANT.

At the thought of the wood-man selecting the pieces and placing them to form the words just for her, Sam feels as if all her insides want to burst out through her skin and whizz off on papery wings, whirling upwards with joy.

It's a poem. A song. A prayer.

For me.

She waits to get her breath back, and then creeps closer to watch him work.

Maybe it's a slight change in the way the breeze blows in through the open doors, or a subtle shift in the light, but in the middle of painstakingly hollowing out a tiny notch for a dovetail joint in a piece of burled olive wood, Charlie suddenly knows *she's* there. Yesterday she wasn't, but today she is, and he doesn't need to look outside to know it. He can feel her gaze, cool like mountain water, sliding over his skin.

She must've seen the message.

Charlie pauses in his work. He doesn't look up, but he smiles. Maybe she can see him do so. He likes the fact that he doesn't know.

'Hello there.' It is very soft, almost a whisper. The girl, if she hears him, if she is even close enough to, doesn't answer. He takes a sip of water from the plastic bottle on the bench beside him, and then reaches for his smallest rasp to continue smoothing the notch.

Silence spirals up around the barn, broken only by the frantic tweet of a fiscal shrike that rises, falls and fades again.

The next day, Charlie throws open the doors of the barn to let the early morning hill shadows drift in and slide over the waiting workbench with the dogs all placed where he put them last night. The air is so still that he can hear the faint far-off sounds of the farm workers in the vineyards. Something about the thinness of the early morning air carries their voices, the snip of their cutters and the scrape of their trowels all the way into the timber-scented hush of the waiting workshop. He steps outside and places a small, twisty-legged stool just beyond the doorway. There's a silky dimple in the top of the stool that, last week, he spent hours sanding with glasspaper, finally using a piece so fine it felt like velvet. He gives the dimple a light pat.

'For you. If you want to sit.' No answer but birdsong and the rustle of grass on the hill. But she's there. He can sense a spot of warmth lurking in the morning freshness. He goes back inside and gets to work.

Charlie's not sure exactly when the girl sits down on the stool, but he looks up some time later to see that she's pulled it into the shadow just inside the doorway. At first glance, she's just a lighter spot of silver against the greying wood of the doorframe, but each time he sneaks a look, he sees a little more of her. There's the slender curve of her calf disappearing into her boyish hiking boot. There's the shape of one arm, like a spear of pale bone suddenly catching the sunlight. There's the impossible waterfall of her ponytail falling over her shoulder and all the way down to the waistband of her shorts.

Charlie doesn't look up long enough to catch her eyes. He doesn't want to scare her off again, but he can feel them on him. Like a fine sheen of linseed oil rubbed into timber, something new in Charlie begins to emerge and clarify beneath her gaze. He doesn't know what it is, but it makes him feel as if he's taking up more space, somehow. When he gets up and walks to where the circular saw is set up, each stride feels choreographed, as if he's performing a strange, ritual dance.

'This is going to be loud,' he warns. Silence from the doorway. He can see a wisp of bright hair lifting up and moving in the breeze. Charlie grins into the buzz of the power tool. Each angled piece of oak he slices drops out clean and sharp and perfect.

That night, after hastily finishing up the World War Two assignment and emailing it off to Mrs McGovern, Sam heads back outside. A white circle of light skips ahead of her as she moves through the black garden, coming from the LED head-torch that Jem got her for her fifteenth birthday. Everywhere she looks, the light circle dances, making her think of the pantomime fairy she marvelled at when a travelling Peter Pan production once came to Robertson. Anneke had insisted they go, despite the fact that she was having a bad week and her joints screamed throughout the long road journey back.

I did close Grandpa's curtains, didn't I?

Sam looks back at the closed-up house. She did, of course she did, she always does, but guilt has made her uncertain.

Beyond the edges of the bright disc, the darkness seems deeper than usual, and Sam finds herself stumbling over familiar obstacles. She's tired. She should be in bed, but there's something she has to do first.

Sam collects the items that she placed at the ready earlier: a trowel for digging, and a large bucket brimming with a collection of small new plants she uprooted from the garden. She's chosen hardy things: baby lavenders that she grew from cuttings last year, two young daisy bushes and a host of little jewel-coloured portulacas and vygies whose low-growing succulent stems and leaves will be perfect, both for the arid ground of their new home, and for her planted words. She's going to write back to Charlie, a message, just for him.

The bucket is heavy with the combined weight of the soil-encrusted root-balls. She can feel her arm pulling, and she's not even out of the garden yet. For a moment, she stands, reconsidering. But then she remembers the perfect little stool. The dip in the top had cupped the warm, secret parts of her body like an upturned hand. She remembers the way the wood-man's eyes crinkled up when he smiled.

She hefts up the bucket and begins to climb the hill. When she looks around her, the head-torch picks out the light-glows of many pairs of eyes in amongst the black tracery of bush. Green, gold, white and even red. Snakes, mice, spiders and hyrax. She's not sure which ones belong to which, but she's glad she's wearing two pairs of thick jeans tucked into her boots.

Much later, Sam drops into bed like a puppet with cut strings. Her hair is still wet from her hasty bath, soaking her pillow through almost as soon as she lies down. In the brief moments before sleep pulls her under, she smells wet, unwashed linen. When did she last launder the bedding? The towels? When did she last sweep up, or wash the kitchen floor, or scrub the loo with vinegar and bicarbonate of soda?

She doesn't know. She doesn't remember. There's no space in her head for anything beside the hot-resin scent of sawn wood, and the newly-cut-pine creaminess of the skin on the undersides of the wood-man's arms where the sun has not been.

Sam dreams of a huge bird with copper-coloured feathers. It rises up on vast, outstretched wings, scattering rosy reflected light in bands across the valley floor below it. She stands on the tin roof of her home and watches the creature come, riding the thermals over the distant mountains and speeding towards her. Warm air rushes into her face as it approaches, and her eyes are held in its steady, golden gaze. The giant dream bird gets smaller as it gets closer, smaller and faster, until it slams right into her chest like a bullet. The air is punched from her lungs as the creature makes contact. Everything goes dark.

And then, there's the sensation of feathers brushing her spine and clawed feet gripping her heart. Wings unfurl inside her until the wingtips brush the bones of her shoulders. Sam breathes in and the bird inside her swells. She opens her eyes to see that the darkness has passed and the valley spreads out before her: vineyards and fields and orchards and dirt roads bright in the sun.

Sam is aware that somewhere behind her pale blue eyes, a pair of golden, predatory ones are looking out too.

Sam is woken by the frantic ringing of Jem's old alarm clock. She slams her hand down on it to silence the clamour. It can't have been more than three hours since she set it. Her hair is still wet, glued to her damp cheek on one side of her head, and it's still dark. *Good.* She switches on the bedside light and blinks. Her eyes are gritty with tiredness. She climbs out of bed and pulls on her clothes. She aches to climb back under the covers, but she needs to be on the other side of that hill when dawn comes. She doesn't know what time the wood-man starts work and she doesn't want to miss the moment when he sees what she's done for him. Will he read the words she's planted, her greening, growing reply to his earlier message made of wood?

As Sam heads up the dark hill once again, with her legs stiff and her damp hair hanging heavy and cold against her back, she notes that a path is now appearing amongst the vegetation on the route that she's been taking. Even with only the headlamp to light her way, it's becoming clear that she's wearing away a channel in the grass, breaking twigs with her boots again and again, carving up the landscape with her need. Even now, in the dawn grey, and with her eyes still dusty from sleep, she navigates with ease. One hiking boot in front of the other, and then again and then again and – STOP.

Sam freezes mid-step, trying to keep her balance. There, in the path ahead, is a snake. Not just any snake. This one is patterned with chevrons in brown, black and cream all down its short fat body, and its head, facing her down, is wide and flat. A puff adder.

It doesn't move, and neither does she. Sam rocks on her toes for a terrible moment, holding her breath. Another step and she'd be on him. Another step and she'd be dead. Carefully, slowly, Sam reverses away from the thick, tapering menace that bars her way.

The first time that Jem warned her about puff adders was on the way to school one morning when he spotted one coiled up at the side of the road. He'd pulled over and switched off the bakkie's engine so that she could take a good look from the safety of his lap. 'Don't let that big fat belly fool you, my love,' he'd whispered. 'Puff adders are the most dangerous of all, and you want to know why? Because they're not scared of humans. They don't just slither off when they hear you coming.' Sam still remembers the warmth of Jem's chest pressing into her back, and the plastic of the steering wheel beneath her fingers, worn smooth from her grandfather's hands resting there, day after day, year after year. 'It's all too easy to step on one of these guys, Sam. Keep your peepers open.'

'OK, Grandpa,' she'd promised.

Taking a different route to avoid the snake adds precious minutes to Sam's journey over the hill, and the eastern sky is turning from peach to pale blue by the time she crests the rise and starts to make her way down the other side. She turns off her headlamp in case the workers, whose voices she can already detect as they make their way into the fields, spot her white light and sound some sort of alarm. She hunkers down and eats an apple and two crackers that she brought along with her. To her left, the sky lightens to a pearly grey-blue, and before her, the farm takes shape, bits of it emerging out of pools of night shadow, until it is only the furrows between the grapevines that seem to clutch on to the dark. The layout of the fields and buildings on this side of the hill are now almost as familiar to her as the garden she's left behind, but it is the barn she knows best.

She creeps down to the boulder, crouches behind it, and waits for him to open the doors.

The first thing Charlie sees when he pushes open the workshop door is a brilliant fleck of colour lying on the ground outside, as if someone has dropped a crumpled piece of orange tissue paper. He squeezes his way through the gap and stares. There's colour all around the spot where he spelled out the note in bits of wood a few days earlier. Not from crumpled tissue paper, but flowers: red, orange, yellow and vivid pink, as well as waving lavender buds on stalks of bluey-green. The plants poke up out of the newly dug earth in a strange row, bunched together in spots, and then set apart in others. The whole odd arrangement is flanked at either end by a daisy bush, each one encrusted with flowers like blue stars.

Charlie finds that he has forgotten to breathe. Behind the astonishment, a faint little note of discomfort sounds somewhere deep inside him. He shakes it off, and walks towards the vulnerable new garden, bending down to touch the satin petal of one of the bright things. It clings to his fingertip, so soft it's almost as if the flower isn't really there at all. He looks up at the hill, searching for the white hair, the pale eyes. There, peeking out from behind that big boulder, the smooth curve of her forehead. Her eyes are in shadow.

'Thank you,' Charlie says in her direction. 'It's really... great.' He knows he should say something more appreciative, give credit for what has clearly been an enormous amount of nocturnal work, but he's not sure which words would be the right ones. There's no precedent for this. The note of discomfort pings a little louder, but it is lost beneath his wondering how exactly all that spun sugar hair smells when it moves against her neck. He remembers the outline of her body silhouetted against the light yesterday, showing clearly though the thin fabric of her frumpy top. He stands, goes inside, and fetches the stool for her once again. 'My name is Charlie,' he says, loud, so he can be sure that she hears.

Charlie. Sam receives the two syllables as if they're a gift he's given her in return for the fresh new garden at his feet.

Some days, when Sam comes over the hill, she brings more plants with her, and now there are a number of succulents nestling in between the blooms, filling out the patterns of colour with clumps of green and grey. The words she's planted are clearer, stronger. Surely he can't fail to read them now?

The dimpled, twisty-legged stool is always waiting for her. Sometimes she uses it, and sometimes she leans up against the wall inside to watch, and sometimes she sits on the floor amid the powdery sawdust. She's become bolder, moving around the workshop as if the space is her own.

Charlie is constantly surprised that his work doesn't suffer in her silent presence. He's keenly aware of where she is at any one time, but instead of it being a distraction, beneath her gaze his hands are surer and his labours result in items of such purity that the wood seems to breathe beneath his fingers. In the hours before she arrives and after she leaves, he can feel the old tension building up between his shoulder blades. *Don't fuck up.* But when she's there, everything he does is close to perfect.

One evening, Sam stays later than usual. The light outside is softening with the lowering sun, making shadows bruise the space beneath the workbench and in the corners of the barn. When Charlie glances up from the bench, he finds himself looking directly into the girl's eyes.

He forgets the measurements he's supposed to be marking out.

She's so close, he can hear her breathing. Her eyes are wide in the lowering light, the dilated pupils deep puddles of black surrounded by translucent blue, and the look in them is unmistakable. Hungry. Charlie feels the blood rushing to gather in his groin. He moves out from behind the bench, stepping closer to where the wordless girl leans up against the wall beside the peg board where he hangs his tools. Her eyes widen further. He reaches across her to take something from the board. A slender metal rasp with a wooden handle. It doesn't matter what he picks, it's the proximity he wants to test. Her breath comes in a little gasp but she doesn't move back from his outstretched arm. His elbow is centimetres from her face. He can feel the puff of her exhale along his skin.

Charlie's heart pounds. Carelessly, as if it's an accident, he brushes his wrist against her arm when he moves back. The bright curtain of her hair shimmers as a shudder vibrates through her body.

She doesn't draw away.

Suddenly, a violent, mechanical beeping screeches through the silence. It's the alarm on Charlie's mobile phone. The shock of the sound makes them both jump as if scalded. Sam bangs her elbow into the wall, and Charlie stumbles backwards before racing across the room and grabbing his phone. It slips in his grip and his clumsy fingers battle to silence the racket. On the little screen, the bright letters beam up at him: *Delia's bedtime story*. He's set the alarm to go off each night so that he has enough time to clean up and get back to the house to put his daughter to bed.

'I have to finish up,' he says, but when he turns back to the room, the girl with the pale hair is gone.

CHAPTER TWENTY-SIX

'COME, MY LITTLE moppet!' Charlie lifts his daughter into the air and over his shoulder. Delia yelps with delight and bangs her small fists on his shoulder blade to urge him on. 'We're going on an adventure, just you and me.'

'Daddy and Delia, Daddy and Delia,' she chants, and Charlie feels a spike of guilt at the fact that a trip into town in a van with her father can bring such delight to this vibrant little person whom he's managed somehow to neglect, without realising it. He's been too full up with the work.

Be honest, Charlie.

And with the presence of someone else.

Two days have passed since the girl from the hill with the pale watching eyes was last in the workshop alongside him. He wants to be able to tell himself that her absence doesn't matter, but he can't shake the worry that he needs her eyes on him to be able to bring the wood to life the way he's been able to do lately. This morning, he was reluctant to go down to the barn for the first time in months. He suggested an outing with his daughter instead: 'I'll take her out of everyone's hair for a bit,' he'd said to Liezette, who now stands with folded arms, watching him buckle Delia into her kiddie-seat. Liezette is wearing her riding boots and an unreadable expression.

'You're sure that's fastened properly?'

'Sure I'm sure.' The air between them has become brittle with invisible little shards of things unsaid. He gives her a clownish grin, ducking and weaving to avoid being sliced by one of their merciless edges. Liezette ignores the smile and brushes past his capering to plant kisses all over her daughter's smooth-skinned face.

'See you later, my little angel,' Liezette says in Afrikaans.

'Bye, Ma.'

Charlie bounces the car keys in his hand. His wife and daughter have been speaking to each other in Afrikaans all the time lately, making him feel even more of an outsider. *We've been in this place too long.* But Charlie no longer wants to leave. He opens the driver's door and pauses, held in the thrall of a sudden mental image of bright hair cascading down a slender back.

'Daddy?'

'Righto, off we go,' he chirps, and slides into the driver seat.

'Off we go!' Delia echoes. And they do.

Liezette waits until the van is well out of sight. In the ensuing quiet, she digs her own car keys out of her back pocket where they've been hiding since Charlie suggested his outing with Delia. She unlocks her little French city car and climbs in. For a moment, the familiar musty smell of its interior transports her right back to Cape Town. She hasn't thought about the ocean in who knows how long, but now she aches for the crash and the spray of it. There's a fine dull film on the inside of the windscreen, and she resists the urge to wipe it with her finger and taste it to see if it's still salty.

The engine starts up with a cough, and Liezette drives off

in the opposite direction to the one Charlie took, making her way towards the barn at the base of the hill.

A strange tightness has recently taken up residence in Liezette's back, and as she navigates the farm road, she feels as if there are steel wires running all the way up it and into her neck. She shakes out her shoulders but it makes no difference. Apart from when she's riding Rolo, the feeling is always there. Some days, she can even feel it pulling from her jaw-bone and all the way down into her stomach. She's taken to eating her food in tiny bites to try and get her swallowed mouthfuls past the cables.

The closer she gets to Charlie's workshop, the more the tension builds, and by the time she parks the car and climbs out into the dusty silence, her whole body is thrumming. She enters the barn by the smaller back door, on the side furthest from the hill. It's been weeks since she last set foot in here. It feels as if she's trespassing, breaking in like a criminal.

Without the big double doors open at the far end, the work-shop is dim, and strange shadowed shapes seem to coalesce and disperse in air thick with wood dust and silence. The heels of her boots send sharp cracks of sound bouncing through the vast space. Liezette walks and stops, walks and stops.

Oh my God.

The moment Liezette sees Charlie's latest pieces, the steel wires pulling on her insides go slack as if sliced clean through. An extraordinary occasional chair emerges out of the gloom and seems to be reaching out with curved arms as if it's been waiting, for so, so long, to embrace her. She sinks down into it, holding her breath. The wood has been sanded and rubbed so satin-fine that the bits beneath her exploring fingertips seem to be spun from petals.

'Jesus, Charlie,' she says out loud, and a laugh bubbles out of her as she looks around and sees more and more of the work he's created. Each piece reveals some intimate secret about the tree it once was: this unique curve whispers of how it feels to dig roots down into the depths of cool earth while singing at the sky, and that whorl right there is about birds tickling your scalp with their twiggy, clawed feet. Liezette, breathless in her embracing chair, suddenly lifts her arms above her head and imagines her fingers grazing the bottom of clouds. 'Magical,' she says, and in the strange presence of these pieces, the word seems to dart from her mouth and dance along the lengths of timber. This isn't furniture, this is sculpture you want to sit on.

Folks are going to claw each other's eyes out to have one of these in their homes, she thinks. *My husband's going to be famous.* Never mind the shop in De Waterkant, her Charlie Rowan is going to take the international market by storm.

It's been a long time since Liezette has allowed herself to imagine playing the role of 'wife of the artist', but now she slips on the fantasy like a familiar, luxuriant velvet coat. She closes her eyes and smiles. She'll need a new wardrobe, for a start. She can see herself in something linen, well-made and deceptively simple-looking. Something that shows off her legs, now leaner thanks to all the horse riding. The impetus of her imaginings push her from her seat and send her pacing through the still workshop. In her mind, she's stepping out of aeroplanes in exotic destinations, being welcomed wherever they land. Liezette has always craved the kind of adulation she imagines is given to a successful, talented artist, but has never had the goods to get there herself. Now, at Charlie's side, she'll be able to taste a bit of it.

She places her hand on the bolt that closes the large double doors at the end of the barn and pauses, the metal chill seeping into her fingers. Charlie and Delia could be back soon, and she doesn't want him to find her in here. Besides which, what's the point in opening the place up any further? There's no furniture out there in the yard. *I've seen what I came to see.*

Liezette trots back through the workshop and out into the bright day wearing a smile of intense satisfaction. *It's all been worth it*, she thinks, all Charlie's distance and strangeness doesn't matter. She's going to be the wife of an artist, an admirable man. Until this moment, sliding on to the sun-warmed fabric of her car seat, Liezette has never quite realised how much she's wanted this all along.

Did she do this? Did she make these incredible pieces happen by bringing Charlie out here to this beautiful valley? She wants to dismiss the thought, but it's too delicious to abandon that quickly. She allows herself the treat of believing it for a little while longer. She smiles all the way to the stables.

Charlie opens the doors to let the summer cacophony of morning birdsong and cicadas flood in to replace the stale, woody night-breath of the barn. He scans the hillside for signs of the 'water-eyed-girl'. It has been four days. Her continued absence distorts his week like a thickening scar, each new layer of discomfort hardening over the last. He takes his time filling an old metal watering can at the borehole pump, and uses it to water the strange garden. He found the can dented and abandoned in the far back corner of the barn along with some other old junk. It has a hole in it, but it's still usable. He pays special attention to watering the lavenders, which seem to be losing some of their oomph. The flower heads sag on the end of their grey-green stems.

Don't die. Charlie makes a silent plea as he watches the water soak into the orange earth. He sits on the stool that he still places ready for the girl, and watches the bees explore the little garden. He's biding his time, reluctant to go back inside and face the piece he's working on. Without her watching, he's unsure of how to approach the timber, and this realisation makes him want to leap up and kick the plants to pieces. He clenches his callused hands into fists, and forces himself to stand up, nice and slow.

'You're a first class fuck-up, Charlie Rowan,' he hisses through clenched teeth. 'You scared her off, shouldn't have touched her.' But he remembers the way her eyes had locked onto his as he brushed his arm against hers. She hadn't been afraid. She'd been something else. His body warms at the memory, and he lifts his eyes once more to scan the clumps of fynbos and orange rocks. Nothing.

Damn it.

Sam stops past the graveyard on her way back home from the Super Saver. Despite the fact that she hasn't been here to water or weed since she followed that horse over the hill, the roses around Anneke's grave are thriving. The limbs seem to have swelled and tangled themselves into a protective thicket, and their luxuriant coating of green leaves is studded with bright flowers. Sam touches a peachy petal with caution, half expecting the rich colour to rub off on her fingers like fresh paint.

She works steadily in the heat, filling the old bucket she's kept hidden in the bushes for years with water from the collection tank and carrying it into the graveyard to moisten the thirsty roots. Load after sloshing load. Sam's aching with exertion by the time she's finished watering. The skin on her nose and the back of her neck is stinging from too much sun, but she's not done yet.

Sam takes the secateurs from her backpack and approaches the plants, aiming to snip off the browning spent blooms, but when she leans across to reach one, she gasps at a sharp, sudden pain on the inside of her wrist. She jerks backwards and inspects a glowing bead of blood seeping from her torn skin. She peers closer at the thick foliage to find that beneath the leaves and flowers, each stem is bristling with an armoury of huge, sharp points. She's never seen rose thorns so big. *And so many of them.*

The rose leaves rub their green selves against one another, and it seems to Sam as if their rustling has become a wall of whispers. *What are they saying?* Sam takes a small step back. The flowers shake admonishing heads on the end of their stalks, and the whispering seems to build. *Betrayer.* A clump of red petals suddenly come loose from their calyx and fall to the damp ground with a soft fleshy plop. Sam stares at the scattered, crimson blobs, very aware of the feel of the blood from her cut arm sliding down over her hand and clinging to the ends of her fingers. She lifts her wrist to her mouth and sucks to stem the bleeding. Slowly, with the taste of metal coating her tongue, Sam walks back to her motorbike, packs her things, and rides away.

CHAPTER TWENTY-SEVEN

JUST AS CHARLIE has begun to wonder if the girl from the hill with the water-cool eyes is real, if he didn't perhaps make her up in a fit of overworked lunacy, she returns. It happens on a clear November morning when the air has a certain thin quality that promises a scorching day. Charlie steps out of the barn with the watering can only to find that the garden has already been watered. He sets the can down on the damp ground and scans the whiskery hill scrub for signs of her. He can't see anything but rocks, bush and grass, but just knowing she is out there somewhere makes his muscles surge like water beneath his skin as if a tide is swelling within, pushing him towards the pile of timber that he's neglected for too long.

It is only hours later, when he finally looks up from the lathe, that he sees the girl. She's standing in the dark corner of the barn. Regardless of the shadow, her extraordinary pale braid glows, as if drinking the light into itself and burning it back at him.

'I'm glad you came back,' Charlie says, and the wood shavings at his feet rustle at the sound, echoing their agreement.

Sam doesn't reply. She is motionless, unable to breathe. Her heart is hammering so hard at the wonderfulness of his words that it blocks her throat.

*

The next day, Sam stands by the open barn doors and looks in to where Charlie perches on a stool at his workbench, working on something with a hammer and chisel. There's a hot wind streaming through the valley, and she can feel it pushing against her back and rushing around her, like a boiling river. Sam is caught up in the pull of the current, barely aware that she's moving closer to the wood-man with each breath until the wide curve of his shoulder fills her vision. The ring of the hammer against the back of the chisel stops, and in the silence, she's aware of heartbeats: hers is violent thunder, Charlie's is a pulsing in the veins of his arm which rise up beneath his skin like cords in the heat. Sam is sure she can almost hear the beating heart of the workshop itself, thudding in time with the battering of the wind on the tin roof, and slow and almost indiscernible in the whorled core of the piece of timber that's gripped in the workbench vice.

She is now close enough to realise that, despite her imaginings, Charlie doesn't smell like wood at all. There's something richer there, like freshly baked bread spread with butter. Something edible. She gazes at the slick of sweat on the back of his wrist. If she tasted it, would it be sweet or salt? Her mouth floods. She swallows.

'You want to know something?' Charlie's voice is hushed. 'The wood is different when you're watching. See?' He unwinds the vice and holds up the freed piece. It is a pale ashy beige and, although she knows it's Charlie who has worked it, it looks as if it has been shaped over time by the slow rub of running water. Waves and streams and rivers have carved this timber, licking it into fluid form. 'It's glowing. It doesn't do that unless you're here.'

Sam holds her breath. The hot wind river has turned the wood-man around in its swell and shifted him closer to her.

She flicks her gaze up just long enough to see that his eyes are dark blue-green and his lashes longer than she would've thought possible. 'You see,' he whispers, 'that's why you mustn't vanish again. I need you.'

The air shivers in the small space between them. A strand of his hair flops down and brushes her forehead.

A sudden gust of wind whips through the barn, knocking tools off their shelves and sending a cloud of sawdust swirling upwards into their faces. Sam takes a step back, and then another. Charlie squeezes his eyes shut and picks shreds of wood from where they've stuck to his lips. When the wind dies down again, Sam is back on her stool by the door.

Her eyes stay on him, though, cool and hot at the same time.

Charlie slots the wood back into the grip of the vice, tightens it, and picks up his chisel.

Because the days are summer-long now, it's still light when Sam returns home in the evenings, the low sun whitening the sky as she makes her way down the path she's worn in the side of the hill and enters the garden beneath the vast, shadowy arms of the oak tree.

Sam-the-horse's grave marker is overdue for replacing, and the letters she chipped out years ago have vanished into moss and rotting wood. The reeds around the pond have thickened with no one cutting them back, and weeds have sprouted in the flower beds. A massive marrow has seeded itself in the compost heap and now blankets the whole mound with a snaking grid of vines and yellow trumpet-shaped flowers. As Sam tiptoes past the vegetable beds, she sees that the snails have ravaged the spinach, the onions need to be pulled up before they ruin, and the fruit is reddening and rotting on the tomato plants.

This is precious food, Sam. Jem's voice echoes in her head. *The vegetables are one thing that you can't just keep ignoring.*

So she fetches her trowel and a basket, and digs up the onions. Most will be salvageable, if she lets the skins dry and stores them correctly. She collects what tomatoes she can, inhaling the pungent green smell of their leaves, and for a while, she almost loses herself in the familiar, steady work of picking and cutting and tying up and pulling weeds from between the toes of the vegetable plants.

But as she makes her way to the house with her full basket, Sam notes that the lavenders are leggy and dry and need cutting back. The leaves on the summer bulbs are browning because they haven't been watered. There are weeds everywhere she looks, and clouds of fruit flies hover in clusters over the mush of fallen plums beneath the fruit tree. There's so much to do, so much that she's neglected. Sam resolves to stay home tomorrow and get stuck in, but even as she thinks this, she knows that she won't. She knows that she can't. She knows that she will go to Charlie.

The air is so still that the late afternoon heat seems to suck the breath from the barn. With Sam following a little way behind, Charlie moves outside to work in the yard which, at this time of the day, lies in the shadow of the building. Out here, at least, there's hope of a breeze. Charlie settles on the ground with his work between his splayed legs. He's doing the final rounds of fine sanding on the pieces which will make up the legs of a slim coffee table. Each leg is pale African pear wood and just different enough in shape to give the finished piece an alive look, as if it might just stroll off the living room rug. He wants to make the one-day buyers of the table feel honoured that the piece is choosing to stay with them rather than leave, much like the owners of a sleek and independent cat.

Even out here, the air is motionless and heavy. Sweat slides down his nose and runs over his ribs.

'Some water,' he says to the watching girl, indicating the half-full plastic bottle at his side. 'Please have. It's a furnace out here.'

She moves closer at a crouch, as if the heat is forcing her to stay low to the ground. When she takes the bottle, the backs of her knuckles brush the fabric of his jeans and Charlie can feel their faint trace like a line of tingling cold on his thigh. He turns to watch her drink, eyes riveted on the movement of her throat beneath her creamy skin.

'Jesus,' he says without meaning to, and her eyes lock on his. 'Don't finish all of it, hey.'

She holds out the bottle, but instead of taking it from her, he wraps his fingers around hers so that they're both holding on to it. Keeping her gaze steady on his, the girl moves the bottle to his lips, into his mouth, tips it. Some of the lukewarm water spills down his chin. In a sudden dart of movement, the girl leans forward to suck it off. He jerks backwards, shocked at the jab of teeth against his skin, and she goes bright pink, appalled. She tries to get her hand out from under his, ready to run.

'Oh no you don't,' Charlie whispers. He pulls the bottle in towards his chest so that she has to follow, and once she is right up close, once he can smell the lemon in her hair, it's easy for him to forget the table legs in his lap, and the farm and the vineyards and the horses and his daughter and his wife. He leans a little closer, she doesn't pull away. He gives her the lightest kiss. Her eyes are wide, unblinking. He gives her another. She makes a little involuntary sound deep in her throat, and he moves in for more.

'What... who are you?' he asks into her trembling mouth.

'Yours,' she breathes into his.

CHAPTER TWENTY-EIGHT

AS THE HEAT of the day softens into evening, the sprawling vineyards with their parallel ribs of plantings look as if they've been soaked in golden syrup. Liezette can almost taste its sweetness on the still air. Everything looks better from up here on Rolo's back. She sways in time with the animal's familiar gait, and leans forward to pat his warm, solid neck.

'You know you got me the best horse in the whole damn world?' she asks her father.

'Don't say that too loud. Mostert will hear.' Le Roux ruffles the coarse hair at the base of Mostert's mane, and the giant yellow bay twitches his ears. 'See, he's listening.'

'Oh, Dad.' Riding out with her father has become the best part of Liezette's day. Rolo just follows Mostert, so she barely needs to guide him. After a day of trying to get her mother not to spoil Delia, and trying to get Delia not to behave like a little madam, relinquishing the reins is a relief. Liezette grins as her father points out the small shape of a bird of prey against the pinking western sky.

'Buzzard?' she asks.

'Bateleaur eagle. See how it twists and turns in the air like that? That's how you know.'

'Beautiful.'

'You're looking very pleased with yourself,' le Roux says.

There's something held back about his expression, a look that Liezette knows well. *He's going to bitch about Charlie*, she thinks. It's been a long time coming. Her father may not have said anything yet, but she knows that he's been stewing.

'I've been wanting to mention…' le Roux says as he steers Mostert around the end of the row of vines. *Here it comes.* 'That man of yours. What's he up to, hey? He's in that barn every moment that God sent.'

'Of course he is. That's why we moved out here, Daddy, so he could concentrate on his work.'

'Well if you ask me, he seems to have forgotten that he's got a family.'

'It's not like that. He's just busy. He comes in to read Delia her bedtime story every night, you know. He hasn't missed a single one.'

'A bedtime story doesn't make you into a father' – he glances at his daughter, so high and proud on her brown horse – 'or a husband.'

'Oh, Daddy—'

'Don't "oh daddy" me. Charlie has been completely absent. He hasn't joined us at the dinner table in who knows how long. Works all through Sunday, even. I can barely remember what the man looks like, Liezette.'

'Oh, come on.'

'My girl, I'm serious. I'm an old man and I know a thing or two. I bet you a million bucks that husband of yours is sitting around dreaming in that workshop, just counting off another nice hour in which he doesn't need to take any responsibility for his family or his future.'

'You're wrong.' At the memory of those pieces that she saw when she snuck into Charlie's studio, a bright plume of bubbles fizzes up Liezette's spine. 'He's an artist.'

'Pfft.'

'What do you know about artists, Dad?'

'I know about men, my girl. I know when someone thinks they're having a nice free ride at everyone else's expense.'

'He's working, Daddy, believe me, I've seen it.'

'So what's he so busy with in there all bloody day and night?'

'Magic.'

'Magic?' Le Roux jerks the reins to stop Mostert from sampling an unripe bunch of Sancerre grapes. 'He does *wood-work*, my girl. Now I ask you, who wants bits of mismatched home-made furniture in this day and age? Who's going to pay good money for that?'

'People do. You should see how nuts they go for his stuff in Cape Town.'

'So where's all this money, then? Why's he sponging off everyone else?'

'These things take time, and anyway, that's not fair. *I* made us move here.' Again, Liezette gets a shiver of satisfaction at the thought. 'I had to force him, Daddy. The last thing he wanted was to live off you.'

'Well, perhaps if he took half an interest in the farm, or in anyone else's life around here, it wouldn't be so bad, but…' Le Roux trails off. Something about the lazy way the low sun glows through the vine leaves sucks the vigour from his argument. 'I'm just saying… he's in that barn a hell of a lot.'

'He's passionate about what he does, Daddy. He's working the whole time.'

'Alone in that old barn all day, he could be up to anything.'

'Yes, well he isn't. I've seen.' Le Roux lets out a bark of laughter when he sees his daughter's self-satisfied smile. Both horses swivel their ears in alarm at the sound.

'You control what he does, do you?'

Liezette thinks about the way she got Charlie to fall for her, how she teased him into marrying her, encouraged amazing work out of him, made him into a father, and then she engineered this move which has resulted in this… *magic*. He's the one carving the wood, but she's the one shaping the man who holds the tools.

'I know what's best for Charlie,' she says. 'Trust me.'

'If you say so, my girl.'

'You probably don't even realise it, Daddy, but I control you too.'

'Oh do you now?' Another loud burst of laughter.

'Of course I do.' Liezette gives Rolo's neck a brisk pat. 'Why else would you have bought me this horse? Right, now are we going to plod along like a pair of old ladies,' Liezette tightens her grip on the reins and jabs her heels into Rolo's ribs, 'or are we going to *ride*!'

Each day brings a new corner of Charlie to discover. Yesterday, it was the fragrant dent at the place where his neck meets his shoulder, the day before that, the velvet lobe of his ear. Today, Sam found the slight ridge of muscle that runs across from each hip bone and dips down beneath the front waistband of his jeans. Now, as she climbs back over the hill in the low light of evening, her fingertips ache with the memory of the hard-soft feel of muscle beneath skin. *What will I discover tomorrow?* The thought runs a shiver through her, and Sam stops in her tracks and squeezes her eyes shut. She runs her tongue over the tender places inside her mouth that have been made raw by his kisses.

When she opens her eyes again, the garden at the bottom of

the hill seems to be staring back up at her. From here, it looks like a dark green pool with a limpid surface, but Sam knows that swirling, sucking depths hide beneath. She watches the leaves on the olive tree turn in the breeze from green to silver to green again. A moment later, the same wind makes the wild grasses whisper at her back. *You can't stay here all night, dear heart.* Jem's voice in her head is gentle, but insistent. Sam thinks of the studying she needs to do for the impending end-of-year exams, takes a deep breath and plunges down the hill towards home.

For most of the time when the girl is at the workshop, Charlie works and she watches, lingering at the edges of the barn, silent and unobtrusive. It is only towards late afternoon that something shifts, and Charlie will suddenly turn to find that she is right up close beside him. Moments after that, her mouth is on his and his hands are on her skin, and the mortise and tenon and hand plane and bow saw no longer matter. The wood is nothing and she is everything, and then his phone pings its bedtime story reminder, and she is gone.

Yours.

Beyond telling him this, she's said nothing else, and Charlie hasn't asked where on earth she comes from, how she came to be here with him in this barn in the middle of nowhere, or where she goes every evening when she walks up the hill. He could ask, of course, and maybe she'd even tell him, but he likes it like this. This way, she's not quite real, and if she's not quite real, then there's no real betrayal.

So while she certainly feels very human as she writhes and gasps beneath his fingertips, Charlie thinks of the not-quite-real girl as a creature conjured up from the valley itself.

She is made of Karoo dust and mountain grass and sunlight on river water. Just for him. There's plenty to delight in, from her exploring fingers to her needy tongue to her lithe, smooth curves, but it is her eyes that he craves the most. Charlie is convinced it is the watery pale coolness of Sam's gaze on him as he works that has brought his recent pieces into being.

Charlie stands back from his latest item, a writing desk on elegant, curved legs. He can barely remember making it. The desk has three slim pull-out drawers in the front, each one sitting snug and perfect inside its cavity. The lines of the dovetail joints themselves are all curved, rather than straight, and seem to have flowed into each other and melded themselves together as if he had no hand in their construction at all.

Water-wood. The words seem to swim up in his mind and bob there, ripe with promise. Like this writing desk, each of his latest pieces look as if they've been worn into shape by waves and rubbed smooth by ripples rather than painstakingly worked by hand.

As Charlie drives back up to the main house, hugs his daughter and smiles at his wife, the new pieces that he's already calling 'The Water-Wood Collection' never leave his thoughts. The whorl of a chair arm, the sweep of a tabletop and the silk-smooth grain of the sides of a shelf, these are the things that pulse through him and set him alight. As for the girl? Well, while she isn't watching him, she doesn't need to exist.

Are you going over the hill, Sam?

No, Grandpa. I'm studying in the lookout. Remember, I told you?

Well something's up. Why do you look so guilty, then?

Maybe that's just my face.

I know your face, Sam. Silence, the dark house pressing in on all sides. *So then why are you never here any more?*

You know why.

This is your home, dear heart.

Sam looks out of the window at the black neglected garden which is growing too dense. Out there in the shadows, she knows that the roses are blooming. Opening up their fleshy, fragrant faces, always looking at her.

Is it?

One boiling hot, white-sunned day, Sam realises that Charlie has been all explored. She has touched and tasted every plane of him, and his reciprocation has left her tingle-skinned and humming all through. Her body feels like a china bowl that wants to sing a high clear note and then shatter, exploding in a shower of fine shards. Could that one, mysterious act that she's read about and wondered over and ached for, set her free? Take her away from the too-silent house, her nagging guilt and the whispers in the garden? She wants to do the thing that will grow her up while it makes Charlie hers. He won't without her asking for it, that much he's made clear, so Sam raises the topic with her fingers and her eyes, and he asks if she really means it and she says the second word she's ever spoken out loud in his presence: 'Yes'.

Something shifts inside Sam when Charlie, encased in rubber, is in there too. At first, the smell on his hands, as they twist and clutch through her hair, reminds her of blowing up balloons for a birthday in Mrs McGovern's classroom. Then there's the edge of the workbench snagging the skin at the back of her legs. Then it's a sudden clench of pain that makes her cry out, her shout bouncing up into the high rafters of the barn. But after that, as the pain seeps away and leaves a new feeling that builds and spills down her legs and into her feet, Sam realises that instead of satisfying her hunger for him, this is opening up a bottomless maw of need. She wants to crack wide open and swallow Charlie into her very being, to have him never leave. Things that didn't matter before, like who he is and what his life is like beyond the barn walls, suddenly become imperative, and she wants to *know* him.

Sam both wishes that she'd never started this, and wants to do it again.

CHAPTER TWENTY-NINE

SAM WAKES, GROGGY and thick-headed, shaken from sleep by the dull thumping sound that worked its way into her dreams. She grasps Jem's old alarm clock from her bedside table and stares at it, waiting to make sense of the numbers. Nine thirty. When did she last sleep so late? She falls back against the pillow, trying to figure out where the thumping is coming from. Suddenly, she sits bolt upright.

It's the garden gate!

She can hear it now: the thumps are interspersed with the metallic rattle of padlock against bolt.

Who is it? No one ever comes here.

Panic.

Sussie?

Sam's heart bashes against the cage of her ribs like a terrified bird as she runs from the bedroom and out of the house. If she doesn't answer quickly, Sussie will know something is up. Her feet, still sleep-tender, slap against the sunny flagstones, and surprised bees, shaken from their flowers, whizz up from the plants on either side of the path.

Sam skids to a halt.

What if it isn't Sussie? What if it's Yolande?

The wood judders. Thump thump thump. Sam freezes. Her vision blurs. Suddenly, she is back inside Poppy's small body, listening to her mother beating on the outside of the bathroom door of Karel's disgusting cottage. This was a time before Karel 'lost' the bathroom key. This was before he sold the TV. This was the time that Yolande was sick and screeching and her eyes were mad with storm clouds and, before Poppy had run in here to hide, her saliva had flown out with her shouts, spattering against Poppy's face. Sam can't remember what her mother had been so furious about, but she remembers thinking: *This is it. This is me, about to get killed.*

How would it happen? With a whack against the side of the head? Maybe with a half-brick, like she'd seen one time on the TV. Karel kept a crumbling, orange one by the front door to stop it from banging shut when he wanted a breeze. Sam flinched. Or maybe it would just be her mother's hands around her throat. Wiry, cigarette-smelling hands that squeezed and didn't stop. Poppy had imagined it would be like one of the Chinese bangles that Yolande liked to give 'in fun', but around her neck instead of her wrist. Whatever it was going to be, it would hurt.

'Sam!' Her eyes snap open. She's Sam again, back in the garden. The padlock bounces against the gate. That's not Yolande's voice. Nor is it Sussie's.

'Keegan?' she queries, breathless.

'Sam! Jesus Christ, I was starting to think I'd have to break this thing down.'

'Keegan! Sorry, I was...' She sways on her feet, rubs her eyes. 'What are you doing here?'

'Are you going to let me in, or what?'

'Um...' Sam casts a desperate look around the garden as if the overgrown, buzzing-insect-green will have a solution to offer. 'I'm kind of in the middle of something, can you... wait for a moment?'

'I've *been* waiting ages already,' he says. There's a pause. 'Sam, are you OK?'

'Of course. I was just… about to have a shower, so I'm not…' Sam swallows, shuts her eyes. 'Ready. I was busy doing some stuff for my grandpa. He's…' She draws in more breath. 'Resting.'

'I'll wait, then,' Keegan says. Sam can hear the thump as he sits down on the other side of the wooden gate. 'But I'm not leaving until I see you face to face. My mom will march over here herself if I don't tell her everything's OK with you.'

'What? Why?'

'Sam.' Keegan's voice is low and serious. 'My mom is freaking out about you. You haven't replied to any of her emails, your biology assignment is late, and your telephone just rings and rings as if the line has been cut off or something.'

'Oh.' *Shit*, thinks Sam. *The phone bill.* She was positive she remembered to sort out the water and lights one, but now she's not sure. She's not at all sure about anything.

'I drove over to—'

'You *drove* here? By yourself?'

'Yes.' He'd had to work really hard to convince his mother to let him come alone. Keegan had driven down the road at the pace of a dying snail to reassure her that he was going to take it slow. 'I've got my learner licence, you know. A lot's happened since…' Keegan trails off and the silence sinks down between them, heavy with things unspoken.

'Oh.' Sam didn't realise that Keegan even knew where she lived, but of course he must. Everyone around here knows of Jem and Anneke's weirdo little corner of the valley.

'Are you going to open this gate?'

'Right.' Sam shakes herself from her daze. 'Just give me a minute to get the key and change out of my… put on something…'

'Sure.' Keegan's voice wobbles.

'I'll be back in a sec.'

Sam races to the house and freezes in the doorway, seeing for the first time just what a tip the place is. There's dust on every surface and unwashed dishes in the sink and it smells... unused. Anneke would be horrified. Sam heads to the bathroom and splashes her face with cold water, over and over, until her jaw aches.

At last she's dressed and back at the garden gate with the key in her hand. It trembles when she unlocks the padlock and slides back the bolt.

'Hi,' says Keegan from his waiting spot on the dirty barn floor. 'Thought you'd done a runner.'

'Don't be daft,' Sam says and ushers him in through the gate. 'We can talk out here in the garden, but not in the house. We have to be quiet, OK? Grandpa's asleep.'

'Is he all right? He doesn't seem to be getting better or anything.'

'Being old is not something you *recover* from, Keegan,' Sam snaps. She leads him to the bench beneath the lemon tree because it faces the pond, keeping the house, which seems to have grown into something huge and echoey now that Keegan is here, at their backs. Sam can feel it looming behind her, peering at them through the greenery with unblinking eyes. She darts a look at Keegan. Despite his unwelcome appearance, she's surprised to find that his presence beside her is a relief. He's not Sussie, and he's not Yolande. Keegan she can deal with.

Keegan is the opposite of relieved. Now that he's seated beside Sam just as if they were two ordinary people looking at an ordinary view, he's lost the nerve he's been nurturing all morning. He clears his throat, wincing at the sound, but can't make any useful words come out. Above their heads, between the yellow globes of the fruit, the little Cape white-eyes, whose round, green bellies give them the appearance of unripe lemons themselves, chatter on with enviable ease.

Sam gathers her hair at the side of her head, divides it into three, and begins to plait it.

Keegan watches the deft, automatic movements of her capable fingers. He's not sure whether he's in danger of throwing his arms around her, or throwing up. Neither one would be optimal.

'So.' She finally breaks the silence.

'Yes. So. Like I was saying, my mom is worried. You seem to have dropped off the planet.'

'Oh, come on. I forgot to reply to a few emails, hardly a crisis.'

'You promised her you wouldn't, though.' Keegan feels a jolt run through him when she flips her finished braid over her shoulder and turns her head to meet his gaze.

'You're right. I know I did. Tell her I'm so sorry. I just…' *Just what?* The garden seems to hold its breath, waiting for her to finish the sentence and bring some sort of reason to the fever of the past week.

'It was conditional, your doing the correspondence thing. That's what Mom said. On condition. You've not been holding up your end of the bargain.'

'I'm legally allowed, you know.' Sam turns to stare at the hump of the hill. She imagines being able to look right through it to where the wood-man works in his airy workshop on the other side. Charlie. His name sits soft like a cloud on the end of her tongue, she has to move it out of the way to get her words out: 'I'm seventeen. At *sixteen*, you're like a grown-up or something, and you can drop out of school if you want.'

'Not if people give a shit about you, you can't.' Keegan stares down at his hands. 'My mom's pupils are like her babies. Her special projects. She's not going to let you ruin your whole future without a bloody good fight.'

'Who says I'm ruining my future?'

'Oh, for God's sake, Sam, I know you're all earth-child-luddite and whatever, but really, you live in the same world I do, so don't pretend you don't. This is the twenty-first century. You know you need an education to get anywhere.'

Where would I want to get to? But it bothers Sam that this garden, this sanctuary that has always been enough, somehow isn't any more. She doesn't know *what* she wants. Except for a hot-coal 'something' that she can't yet define, something that has everything to do with what waits on the other side of that hill. The memory of Charlie's skin against hers, his face, so close, as he'd moved inside her, stops her heart for a moment, and then sets it galloping.

'Sam?'

'It won't happen again. I promise. I'll do that biology thingy today. It'll be in Mrs McGovern's inbox by morning.'

'If it isn't?'

'It will be.'

'If you say so.' Keegan looks out over the pond to the dense shade beneath the old oak. A jagged shape pokes up out of the plants. He squints against the glare of the water. *Is that a grave marker? Is something buried there?*

'OK then,' Sam says with finality in her tone; she begins to stand.

'You still haven't explained your radio silence, Sam,' Keegan says, and she lowers herself back down to the bench. 'What's been going on?'

Sam is utterly lost about what to say. Her whole existence

has become a dense forest of lies, but there are no reasonable ones she can think of to explain away her recent behaviour. She glances at Keegan. He is clearly nervous, glaring at the twisting fingers in his lap as if they don't belong to him. She knows now how he feels, why he tried to kiss her all those years ago. Now that she's met Charlie and felt the gushing heat inside her own body, the needle-sharp point of focus in her mind, she knows.

I could use that.

It's a horrible thought. She tries to think of something else, anything that will distract him, get him out of here. She remembers, for a moment, the predatory golden eyes of the eagle from her dream, peering out from behind her own. She shifts on her seat, trying to rid herself of the sensation of dark feathers rustling beneath her skin, but what replaces it is worse: her whole being vibrates with a low growl of panic that runs through every thought, even her thoughts of the wood-man: *no one can know what I've done.* A knot of panic, like a fist punching up the back of her throat, almost stops her breath. What will stop him from asking? What can she do to change where this is going?

'Keegan?' she says, and when the boy turns to her, she jerks forward and places her mouth on his. It's a clumsy move, at first, but she knows how to do this now. Keegan's eyes widen, and his breath through his nose comes in little startled snorts. When she pulls away, he stares at her, red faced. She swears she can hear the thudding of his heart.

'What are you—'

'Everything's going to be fine, Keegan.' She smiles.

'But—' Sam silences Keegan with a touch on his trembling hand. 'Tell your mom I'm sorry I went AWOL for a bit there, but I promise, everything is fine and I'll be working harder than ever.'

Keegan leans into her, hoping for more, but Sam uses the momentum of his movement to get them both standing. Before he knows what's happening, Keegan is being led back to the gate. Her hand on his arm burns into his skin. The garden seems to swim and shift before his dazzled eyes.

'Tell Mrs McGovern I'll be in town on Monday, and she can check on me herself.'

'I—'

'It's going to be fine, Keegan.' Her face is close, she puts a burning hand on his chest, over the place where his heart thunders, runs it down to the base of his belly, stops. 'Trust me. I'm OK. Everything will be back to normal before you know it, right?'

'Um…'

'I'll see you next week.' And suddenly, Keegan is on the other side of the gate. Slices of sunlight dance through the gaps between the barn boards. He breathes in petrol from the Yamaha, blinks at the sight of his mom's blue car, waiting in the sunlight. Everything is so ordinary.

But it isn't.

The part of him that has ached for so many years feels both full up and somehow emptier than before. Keegan walks to the car on numb feet, gets in and starts the engine, letting the dull grind of it soothe his fractured insides, as if the vibration might shake him back together beneath his skin.

Sam stares at the gate for a stupefied minute, listening to Keegan start the car, and pull away. Then she hurls herself against the wood, slams the bolt home, and locks the padlock.

It's going to be fine, Keegan, she'd said. But it isn't. It's all falling down and apart and soon, soon, everyone will know.

Her secret isn't safe. How long did she think she could fool everyone? Even after kissing Keegan, what's going to stop him from telling everyone how neglected and wild the garden is? How she wouldn't let him in the house? How Jem was nowhere to be seen?

With slow steps, Sam turns and walks towards the rose garden. Her stomach churns. Her mouth tastes of earth and tin, and suddenly, she's right back where she was that morning three months ago when everything changed.

It was July, a Saturday.

Sam woke late to the patter of rain on the tin roof, and an astonishing yellow light in her bedroom, instead of winter morning grey. She opened the curtains to see that the sun had found a gap in the grey cloud cover and was shining through the rain, dripping gold onto the garden. She watched bright droplets stream down the freshly pruned rose stems, turning the thorny stalks into lit candles, dripping wax.

And then, in a moment, the gold was gone and the sky was damp-winter lead again. Sam took Anneke's old watch from her bedside table and slipped it on. *Nine o'clock!* The house was too quiet for it to be so late. Jem was always up early, and by this time he should already have brought her coffee in bed and made some comment about her sleeping the day away. She got up and put on her weekend stuff – thick layers of old clothing that were good for garden work – and opened her bedroom door to a silent house.

'Grandpa?'

Nothing.

As she walked towards his room, the air felt oddly tight, as if it was threaded through with rubber bands that pulled at her limbs and distorted everything she passed. The familiar bookshelves became rows of grinning teeth, and the floor swung down and away from her cautious footsteps. It was cold. Jem hadn't lit the stove. He always lit the stove first thing when he woke up on winter mornings.

Sam paused on the threshold of Jem's bedroom with her hand on the door. The wood seemed to pulse beneath her touch. Just then, the sun must've made another grab for the sky, because a sudden flood of bronze light lit up the lounge behind her and lines of warm colour glowed around the edges of the door. Her grandpa seldom slept with his curtains closed.

Sam opened the door, blinked at the light, and peered in. She didn't need to take another step to know, she could see right away from where she stood that whatever it was that had made Jem Jem, was gone. She pulled back with a gasp and slammed the door shut. She swayed on her feet and her ears hummed as if a hundred bees were beating their busy wings against the inside of her skull.

If I look again, it will be different. He will just be sleeping. His eyes will not be open and staring like that. She tried to push the handle down and take another look, but she couldn't. Instead, a hideous wash of hot bile swept up her throat and she stumbled from the doorway and into the bathroom. It was a long time before she could lever herself up from the icy floor.

By the time Sam managed to drink water from the bathroom tap, the last of the opportunistic sun glow had gone, and the rain had stopped, leaving a damp, dripping hush behind. She was shaking so much that the whole bathroom seemed to vibrate around her. Slowly, she walked back towards the closed bedroom door and pushed it open.

'Grandpa?' she whispered, although she could see it was pointless. 'What happened what happened what happened what happened...' The words tumbled from her mouth and lay scattered and unanswered at her feet. Jem was on his side with his eyes open wide and his mouth in an awful shape as if something mechanical had crept in and pulled it this way and that during the night. Sam's tentative touch revealed that his forehead was cold. Everything inside her wanted to climb out of her skin. Her legs lost their bones and she slipped to the floor in a shuddering pile of grief.

Time passed, or maybe it didn't. And then suddenly Sam sat upright and thought: *the survival book!* There was something in there, she was sure of it. Something that would tell her what and how. Something that would tell her why. She ran from the room to find it. The pages felt damp and fragile beneath her fingers.

Searching.

Sudden cardiac death.

Sam could only guess that this was what had happened, and the fact that her grandfather's body was rigid, meant that, according to the book, he'd died some time ago. Hours ago. Alone, in the night. There was no way to bring him back. She clutched her book to her chest, closed her eyes and screamed.

She screamed long and loud and hard. It felt as if the sound was coming from the centre of her spine, carrying splinters of bone with it that ripped against the sides of her throat as it poured out. She gasped and panted for breath. She tasted blood.

What am I going to do?

She went back into the room. It was gloomy now without the sun, and starting to smell slightly of urine. *Ouma wet herself too that time.* Her beloved grandpa's face had become strange in death, but not a stranger's. With a start, Sam finally saw the family resemblance it had been impossible to spot before: she could see her mother's face in Jem's dead one.

With Jem's features now slack and vacant, she was reminded of how Yolande had looked, passed out on the couch in a drugged stupor.

Yolande.

No.

Now that she was without an adult guardian, they could force her to go back to Yolande, couldn't they? And what if her mother hears the news that her father is dead and comes back to claim *her* house, *her* inheritance? Her daughter.

Sam left the house, and in the garden, gulping down mouthfuls of fresh wet garden air, she paced back and forth beneath the olive tree, churning the ground to mud beneath her sodden slippers as a hundred awful scenarios played themselves out in her head. Every single thought led back to one, unavoidable truth: she was going to have to hide this. Nobody could be allowed to find out that she was now alone.

Yolande *cannot*, under any circumstances, know.

That evening, as the light began to dim, and the drizzle started up again, Sam began to dig a grave for her grandpa. The obvious spot was beneath the oak tree, beside Sam-the-horse's resting place, but with raw hands and aching shoulders, she finally had to give up in a rage of tears and exhaustion. There was no way she could dig through the roots that snaked and snarled through the compact ground. Sam trudged back to the dark house, ran herself a bath, and sat in it, sobbing, until the water was too cold to endure any more. She spent the rest of that endless night buried in a pile of blankets on the couch. Awake.

When the light changed and the birds began to sing, Sam went back outside, jerking like a marionette on stiff, sore legs. The sky was clear and the air mild. She marched to the oak tree to review the damage she'd made on the root-twisted earth. Definitely not an option. She needed a patch of ground that had already been cleared and dug over, somewhere where her puny muscles wielding a gardening spade could make some kind of progress.

The roses.

Only last week, she and Jem had laboured to prune each one. Then, they'd dug down deep to lift the root balls of the dormant plants so that they could dig in fresh compost and bone meal beneath.

Bone meal. Grandpa.

Sam's stomach heaved, but after a minute the feeling passed and something calm crept in to take its place. Yes, her grandpa, nourishing her ouma's precious roses for decades to come. He'd have liked that.

It took Sam the whole day to dig a hole large enough. Her grandfather had been tall, and she didn't know how deep she would have to make it. Tears leaked out as she worked, and she imagined the hole to be full of them. Salt. Not good for plants. She hoped the roses, now lying on their sides with their roots covered in sacking to protect them from the winter sun, would be OK once she replanted them.

When, at last, the moment came that Sam had to return to the bedroom, something switched off inside her. She entered Jem's room with mechanical steps and lifted the covers off the bed and onto the floor. In the small gap between Jem's pyjama top and bottoms, she could see that his skin on the side of his body facing the mattress had turned livid purple, and the bits facing up were bone white. She quickly covered his face, and then swaddled his body using the sheet he'd been lying on, wet bits and all. As she pushed his stiff, heavy cadaver over to wind the sheet around it, a piece of her mind snapped off and went floating away, up towards the ceiling and then further, out above the roof. So it was only an empty automaton that pulled the heavy bundle to the floor and dragged it out of the house, sweating and panting and wincing at the thud of a head knocking against the steps that led down from the stoop to the garden.

She pushed the wrapped body into the yawning, muddy hole with a thump that seemed to echo against the house, the barn and the hill, the sound intensifying until it filled up the whole world.

The moment Jem was in the grave, however, Sam thought: *I can't.*

There was no way she could cover him up and have him gone for good. Sobbing, she tried to lift the body out again. Bits of the wet sheet came unwound and slapped against her face. She slid and slipped on the mud, and then went crashing down onto the soil herself. There she lay beside the wooden, discoloured body in its inadequate shroud, staring up at the darkening sky.

It was the call of a bird that forced her back into action. Something about the sound made her think of Sussie's 'koewee', and although her aunt hadn't set foot here since the *desecration*, Sam imagined her arriving and seeing the piles of muddy-toed roses lying on the ground with the great big gaping grave in the middle, and peering in...

At the thought, she scrambled out of the hole and began to push the clumps of earth back into it, aware all the while that she was sending bits of her crumbling heart in along with it. Once it was finally done, and the roses were back in their places, night had cloaked the garden in black, and the temperature plummeted. Sam lay on the cold ground beside the rose garden until her whole body was shuddering and aching with chill.

Finally, she went back inside the house.

Inside the bathroom, she caught sight of herself in the medicine cabinet mirror, and paused, transfixed. Her face was almost featureless with mud and her eyes were bloodshot pink from crying. *I'll have to go to school tomorrow and pretend that nothing has changed.* The reality of the deceit she'd now have to carry hit home and she drew back from her reflection, sick with horror. *I can't do this.*

The wind rattled the branches on the trees outside the bathroom window, and amid the clatter, an exhausted Sam thought she could hear her grandpa's voice:

Have a bath and get warm, my love.

She obeyed, turning on the hot tap and pulling off her mud-caked clothes before climbing in to the water.

Tomorrow you can take the Yamaha motorbike to school. Lucky thing we got it going last month, hey? She nodded, staring at the islands of her kneecaps rising up out of the brown murk. *Just take it one thing at a time, dear heart. Everything is going to be fine.*

But even as she heard the words and lay back in the warmth, Sam knew that this was a lie. Grandpa, as always, even from beneath the rose bushes, was just trying to be kind.

CHAPTER THIRTY

'WELL, IF IT isn't the lesser-spotted Sam Harding,' Mrs McGovern says as Sam walks in to the classroom carrying her motorcycle helmet under one arm and her book bag over the other. Sam shifts beneath Mrs McGovern's gaze. It is the first time in all their years together as pupil and teacher that she can remember being greeted without a smile.

'I'm really sorry, Mrs McGovern.'

Sam tries to tread quietly as she approaches Mrs McGovern's desk, but both Dale and Keegan have looked up from their work and are watching her every move. Sam doesn't look at Keegan. She has no idea how she's going to deal with him, but she knows she's got to make it through this first.

'And?' Mrs McGovern looks stern, but her voice is soft with concern. 'What happened to you, Sam?'

'Did you get my biology assignment?'

'Yes.'

'Was it OK?'

'It was, but that's not what we're talking about and you know it.'

Now. She has to do it now. Sam fumbles inside her backpack. She is not breathing. She pulls out a beige envelope and hands it to her teacher with shaking fingers.

'It's from my grandpa,' she says in a voice that's little more than a whisper. 'It explains… stuff.'

When Mrs McGovern takes the envelope, Sam feels a dark seam ripping open inside her, spilling soil and leaking watery fluid into her chest cavity until she is filthy inside. She busies herself with her bag so as not to have to watch the reading of the letter. She imagines the lies it carries as a thick smearing of bitter-molasses-black over the page. After Keegan's visit yesterday, she'd sat up for hours composing what it would say, working and reworking it until the words made no sense at all. To get the tone right, she'd lifted and changed phrases from Jem's letters to Anneke. Being love letters, there was not much she could use directly, but she hopes that they've made this forgery appear genuine.

After that, she'd practised her grandfather's handwriting over and over, forcing her hand to follow loops and jags of his familiar scrawl.

When the letter was finally done and sealed into its innocuous envelope, she'd run to the bathroom and vomited, heaving and gasping over the toilet bowl until all she could throw up were thin green strings of bile and spit.

And now, here in the classroom, Sam imagines her grandfather's corpse, all run through with the roots of roses, jerking and twisting on the end of wires like a terrible marionette. It feels as if she's dug him up and brought him to hideous life, and now she's holding the strings, making him dance as soil crumbles from his shoulders and dark, shiny beetles crawl out of his ears. The weight of this is almost harder to bear than the act of burying him itself. Sam stands before Mrs McGovern's desk as darts of agony shoot up from her fingers and into her skull, blinding her. What is she doing? What has she done?

'Did you read this before Jem sealed the envelope, Sam? Do you know what it says?'

'Yes.' Speaking this small truth is a rush of relief. Sam blinks, and the blinding shadows scatter. She's just here, in this bright familiar room. And the look on Mrs McGovern's face makes her think that her plan may have worked. The hellish dance of the marionette was not for nothing.

Dear Meg,

I was appalled to hear of Sam's recent lapse in both her school work and her communications with you. I must confess that I have been down with the flu recently, and was not paying quite as much attention to Sam's needs as perhaps she was of mine, nevertheless, that does not excuse the fact that I was so unaware of what was going on with my granddaughter of late. It took some courage for her to come to me and tell me that she was in trouble for having 'dropped off the radar' as she put it, and that her being in constant touch with you was a condition of her being able to continue her studies at home, which as you know, suits us both far better since my health has not been so great.

When pressed, Sam finally confessed that she has been suffering a sudden relapse of the old 'technophobia' that you will no doubt remember was such a feature of her childhood at one stage. Apparently, the reawakened, irrational fear of having to touch the computer sent her into a downward spiral. This meant that she was unable to respond to your communications, and felt unable to speak to me about it, due to her resulting guilt. Sam's recent relapse is over, and I assure you that I will watch out for any signs of it rearing its head once more.

I am getting the landline phone bill sorted out too. It seems that Sam forgot to pay it when I asked her to do so at the post office, as she has been, as she puts it, 'out of it'.

Please accept my apologies for any worry that this episode may have caused, and be assured that it will not happen again while Sam continues her studies from home.

Kind regards,
Jeremy Harding

'The technophobia thing just suddenly happened again,' Sam says into the silence. 'Like he said.'

'What brought it on again, Sam?'

'Don't know. Stress, maybe?'

'Because if it is going to continue to be an issue, we may have to rethink your doing your school via correspondence.'

'I know.' Sam arranges her face to give the impression that this could be a real possibility. Just another move in the dance.

But if I'm the puppet now, who's pulling the strings?

'Well.' Mrs McGovern puts the letter back into the envelope. It's a relief to have it tucked away again, out of sight. 'We're going to have to monitor this more closely from now on.'

'OK.'

'Wait.'

Sam stops on her way to the gate and turns to see that Keegan has followed her out of the classroom. He trots towards her, shielding his eyes from the sun.

'Hey,' she says. It's hard to make a smile happen after what she's just been through, but Sam manages. She must be getting good at this. 'Sorry I ran out. I didn't want to disturb your studying and cause even more trouble.' Little lies spin from her mouth and fill the air as if they're windborne seeds. They melt on her tongue, sharp and sour, and tickle the sides of her throat. Keegan breathes them in without seeming to notice.

'I overheard you and my mom talking in there. What you said about the technophobia stuff.'

'I figured. Not exactly a private discussion.'

'Why didn't you tell me all that yesterday?'

'Don't know.' Sam clutches her backpack against her belly so that it bulges out between the two of them. She wraps her arms around it. 'I was embarrassed, I guess.'

'So instead you...' *kissed me*. Something about Sam's expression, shut down and carefully impassive, makes Keegan suddenly afraid that she did nothing of the sort, that he imagined it all. *She'd tasted slightly of toothpaste.* He wouldn't make up that sort of detail, would he? Her eyes are steady on his, as if daring him to mention it just so that she can deny it. Keegan's head swims. The smell of lemon thyme crushed beneath their feet and the white hard sunlight pressing down on the top of his head is overwhelming.

'Anyway,' Sam hugs the bag closer, 'I wanted to say thank you. For coming round to see that I was OK, and stuff. You're a real friend.'

It's a good word, it shouldn't sting, but Keegan can feel the burn as the soft syllable burrows into his skin. He turns and glares up the road, squinting against the light that rages off the orange dirt. Nathan's sneering voice echoes through his head, but for once, his brother is right: *You need to get out of this dump and meet other girls and get a life and get laid. This shit is getting old.* A sob-shudder builds behind his breastbone, and he fights to keep it down.

'OK, well I guess I'll see you in two weeks for the next bunch of tests,' Keegan says, and before the tears have a chance to come, he dashes back to the classroom.

CHAPTER THIRTY-ONE

'HEY, SKANK.' THE voice barely swims in to the edge of Yolande's consciousness, but the jolt on her shin fires pins and needles up through her body and into her brain. 'Wakey fucken wakey.' She draws her limbs inwards, protecting, and forces stitched-together-feeling eyelids to part. A big white trainer with red laces blurs into view. She watches it pull back and bounce into her lower body again, not too hard, but insistent.

'The fuck? I was sleeping.'

'You weren't fucken sleeping, Ratty, you were cased-out.'

'So?' Yolande drags herself into a semi-sit, legs still pulled in close. She rubs the spot where the trainer made contact. She blinks. 'What's the problem? It's what keeps you in business, isn't it?' In the gloom of the abandoned parking garage, she can see the slumps of clothes and hair that indicate fellow users, still in dreamland. 'This is your empire, Sterre.'

'Not mine, Ratty, not mine.' Sterre's gold front teeth gleam as he grins. 'You *know* who I work for.' He wipes the tip of the trainer that made contact with Yolande on the ankle of his tracksuit. 'And I'm here with a message for the "missus".'

'I was going to pay. Tonight I was going to come. I am.'

'Well then, how about paying up now?' Sterre holds out his hand, waiting. It's thick-knuckled with a scar along the palm, a shiny, puckered ridge bisecting the coffee-stain brown. Yolande thinks it looks like the scar could be the lair of some terrible, flesh-eating demon-worm. She pulls back and away from the hand in case something hideous shoots out of it.

'It's my fist you need to worry about, Ratty, not my old cut.' Sterre beckons, and the poorly executed gang-tattoos of a star on each of his fingers twinkle at her and then vanish. 'Come on, pay up.'

'I don't have—' Yolande's sentence is squeezed short when Sterre's hand shoots out and grips her around the throat.

'Then you'd better get,' Sterre whispers. Yolande squirms as the hard cord of the worm-scar digs into her flesh. Sterre releases his hold, dropping her like a soiled rag. 'Make a plan.'

'I—'

'You're not making friends in this town, lady. Just remember where your sweetness is coming from, hey? You pay what you owe or you're going to have the worst comedown of your life.'

Yolande lifts her fingers to her throat, swallowing down acid as she watches Sterre walk away.

'Can't treat me like your shit,' she mutters at his retreating back, her voice low to ensure she won't be heard. 'I've got inheritance, and one of these days I'm gonna get what's mine and I won't buy from you fucks any more. I'll take my business elsewhere.'

She shuts her eyes, but her body is buzzing and her skin itches. No more happy for Ratty today. *Fuck.*

Yolande pictures her shiny rings, can feel their weight in the warmth of her hand. She heaves herself up off the floor, dusts herself down, and walks towards the grey light of the street.

CHAPTER THIRTY-TWO

DRIVEN BY AN even fiercer need to keep protecting her secret, and haunted by the possibility of having to raise the awful zombie marionette again, Sam studies every night for her end-of-year exams. The week before they begin, she works through into the early hours, and only wakes late when the sun is high and hot above the hills. After that, she bathes and eats her oats and bits of fruit that she's saved from the ants and beetles in the garden, and only then, as the day slips from morning to afternoon, does she hike over to Charlie's.

His evident relief at her arrival always brings a steady wave of delight that rises up inside and seems to slosh over the edges of her, spilling joy all over the floor at her feet. But on the day of her first exam, when she has to ride back home from town on the old Yamaha and only makes it to the barn after four, Charlie's expression is full of reproach, and the hunger with which he pulls off her clothes feels a little like fury. For the first time, Sam feels small in the hard brown circle of his arms.

'I'll be late all this week,' she whispers when they are done, and the sweat sticks her arms to the back of his neck. Charlie pulls away a little and looks at her then. Something softens in his eyes as if he realises, suddenly, how rough he's been. 'But I will always come here. Never think I'm not going to,' she says and he smiles and kisses her, and then kisses her again.

Keegan sits on the warm grass outside the classroom and waits for Sam to finish writing her geography paper. He presses his back against the cool plaster and looks up at the sky. It's the colour of dirty metal and makes Keegan think of a lid slamming closed on a cooking pot. He scowls, and tugs at a shred of lawn by his knee until it comes free from its brothers, then he begins the methodical process of tearing it to bits.

When Sam exits the classroom, she comes and sits down beside him in silence. Keegan glances at her to see that she's looking to the far side of the garden where cool blue agapanthus flowers are blooming on the ends of their long straight stems.

'Agatha's panties,' he says.

'What?'

'It's just what Nathan and I used to call them.' He chucks a bit of ripped-up lawn in the direction of the flowers, and immediately searches out another to keep his fingers busy.

'I remember you telling me that once.'

'I mean, what kind of a daft name is agapanthus anyway?'

'It comes from some Greek words, but I can't remember what they are now.' Jem always used to tell Sam this sort of thing, and it seems that despite all that's happened since he last said anything at all to her, the facts are still inside her somewhere, waiting to spill out.

'Right, I forgot, you're a botanical genius.'

'I know they mean love flower.'

Love flower, thinks Keegan, *what a load*.

'Speaking of flowers, how's your garden doing, by the way?' Keegan immediately wishes he hadn't asked. Thinking about that strange, dense, scented wonderland reminds him of the kiss, and the kiss reminds him of everything that is wrong with him that will never be right. A whole chunk of lawn is tugged from the ground then, scattering sand over his jeans.

After a long time, Sam answers 'OK,' in a voice that sounds strange, as if she's lost all the air in her lungs. Keegan dares another peek at her. *Does she remember too? Does she think of it and regret it, or...* No, he knows she won't kiss him again. There is something new about Sam, something changed, as if, somehow, she's moved into a separate atmosphere and is breathing different air.

'How did you find it? The geography?' Keegan tries a change of subject, but his fingers still brutalise the tuft of grass. Rip, shred, break.

'Fine,' she answers.

'Just one more year to go, hey, and then we're grown-ups.'

'Yeah.'

'Don't suppose you and your grandpa have any plans for the holidays?'

'Nah. You?'

'We're going away. To Betty's Bay with Nathan and his new girlfriend. Her folks have a place there or something.'

'That sounds...'

'Horrible?' Keegan asks, but he doesn't mean it. He can't wait for the clean tang of salt in his nostrils and the punishment of the ice cold Cape sea on his skin. Most of all, here in the still hot bowl of the valley, he craves the ocean breeze.

'I was going to say, *refreshing.*' Sam went to the sea once with Anneke and Jem. She was about nine years old. She remembers being astonished by the waves, which never took a break from their endless moving and crashing, and digging her toes into the soft, warm sand. She remembers watching the ceaseless rush of the water, and missing the green silence of their garden back home. Now Sam pictures walking along a beach with Charlie, her hand in his. 'It would be nice to get away for a bit.'

'You want to come?'

'Yeah right. You know me, I've got to look after my grandpa and… stuff.'

'Of course.' Keegan tosses a palmful of torn-up grass bits into the air, and watches them fall. 'Stuff.'

Sam steers the Yamaha into its usual spot in the barn and pulls off the motorcycle helmet. A light breeze ruffles the damp hot hair that's become glued to her forehead. She climbs off the bike in the dusty silence and readjusts the heavy pack on her back. As soon as she'd finished her algebra paper, she'd headed off to the Super Saver, and the whole ride home she's been aware of the small tub of strawberry yoghurt that's been waiting between the sensible oats and rice and cheap packets of powdered soya mince. She's more aware of rationing than ever, especially with all the petrol she's using to get to town and back for her exams. Withdrawing money using Jem's bank card at the service station always makes her edgy. There are cameras at the ATM, and she worries that someone will watch the footage and wonder why it's always the granddaughter who draws the cash these days. *What has happened to Jeremy Harding?*

Despite the fact that Sam has no idea how long this money is going to last, or whether something baffling and administrative will suddenly prevent her from being able to access it, she couldn't resist the yoghurt. She can almost taste the creamy sweetness on her tongue and feel the soft slip of it down her throat. Sam is so busy thinking about eating that little pot of goodness that she only sees the envelope when she clicks open the padlock.

The paper corner of it sticks out from between two of the wooden slats of the gate where someone has shoved it, white and clean and out of place in the dusty, petrol-scented barn. Sam pulls the envelope free with shaking fingers. *Someone was here.* She looks behind her, scans the road and the scrub for signs that they might still be somewhere close. Could Yolande be hiding behind one of those bushes, watching her? Sam is sure she can smell something familiar on the air, a sick, chemical stench. Her stomach swoops.

Clutching the envelope, she darts in through the gate and slams it behind her, sliding the bolt home and snapping on the padlock before she allows herself another breath.

The garden is a wall of growth pressing in. The flagstones of the path have shrunk in the onslaught of the tangled weeds which are overpowering the clover. Sam takes a breath. The chemical smell is gone, or maybe it's just lost beneath the rich scent of roses, lavender, herbs and star jasmine which are now tinged with the smell of rot from the fallen fruit and the dying plants that she's abandoned to the snails, slugs and caterpillars. Sam makes a run for it, crashing through the greenery towards the house.

In the untidy kitchen, with the garden at her back, surrounded by the reassuring hum of the fridge that means she wasn't too late with the electricity payment, Sam lets the pack slide from her shoulders to the floor as she inspects the envelope. Now that she's looking closer, there's no way it could be from Yolande: it's too clean, white and perfect. She turns it over. The rounded cursive on the front is unmistakably Sussie's, and seeing the words *Jem and Sam* written there together as if nothing has changed, weakens her legs so suddenly that she has to reach for a chair and sink into it.

Jem and Sam. Jem and Sam.

Jem.

Her eyelids prickle and sting and the white oblong blurs in her hands. She makes the first, cautious tear in the envelope. It's a greetings card. Sam pulls it out and lays it on the table. It's thick and glossy with a solemn painting of the three wise men on it, following their star. Before Anneke died, Sussie sent a Christmas card each year, but since the *desecration*, nothing. Why now? What's changed?

Inside it is a short message written in Afrikaans: *Dear Jem and Sam, may you both be blessed this Christmas. Sussie.*

Sam remembers the way her great-aunt's eyes had filled with tears when they encountered each other at Anneke's grave months ago. Her shocked whisper: *My God. You look just like her.* Is Sussie hoping for some kind of reconciliation?

'Jesus,' Sam says out loud, shoving the card away from herself as if it's contaminated. She imagines Sussie, in full family mode, descending on her in a fever of well-intentioned Christmas spirit. 'That's all I need.'

Is one padlock enough?

CHAPTER THIRTY-THREE

WHEN SAM MAKES the hot journey up and over the hill after her final exam, she's stunned to find that the barn is closed up, and there's no sign of Charlie. A high whine of panic builds in her ears as she creeps around the far side of the building and looks through the windows to see that the workshop is dark and silent. In the yard at the far side, where she knows Charlie parks his van, she finds nothing but tyre ruts and a small shred of bubble wrap caught on the branch of a tree.

Sam clutches the plastic in sweating fingers and stares up the track that he must take every day when he goes home to whatever he goes home to. The dirt road curves away into an orchard of pruned plum trees planted in even rows. Sam tucks the bubble wrap into the pocket of her shorts and moves towards the trees. They smell of sun on sugar, and unlike the ones in the garden back home, these have been tended and sprayed, and the fruit she finds is firm and perfect. She recognises Santa Rosas. They'll be harvested soon then, next week, most likely.

She eats a red-skinned plum. It's not ripe, but warm and sweet just beneath the skin. No worms. She picks another and bites into it as she makes her way deeper into the orchard, following the track. *Where's Charlie?* She licks the tart juice from her fingers. Her heart is going at a gallop, and her legs feel wobbly. *Is he coming back?*

When the trees end and the farm opens up before her with its blocks of green lucerne, rows and rows of vineyards and its buildings in the distance, very white in the late sun, Sam stops. She's breathing hard. The fragrant sweetness from the plums has gone from her tongue, leaving only the sourness behind.

Keeping in the shadows of the trees, Sam scans the farm for any sign of Charlie. She spots two horses and riders heading out of the far paddock, and remembers, with a rush of guilt, how decrepit Sam-the-horse's grave marker is looking back at the garden. She doesn't want to think about that place. She doesn't want to go back. *Perhaps I can stay here?* The thought sidles into her head and lingers, even though she knows it's ridiculous. What would she do for food? Swan up to the distant white house with its pristine gable and raid the kitchen? Eat unripe plums until she's sick? Her uneasy guts give a little growl in protest at the idea.

But Sam feels unravelled and lost without her fix of Charlie, and the longer she waits beneath the trees, the less possible leaving becomes. She stands, motionless. A bee buzzes past her ear, lands with a tickle, and then takes off again.

Eventually she forces herself to move. Her legs feel strange and stiff as she makes her way back through the orchard, as if they've got hinges that need oiling. When she arrives back at the barn and tests the handle on its small back door, it opens easily beneath her hand, and she almost falls into the dark, woody silence. She blinks as her eyes adjust, and then closes the door behind her. Without Charlie in here, the mood of the place is different, solemn, as if, like her, the wood is biding its time until he returns. She notices that there are more bits of bubble wrap lying around, and it soon becomes clear that almost half of his finished items are gone.

Sam has never thought of Charlie's pieces being wanted

somewhere else, but of course they must be. Why else would he be working so hard to make them in the first place? He must've taken some to be sold. That means he's coming back. He's not gone for good. She walks between the items that remain. They're familiar, like old friends. She's watched most of them come into being from chunks of raw tree. She touches each one as she moves through the barn, then walks back and counts them again, searching. *It's gone.* The little dimpled stool with the curving legs has been wrapped up and taken off and sold to someone else.

I thought he made it just for me.

Sam's first sob is a brutal hammer smack on the inside of her chest bone. The force of it pushes her to the sawdust-coated floor. She drops her head into her hands, still sticky from sour plums, and weeps.

CHAPTER THIRTY-FOUR

CHARLIE CALLS SOON after Delia's bedtime story.

'Hang on,' Liezette whispers into her phone, and leaves the darkened bedroom as quietly as she can. 'Charlie?'

'Babe!' Charlie's voice is overly loud, punching into her eardrum. She winces, although she knows it's impossible for Delia to hear it, and moves further away from her daughter's bedroom.

'How are you? How did it go?' she asks. The line gives a hiss and a crackle and when the reception clears, she hears that Charlie is laughing. He sounds a little drunk.

'It went like a bomb, Liez.'

Liezette adjusts her grip on the phone. Her fingers are sweating. 'So? Did they love the stuff, Charlie?'

'They sure bloody did!'

'Really?'

'You better believe it. I thought that one guy, what's-his-name... Craig. I thought he was actually going to burst into tears.'

'Oh my God. That's great, babe.'

'Get this, Liez: they want to do an exhibition, launch the Water-Wood Collection like it's a goddam work of art.'

'It *is*, Charlie. It deserves that.' Liezette is grinning, her head feels light and swimmy. It's really happening, all the things she's been dreaming about for them. 'I'm so proud.' And then: 'Are you staying the night?'

'Yeah, sorry. They insisted on taking me out and I've had a few beers. And anyway, it's too late to set off now.'

'No, of course.'

'I'm going to have to make another trip in the next few days to deliver the rest of the stuff that I couldn't fit in your dad's van.'

'Oh really?'

'Yeah, they think there's still time to do this before Christmas. Take advantage of the holiday-shopping madness.'

'Awesome, babe.'

'I know, hey?' He sounds young, like a schoolboy winning a longed-for prize. She laughs and he joins in, and neither of them seems able to stop for a long time. The cell phone is warm in Liezette's hand.

Charlie drives back from Cape Town early the next morning, and by nine o'clock, he's showered and has spooned cereal into his mouth while Delia read him a story: turning the pages of her mother's magazine and making up nonsense rhymes to go with the bruised-eyed skeletal fashion models that sulk across the glossy pages. He's returned the van keys to le Roux and, at last, is in his old van and driving through the orchard towards the barn. He taps his fingers on the steering wheel, impatient to get back to the wood and finish up those final touches. Last night, in his beer-soaked sleep in Craig's guest bedroom, Charlie had dreamt that the barn was flooded, and that his precious water-wood babies were swelling and warping in a sludge of brackish water. He'd woken at dawn, breathless with longing to get back. Now he sprints from the van to the barn.

There they are, waiting for him in the shadowy gloom of the closed-up workshop, their curves aching to be stroked. No flood, no fire, all present and correct. Charlie touches each piece before throwing open the wide double doors. When he does so, he stops, and draws in a sharp breath of surprise.

The water-eyed girl is sitting in her gift-garden, in the midst of her freshly watered plantings. Her hair is so white in the glare of the late morning sun that Charlie has to blink and squint, but when her eyes meet his, they're cool as shade. Never shifting her gaze, she stands and walks towards him, pulling off her clothes with quick tugs, so that by the time she's up close, she is utterly bare but for her hair, which is loose and moves across her back and shoulders like a cape woven from living white snakes.

'Woah,' he whispers as she crashes into his body and pulls him closer. 'No waiting this time, hey?' Her fingers fight the fastenings of his belt and jeans. 'I guess you missed me.'

In reply, she wrenches his T-shirt up and off, and when he blinks in the wake of the scrape of fabric over his face, her eyes, with their strange unreadable expression, are still staring into his. She hangs onto the back of his neck and uses her weight to draw him to the floor before climbing on top of him. Charlie, on his back on the ground with the girl above him and sawdust sticking to his skin, surprises himself by wishing she would say something. There is too much feeling in her silence, and a word or two would lessen the intensity that radiates off her boiling skin. But there's no time for words, her mouth is already on his, devouring.

Later, when Charlie is, at last, back with the timber and the tools in his hands, and she is dressed and sitting in the shadow by the wall, the water-eyed girl finally does speak. The sound of her voice is so strange, so unexpected, that the small hand-saw Charlie is using slips from his grip and clatters to the floor.

'I was here, yesterday,' she says. 'Without you. I waited.'

Charlie goes cold and a rash of goosebumps rises up on his skin.

'Oh?'

Yesterday. He remembers holding his cell phone, about to call Liezette and ask her to drive down to the barn and take some photos of the pieces he'd left behind and email them back to him for the gallery guy to look at. He remembers getting distracted by the conversation, and never making the call. If he had. If she had come here. If this girl had been…

Fuck.

He picks up the saw and tries to focus on the join he's working on, but his head is whirling and the sudden tightness in his chest is making it impossible to breathe.

'I figured you were making a delivery.' That voice again. It makes her sound so young. *Jesus, how young* is *she?*

'You were right. I was in Cape Town. Didn't I mention I was going to go?'

'No.'

He readjusts his grip on the worn handle of the saw. His fingers are sweating. He doesn't have a clue how to navigate this new, strange space with the water-eyed girl: she is talking to him. Like a girlfriend, or something. A wife. He swallows.

'Sorry,' he says. That's usually a good start.

Silence. From outside somewhere, softened by distance, comes the high wild sound of a horse's whinny.

'Well, I'd better let you know that I have to go again in a few days. They want the rest of this stuff.' Charlie gives a nervous laugh. 'They want to have an exhibition.'

'When?'

'Soon, before Christmas. To capitalise on the holiday shoppers, you know?' *Does she?* Charlie has no idea what she knows. He imagines her being born, new, each morning as the sun touches the tops of the hills, rising out of a stream like a nymph. But there's nothing nymph-like about her questions:

'When are you going again?'

'Hey?'

'To Cape Town. When?'

'Oh, right. In two days' time.' Charlie places the saw to the wood and then pauses, alert to the weight of the silence. 'I'll be packing up this lot on Friday morning and then heading off.'

Sam tightens her arms around her knees, holding herself in place. He's leaving again. And she'll be stuck here. Alone in the garden with the roses and the silence. The idea is sickening. Unbearable.

It is still early when Sam gets back to her side of the hill. As she walks past the sun-drenched rose bed, she notices that the blooms are vast and fleshy and vibrant with colour. She imagines the roots of the plants twisting down and nuzzling in between the cells of her grandfather's flesh to feed on his corpse.

Fuck you, she wants to scream. *How dare you devour him and flaunt yourselves at me? Damn you with your flouncy petals and your fat, greedy buds.* She stands at the edge of the flower bed, shaking, and then marches with determination to the tool shed where she keeps the secateurs. With vicious, ragged snips, she decapitates each lovely, fragrant rose. She stamps through the clover and scratches herself on thorns to get to the hard-to-reach blooms. When the flowers are all gone, it's still not enough. She slices off the buds too, even the tiny, whiskery green ones.

Sam steps back, sweaty and tear-streaked, suddenly appalled at what she's done. The fallen flowers blink their brilliance at her from their spots on the ground. Still beautiful. Still scented. Sam drops to her knees and starts to gather each one, crawling through the dirt to get to them, running inside to fetch a bag to put them in when they start to spill from her arms.

When they are all collected, she opens the bag and peers in. The petals quiver up at her, blood and peach and sun and snow and blushing pink. Each perfect, frilled oval carries something of her grandfather's life inside its sap. She thinks of his strong, wide hands and his blue eyes filled with kindness and his metal-coloured hair. How could she have done this?

I didn't mean it. I'm sorry. But the roses cannot be glued back.

There is only one thing that Sam can think of to do with them.

Before she gets to the graveyard, Sam stops at the top of the rise and scans the road for a puff of dust that could mean Sussie's SUV is on its way. The lucerne fields look like blocks of emerald, and the grapevine rows flaunt their exuberant leaves, but the only companions in sight are a pair of small brown birds that flutter up and then wait in the long grass for her to move on so that they can resume their pecking on the road.

She rides the motorbike down to the graveyard and parks it by the fence. The roses here are blooming too, an echo of their parent plants across the valley. She takes a trowel and the bag of flower heads from her knapsack, and walks to Anneke's graveside. Sam drops to a crouch, and proceeds to bury each and every cut flower into the soil amongst the plants around her grandmother's grave.

Her grandpa and her ouma together. Sam thinks of all those love letters in their tin at home. She clenches her fists into the mud. Charlie is leaving her again. Why can't she have the kind of love that Jem and Anneke had?

Why is he going without me?

She brushes the soil from her fingers, collects the empty packet, and scrunches it into a ball.

Maybe he doesn't have to.

Sam starts to formulate a plan.

Two days.

She'll be ready.

CHAPTER THIRTY-FIVE

CHARLIE HAS BEEN driving for close on an hour, and is approaching the vast rocky backs of the Du Toitskloof mountains when he hears the noise. At first, he thinks there's something wrong with the engine, but the knocking seems to be coming from the back of the van. *It can't be.* He packed so carefully, wedging the pieces against one another and jamming rolled up bits of bubble wrap in the gaps to prevent slipping and rattling and possible damage. He glances at his rear-view mirror, adjusting it so that he can see the little window behind the back seats, a pane of glass between the back of the cab and the cargo area of the van. At first, he can see nothing but a dark block reflecting the inside of the cabin, but then suddenly, a pale flash of movement. His guts drop in fright. He focuses on the road ahead for a moment to steady his nerves before daring another look.

Jesus!

A face appears in the glass for an instant, and then is gone again. Charlie's heart halts and then gallops. He looks again. Yes, a face, and a set of slender knuckles rap-rapping on the glass. *It's her!* It's the girl from the hill with the eyes like water. What in the name of all that is holy is she doing back there in amongst the furniture?

Charlie pulls over onto the side of the road. He switches

off the engine and waits for his heart rate to slow to something approaching manageable. He climbs out onto the tar, taking a moment to steady himself on his shaking legs before walking to the back of the vehicle, bracing himself against the wind of the highway traffic rushing past and the hot dry breath of the air that pours down the sloped rocky backs of the mountains ahead.

He opens the back of the van.

'Hello?' He is dry-mouthed, and it comes out as a whisper. A pause, a rustle of movement, and then a hand appears around the back of a bubble-wrapped chair. A hiking boot pokes out, testing for a solid spot, and then the pale leg, as, a bit at a time, the girl twists and clambers her way out from the barricade of the Water-Wood Collection. 'Watch it,' he cautions when it looks like she's going to ding her head into the edge of a shelf.

After the close darkness of the van, the scrub-covered ground seems to race away towards the edges of the distant horizon with dizzying speed. Sam grips the hot painted metal of the van door and waits for the vertigo to pass. She can't look at Charlie yet. She shades her eyes and stares back down the ribbon of highway in the direction that they've come. It's the first time since before Anneke died that she's been so far from home. She feels floating, free, untethered. She turns to Charlie with a laugh of delight in her throat, but gulps it back down when she sees the look on his face.

'What the hell are you doing?' he demands. She blinks at him, wordless. Charlie crosses his arms across his T-shirt. She can see patches of sweat bruising the fabric a darker blue beneath his armpits. *I thought he'd be pleased.* The only words she can think of to say are *Don't leave me here*, but she holds them in.

To Charlie, in the brittle highway sunlight, suddenly materialising from out of the back of le Roux's van, the girl seems even less real than she ever has before. He resists the urge to prod her shoulder to prove that she isn't a figment of his imagination. 'Hey?' he asks, his voice softer this time. 'Why did you hide in there?'

Sam can't understand why he is asking. Surely it's obvious? He was leaving her alone again and she wanted him not to. She wraps her arms over Anneke's old cotton blouse, the one with the tiny lilac flowers printed on it, and looks down at her feet.

'Come on, then.' Charlie marches to the passenger door and swings it open. 'I guess you'd better sit up in the front with me.'

From her seat beside Charlie in the front of the van, Sam watches the mountains draw closer. As they drive deeper into the valley, the stern flanks of scored rock rear up like waves of earth on either side of the road. Looking up at them leaves her breathless. Back home, the space between the mountains is wide and undulating, and the peaks themselves are soft, bluish and distant, but these mountains are front-and-centre, in your face, a challenge.

She's leaning against the passenger window, gazing up, and so is not prepared for the sudden swallowing dark as the vehicle hurtles into the mouth of the Huguenot tunnel. Sam gasps in surprise, and then smiles, mesmerised by the ribbons of ceiling lights curving away ahead.

Although he knows it's absurd, Charlie has been half expecting the girl to vanish the moment they enter the tunnel, perhaps unable to leave the landscape that conjured her into being, like one of those hitch-hiking highway ghosts he's heard of in suburban myths. But she doesn't dissolve, she's solid and breathing beside him as they plunge deeper into the black heart of the mountain. *It's time to stop kidding yourself, mate. The girl is real.*

And alive, and very young.

Away from the barn and the smell of sawn timber, Charlie finds her new human-ness alarming, and he's plagued by the questions he knows he should've asked months ago. Who is she? Who has she left behind to be with him out here on the road to Cape Town? *Parents? Is there going to be a big stink when someone discovers she is missing?*

'Hey,' he says, breaking the silence.

'Yes?' She turns to Charlie, her eyes luminous green in the electric yellow of the tunnel lights.

'Is this OK, your coming with? You're not going to... get into trouble?'

'No.' She smiles and shakes her head. 'Everything is fine.'

'Right.' He swallows, adjusts his grip on the steering wheel. 'Good.' All the other unasked questions bank up at the base of his throat, solidifying into an unmanageable lump.

Sam reaches across and touches his denim-covered thigh. She can feel the vehicle's engine thrumming through his muscle and into her hand. Here in the mountain, with the garden and the rose bed so far behind her, she starts to believe that she can be new. She can be more than she's ever been. *Maybe Charlie will love me like Grandpa loved Ouma. Maybe he will ask me to marry him one day.* It's a luscious, ludicrous thought and she almost laughs out loud at the loveliness of it. *I can live with him on the other side of the hill and none of that old stuff will matter any more.* She moves her hand over his leg and on to the zipper of his jeans and draws it open and, with the burning heat of her fingers, feels as if she is melting him, moulding him, making him hers.

Sam is not prepared for the claustrophobic busyness of the City Bowl with its stinking strings of traffic and knots of people waiting to cross the road at each intersection. She shrinks back from the car window at the onslaught of Cape Town, open-mouthed, trying to take everything in: the docks, with their massive stacks of shipping containers and swinging, metal-necked cranes, the buildings that jostle for space and soak the narrow streets in shadow, and the people. So many faces and eyes and arms and moving mouths. The frantic-seeming churn of humanity and progress and commerce clings to the hem of the famous flat-topped mountain and pulses and breathes beneath its stony gaze.

'I'm going to drop you off somewhere so you can look around and chill. I'll give you some money to go and get lunch.' Charlie's voice is casual, but she can see his knuckles are white on the steering wheel. *Drop me off?* The words make Sam think of swaying from the end of one of those giant metal hooks on the tip of a crane, waiting to fall into the hold of a ship.

'Can't I stay with you?'

'Look, I've got business to do, lots of boring stuff to discuss with all sorts of people.' Charlie works at keeping his voice level with reason, like when he's trying to get Delia to do something she doesn't want to. 'It's not... possible.'

Charlie is going to have to double back to get to De Waterkant, but better that than the girl being spotted by anyone from the gallery or the shop. He drives her all the way up Kloof Street to where the cafés and bars are clustered. The mountain looms above them, watchful.

'Here?' Sam whispers in horror as he pulls over and takes two blue hundred-rand notes out of his wallet. Charlie waves them in front of her face to get her attention, and when she turns to him with huge, frightened eyes, he forces a smile. He presses the bills into her limp hand and folds her fingers over.

'You can get a drink, something to eat, whatever.' Charlie's tone is carefully casual as he points to a vibey café where a dreadlocked waiter in too-tight pants squeezes between the tables set out on the pavement. 'Sit there and chill and wait for me. I'll collect you when I'm done.'

Sam battles with the catch on the passenger door. She glances back at Charlie, imploring him to change his mind, but he's watching the traffic, looking for a gap.

'Promise you'll come back?'

'Of course!' He turns to her then, gives her a reassuring smile and a brief touch on the back of her wrist. 'I won't be long. Just enjoy yourself.'

'Can't I just wait in the van?'

'Please, babe, I need to get a move on. We're holding up the works.'

Sam climbs out onto the kerb. The tar at her feet is greasy and emits a sour sort of smell in the sunlight. Everything smells. Her nostrils flare at the city cocktail of frying food and traffic fumes and garbage.

'See you soon,' she says in a small voice, and the moment she closes the door, Charlie revs and pulls off and away, joining the other cars to snake up the hill.

She stands on boneless legs and watches him go, clutching the money in a quivering fist.

PART FOUR
THE SPIDER IN THE JAR

CHAPTER THIRTY-SIX

YOLANDE DRAGS THE back of her arm across her nose and wipes the resulting wetness off on her jeans. She's stoked about these jeans. She found them in a bedroom in a crappy little hole that she snuck into in Belville last week, and unlike most she scrounges, which are far too roomy, these fit nice and snug. Probably belonged to some kid. She'd taken a cell phone too, and a not-even-close-to-being-gold necklace that was hanging over the spotted mirror. The cell phone was an old Nokia. Barely worth selling, but still. *A few rands is a few rands and – oh, that's more like it!*

From her spot beside the dustbins, just up from the café, Yolande can see the telltale blue of a couple of hundreds being passed from hand to hand through the front windscreen of the big, dusty van that's just pulled up at the kerb. The van's licence plates tell her it's from a farm out east, just like she is. Yolande wants nothing to do with anything from the valley, but...

But those hundreds.

Who's holding them now? Just a scared slip of a girl with country bumpkin clothes and dirt on her clumpy boots. Easy-peasy. Yolande grins, even though she can see the girl is gripping those buggers tight. She lights a fresh cigarette and waits to see what the bumpkin will do. Yolande takes a small step closer to get a better look, and as she does so, something cold and terrible slips down her spine and freezes her limbs and threatens to squeeze her guts out, to make her shit herself, right here on the street. In her 'new' jeans.

It's the hair. The hair the hair.

No one else in the world has hair that colour, that silver.

The hair.

Long, braided, fat like an albino snake hanging down the centre of the girl's back.

Mama.

The word slams into Yolande's centre, right into the bits that she thought had all hardened up and dried out. *My mama.*

But her mama is dead. Remember? Thanks to the message she got years ago from her old busybody bitch of an aunt, she saw the hole they put her in with her own eyes. She'd hidden herself at a distance and watched them bury her. Yolande's blanked a lot over the years, but my God she remembers that. She even saw her father, tall in a dark suit, standing beside a child. She remembers how it felt to suddenly know that Anneke, the old cow who saw fit to push her out into this horror-show of a world and then spend the next sixteen years retreating from her, was no longer. She remembers laughing. She remembers that she was not really laughing. She remembers the hollowness that now hurts, all over again. Maybe they lied to her? Maybe she's not dead after all?

But no. It cannot be her mama.

Of course not. She's too young, far too young. Barely a woman even.

But.

Yolande bites her lip, tasting bitter chemical snot and ash, and watches the girl as she takes her first cautious step towards the café. A corner of a blue hundred pokes out from between her fingers, but Yolande is no longer interested in the cash. All she can see is the very living likeness of her dead mother walking to a table and sitting down. Facing her. With that face. The same.

The hair.

Not possible. Not not possible. *What have I taken today? What could it be that's making Yolande hallucinate, making her see ghosts from her past?* The shit she smokes is supposed to do the opposite, for fuck-sakes. It's supposed to send the ghosts scuttling back to their wide valley with its fruit trees and bare blue hills.

Yolande steps back to the safety of the dustbin, sliding into the shadow to watch without being seen. She does her little tricks, the ones she uses to tell real from not-real in the too-bright, slidey stupor of a high. She takes a big drag of her cigarette, holds it in, lets it go. A special pinch here. More this toe, move that finger. Close the eyes, open them. Look down, look up.

She's still there. The girl. The hair.

If it isn't Anneke, if it isn't her mother, which it can't be, because she's dead, and because this *thing* is too fresh and new and babyish, then who is it? Why is she wearing Anneke's face, her hair? *My God, her fucking blouse. I remember that blouse. I hated that blouse.*

The child at the funeral, standing beside Jem, holding his hand like a daughter.

Yolande remembers now. The child's hair had been pulled tight into two, neat braids with black ribbons on the ends. White silk against black velvet.

Yolande slides down against the wall and onto the pavement. Her unpadded bum bones jar against the asphalt.

Her head is splitting, her temples burning with white fire. Something nags and scratches and screams inside her.

There's something she's supposed to remember about the child, the girl a few metres away, but she knows she cannot.

Who?

Who is the girl with the hair?

CHAPTER THIRTY-SEVEN

AS CHARLIE PROMISED, he is not gone long, an hour forty-five at most, and when he returns to Kloof Street and takes the seat opposite Sam on the pavement café and reaches out to take her hand in his, she comes back to life. Her skin pinks and glows, and after sitting rigid, like a frozen doll, she softens into the back of the chair at last.

'What have you eaten?' Charlie asks and when she shakes her head *nothing*, he calls the waiter over to order toasted sandwiches for the both of them.

After the barrage of fawning from the gallery owner and the interior designers and all the other folks in their immaculate outfits and expensive haircuts, all of them stroking his Water-Wood Collection, sighing over each curve, Charlie feels vast and powerful inside his ragged jeans and faded T-shirt. Knowing the part she played in those pieces, he feels particularly tender towards the girl with the water-blue eyes. He knows, now, that he needs to take care of her, keep her sweet, keep her at his side when they get back to the workshop so that beneath her gaze he can make more of the stuff they want, more of the stuff that makes him feel worthy and alive and part of the world. For some reason, she is the key. He reaches across the small table to brush a wisp of hair from her face and she leans in to his touch like a cat.

'Forgive me for leaving you here when you didn't want me to. I'm sorry.'

'It's OK. You came back.'

'They loved the pieces, by the way.'

'Are you going to make more?'

'Sure hope so.'

'Then we'd better get back.' She smiles, and it makes her look older, somehow.

'Lunch first. I'm starving.'

'Me too.'

'Why didn't you order something while I was gone?'

Sam wraps her fingers around her empty glass. The hell of the past two hours has dissipated in Charlie's protective presence. With him right there, across the table, with that brown soft piece of hair falling over his eyes, it's as if she was never terrified and confused and bereft at all. It's like a dream she's forgetting already.

'I had a Coke,' she says, and Charlie smiles.

'It's a start, I guess.'

'In Cape Town, you say?'

'I've told you already, Dad. Yes. He's delivering the final stuff for that exhibition.'

'Right.'

'You know what? I'm really sick of you constantly implying that my husband is a loser.'

'Implying?'

'Tertius.' Antoinette interjects in a placating tone. She ladles a heaped spoonful of mashed sweet potato onto her husband's plate as if doing so will slow his anger with stodge. 'Come now. Not at the dinner table.'

'*She's* the one you need to tell that to.' Le Roux points a fork at his daughter. 'She's spoiling for a fight. You know how she gets.'

Liezette waves away her mother's freshly refilled potato spoon. Her own plate is a spare selection of green vegetables and two lamb cutlets. No carbs are allowed anywhere near it.

'I'm right here, you know, Dad. You don't have to refer to me in the third person. I'm not twelve any more.'

'Nope? Well you've got no more sense now than you had when you were, my girl.'

'He's cross with me, Ma.' Liezette pouts at her mother like she did when she was little, hoping to get an ally. Delia, fingers deep in her own sweet potato portion, watches with unblinking eyes.

'You will be too, Antoinette, when you hear what she had to say to me this evening when I mentioned our little idea.'

'Oh,' Antoinette says in a soft voice. 'You had the talk.'

'We had "the talk".' Le Roux bites and chews, and while he does, everyone waits. Delia swirls her fingers in the orange goo, Liezette looks down at her unexciting plate, and Antoinette, who seems unable to relinquish her serving spoon, doles out another dollop of stuff onto her own.

'And?' Antoinette asks at last.

'And our dear daughter seems to think that our idea of having her and Charlie take over the running of the farm when we retire is ridiculous.'

'Liezie?' Antoinette pleads.

'Well it is. Come on, Daddy, how many times do I have to tell you that Charlie's *got* a career. He's not just waiting around for me to inherit the farm. He's making huge waves in the design and interior decorating industry already.'

'His work is very lovely,' Antoinette says to no one in particular.

'You've got it all planned out, don't you, Liezette?' le Roux growls at his daughter. 'Your precious Charlie is going to be rich and famous, he's going to take you places, isn't that it?'

'Who says it won't happen? What the hell do you know about life outside this backwater valley, Dad? There's stuff happening out there. Art. Fashion, design. These things might not be "from the land" but they matter, and Charlie is a part of that. You're just too out of touch to see it.'

'And you? How do you fit into all of this, Liezette? Who says there'll still be a place for you when the man is big and famous and he can have his pick of any bit of skirt he wants?'

'Thanks, Dad. That's lovely.'

'No, listen to me, my girl. It's not all about Charlie this and Charlie that... what about you? I want to leave the farm to YOU.'

Liezette looks at her father with tear-varnished eyes.

'But I don't want it, Daddy. I want the future that *he's* going to give me.'

'Well then.' Le Roux takes a sip of his wine. The base of the glass shudders against the tabletop when he places it back down again. 'I hope you're not too disappointed.'

'With what?'

'When the people who think he's such hot stuff today suddenly swing their favour to the next guy and forget all about Charlie. Fashion is fickle, that much I do know about it. You need something solid. Earth and fruit have been here for centuries, the co-op will always need grapes. This place could give you a real future.'

'I already have a future.' Liezette's voice wobbles. 'If all you can trot out is a tired old cliché, then...' She cuts a piece of meat, lifts it to her mouth, puts her fork back down again.

'Then what?' Delia asks. They all turn to look at the child, who took the opportunity, while everyone was arguing, to cover her face and hair in a thick coating of mashed sweet potato.

'Good Lord, look at you.' Liezette bursts into tears, jumps up from the table and collects her sticky child in her arms. 'We need to get you cleaned up.'

'Mama, why are you crying?' Delia asks as she's whisked from the room.

The dining room is quiet. Le Roux takes another sip of his wine. Long minutes pass.

'But what about our plans to move to Hermanus one day?' Antoinette asks at last.

CHAPTER THIRTY-EIGHT

SAM WAKES WHEN the sun is already high and the heat has burrowed its way into all the hidden corners and hollows of the valley. She lies on her back, sweat-damp covers thrown off, and stares at the large, soft-bodied rain spider that's squatting in the corner by the ceiling.

For the first time in years, Sam doesn't bother to apologise to the rain spider for the 'spider-jar' incident from when she was little. She just rolls over in bed and luxuriates in the memory of yesterday, and how she felt, sitting there and having lunch with Charlie in Cape Town: just like a normal woman, out with her boyfriend.

Boyfriend. Can I use that word yet? How do you know when it's time? She runs through what she can remember of Jem's love letters to Anneke, hunting for clues, but there's nothing helpful there. She thinks of the message Charlie spelled out in wood for her, months ago. When is he going to write another one to tell her that he's in love with her? He must be, or else he wouldn't have held her hand over the table, in public. Isn't that how it's supposed to go?

Sam and Charlie had spent the long drive back to the valley in companionable, air-conditioned silence. It was late when they finally got to the barn, and in the dark beside the plum trees, Charlie had ruffled her hair and given her a quick pat on the bottom to send her on her way. There was no chance for her to voice the question she'd been planning to ask him: *Can I stay with you?*

So here she is, again. On the wrong side of the hill. Alone.

Except for the spider.

Sam gets up and pulls off her nightshirt, dropping it on the floor on the way to the bathroom. What would she sleep in if she were sharing a bed with Charlie? Not that old thing, surely? It was once a vest belonging to Jem, and has coffee stains on the hem.

I guess, she thinks as she turns the taps to start her bath, *I could just wear nothing*. She places her hands on the warm flat of her belly and then runs them up her ribs and then down again.

With the exams now past and passed, and no more school assignments till next year, Sam has nothing to prepare for but the walk up and over the hill. Today, she's packed a small backpack. It's the one she usually uses for carrying supplies from the shop along with her schoolbooks and pencils, but there's none of that inside it now. Sam has packed a few clothes and some toiletries, and her precious old hunting knife that once belonged to Anneke's father. She slides the bag's straps over her shoulders and descends the steps from the stoop to the garden, buoyed up by the presence of her toothbrush nestling in amongst a few bunched-up clothes inside it. The press of the canvas against her back makes her think of the shell of a tortoise. She's protected by that little toothbrush and what it signifies. Strong. She marches past the rose bed without even needing to speed into a run.

The roses are already sending out new buds, despite their

recent massacre. *I should water them.* It's an automatic thought, a throwback to the 'old Sam'. With a slap of wet braid against the bag, she tosses her head to dismiss it, and walks on.

'Hello?'

Charlie looks up to see the water-eyed girl stride into the workshop, smiling and radiant. He smiles back, although he's not entirely comfortable with her announcing herself. She used to just slide in like a shadow. Also, she's brought a bag with her today. *What's that about?* He watches as she places it on the floor and then sits down beside it.

All morning he's been at a loss without the Water-Wood Collection, which, at this very moment, is being artfully arranged inside the blank white space of the gallery by a bunch of trendies. But now, as soon as the girl's strange full-moon eyes come to rest on him, he can feel the edges of his new piece rising up inside him, pushing on the insides of his veins and stretching his skin.

It's going to be a chair. There's something both spare and complex about a chair, something satisfying. He crouches down beside a pile of raw timber, touches one plank, and then another. He can feel Sam's gaze on the side of his face, making his skin feel hot and cool at the same time. *How does she do it?* The question is forgotten almost as soon as it comes, because suddenly, Charlie *knows* this new chair. It's going to be hard-edged and linear with sharp corners and geometric dovetail joints so tight that the whole piece will look ironed. It will need an upholstered seat, and will be hewn from something dense and dark. Kiaat? His fingertips dance over the grain of a wide piece of timber the colour of black tea that's been brewed too long. Teak.

Liezette unhooks Rolo's bridle from its spot in the tackroom and, ignoring the offers of assistance from the hovering stable hand, strides out into the paddock. The leather straps swing from her hand, and the metal parts jingle with false cheer. It's late for a ride, already too hot, but Liezette is determined to have one anyway.

'Rolo,' she calls, 'here boy!' The brown horse looks up from the snack he's enjoying alongside the other horses in the cool shade beneath the karee tree, but doesn't move. Liezette shades her eyes against the glare, almost slapping herself in the face with the bridle. She calls as sweetly as her black mood will allow: 'Come on, big boy, let's go for a ride. Won't that be nice?'

In response, Rolo shakes a fly from his nose and lowers his vast head to snick off another bit of grass. Liezette can already feel rivulets of sweat streaming down her back beneath her shirt. A ride out now would be lunacy. It would be hell. She squares her shoulders and sets off across the bright field towards the horses.

'ROLO!' she demands when the animal shies away from her attempts to slip the bridle over his head. 'For heaven's sake.' The horse steps away and stares at her. His always-huge eyes seem even larger and his ears flick back in alarm. She tries again, and although Rolo is happy to have her stroke between his ears and run her hand down his bony muzzle, as soon as the bridle comes near, he shakes her off.

The sun pounds down onto Liezette's skull. It feels as if her brain is melting from the combined onslaught of the heat and the unreasonable rage that's been boiling up inside her since her father proposed his 'retirement plan' to her yesterday. She was hoping to talk to Charlie about it when he got home from

Cape Town last night, but he was monosyllabic with tiredness and had pushed her aside with a 'not now, Liez'. This morning, he'd been up and out of the house by the time she'd gotten Delia up, and Liezette's been churning ever since. A ride, even a hellish ride through the noon furnace, is what she needs. It's what she wants. Liezette always gets what she wants.

Apparently, Rolo is unaware of this.

'Come on, you goddam horse,' she yells when he trots beyond her reach for a fifth time. He swishes his tail in response. The other horses have backed away from her, too, ears back, unnerved by the shouting. Liezette can feel the frustration burning at the back of her throat, threatening tears. She glares at Rolo, who puts his head down and nibbles at another bit of turf. *My father just bought me this stupid horse to control me, didn't he?* Liezette thinks. *To buy me off so I'd do what he wants me to. As if I'm still a child.* She clutches the leather very tight, and then opens her fingers to let the bridle fall onto the dry grass. *Screw that. I'm tired of it always being about what everyone else wants.* She turns and walks back to the stable, boiling beneath her skin. *What about me?*

'Aren't you riding today, missus?'

'I don't know, genius,' she barks at the startled stable hand. 'What does it bloody look like?' The young man gulps and shrugs, unsure of what's expected of him. 'Oh, for heaven's sake, just get out there and fetch the bloody tack, please.'

'Yes, missus.'

CHAPTER THIRTY-NINE

FROM HIGH UP on the front bench of the delivery truck that she flagged down earlier, Yolande approaches her hometown as if she's in a glass tunnel that's been fogged up around the edges. The only clear spot in her vision is a disc of grey road directly in front of the vehicle. All the rest: the fynbos, the dry earth, the vineyards, the fruit trees in full leaf and the far blue mountains, are a blurry, indistinct madness on the periphery.

'I don't know why they bothered to tar this road,' she says. 'I mean, as if anyone would want to get to this dump any faster!' Yolande opens the window a slice so that she can ash her cigarette out into the valley.

The driver who picked her up and then, in a half-hearted fashion, felt her up, glances across at Yolande as if she's just sprouted horns.

'You're getting out here, right?' He speaks in that particular, local sing-song Afrikaans that makes Yolande think of the time when she was too young to leave. It's the sound of the workers amongst the fruit trees. She can practically smell salty sweat mixed in with the bitterness of leaf-sap in the sun. 'Because I have to drop you off at the next turn-off,' the driver continues. 'I'm not supposed to pick up hitchers, and—'

'Yes, yes, no need to panic. I'll be out of your hair in a minute.'

Silence. Yolande blinks at the tatty vinyl of the truck's dash. She's got it figured out. Who the girl with the hair is. *Fuckers.* A chemical belch leaps out from her guts and into her mouth. *Think they can pull this one over on me? They've got another think coming.*

Yolande remembers the way Jem had looked down at the child that day of the funeral, the care so evident in the tilt of his head. Even from Yolande's hiding place, through a fog of chemicals, she could see it. Like she was his daughter. Yolande snorts now at the memory. *But one that he wanted.*

Well she's not getting what's mine. Yolande almost speaks the words out loud. *She's got to be stopped.*

Oh yes, Yolande is on the road and ready. Rat-ready. Rat-a-tat-tat.

But now that the driver is steering the truck towards the shoulder of the highway by the turn-off, and motioning for her to climb out, the blood in her veins feels thick and sludgy, like fruit juice that's been left to evaporate and is getting all sticky. She clutches her bag. She's got her rig in there, and a few nice fresh packets of stuff that she's been itching to cook up ever since she scored this morning. That would thin her out a bit, give her some breathing space. But not yet. She's been good about saving it. She's being patient. She's had to be. Out here in this backwater shithole, she's going to need all the help she can get.

Sam waits for Charlie to pause and take a break. She waits for him to let go of the rough timber and hold her body in his hands instead. She watches from the floor in the shade of the wall, and wonders where her dimpled stool is, and who is sitting on it now. She takes a drink of water from the same plastic bottle that they shared that once, the first time he kissed her. She's kept it ever since, despite the fact that the cheap plastic is dented and foggy with use. She presses her tongue into the bottle rim. She watches, waits, but Charlie works without a pause. To Sam, he doesn't even seem to be breathing.

Mr Vosloo leans across the shop counter, bumping an unthinking elbow into Betty's arm, and gawps at the creature with her yellow skin and scabby lips.

'Yolande?' His grin fails to shift the scarecrow stranger's scowl. 'Jem and Anneke's Yolande?'

'Yes,' Yolande says again, exasperated. 'I remember *you*, Kobus.' They were in the same school, but Kobus Vosloo was years ahead of Yolande. She's not surprised to see that he's running the Super Saver now. Just like his father did when they were kids. Jesus, imagine she'd never left this place either? Who would she be now? The thought brings a splutter of cracked, bitter laughter.

Kobus Vosloo joins in because something *must* be funny. This woman-snake creature has to be a joke of some sort. She can't be Yolande, that's for damn sure. Yolande was a pretty, curvy thing with dimples and a shiny ponytail. She used to give handjobs to the boys behind the church sometimes. Did she ever give one to him? He wishes he could remember.

'So anyway. I'm on my way to see them. Was wondering if someone could give me a lift to the farmhouse.'

'To visit Jem, you mean. Anneke's passed.'

'I know that. I'm not stupid.'

'Well, he's not at the farmhouse any more.' Vosloo is still trying to remember his high-school handjobs, and this scary stick of straw is not helping. She's got a weird look in her bloodshot eyes that he's not keen on at all. 'Sussie and François live there ever since Jem and Annie sold off the farm.'

'They sold the farm?' Yolande's lips go white. That's *her* inheritance they've chucked away, thank you very much, and without that, this whole trip is pointless.

'Well not *all* of it. They kept a little corner. They went to live in the old stables. Made the place beautiful, Jem did. Put all his heart and soul into it when Annie got sick.' Vosloo rubs the side of his meaty jaw with a hairy-knuckled paw. 'Mind you, he's not doing too well himself, these days. Haven't seen him around town in months. He's lucky that kid is there to…'

But Yolande is already walking out the door and into the stark noonday sun.

'Goodbye to you too, scarecrow,' Vosloo mutters. He turns to see Betty staring at him with her unfathomable black eyes. 'Hey, don't look at me like that, *klonkie*.' He's in a bad mood now because he's just remembered that he never got a hand-job behind the church. Ever. Little slut was too full of herself. She wanted you to grovel for it, to beg. 'Remember, Betty, my girl, you're replaceable, hey? Any cheek from you and I'll give your job to someone else. There's plenty waiting in line, believe me.' He manoeuvres his beer gut out from behind the counter and makes his way to the far end of the store to where his saggy old sofa waits on the porch out the back.

Now that he thinks about it, he *did* beg.

How did decent folk like Jem and Anneke ever spawn a little tart like that?

'No.' Charlie's eyes are wide and shocked. His mouth has gone from kissing-soft into a thin, stiff line. He picks up her blouse from the floor where she dropped it earlier, and offers it to her as if to say 'cover yourself'. Sam takes the bunched-up fabric, but she doesn't get dressed. She stays on the floor with sawdust sticking to her skin and watches him pull on his clothes. He does it fast, as if he's running late for something. 'That's not possible, I'm afraid.'

'But I thought...' Sam thinks of the love letters that Jem wrote, all that devotion, that attention. Isn't that what it's supposed to be like? Not like this. Not this captured, frightened look in Charlie's eyes. The Cape Town trip, their lunch together, her talking and him answering just as if they're a regular couple, she thought all of that meant the *next step*. Sam glances over at her bag in the corner with her toothbrush in it. But did she really? How much of this plan was just about her wanting to get away from the roses? Goosebumps break out all over Sam's naked skin.

'I can't go back.'

'Of course you can. Don't be crazy.' Charlie is fully dressed now. He stands over her, looking down. 'Come on, please.' He's trying to keep his tone gentle. 'Get dressed.'

'But I need,' it comes out in a whisper, 'to stay.'

'Shit.' Charlie turns and paces across the floor and then back again, kicking up little dusty puffs of sawdust with his trainers. 'Honey, you just can't. I'm sorry.' Sam stares at his feet. The wood shavings cling to his laces like fur. 'This barn, the whole farm... it's not mine, you know. I'm just sort of staying here and using it, they're doing me a favour. I'm just...' He sounds lost, panicked. She looks up, then, and sees that his face is pink with strange bloodless patches around his eyes. 'I want you here with me every day like always, but you can't...' he gulps under the force of her deep-water gaze, 'stay over.'

Sam takes shallow little breaths to stop her chest from bursting open. With trembling fingers, she pulls on the blouse, not bothering to brush the sawdust off first. Splinters prickle as she stands to pull on her underpants and jeans.

'Promise me you'll come back tomorrow?' Charlie pleads as she hunts down her socks and her hiking boots. 'I can't lose you.' He walks up and pulls her into his arms. The sawdust clinging to her back stabs into her skin as he presses her body into his. 'Let's just keep things the way they are, hey?' She is limp in his embrace, still battling for breath. He turns her around, like a doll, to face him.

'I need you, water-eyed girl. Don't forget that.'

She nods. She cannot speak. She closes her eyes as he cups her face in one warm, timber-scented hand. He kisses her eyelids, the tip of her nose.

'We're OK, aren't we? You understand?'

Yes, she nods. *I understand*.

But this is just another thing in Sam's spiralling universe that makes no sense at all.

CHAPTER FORTY

AS SOON AS Sam descends the hill and enters the garden, she knows that something is different. The thicket of green and gold seems to throb before her in the soft evening light, pushing her back the way she's come. 'I know you don't want me here, but I don't have a damn choice, do I?' she says as she stomps past the pond. 'It seems that I've got nowhere else to go.' Her back is prickling with sawdust and sweat beneath the weight of her bag with its stupid toothbrush in it. For a moment, she's tempted to rip the thing off and hurl it into the water, but her knife is in there, the one Jem gave her for her eleventh birthday.

And then Sam sees the roses.

This morning, the plants had been healthy, studded with buds and haloed by bees, but now the new buds have shrivelled into sad, crumpled clusters, sagging and soft on their drooping stems. Even the leaves, so luxuriant earlier, hang limp, some even browning at the edges. A dart of fear shoots up from her gut and into the back of her throat, carving a burning scar through her centre. Sam moves past the rose bed and through the herb garden, trying to place the other oddness that persists in the air.

What? What is it?

Then she realises that the cicadas aren't singing. There are no crickets winding up for their nightly serenade. The raucous clamour of the pond frogs, so constant on summer evenings that Sam hardly hears them any more, is missing too. Sam's footsteps sound too loud in the heavy hush. Her key in the lock of the kitchen door is a metallic clatter, and the hinge screams when she pushes her way inside.

As soon as she's in, her nostrils twitch. The smell is so slight that it's almost lost in the fug of unused rooms and unwashed dishes waiting in the sink, but it's there, unmistakable: chemical sweat and cigarettes. Breathing it in brings a wave of memory that rises up and crashes down onto Sam, drenching her with the past. She gasps for breath, stumbles, almost falls. She reaches for the edge of the table and grips the wood to steady herself.

Inside Sam, Poppy shrieks, panicked, dashing from side to side as if trying to escape a locked room.

Sam makes it to the kitchen sink just in time. She bends over and throws up into that morning's used oatmeal bowl. She runs the tap to wash the thin mess down the plughole, and then sluices out her bitter mouth.

Slowly, on unsteady legs, Sam follows the smell into the lounge. There, sitting on Anneke's favourite chair with her dirty boots pulled up under her and a cigarette in her hand, with her stringy hair and hard expression exactly as Sam remembers them from eleven years earlier, is her mother.

'So.' Yolande take a drag of the cigarette, squinting her eyes up against the smoke. 'Who the fuck are you, and what have you done with my father?'

CHAPTER FORTY-ONE

SILENCE.

Sam can taste her own vomit on her tongue. She stares at Yolande and Yolande stares back. Long minutes pass.

'Are you simple, or something?' Yolande asks. Her brow wrinkles as she studies the girl. 'Why don't you speak?' The column of ash on the end of her cigarette trembles and then collapses, dropping on to the embroidered arm of Anneke's chair in a puff of grey.

'You don't know who I am?' Sam hasn't spoken Afrikaans in a long time, and the words feel rough and strange in her mouth.

'Why would I? Clearly things have been going on around here that I was never meant to find out.' Yolande waves her hand around at the room, leaving a trail of smoke in its wake. 'My father might be an asshole, but he would never live in a mess like this. I can tell right away that he's not here. But then, all of his stuff is. So what? What have you done with him?'

'Me?'

'Yes, *you*.' Yolande leans over the arm of the chair and grinds her finished cigarette out on the floorboard. Sam stares at the little crumpled thing lying on the yellowwood. It makes her think of a caterpillar with its head staved in. Her own head

293

is spinning. 'You with your Anneke-braid, wearing my dead mother's clothes, living in the house that is mine by rights.'

'Yours?'

'Jesus, I'm starting to think you really *are* simple.' Yolande picks at one of the scabs at the corner of her mouth, and a bright pinhead of liquid red swells up beneath her fingertips. 'But no wonder. My mother must've been all dried up and finished by the time she had you.'

'*Had* me?'

'Are you just going to stand there like a moron and repeat everything I say? Yes, *had* you. I've been thinking about this ever since I saw you in Cape Town yesterday. You look just like her, so there's no other way to explain it. I bet they decided to give it one last try, hey? To have a good daughter, one they could control and mould into another boring farmer, obsessed with cow shit and worms.' She glances around the room. 'They didn't get it right though, did they? I mean, look at this place.' Yolande snorts out a laugh, and the prick of blood by her lip bubbles out further, quivers, and turns into a trickle that snakes down her chin. She wipes it away with the back of her wrist. 'It's been left to rot. Stuff lying everywhere, nothing clean. Looks more like somewhere I might live. Proves we're sisters.'

'Sisters?'

'Oh, for fuck's sake, say something original, why don't you?'

Sam sinks down to sit on the floor. She is numb all over. Dark spots appear and then fade before her eyes. She can feel the bag squashing up between her spine and the wall. Something hard presses against her back. The toothbrush? The knife handle?

Yolande gets off the chair and strides towards Sam, shedding bits of filth from her decaying boots on to the rug that

Sam hasn't vacuumed in weeks. She crouches down in front of her. She smells sour, like the filthy street in Cape Town. She smells of the same seeping chemical-sweetness that she always did when Sam was Poppy.

'Enough playing dumb, you sneaky little bitch,' Yolande hisses into her face. 'You can do that later, on your own time, but for now, for right now, you're going to tell me what you've done with my father.' She leans in closer and peers into Sam's eyes. 'And let me tell you this, baby-girl, if he's dead, then you're living in *my* house now.'

'Daddy, I don't want to go to sleep,' Delia says when her story has been read, and her nightlight switched on. 'Can't you stay here with me a little bit longer?'

'Ah, moppet, what's the matter?' Charlie smooths the hair back from his daughter's forehead and bends down to kiss her damp skin. 'Aren't you feeling well?'

'Don't put ideas into her head, Charlie.' Liezette is leaning against the door frame, waiting to have 'a discussion'. Her folded arms and rigid expression make Charlie think that an awake Delia might be preferable.

'I'm not sick, I'm just…' Delia scrunches up her nose, pokes a chubby hand out from beneath the bedding, and beckons him closer. 'I'm scared, Daddy,' she whispers into his proffered ear. Although Charlie is pretty sure she's just stalling, the words send a strange chill down his spine, at odds with the bubblegum sweetness of the junior toothpaste on Delia's breath.

'Of what, Dells?' She looks up at him with very wide eyes, and then shakes her head. 'Tell me. It's OK.'

'Of the lady in the trees.'

'What lady?'

'The one with the long, white hair,' Delia whispers, and Charlie goes very still. 'Granny didn't see her and says she's not real, that she's just my imagination, but if she's not real then I saw a ghost even though it was the daytime.'

'A ghost?'

'She was standing under the plum trees.'

'When?' Charlie asks. Delia swivels her large eyes towards where her mother waits in the doorway. 'When did you see the ghost lady, Delia?'

'When you were in Cape Town the other time.'

'I've already told Delia there's no such thing as ghosts.' Liezette is losing patience. 'Come now, lovey, time to say night-night.'

'And what did she do?' Charlie whispers to Delia.

'Nothing. She just stood there, and then next time I looked she was gone.'

'Stop encouraging this ridiculousness, Charlie.' Liezette strides into the room and straightens the bedcovers, tucking them tightly under her daughter's chin. 'We've already had this discussion at length.' She switches off the overhead light and the room glows pink from the My Little Pony nightlight on Delia's bedside table. 'Haven't we, Delia?'

'Yes,' Delia admits.

'And what did we learn?'

'That Jesus won't let there be ghosts, so it's not real.'

'Exactly. So there's nothing to be scared of.' Liezette takes Charlie's arm and tugs at him. 'You just need to pray to Jesus if you're scared and then nothing bad can happen to you.'

'Really, Liez?' Charlie asks, eyebrows raised.

'Yes.' Her eyes glitter in the rosy dimness, challenging. 'Now have you said your prayers, Delia?'

'Yes.'

'Well then. Nothing is going to hurt you. Now say night-night.'

Charlie kisses his daughter and then follows his wife out of the room and down the passage towards their own bedroom.

'Jesus?' he asks when they're safely out of earshot. 'Since when did *he* start playing a significant role in the raising of our daughter?'

'Since you've had better things to do,' Liezette hisses at him. She closes their bedroom door behind her. Her eyes now look flat and gunmetal-hard. Charlie sits on the edge of the bed. He's still feeling shaky about Delia's white-haired lady in the trees. *The water-eyed-girl. It had to have been.* This is getting out of hand.

'OK, so what did you want to talk about?'

Liezette sits down beside him with a sigh.

'My dad.' The fury has leaked from her voice. She sounds exhausted. 'He's got this idea in his head that we're going to take over the farm so he and Mom can move to Hermanus.'

'What? That's nuts.'

'I know. I said the same thing.' Liezette puts her hand on his arm. Her palm is very warm. 'He just can't seem to get it into his head that I've married an artist, someone with a real calling. He's been trying to undermine our whole way of life ever since we got here.'

'That's a bit harsh, Liez. He's just old-school. The guy must be worried about the future of this place. It's understandable that he wants it to stay in the family after all the work they've put in.'

'Why the hell are you taking his side?'

'I'm not taking any side. I'm just saying.'

'Well don't. You've no idea what you're talking about. You're never bloody here.'

'Oh God. This again. I'm not working enough, then I'm working too much. You want to live out here with your parents, and then they're wrecking your life because they're too involved in it. You can't have everything both ways, babe.'

'Yes, thank you, Charlie. That's so helpful. How kind of you to explain it all to me so clearly.'

'Liezette—'

'No, this is all bullshit. Everything has become screwed up since we moved out here.'

'I thought you were loving it?'

'Again. How would you know? You're never around.'

'Right. So what are you saying then?'

'I'm saying we should make plans to move on. There'll be some serious money coming in from this exhibition. We can put down a deposit on a house. A nice one. Maybe in Claremont or something. We need to start thinking about schools for Delia and...'

Charlie's mouth has gone dry. It feels as if someone's stuffed it with grit and dust.

'I can't leave the workshop,' he blurts out. Liezette looks at him, startled. 'I mean,' Charlie swallows, 'I am doing great work out here. I don't want to risk messing with that.'

'It's *you* doing the work, not the place.'

'But...' *I need her watching me.*

'You said the same thing before we moved out here, remember?'

'I know, but there's something here that... It's... I don't know if I can do this anywhere else.'

'Since when did you become so superstitious, Charlie?'

'Oh for God's sake, let's be honest, Liez. This has nothing to do with me and whether I'm superstitious or not. You just want us all to do what you tell us to, don't you? Move, stay, leave, it's all the same, as long as we're doing what you want.'

'I only want the best for—'

'Well I'm sick of you calling all the fucking shots. We're staying. That's final.'

'Oh, now you've decided to grow a pair, have you? Well done you.' Liezette stands and marches to the door. 'Well, seeing as this is *my* family home, and we're here because of the generosity of *my* parents, have fun making that stick.'

The heels of Yolande's boots go bam-bam on the yellowwood floorboards and then thud-thud on the carpet. Up and down, down and up she walks, back and forth, to and fro, stepping on a folded-up piece at the edge of the carpet each time she crosses it. Sam is still sitting on the floor against the wall. One of the straps of the bag is cutting into her shoulder. She keeps thinking about shifting it around and digging her hand in to grab her old hunting knife, longing to feel the comfort of its worn handle in her palm, but she hasn't moved.

'I remember this place, you know,' Yolande says. 'Me and a guy called Hendrik used to come here and smoke grass and snog, once upon a time. He used to drive me out here on the back of his crappy old motorbike.' She rubs her hands up and down her arms, hard. She looks at Sam, lights another cigarette. 'In those days, it wasn't a precious little hidey-hole with nice wooden floors and things, it was just an abandoned old wreck. You could still smell horse piss in the stables. There were mice. Mouse shit everywhere.'

Yolande laughs. It's a terrible, broken sound. Sam looks at the floor. Inside her, Poppy curls up into a tight ball.

'It's fucking funny, you know: my sainted folks moving in

here and living their feeble little soil-encrusted lives in the very same spot where I first got high and lost my virginity.'

Bam bam, go Yolande's boots. She's walking faster now, and rubbing her arms so much she's leaving red, angry marks on her mottled skin.

'Don't think just because I've shared my little memory with you, that I'm letting you off the hook, kid,' she snarls into the silence. 'I'm going to get you to tell me where my father is.'

Sam doesn't move. She watches. She remembers the signs of Yolande's itch. It is as if no time has passed at all since she last watched her mother pace up and down a dirty room: no years of Anneke's cuddles and cakes and roses in vases, no Jem reading *The BFG* and showing her how to plant cuttings and prune fruit trees. Without realising it, Sam has raised her fist to her mouth and is sucking the same knuckle she used to bite when she was Poppy and Yolande was itching.

Soon, Sam knows, Yolande's itch will be too much. When that happens, Yolande will take something to make it better, and Sam will get a chance to think.

Bam-bam thud-thud thud-thud bam-bam.

'Fuck.' Yolande gives her upper arms an even more vicious rub. She tugs at the skin beneath her chin. She hunches her shoulders up and then down again. Itching. 'Where's the bathroom in this shithole?'

All Sam has to do is wait.

CHAPTER FORTY-TWO

FROM HER SPOT on the floor by the wall, Sam can see that Anneke's cuckoo clock now reads ten to midnight. She's been rigid and motionless since her mother went to the 'bathroom' half an hour ago, but now she forces her body to move. At last, she's able to take her sheathed knife out of the backpack and tuck it into her belt. On stiff, uncertain legs, Sam tiptoes from the lounge and up the passage. The bathroom door is closed. A strip of light glows beneath the wood. Sam watches for flickers of movement in it, but the light stays steady, undisturbed. Sam's breath comes in short, ragged gasps. She holds it in and leans her ear against the wood.

Silence.

She tests the handle and it moves beneath her hand. Carefully, she pushes the door open. The bathroom smells of old sweat, beer-stained fabric and the faint reek of vinegar with something sweet behind it.

Yolande is lying on the floor by the bath, on her side. Sam creeps in and watches Yolande's chest moving up and down with each breath. Slow up, slow down. So slow. She waits for it to stop, just like she used to do when she was Poppy, only this time, she *wants* it to stop.

It doesn't.

Sam looks around the room. There. Lying on the unwashed

bathmat beside Yolande's messed-up old canvas bag: the empty syringe. Sam tiptoes forward and peers at it, holding her breath, hand on the hilt of her knife, waiting for a movement from Yolande, a change. But of course, there is none. Sam remembers now: this can last for hours, this slack mouth with its stubs of brown teeth, and those eyes showing a rim of horrible white between the half-shut lids.

Sam uses the toilet, wincing at the roar of the flush, and then pauses again, frozen in the middle of the bathroom, staring at that syringe. Her thoughts are racing, and all mixed up with dark streaks that she can feel rippling through her, trailing tattered shadows. How much would it take? How much stuff in her mother's blood would cause those slow, stinking breaths to stop? Sam moves towards the syringe and then pauses. The ancient leather from the sheath of the old hunting knife is warm against her skin, as if it is part of her. One breath. Another.

Sam gives a sudden gasp, and turns and dashes from the bathroom, ripping the key from the door as she does so. She shuts the door behind her and the click of the lock sliding home seems to drown out her frenzied heartbeat. She slides the key into her pocket, and backs away from the bathroom door.

And now? The bag with her toothbrush still in it tugs at her shoulders.

Now it's time to run.

Sam heads to her bedroom and stops, confounded by the drawings on the walls, the old school notes heaped up by the bed, and the piles of crumpled, unwashed clothes. *Move.* She needs to pack and get out of here while she can. *Quick.* But her body has turned into a heavy lump of dough with a ticking bomb racing inside it. The floor tilts when she takes a step. She blinks to refocus. She takes another.

Move.

Sam jerks forward and starts grabbing things and shoving them into the bag alongside her toothbrush. Her thick fingers grasp and fumble, dropping half of what she collects before it makes it into the bag, and in her panic, she knocks the framed photograph of young Anneke on Sam-the-horse from her bedside table. The picture hits the floor with a sound that Sam seems to feel right inside her skull, as if it's her teeth that have broken. She picks up the frame and turns it over. The old glass has splintered into a spider web of cracks that radiates out from the centre of Sam-the-horse's face, obscuring his gentle features behind jagged shards. She thinks of buried Sam in the garden, how he used to visit her in her dreams, how he gave her his name and helped her not be Poppy any more.

I can't leave him behind. I can't leave him here with her. A sudden violent sob shakes her body from its heaviness, and she sets the picture back down, taking care not to spill the fragments of glass.

And what about Jem, lying beneath the roses?

If she leaves, then everything that Jem and Anneke built and cared for and loved will be Yolande's. Sam drops her bulging bag and backs away from the bedroom.

Around her, the neglected house seems to sag beneath its layers of dust. Everything that Jem and Anneke loved.

'I'm sorry, I'm sorry, I'm sorry,' Sam gasps. She races through to the kitchen and begins a furious hunt for buckets, cloths, brushes and soap. She needs to make it right. 'I'm sorry, Ouma. I'm sorry, Grandpa.' She fills the bucket at the tap, blinded by tears, and races through to the lounge. First, she beats the pillows and shakes out the throws, then she brushes up the dust from the rug and the floor. She vacuums everything in sight using wild, frantic sweeps and changing attachments with flustered, shaking fingers.

'I'm sorry. I'm so sorry.' Sam begs forgiveness as she scrubs the floors and rubs down tables. 'I didn't mean to neglect our home. I didn't mean...' She empties bucket after bucket of dirty water down the sink and then moves on to the kitchen, cleaning until her hands sting and her muscles ache and she's raw from weeping, inside and out.

There's so much to do. Too much. Load after load of laundry waits to be washed. Her clothes and bedding, all the cushion covers, the towels, the dishcloths. She wants everything to be clean, to be done, but it can't be because the washing machine is in the bathroom. With Yolande.

Sam stands outside the bathroom door once more, and pushes against the wood, listening to the feeble metal lock jiggle in its slot. Too flimsy. She needs a barricade, bars of iron, concrete blocks...

CHAPTER FORTY-THREE

AFTER A RESTLESS night, in which he could feel Liezette's fury pouring off her rigid body and over his in numbing waves, Charlie is up and showered and out of the house as the eastern sky turns from charcoal to pink.

In the quiet cool of the workshop, the chair he started making yesterday with such vigour looks raw and a little alien. Charlie gives it a wide berth, and sipping sweet coffee from the flask he prepared in the farmhouse kitchen, he begins to tidy the workshop, sweeping up sawdust and oiling his tools and lining them up neatly.

Through the open double doors, the day brightens and warms. He goes out and waters the garden that the water-eyed girl planted for him. The fresh new stalks on the lavender bushes bend beneath the spray from the broken watering can, releasing their clean, tingling scent. He breathes it in and stares at the peculiar arrangement of the plants, turning his head this way and that to try and devise the logic of the pattern, but there doesn't seem to be any. He gazes up at the brown hill. No sign of the girl herself yet, but it's early. She'll come.

Charlie goes back inside the workshop and sorts the off-cuts by size, and then by type. It's getting warmer. He stands at the door again, eyes on the hill. Behind him, the pieces of the new chair wait to be smoothed and worked, impatient to be assembled into something solid.

It's OK, she'll be here soon.

As the morning sun seeps into the valley, Sam finally falls into an exhausted sleep. She half-sits-half-lies, slumped and shattered against the wall outside the bathroom door. The door itself has undergone some changes: a thick plank of wood has been inexpertly sawn to fit beneath the handle, jammed between the lever and the floor, so that anyone trying to open it from the other side won't be able to budge it. The rough plank is further held in place by the back of a low bookshelf, which has been emptied of its books and dragged into place and then refilled for maximum weight.

Beside the makeshift barricade, Sam sleeps and dreams.

She dreams of the spider that she once caught and held captive in an empty glass jar, only this dream-spider is different. It has strings of lank hair on either side of its arachnid head, and its limbs are thread-thin and mottled. The abdomen is shrunken too, like a yellowish raisin. The spider tries to find a way out of the jar, scrabbling with its terrible legs on the inside of the glass, scattering spider hairs and leaving smears that look like brownish blood.

Dream-Sam hides the jar beneath the shrubbery, just as the real Sam did, over a decade before. But it is not enough. She can still hear those spider claws sliding down the glass. She tries to bury the jar, digging deeper and deeper into the ground until her scraping uncovers a large, grey bone. Then there are more bones. Suddenly, she's sitting in the midst of a buried skeleton. Large curved ribs, vertebrae like sawn logs all in a row, and a long-nosed skull with vast sockets where the eyes would once have been.

A horse. Sam-the-horse.

No! What have I done?

Frantic, she tries to bury it again, to make everything right, but there's not enough sand, and Sam-the-horse's eyeless skull stares back at her, no matter how hard she tries to cover it up.

'What the fuck?' The screech wrenches Sam from her tormented sleep. She blinks at the piercing daylight. Her body aches. Pins and needles dance through her stiff limbs when she tries to move.

THUD.

'Let me out!'

Why was I asleep on the floor?

THUD.

Yolande.

Sam is wide awake now. The door handle rattles, banging uselessly against the wooden plank as Yolande tries to open it from inside.

'What have you done, you mad little bitch?'

The air smells of sun-on-soap from Sam's furious cleaning the night before. She takes in big gasps of it, trying to clear her muddy head. In the dark, awful hours before dawn, barricading the bathroom seemed to be the only possible action she could take, but she didn't think any further than that. She couldn't. *What now?*

The books judder inside their shelves as her mother pounds on the solid wood of the door. After a while, they stop. In the ensuing silence, Sam can hear the throaty whoop-whoop of a hoepoe outside in the garden. Jem's favourite bird. She folds her arms around her legs and puts her head on her knees, pressing her forehead hard into the bone.

'Hey?' Yolande tries a different tone, but the rage is barely concealed beneath the wheedling. 'I know I freaked you out arriving out of the blue, yesterday, but honestly, I just want to talk to you.'

'So then talk.' Sam's mouth tastes bitter, like a burnt pot that's been left to soak in used dishwater.

'Open up, first. Let's discuss things like adults.'

'No. You can talk from in there.'

'Ooh, aren't you big and brave when you've got a locked door to hide behind? Not so simple now, are we?' Sam says nothing. She presses her forehead harder into her knees. 'You tried to make me think you were, but you can't fool me, you know. I can see right through you.'

'No you can't.' *If you really could, you'd know who I am, Mother.*

'Oh yes, acting like the little madam, all country-sweet and good as gold, but you're just a whore like your big sister, aren't you?'

'What?'

'Takes one to know one, baby-girl. I saw that guy giving you money the other day in Kloof Street and I had to laugh because despite Jem and Anneke's best efforts, you're just like I used to be, hey? Turning tricks for cash. Screwing around with married men.'

Something wild swoops through Sam's belly. Fast down and then up again.

'Married?'

'Oh my God.' Yolande yelps out a high, delighted laugh. 'You didn't know!' The laugh becomes a hacking cough, and then a laugh again. 'Poor little fool. I could see you were all moon-eyed over the guy. Probably think he loves you, don't you?' In place of a beat, Sam's heart gives a little shudder in her chest. 'Yes, he's married. Even a halfwit knows what a wedding ring is.'

If she closes her eyes, Sam can feel Charlie's hands on her skin, his warm-rough fingers, gentle then strong, then gentle again. She can feel the ring he always wears, a thick band of metal that, until this moment, was just another part of Charlie, like a fingernail, or a freckle. Her breath stops and then starts again. *You can't stay over.* Acidic bile burns the back of her throat. She swallows it down.

'Not just married, he's got a kid too. A little girl, I'm guessing, judging by the colour of the kiddie seat in the back of his big fancy 4 x 4.' A kiddie seat. Sam can see it now, so clearly, with its grubby plastic buckles and collection of unidentifiable crumbs on the chair cushion. There was a plush bunny lying beside it too, once pink but now faded and hugged to a dusky grey. How is it possible that none of this registered before?

'I hope you charged extra for that little sex-trip to Cape Town with Mr Daddy-man.' Yolande's gleeful voice seems to be coming from a very long way away. 'When I was tight and fresh like you, I used to make them pay for my time, even when we weren't fucking—'

Sam scrambles to her feet and runs from the voice and the door and the smell of soap. She bursts out of the house and the hoepoe, which had been pecking for morsels in the clover beneath the roses, flaps up and away into the sky, a flutter of russet against the blue.

CHAPTER FORTY-FOUR

CHARLIE ITCHES ALL OVER. He wipes the sweat from his face with the back of his wrist and squeezes his eyes shut. They sting. The workshop seems too bright: full of glancing planes of reflected light and blinding pools of sun. He takes another drink from the water bottle at his side and gets a mouthful of sawdust along with the lukewarm, plastic-tasting liquid. He forgot to close the top. He spits out tiny bits of wood, and then tries to pick the rest off his tongue with fingers that are already coated in a fine layer of the stuff.

She's not coming.

'Fuck.'

He flings the water bottle away from him, and it flies through the air sending vivid droplets spinning in a wild arc. Charlie doesn't see where it lands. He's staring, again, at the timber in his hands. The cut-outs for the complex dovetail joint he's been trying to work on look like something Delia might make if she picked up his tools. He wouldn't have done much worse if he'd gnawed the thing with his teeth. He raises his arm to send the ruined piece of wood flying after the water bottle, and then restrains himself.

Stop acting like a petulant child, Charlie.

For the first time, Charlie realises that he admonishes himself in Liezette's voice. Has he always done that, or is it just

310

a recent thing? Still gripping the offending piece in his fist, he walks towards the double doors. The endless zither of invisible cicadas make the brown hill seem as if it's sizzling beneath the sun. He glares at the boulder that Sam used to hide behind in the early days. Maybe she's hiding out there, afraid to come to him after yesterday's misunderstanding?

'Hey?' he calls, but only the cicadas sing back. He loosens his grip on the chewed wood and it falls to the ground with an empty clunk.

'I need you,' he whispers.

Out in the garden, Sam drinks long and deep from the borehole tap. The water tastes like stone. She splashes her face and then the back of her neck, gasping at the shock of cold. She can hear her mother calling from the bathroom. The cries alternate between scalding acid curses and saccharine offers of peace and reconciliation, but Sam is numb to both. She feels strange and disconnected, as if she's coated in cotton.

Sam dries her wet hands on her blouse and wades through weeds and overgrown shrubbery before coming to stand at the base of the hill. She looks up. Her lookout shelter is still there, long last used, and needing some repair work on the roof. Perhaps she can stay in it until...

Until what?

Until Yolande withers away like the spider in the jar?

Is that how this is going to end?

Sam gives a shudder, and as she does, the merciless truth seems to rattle free. She staggers backwards, stumbles, and sits down, hard, amid the ragged undergrowth. There's no escape from this. Charlie is married, he has a child, he is not coming for her, not going to rescue her, not going to love her and marry her and take her away from the awful secret that's sinking into the soil beneath the rose bushes, nor the woman that wails inside the barricaded bathroom.

Charlie belongs to someone else.

Sam knows, with a sudden cold clarity, that she can never climb that hill again. Her mouth opens wide, but instead of a cry, all that comes out is a voiceless rush of escaping air.

Yolande jams her face against the open bathroom window. It's small and high up, with mottled glass and steel burglar bars, but if she stands on the closed toilet lid, she can just see a slice of garden through the gap. Her cheekbone aches from where she's pressing it into the frame, and her vision swims with green, giving her light-headedness an otherworldly, underwater feel. Even a rat-burglar couldn't get out of this. Her mouth is dry and her chest achy. In her canvas bag on the floor by her feet are her rig, matches, the remainder of her stash, and three cigarettes. Just three.

That's all.

Three.

'Goddammit, you lunatic, let me out of here!'

In reply, a guinea fowl somewhere close by squawks like the rusty hinge on an old farm gate. The sound reminds Yolande of endless, featureless afternoons spent waiting for her parents to do something more interesting than play with mud.

'Shut up, you retarded bird.' The guinea fowl does not shut up. It continues its mindless calling. To drown it out, Yolande starts shrieking too. The high, fractured sound doesn't seem to come from inside her at all. She feels as if she's pulling it out of some other, wilder dimension where beasts with frayed wings flutter through the dark, and is sending it streaming out of her mouth. Now Yolande's loving it. It's powerful. A rush. She shrieks louder, throwing back her head to allow the sound freer passage through her throat. Her ears hum and her head spins and she clutches the bars of the window to keep from sliding down on to the toilet seat.

Behind her closed eyelids, black figures whirl on talon-toed feet. Yolande is so engrossed in their shadowy dance that she doesn't even realise that her shrieks have become words, words that pour through the window and into the garden until they stain the sky:

'I want what's mine. What have you done with my father? What have you done with Jem? Where's Jem? Where's Jem?'

'Where's Jem?'

Sam is on her knees with her face pressed to the ground and her hands over her ears, but it doesn't help. The sound of her grandfather's name throbs through the valley, loosening the soil beneath her, shaking the trees till their shocked leaves spin from their branches.

'Where's Jem? Where's Jem?'

Sam crawls on her hands and knees towards the house and the source of the noise, scraping and splitting her skin on stones and stems. She grinds her teeth together, so hard that her temples pulse, but the sound keeps coming and the answering call is rising inside her, straining to be let out.

'Where's Jem? Where's Jem?' The banshee howl seems to be drawing Sam towards it. She gets to her feet, moves faster, run-stumbling towards the high little window in the dove grey wall.

'Where's Jem?'

The screams are so loud now that Sam's body is vibrating

in response. She is on the stoop, right under the bathroom window, she jumps up, grabs one of the metal bars and pulls herself up so that she's looking at the demon, staring down its vile throat.

'Where's Jem!' it shrieks.

'He's dead. Jem's DEAD!'

At last, the words that have manacled her and dragged at her belly and tortured her for months, have been spoken.

CHAPTER FORTY-FIVE

CHARLIE PLACES HIS hand on the boulder that the water-eyed girl used to hide behind. It's hot beneath his palm. This is the furthest he's ever been up the hill. From here, Charlie can see the faint path through the bush where the girl made her daily journey to his door from wherever it was that she came from. He stares at the little gulley of sand and stones that winds its way upward. All he needs to do is follow and he'll find her. Just a step, and then another.

He glances back at the barn. Through the yawn of the open doors, the discarded bits of the failed chair lie on the floor like a set of misshapen, knocked-out teeth.

Maybe it's not his fault that she didn't come today? Maybe it has nothing to do with him telling her she couldn't stay? Maybe she cannot leave, for some reason?

Charlie turns again to look up at the hill. The breeze is warm, it's late, but there are hours yet till the sun's going down. After a moment, he steps out on to the path, following in the footsteps of the water-eyed girl.

Up the hill and over, she's waiting on the other side. It's so simple, all he needs to do is climb.

'I knew it.' Yolande's eyes are open now. Sam's words have

stopped her hideous shrieking. 'But when my mother died, Sussie made sure to get the news to me, so what's different? Why the hell wasn't I told about my father? You're trying to keep my inheritance from me, aren't you? You're trying to take what's mine!'

Sam is quiet again. She lets go of the window bars and drops to the ground. She sinks down to sit on the stoop, leaning her back against the cool of the wall.

'You killed him, didn't you?' Yolande whispers.

'No!'

'How can you expect me to believe you, when you're planning to kill me too.'

Beyond the garden, the guinea fowl gives one more rusty screech and then falls silent.

'I'm not.'

'Oh yeah, right. So you just locked me up in here with no food or anything for my own good, hey?'

Sam stares out at the garden. She can see the edge of the rose bed from here. The buds are still limp, and some of the leaves have yellowed and fallen off.

'Jem died in the night,' she says. 'Sudden cardiac death.'

'You just made that up.'

'No I didn't. It's a real thing. I looked it up in a book when I found his body. Cold. And white with purple bits from where he'd been pressed into the mattress. Then much later, I checked on the internet.'

'Looked it up in a book?'

'Yes.'

'Why didn't you call someone or get Sussie or the police?'

Because of you. The words burn in her throat, but Sam holds them in.

Something in Sam's silence makes Yolande pause. The first

eager frogs by the pond start their evening song, winding up for their nightly racket like little mechanical buzz saws. Sam closes her eyes. She feels tired right down to the marrow of her bones. If she could just lie here... curl up...

Then nothing would change.

The spider would still be trapped in the jar, the body would still lie beneath the roses, and she'd still be wrapped up in a man she cannot have.

'Enough.' Sam gets to her feet and walks away from the house.

'Hey, come back! Come back!' Yolande reaches an arm out of the window, grazing her elbow on the rusty frame. 'Don't just leave me here like a rat in a trap!' She waves a useless claw at the cooling, darkening sky.

'Where's Daddy?' Delia's wide eyes look like two shiny chocolate buttons over the top of her blanket. 'Why isn't he doing my story?'

'I'm sorry, my darling. He's working late tonight in the workshop. He must be so busy that he's lost track of the time.' Liezette smooths open the page of the picture book with fingers that tremble, ever so slightly. 'I'm sure he didn't mean to. I'm sure he's realised and is on his way back as we speak.'

'But do you know that for definite?' Delia asks. She sucks her bottom lip over her teeth and bites down. Liezette doesn't answer. Outside the heavy curtains, the sky is still bright, and birds twitter in the blue gum trees at the edge of the lawn. 'Maybe the ghost-girl got him.'

'Delia, there's no such thing as ghosts. We've talked about this. Don't make Mama cross now.'

'But I saw her,' Delia whispers. Liezette looks up from

the book, softening when she sees the fear in her daughter's round eyes.

'I know you thought you did, sweetie, but I can promise you, there's no ghost in the fruit trees, and your daddy is just fine. I'll tell him to come and give you a kiss when he gets in.'

'Even if I'm asleep?'

'Even if you're asleep.'

'OK.' Delia wriggles down further under the covers, making herself comfortable. 'Now read the story, Mama.'

When Sam opens Jem's tool shed, she reels backwards at the smell of Charlie-reminiscent sawed pine. The saw is still lying on the floor from where she dropped it last night while she was preparing the bathroom barricade. She steps over its metallic teeth, grinding the fresh sawdust beneath her boots, and marches over to where Jem's old tools hang from their pegs against one wall. There's the spade she used when she buried him, with its corners dull from decades of use, and its wooden handle stained the colour of earth. There's the chisel that she once used to carve out the letters on Sam-the-horse's grave marker, what feels like a lifetime ago. There are some pliers, a hammer, a pickaxe, a garden fork, and a mallet. She touches the cold metal of each.

Sam has decided. It has to end. All of the lies and the fear and the madness, it has to end. She closes her fingers over the handle of the mallet, and lifts it from its peg.

Now.

Sam pulls the books from the shelf and shoves the piece of furniture away from the bathroom door with a shriek of wood on wood. She whacks the mallet against the wooden plank that's pushed up under the door handle. Once, twice, and the third time it knocks free, clattering to the floor. Sam pushes it out of the way, and digs in her pocket for the key. In her haste, she misses the lock at first, scratching metal against metal, but then the key's in and turning and, at last, the bathroom door swings open.

Yolande is standing beside the toilet beneath the window. Her wide eyes flick towards the escape promised by the now open doorway, and then to the heavy mallet clutched in the girl's hand. It was once green, but much of the paint has chipped off, revealing the metal beneath.

'You want to know why I didn't tell anyone about Jem's death?' Sam's voice is soft and low. She steps into the stuffy room, her gaze fixed on the woman by the window. Yolande doesn't move. She doesn't breathe. The girl's pale, other-worldly eyes seems to be burning with a kind of terrible, blue heat. The mallet waits against her thigh. 'Because of YOU, Yolande.'

Somewhere out beyond the open window, the guinea fowl starts up again, its high, squeaky-hinge cry grating through the evening air.

'So I lied and I hid things and I buried things, but I've had enough. I don't care what you try to do to me, I don't care if they take everything away from me, but I can't feel like this any more.' Sam takes a shuddering gulp of breath and squeezes her eyes shut. 'Because the worst thing I could possibly imagine, the very worst thing, was you coming back for me.'

'For you?' Yolande blinks. Soft grey shadows, like clouds of ash, have crept in to the edges of her vision.

'For Poppy,' Sam says.

Poppy.

The word hangs in Yolande's mind for a moment, shimmering, and then it explodes, sending waves of orange flame roiling outwards, licking against the walls inside her and melting them. Hidden memories, molten hot, course through her, dragging all the barricades with them and scouring her insides out.

In the blank raw space that is left behind, Yolande can suddenly see the girl in front of her as she was as a child: tiny and twitchy with fright and coated with grime. A baby mouse. A rat-baby. *My baby.*

'Oh.'

Yolande sinks down on liquid legs, banging her hip against the side of the toilet as she falls. Not sister. There is no sister.

'Oh.'

She shuts her eyes and grinds her crumbling teeth against each other as the truth rides in. It is armoured in shining metal and rides on bright horses. Lances stab at her from every side, until Yolande is pierced through and through.

'Poppy,' she breathes.

'You remember now?' Sam's voice floats in from miles away.

Yes, Yolande remembers.

For the first time in over a decade, Yolande remembers waking up too late about the pregnancy and thinking that perhaps this was it, this was the thing that would make everything right. She remembers the ripping and the shrieking and then the months of squalling, the slapping and the shaking. Worse. The child made things *worse*. Now there was a little hungry face always looking at her and wanting something and her never being able to give it. She remembers hating herself and then hating it and then hating herself more. She remembers thinking she could get some money for it. Sell it. Use it.

But she didn't.

And now Yolande remembers her one moment of mothering, her one kindness: she remembers letting her father take the child away.

CHAPTER FORTY-SIX

THERE'S SAND IN Charlie's canvas trainers. Just a little, but enough for the fine particles to grind between socks and skin until his feet feel peeled raw. He can now see why the water-eyed girl always wears hiking boots. He sits down on a rock, checking first for scorpions, and pulls off his shoes. His socks are damp with sweat, making the sand hard to dislodge, so he tugs them off and whacks them against the side of the rock to loosen the grit. Now that he has a chance to take in his surroundings, he's surprised to see how little ground he's covered. He's not even halfway up the hill. How many hours did the water-eyed girl spend hiking every day to see him? It's an uncomfortable thought.

The sky is turning mauve in the west, and down below, spreading out towards the horizon, le Roux's magnificent vineyards look like a roll of ribbed green corduroy, spread out and waiting to be cut and stitched. Charlie's workshop seems shabby from up here: the roof is a patchwork of corrugated metal in various stages of disrepair. He'll have to get that fixed before the next rains. In the scruffy yard between the barn and the hill, the water-eyed girl's little garden is bright against the dusty ground. Charlie gazes at it as he picks burrs from the hems of his jeans, wishing he'd thought to bring a bottle of water.

And then, suddenly, the coloured blobs of the plantings

no longer look so random. There's a pattern there. Charlie's mouth goes dry. *It can't be.* He stands to get a better look, unaware of the sharp stones and scratchy scrub beneath his bare feet. *It's impossible.* A cold fog seems to bloom at the base of his gut and blossom outwards, filling his body with ice. He remembers his own clumsy little note laid out in that yard with bits of wood, meant to be read from just such a vantage point. Did the girl purposefully plant those flowers to form words too, or is he just seeing things?

I must be making it up, he tells himself. Why would she spend so much time planting words that he would most likely never be in a position to read? He wants to shrug it off, but the longer he stares, the clearer it becomes that the garden was laid out with consideration and care, the colours arranged to form two short words in amongst the low-growing green succulents.

LOVE ME.

Is it a salutation, or a plea?

A command?

An incantation?

He's been watering those words all this time, making them grow.

What the fuck have you been thinking, Charlie?

Charlie forces his feet back into his grainy socks and then into his shoes. He makes his numb legs move, back the way he's come, back down the hill. He feels ill. He goes faster and faster, skidding and stumbling and sending insects scurrying out of his path, but he can't outrun the feeling, and with each step, he sees himself clearer.

This is a life you've been messing with, man. A heart. Did you think that just because she was quiet and strange and seemed to appear out of nowhere that she didn't have one?

He keeps remembering his stupid timber note. What was he thinking when he laid out those pieces? What was he hoping would happen? How the hell did he think it would all end up? As Charlie slips and scrambles down the slope he feels the full weight of the life and hopes of the water-eyed girl hanging heavy from his shoulders. When he reaches the yard, he doubles over with his hands on his knees, panting. Indigo blotches swim across his vision, darkening the ground beneath his feet. He squeezes his eyes shut, appalled at how close he came to climbing over the hill to get the water-eyed girl back again, just when she was trying to get free.

Sam leaves the bathroom and goes outside into the garden. Her old name is still burning on her tongue. She goes to the borehole tap, and then connects the hosepipe to the faucet. The plastic tubing is warm from the heat of the day, and coats her hands with dust when she pulls it over the ground towards the rose bed. It's been too long since she watered. Perhaps it's too late.

Perhaps it isn't.

She stands with her back to the hill and directs the spray onto the thirsty ground. The droplets glitter in the air for a moment, catching the last of the daylight before sinking into the baked, dry earth, towards the waiting roots beneath. Her head swims with the loamy scent of newly wet soil. Sam breathes it in in huge gulps. She waters the base of each rose bush, taking care not to get too much spray on the leaves, repositioning the hose until the sky is navy blue above her head.

In the gloom, the black shapes of the trees and plants look like the backs and shoulders of benign creatures clustering close. The warm wind sighs like breath through their branches as they encircle Sam to keep the dark away.

When she's finished with the roses, Sam drags the hose around the entire garden, watering the vegetables and then the fruit trees, moving on to the herbs and the flowers and the fragrant-leafed shrubs that line the path in the place where the poppies used to grow.

Yolande lies in a crumpled heap with her face to the wall. Through the bathroom window comes the chorus of crickets and frogs, and the sound of water rushing out of the hose attachment. After long minutes, her one arm snakes out and her searching fingers find the corner of her bag. She drags it towards her, bringing it in close, holding it like a baby against her body. Then she reaches out again, feeling for the syringe which still lies on the bathmat. She holds it tight, fist pressed against the bones of her chest. Beneath it, her heart flutters and fumbles, trying to find its rhythm.

Yolande's memories continue to come, streaming like blown ash through her skull. When she let Poppy go with Jem, she shut them all down, but now they're loose and flapping free, whipping against the empty insides of her until she's bruised all through.

I could cook up some stuff to stop it.

The vitamin-and-vinegar smell of the remnants in the syringe make her whole body salivate.

I could cook up all of it.

Yolande bought enough for a few days, and she's only used once. There should be enough in the bag. But then she thinks of the tiny girl with her broken tooth and snotty, tear-stained face that always made Yolande feel sick and empty and full at the same time. *The child needed a mother, and that was supposed to be me.* And now? A girl on the brink of womanhood with no one to look after her, letting some unsuitable man use her, doesn't she need a mother right now?

Could I be that?

But with her next breath Yolande knows that there's no more chance of that happening now than there was all those years ago. The very idea of it is ludicrous. But she did do one thing right, when Poppy was little: she remembers watching the child reach up to take Jem's giant hand in her small grubby one, and she remembers thinking *Poppy will be safe now*, and she knows that if she has any more acts of kindness left in her rat-self, it is this: she needs to abandon the girl one last time.

This time, Yolande thinks as she pulls herself up to sit against the icy wall, and puts the needle back into its pouch inside her bag, *I need to stay gone. Not the dead-and-broken-and-covered-in-vomit-on-her-bathroom-floor kind of gone.* She gets to her feet and drinks long and deep from the basin tap.

Away-gone. Never coming back.

For good.

CHAPTER FORTY-SEVEN

THE TIMBER OF the doomed chair is a liverish colour in the flat blue of the barn's neon overhead lights. Charlie stares at it for a full minute before shutting the workshop door behind him.

He makes his way over to the van in the dark and climbs in, but before he can start the engine, Charlie suddenly remembers, as if it were yesterday, sitting at that little yellow craft table on the evening after his mother's funeral. He'd felt so numb and light that he'd had to hold on to the painted table-top to stop himself from floating up and drifting around the room like a crumpled leaf on a breeze.

He forces himself back to the present and turns the key in the ignition. The van's headlights blaze into the orchard, casting sharp shadows between the espaliered branches, and catching the rosy globes of plums almost ready to be picked. For a second, he thinks he spots the pale flicker of something move between the trees. As he drives towards the house, he can't shake the feeling that Delia's ghost-girl is out there with her pale eyes and white hair, watching him from the dark.

Sam enters the kitchen with bare feet, leaving her hiking boots, wet from watering the garden, on the stoop to dry out. The tiles she cleaned the night before are smooth and cold beneath her soles as she stands and watches her mother spooning instant coffee into a flask.

'There's no sugar.' Yolande keeps her back towards Sam as she lifts the steaming kettle and pours its contents into the flask. Sam can see her elbow shaking as she battles to hold her arm steady.

That was Jem's flask. He used to use it on mornings when he wanted to get an early start in the garden, or was about to take a drive. Sam can remember Anneke filling it with fresh filter coffee, standing right where Yolande is now, the skin on her misshapen fingers cream and rose against the dull metal.

Yolande closes the top and gives the flask a shake to mix the coffee up. 'That should keep me awake till Cape Town.'

'You're leaving?'

'Yes.' Yolande still hasn't turned around. Sam stares at the points of her mother's shoulder blades which jut like sharp, stunted wings beneath the fabric of her dirty T-shirt. Then she looks around the kitchen. On the table, beside Sussie's Christmas card that's been lying there ever since Sam found it, are Yolande's bag, and the key to Jem's bakkie. Sam glances at the shelf to see that Jem's house keys are still hanging from their hook. All present and correct, minus just that one. The bakkie key looks lonely lying on the table, uncoupled from its fellows after decades jingling beside them. Sam feels unshed tears sting behind her eyes.

'You're taking Jem's bakkie?'

'Yes.' Yolande turns around at last, but she doesn't meet Sam's gaze. Her eye sockets look like bruises in the waxy yellow of her face, her toothless mouth a puckered scar. 'And his flask. And my mother's rings.' There's a note of challenge in her tone, as if she's waiting for Sam to object. 'I found them in the drawer of her bedside table.'

'They've been there since she died.' Sam's voice is flat.

'That's all I'm taking.'

'Is it?'

'And I'm not coming back.' Yolande looks up at Sam then, but only for a second. She doesn't think she'll ever be able to bear Poppy's gaze again.

'I don't believe you,' Sam whispers, and Yolande shakes her head.

'I could've stopped him taking you, you know, all those years ago. I could've made him give you back, but I didn't.' Sam can feel the dark garden pressing in against her back through the open kitchen door. She can smell roses. A cricket chirps from somewhere close by. 'Instead, I forgot about you. I can do that again.'

Finally, Yolande steps forward and picks up her bag, placing the full flask inside it. She takes the bakkie key, testing its small silver weight in the palm of her hand before sliding it into her pocket, and Sam stands aside from the kitchen door to clear the exit. Yolande pauses. Sam's mouth goes dry.

'Sussie,' Yolande says, and taps the greeting card with a grey-rimmed fingernail. 'Whatever it is you think you've done that's so terrible, she'll forgive.' Sam's heart starts up again, but she's still holding her breath. 'She might be a bossy old bitch, but that woman is all about family. And her family is *you*.'

Silence.

Yolande shrugs her thin shoulders and then, without once looking at Sam, walks past her and out into the night. The heels of her boots are loud on the slasto of the stoop, and then softer down the steps, and then even fainter on the overgrown path. Sam listens for the rattle of the bolt on the gate and the sound of wood on wood as Yolande closes it behind her.

The bakkie engine turns but doesn't take. The ignition

whines and shudders. Sam closes her eyes, clutches her hands into fists, takes tiny little breaths. Again, it grinds, chokes and stops. Sam's fingernails dig into the palms of her hands.

And then, the bakkie kicks into life with a glorious roar. The wheels spin and it drives off, the familiar sound of its motor fading until it is swallowed up by the valley.

Taking careful, deliberate steps, Sam walks over to the kitchen door, closes it, locks it, and covers her face with trembling hands.

CHAPTER FORTY-EIGHT

IT TAKES HALF the day to do all the laundry. Sam spends the morning hanging it up on the washing line, and then backs of chairs, and then some of the garden shrubs, rotating the pieces when they dry, and folding the clean, sun-smelling cloth to carry inside.

Last night, after Yolande left, she ate a tin of pilchards, standing up at the kitchen counter, and then went to her room and slept through till the morning. Her dreams were jumbled and nonsensical, but she does remember a brown horse standing beside her at one point. She could feel its breath and the heat radiating off its skin.

She woke to the call of the hoepoe, too numb inside to form any useful thoughts about what to do next, so with sleep still crusting the corners of her eyes, she began piling the first load of waiting laundry into the machine.

She's eaten her milk-less oatmeal, and drunk her sugarless coffee, and scoured the bathroom with vinegar and bicarbonate of soda, and now she stands in the blazing bright garden, with drying clothes flapping on the line and pillowcases spread out behind her, and stares at the rose bed.

Although the clover is littered with fallen leaves, she can see the beginnings of new buds on the ends of some of the bright green stems. Maybe her nocturnal watering has helped. Sam goes to the shed, fetches the secateurs, and begins to clip, cutting away the dead buds and the broken stalks, and tidying up the canes that have grown too wild. Every time she glances at the hill, she feels the edges of a raw, sharp pain that she's not ready to face. Instead, she folds laundry and sweeps up the plant trimmings and piles them on to the compost heap.

When she's done with the roses, and is walking back to the shed to put the secateurs away, Sam is startled by a loud, insistent bird call from high up in the oak tree. She stops, listens. There it comes again: *koewee*. She looks up and shades her eyes, trying to see what creature could be making such a sound. Such a Sussie sound. It is a call that taps right back to a time when Anneke was the one tending the roses, and Sam was not alone. Could it be an oriole? She waits for another call, but none comes. She stares hard at the oak tree, searching, but apart from the movement of leaves up in the high branches, Sam can see nothing.

Whatever it is you think you've done that's so terrible, she'll forgive.

Sam closes her eyes and then opens them again, and suddenly she knows. She knows that this is finished. There are no more options, no more choices, no more lies.

Sussie opens the front door while Sam is still halfway up the path. She darts out onto the porch and then stops. Sussie's forehead is a crumple of uncertainty, and her mouth quivers, wanting to smile but not sure if it has permission to do so.

'Aunty Sussie,' Sam says as she climbs the porch steps. 'I...' Sam's speech deserts her in the face of what she has to tell. She adjusts her grip on the motorcycle helmet and looks down at her feet. Sussie waits. Somewhere in the grounds, a lawnmower starts up, and the sound judders through their silence.

'Yes, Sam?' Sussie's voice is soft, and Sam thinks she can hear tears waiting at the edge of it. Jem always used to say that Sussie was quick to 'get the mistys'. Sam can remember her grandpa grinning when he used to say it. Grandpa, with his crinkle-cornered eyes and too-big hands whose fingernails were always edged with earth-brown, no matter how much he washed them. Grandpa, with his blue-white rigid face showing above the slipping, mud-covered sheet. In the bottom of a hole.

Sam's vision blurs, and for a moment, all she can see is a swirl of dusky purple. *Sussie's trousers*. Sam realises that she's been staring at them. They're immaculately ironed and are the exact colour of dried lavender flowers. Sam tries to force words past the fullness in her throat. They don't come.

'It's all right,' Sussie murmurs. She steps forward again, but holds herself back from embracing the girl; instead, she clutches the top of Sam's arms. It's an awkward gesture, but the two of them seem frozen within it. Sussie smells powdery and clean, with notes of lemon and floral, and with a rush, Sam remembers that Anneke used to smell like that, but with more soil mixed in.

'Aunty Sussie,' Sam begins again. She swallows, then clears her throat. Something in her look makes Sussie release her grip and step back a little. Her eyes widen.

'What is it, my child?'

'Jem died, Aunty Sussie. He died in the night in the middle of July.'

And then Sam breaks in two.

Sussie catches her as she falls.

PART FIVE
THE KOEWEE-BIRD SINGS

CHAPTER FORTY-NINE

'DID YOU HAVE a good day with Daddy, my love?'

'Look, Mama, come look. See what he made me!' Delia grabs Liezette's hand and pulls her in through the front door of Charlie's small flat. Charlie nods an awkward 'hello' to his wife. He notices that Liezette, in a new dress, looks fresh and immaculate, like a pile of just-laundered linen. She's wearing less eye make-up than she used to. It suits her.

Charlie wrenches a window open, despite the fact that a vicious south-easter is blowing hot and mad through the streets of the City Bowl, whipping up dust and drinking up all the moisture it can find. Liezette looks so alive, so full of purpose. *Is she seeing someone else?* A brief scorch of rage, that Charlie knows he has no right to feel, burns through him and out again, leaving a hollow emptiness. Papers he left lying on the coffee table earlier flap and scatter, and deeper inside the apartment, the bathroom door bangs shut with a thump.

'See, look.' Delia shows Liezette her brand new, miniature-sized table and chair, all set up in the corner of Charlie's lounge. 'It's a craft table. For making things.' She shows her mother the tubs of beads and buttons, the piles of coloured paper and the tubes of glue, both glitter and plain. 'Daddy made it for me special.'

'It's lovely, Delia.' Liezette bends to touch the bright,

yellow-painted surface, and shoots Charlie a look that seems to say: *This, you can make? Why not anything else? Why not anything that's been goddam ordered?*

'And this is where Daddy sits when he helps me.' Delia pushes a short, three-legged stool at Liezette, who runs her fingers along the dimpled timber top. Charlie hunches his shoulders and jams his hands into his pockets. The stool is a replica of the one he once gave the water-eyed girl to sit on, and then wrapped up and sold on without a second thought.

'Checking my workmanship, are you, Liez?' When the three of them, still a family, moved back to Cape Town nine months ago, Liezette had promptly organised herself a job at the same furniture shop in De Waterkant that had been so thrilled with Charlie's Water-Wood Collection. Now, with Delia at day-care, she spends her days scouting for pieces and new artisans, arranging displays, and managing orders. *Hunting for a replacement 'Charlie', are you?* he'd accused her during one of their bitter, pre-trial-separation arguments. Long, aching months had passed since he'd been able to build a single piece of merit. *No, I'm not*, she'd retorted, *I'm trying to earn a bloody living. One of us has to.* And now, Liezette is thriving with new-found purpose. It seems she's found her calling.

When Charlie had then applied for the position of woodwork teacher at a nearby boy's high school, his new job had only incensed Liezette even further. *What the hell do you think you're doing? You're just wasting your talent, wasting time.* Charlie had tried to explain that he might be able to inspire some boy the way he was redeemed by his own woodwork master in the black, empty hell following his mother's death. But Liezette had just stared at him, mystified. *It's as if you're making yourself do penance, Charlie*, she'd said, *but in all the wrong ways.*

Not long after that, Liezette asked Charlie to move out. *Just for a while. Just to get some space and perspective.* He moved back to his dad's place first, and then, last month, to this small flat in the heart of the City Bowl. It's a longer drive to the rented workshop space in Woodstock that he goes to on weekends when he's not teaching, but that's just fine by him. The more time it takes to get there, the better. For the most part, it's war that waits for him on the other side.

'Right, come, Deelie, say goodbye to Daddy for now. You'll see him on Friday,' Liezette says, and then to Charlie, 'We're driving to the farm early Saturday morning to see my folks, so please have her back on time.'

'We're going to see Rolo,' Delia says, grinning.

'That's nice. Tell the old chap I say hello.'

'OK. Bye, Daddy.' Delia's hug is all clinging arms and legs, making Charlie think of the koala clutching a tree trunk in one of the picture books she likes him to read to her. Charlie, in turn, holds Delia longer than she's happy with, waiting till she's squirming and wriggly before letting her go.

He watches his wife and daughter walk down the corridor towards the stairs, and as always, after saying goodbye to Delia, skids into a slump of unnavigable despair. He closes the door and gazes at his little lounge with its one sofa and piles of books with no shelf to sit on (oh, the irony), and Delia's bright yellow table glowing in the corner. *Just temporary,* he tells himself for the thousandth time. But as soon as he does, he remembers Liezette's look of shocked disappointment at the pieces he began, at last, to produce without the water-eyed girl to watch.

You're like timber yourself, Charlie, she'd accused him on one of the nights they stood in battle in their small, Claremont kitchen, trying to keep their voices down so as not to wake Delia. *It's like you've been sawn off from your roots, a dead chunk of wood, and nothing grows or changes unless someone else picks you up and shapes you.* Charlie had been unable to meet his wife's eyes, remembering the water-eyed girl, and how, beneath her cool gaze, the pieces seemed to purr into being beneath his hands.

Charlie remembers the way the girl's huge, light eyes had looked when he last saw them: cut through with pain. What is she doing now? Has the little garden she planted for him outside the barn died without him there to water it? Her words withered to meaningless stalks?

Alone in his dingy flat, missing his family, and aching for his lost way with the wood that used to want him back, Charlie often wonders what would've happened if he'd been less of a coward and climbed the rest of that bloody hill.

CHAPTER FIFTY

'SEE HERE, THIS is where they can go to fill out the booking form,' Keegan explains, clicking his mouse on the 'contact us' link. 'It will then get emailed automatically to Gerrie so that he can get in touch with whoever wants to stay.'

'It's great,' Sam says, 'it really is, Keegan. So professional.'

'Yeah, well,' Keegan tries to force his blush back into hiding by scrolling through the image gallery, 'you've got to be, to stay competitive. Practically every second farm out here is offering holiday accommodation and stuff these days.'

'But none as nice as this.' Sam stares at the photograph on the screen. It was taken from beneath the lemon tree, facing towards the house, and at the top of the frame, one vivid corner of a lemon peeks into shot. Beyond the fruit, there's waving lavender and columbine, then the radiant roses, and further off, the dove-grey walls of the old stable itself.

'I'm thinking we'll need to add in a 360 degree tour,' Keegan says, and Sam nods, not really listening, lost in the image on the screen, staring at the play of sunlight on the leaves. She's sure she can almost feel the breeze tickling her skin. The sudden scent of roses billows up from nowhere, and she sways on her feet. 'Are you OK?' Keegan asks with a worried frown. 'You look weird.'

'I'm fine.' Sam steadies herself with a hand on her desk. 'I was just... can you smell... anything strange?'

'Nope.' Keegan hopes his armpits are not taking over the world again. He bends his head to give them a surreptitious sniff. 'You sure you're OK?'

'Yeah.' The image on the screen dissolves and is replaced by one featuring the pond, looking across the reflective water to the oak tree. In the shade beneath the leaves, Sam can see the faint outline of Sam-the-horse's new grave marker. She had been weeping as she'd carved out each letter because the smell of wood and the tap of the chisel in the grain had made her think of Charlie. With each dig of the spade into the ground to make a hole for the new plank, she'd whispered a goodbye to her wood-man under her breath, and after patting down the soil, she'd walked out of the shade with sore eyes and blisters on her fingers and a fresh empty space inside her which Charlie used to fill.

The website picture doesn't show it, but Sam made another marker and buried it beneath the bushes near the quince, where once she'd hidden a jar with a spider inside it. This other marker was small, little more than a slender stick with the carved letters running down it, one below the other:

Y
O
L
A
N
D
E

Not the marker for a grave, or a dead person, but for someone gone. For something finished.

As Yolande promised, she's vanished without a trace. Sam

has decided to imagine her in a rehab somewhere, getting clean, starting on a new life. If she's going to make up stories about her mother's life, they might as well be good ones.

'Yo, earth to Sam. What are you thinking about? You look like you're miles away.'

'Sorry. I was just wondering… Do you think this whole guest house thing is going to work?'

'Well, to hear your uncle Gerrie go on about his business plans, this place is going to be marketed so hard it's not going to know what hit it. Holidaymakers are going to be jammed in there like sardines in a can, if he's got anything to do with it.'

'Yeah.' *Or maybe pilchards. Pilchards in a can. Especially for you, Jem.*

'I think it's cool, but it will probably take a while, Sam. I know you want to use your share of the profits to pay for university next year, but I don't know… it's a big ask.'

'It's a start, though, hey?'

'Yup.'

'Anyway, thanks again.' She leans across him to press a button and the laptop screen goes dark. 'You'd better head off. I have to study for the next final, and Sussie will get twitchy if there's a boy in my room for too long.'

'Right.' Keegan feels his traitorous face pinking up again. 'Of course. English lit on Wednesday.' Keegan follows Sam through Sussie's house and to the front door. 'My mom says she'll fetch you on our way to Robertson.' Sam and Keegan are writing their final exams with a real invigilator from the Department of Education, sent out to make sure the home-scholars get a proper matric.

'Thanks.'

'Urgh, I suck at English lit.' Keegan pulls a face.

'I know.'

'My worst.'

'Shut up, you'll do fine.'

'If you say so.'

'See you Wednesday. And thanks again for the brilliant site.'

'Anytime, Sam.' Keegan stops at the bottom of the steps and turns back, shading his eyes to look up at the girl with her lemon-pith hair and guarded expression. Ever since Sam's grandpa died at the end of last year, and she moved in with Sussie and started coming to class again, she's seemed lighter somehow, less remote than she was last year, but Keegan's sure that Sam's got secrets, hidden things she'll never share. Not with *him*, anyway. He's under no illusion that when they both go off to university next year, Sam's going to be pounced on by some third-year guy brave enough to approach her long-limbed loveliness, and that will be that.

'Bye, Keegan.'

'Bye.'

Sam goes back to her bedroom and sits down at her desk. Beside her laptop is a freshly made mug of coffee and a rusk on a plate. She loves how, in Sussie's house, these comforting wonders sometimes appear as if by magic.

'Thanks for the coffee, Aunty Sussie!' she calls, and pulls her English notes closer.

Someone is mowing the lawn outside her bedroom window. As the mower moves closer, Sam can hear little stones flying up and clattering between the blades.

Sam opens her file and stares at a poem by T.S. Eliot, but she's not seeing a thing. She's thinking that the lawnmower had also been going that day, almost a year ago, when she'd ridden over here with her terrible truth lodged in her throat. Once she'd said the words at last, spilling them out onto the front steps, she'd felt like an empty husk, light and dry. Afterwards, she'd sat in Sussie's lounge and somehow, all her insides had felt as if they'd relocated from her body to somewhere else, curled up in a dark corner, perhaps, where she didn't have to see them. The only thing that had weighed her down and kept her anchored to Sussie's couch was the mug of coffee in her hands. The curve of the porcelain handle was smooth, and the surface against her knuckles burning hot. She remembers lifting it to her mouth. Sipping, swallowing. A husk with a thin thread of hot coffee melting through its centre. Close to her knees, on the table, had been a plate of Sussie's home-made butter cookies. She'd reached for one and placed it in her mouth, and for long minutes she'd been little more than dissolving buttered sugar and liquid warmth.

'Right, I've spoken to François, and he's spoken to Dr deWildt,' Sussie had said as she strode back into the lounge. Her eyes were still rimmed with red, but the rest of her face had regained its regular colour, and now that she had something to do, something to plan and sort out, she seemed to be back in her stride. 'Dr deWildt listened to your situation, and he says he's willing to issue a death certificate. He owes Fransie a favour.'

The last bite of Sam's biscuit had stalled in her throat. 'So we won't have to…' she swallowed hard, 'to dig him up?'

'No, child.' Sussie came over and sat beside Sam. She gave her a tentative touch on the knee and then folded her hands together in her lilac lap. 'We don't have to disturb him. You chose just the right resting place for the old man, my dear.'

'I didn't know what else to do.'

'Shush, child. I understand.' Sam didn't know what to expect when she rode over to Sussie's house with her heart in her mouth. She thought there'd be anger and horror, and a trip to the police station. *You're going to be in big trouble, Sam.* She'd imagined men stomping through the garden and ripping up the roses, coroners reports, a criminal record, questions to answer about using the money in Jem's account. Even now, almost a year later, she's still trying to process the unconditional understanding that she'd gotten instead, not to mention the lies that Sussie, her husband, and the favour-owing doctor have cheerfully told about the date of Jem's death. All for her. *All to protect me.*

Yolande, it seems, was right.

'The thing is, Sam,' Sussie had said next, 'you need never have worried that Yolande would come and take you away. Your grandparents thought of these things, my child. In Anneke's will, she stated that I was to be your legal guardian in the event of Jem's death. I would've fought for you.'

'I didn't know.' Sam had been numb in the face of all the things that she didn't know. She'd placed her empty coffee mug on the table, and drew a big breath.

'And there's something else.' Sussie had leaned forward and neatened up the tray, brushing crumbs off the linen cloth and stacking up the plate and the mug. 'Before she died, Annie left the land to you in her will, so that if something happened to Jem, there'd be no doubt as to who had rights to it.'

'So the house is mine?'

'It always has been.'

When Sam and Sussie climb out of the SUV, the late-setting sun is fat and gold in the western sky. In silence, carrying a bucket and a small basket of gardening tools between them, they walk to the graveyard that sits in a pool of shadow at the base of a low hill. Sussie wears a new pair of gumboots in a shade of powder blue that makes Sam smile. Hers, as they always have been, are olive green, workmanlike, just like Jem's.

Together, they clip and snip and weed and water, Sussie following Sam's whispered instructions, until the light is almost gone. The roses and dahlias around Anneke's grave look like dim dots of colour against the coming night.

While Sussie sits in the car and wipes the mud off her powder blues with a pack of wet-wipes that she carries in her glove compartment for such occasions, Sam stands and looks out towards the humps of the surrounding hills. The landscape seem to soften, melting into sky as the twilight deepens. On evenings such as this, when Sam was little, she, Jem and Anneke would often wait in the kitchen, with all the lights off, staring out through the window.

'Hush,' Anneke used to whisper, 'let's see who comes visiting tonight.' After sunset, the garden ceased to belong to them. It was now a world for the elusive little creatures that only came to life at night, stalking between the tame plantings on ash-soft feet.

'Ah look, it's the Cape genet.' Jem lifted Sam close to the window so that she could catch a glimpse of the spotted cat-like creature creeping across the stoop. Sam still remembers how it felt to have that shy genet turn its serious, foxy-face in her direction. The blotches of white on either side of its snout seemed to hover in the darkness. Above them, its eyes were a glossy, impenetrable black.

All three humans held their breath and watched as the animal sniffed the air for a moment before turning tail and darting off into the dark.

'So beautiful,' Sam breathed.

'See what can happen if you're still and quiet?' Jem

whispered, hugging her against his chest. 'The wild things aren't afraid to come up close.'

'It's true,' Anneke added. 'That's how it was when we got you, Sam.'

'It was? Was I wild?'

'And afraid,' Anneke said. 'The most interesting kinds of creatures often are.'

Sam absorbed this, then clambered down off the kitchen counter and dashed towards the light switch. 'Is it time for hot cocoa, yet?'

'Yes, dear heart,' Anneke had laughed, blinking in the sudden electric blaze. 'It's time.'

Sam shuts her eyes and breathes in the scent of roses on the wind.

Despite the funeral that Sussie organised here a year ago, and the fact that his name is now carved beside his wife's on this granite headstone, her grandfather rests at the bottom of another hill.

'Are you ready to go, Sam?' Sussie calls from inside the SUV.

Sam thinks of the bed of roses that gave rise to these ones. She can picture them bowing and dipping their blowsy heads beneath the same darkening sky. If she waits, and stands very still, she's certain she can smell their rich fragrance mingling in alongside the smell of the ones here beside her.

'Yes,' Sam says. She makes her way back to the passenger side of the vehicle, and opens the door. 'I'm ready.'